THREE WEEKS
IN DECEMBER

P9-DBY-741

Audrey Schulman

THREE WEEKS
IN DECEMBER

Europa
editions

Europa Editions
214 West 29th Street
New York, N.Y. 10001
www.europaeditions.com
info@europaeditions.com

This book is a work of fiction. Any references to historical events,
real people, or real locales are used fictitiously.

Copyright © 2012 by Audrey Schulman
First Publication 2012 by Europa Editions

All rights reserved, including the right of reproduction
in whole or in part in any form.

Library of Congress Cataloging-in-Publication-Data is available
ISBN 978-1-60945-064-9

Schulman, Audrey
Three Weeks in December

Book design by Emanuele Ragnisco
www.mekkanografici.com
Cover photo © iStockphoto.com/Chase Swift

Prepress by Grafica Punto Print – Rome

Printed in the USA

THREE WEEKS
IN DECEMBER

Historical Note

In the late 1890s, by the River Tsavo, in the country now called Kenya, two lions began to kill and eat people. Working in concert, they preyed on Africans, Indian railroad workers, and British administrators.

Dozens of men hunted the cats. Extensive barricades were built up around all human habitation. Still, every few nights, the lions would somehow appear by the firelight inside a camp or village. They seemed bigger than any lions previously recorded, and stronger. They would drag someone away. In the darkness the screams of the victim were suddenly cut off.

They ate over a hundred people.

THE STEAMSHIP GOLIATH,
EAST INDIAN OCEAN

DECEMBER 7, 1899

T hree hundred miles from Mombasa, the steamship Goliath happened upon an Arabian dhow becalmed on the Indian Sea. The sail hung slack, the rope trailing loose, and no person was visible aboard. The steamer rumbled deep in its guts to begin its emergency halt.

Carrying his iced tea, Jeremy got up from his lounge chair to walk to the railing where he could view the boat better. Even at eight in the morning, he narrowed his eyes as he stepped into the weight of the tropical sun.

As the shadow of the steamer crept over the tiny wooden boat, its single sail slapped listlessly from side to side. Peering down, it took Jeremy a moment to make out the sprawled forms of the five Mohammedans, their white robes appearing at first like discarded sailcloth. Only their faces showed, burned so dark they appeared black. Although none of them were able to sit up, two of them beckoned weakly as they stared up at their rescuers. A crew member from the steamer unrolled a rope ladder down the side of the ship and then clambered down, balancing a cask of water on his shoulder. For the next few minutes, the five men took turns drinking. One of them cupped his fingers over his mouth after each turn as though to ensure no water trickled back out. Jeremy could see them talking, but could not hear, over the steamer's rumbling engines, what language they used. The white man listened attentively, asked a few questions and then clambered back up the ladder to head toward the bridge. Jeremy watched him in the cabin there, reporting to the captain. The captain's face was obscured by a harsh streak of sun on the window, leaving only his white uniform facing Mombasa, their destination. At no point did the captain turn toward the stranded men.

After what seemed a long wait, the crew member reappeared at the head of the ladder. He did not climb down this time, but just lowered another cask of water on a rope, yelled some last words down to the Mohammedans, pointed emphatically twice in a westerly direction, and then rolled up the ladder. The engines surged and the ship chugged away.

Surprised, Jeremy watched the dhow bump off the steamer's side and twist in its wake.

He stopped a crewmember walking by. "Where are they trying to get to?"

"Get to?" asked the purser. "Those poor buggers? Dar es Salaam, sir. They ran out of water two days ago. They're lucky we stumbled onto them."

"Will they be all right?"

"What, them?"

Here, he would be working for the British: a detail about his employment he rather regretted. They frequently repeated questions as though shocked at the rest of the world's lack of basic comprehension. Already, he had met several men who each spoke with as much stiff-necked propriety as though the papers to the whole of the ever-expanding British Empire were secreted about his clothing. The titles to the Suez Canal and Canada stuck down his collar; Uganda and Nigeria tucked into his socks; Singapore and Australia snug along his thighs; India supporting the small of his back; British East Africa, Rhodesia, and all the rest in the armpits. No matter what exotic sights passed by, no matter who tried to interact with him, the man's expression stayed internal as he struggled not to perspire on the paperwork.

"Why, they're Arabs," said the purser surprised. "They'll be fine, sir. Like camels, they are. Be able to deal without water much longer than you or I could."

Pausing, the purser leaned forward to add confidentially, "You know, those people still buy and sell slaves in this day and age. That boat could be heading into port to pick up part of a caravan and auction them off in Persia." He shook his head. "Inhuman what they do."

Jeremy threw one last look astern at the dhow getting smaller in the distance, bouncing in the steamer's wake. Three of the men had struggled up into a sitting position, turned to watch the boat steam away. The distance made it impossible to see their expressions.

BANGOR, MAINE

DECEMBER 7, 2000

TWO

The moment the two of them stepped into her office, she didn't like their smell. The younger one reeked of cigarette smoke, as well as an over-reliance on hair gel. He said his name was Stevens, head of R&D, and he didn't wait to find out if she would hold out her hand for a handshake, but instead he picked her hand up from her side in order to shake it. Eye contact was something he could manage all day.

The older one was called Roswell. Wafting along with him came the essential oils of lavender and lemongrass—aromatherapy—unexpected from the CEO of a pharmaceutical. Since Stevens was still busily pumping her hand up and down, he just nodded to her.

Max stepped back as soon as she could. Took away her hand, rubbed it on her hip. "Yes?" she asked, sitting down behind the safety of her desk.

"As we said over the phone, we have a job proposal we think you might be interested in." Stevens's voice was rich and emotive, the kind a morning-talk-show host might have.

She cocked her head, listening, but kept her eyes directed down toward her papers. She could listen better without the distraction of faces, especially those of strangers.

She strongly doubted this job proposal would be realistic. Just three years ago, Genzyme had four separate expeditions out in the field; Sanofi had two. Now there was nothing. Still she had to listen. Her postdoc ended in a month. The only offers she'd gotten had come from the fragrance industry.

These men, however, seemed serious. From the edge of her eyes she could see them lean toward her in their chairs: big men, ruddy skin, the sheen of expensive clothing, their hands clasped in front of them in a position reminiscent of prayer. On the phone, making the appointment, Stevens had said they were flying in from Denver just to talk to her.

This pause was too long. It must be her turn to talk. She still sometimes had difficulty with the rhythm of conversation, understanding what was required.

"Yes," she said, "Go ahead."

Stevens ran his hand over his tie, smoothing it down. Maybe he'd thought she was about to refuse even to hear the proposal. The combination of her height and averted gaze could make her seem haughty. He skipped over the pleasantries. "Three weeks ago a rather battered envelope arrived in the mail, addressed to a chemist in our labs. Inside was a vine. Not much of a sample, three, maybe four ounces. Badly preserved and wilted. Still the chemist gave it to her lab tech to run a crude extract." He angled his head a bit, trying to get his face closer to the path of her vision, preferring to look into a person's eyes. She was surprised he didn't work in sales.

Roswell's voice was flatter, more factual. He was the CEO, didn't have to charm anyone. He cut to the point. "The extract contained five times the beta-blockers of anything known to science."

At this, her eyes jumped, involuntary. The two of them. Heavy faces, manicured hair. Human eyes. Like touching an electric fence. The glittering shock.

She turned away, to the window, to the oak outside. On the wall behind her, the clock whined and thunked.

"Five times?" she repeated.

They nodded.

"Also a mild vasodilator," added Roswell.

"Any vine left?" she asked.

"No."

"The crude extract?"

He shifted in his chair. "Tossed. Before the tech read through the printed results."

She studied the oak outside. It was at least 100 years old. Earlier in the fall she noted it had a mild case of anthracnose, the brown blotches spreading across the leaves. With luck, this winter would be severe enough to kill the fungus. "Any description of what the vine looked like? The shape of the leaf? The type of branching?"

"From the tech? He's just out of college, doesn't notice plants."

Max was derailed for a moment, trying to imagine that. Then continued, "Foreign or domestic?"

"What?"

"Where'd the vine come from?"

"Virunga National Park, Rwanda."

"Foreign." She eyed the oak. She'd always been honest to a fault, uncomfortably honest. "Well, I'm sorry then. This won't work. You won't be able to get the plant out through customs. Not legally. It's the property of another country."

Stevens responded, his voice smooth. "The Rwandan president himself has given us the go-ahead, requesting immigration render us every assistance possible."

She was careful this time to glance only so far as his mouth. A mouth wasn't as shivery as eyes, not so shocking. His lips were stretched in a proud smile, indents at the corners of his mouth from the contraction of the buccinator muscles. However, none of his teeth were revealed.

"How'd you manage that?" she asked, turning back to the oak. Plants were so much more understandable. This tree, for instance, whatever gesture it made was how it grew, its limbs hardening into its intent. She could comprehend it at a glance, its past struggles for water and sun, its future needs there in the angle of its trunk, the reach of its branches. Never a hidden agenda.

The two men looked at each other. Then Roswell said in his flatter voice, "Since the genocide, the country's not doing so well economically. They *need* money."

Stevens continued, "If any drug made it to market, the Rwandan government would get a share of the profits. Also we're in preliminary negotiations to build a factory in Kigali."

She glanced over. His smile wider, lips parting, visible teeth.

(Most humans were born able to read the facial expressions of others—not even knowing they should be thankful for that immense power. They could afford to be sloppy, satisfied with approximations of sincerity. Max, on the other hand, had labored for a solid year before college, studying flashcards and videos. Her mom and her, on the couch, went frame by frame through *Bambi* and *Dumbo*, analyzing each close-up. Animated talking animals were much less threatening and had such telegraphed emotions. They became her seminar in humanity. She could reel off every facial muscle. Zygomaticus major, caninus, procerus. She'd memorized action units and rules.)

Stevens's grin wasn't honest, for it didn't extend to the muscles under his eyes.

Her mother had always repeated that, yes, Max had deficits, but through them she could attain unusual strengths.

"You're not going to build a factory there, are you?" she guessed.

A beat passed. His voice wasn't quite as smooth when he responded. "That hasn't been determined yet. The important thing, in terms of us getting hold of this vine, is that Rwanda *needs* this facility."

Five times the beta-blockers of Carvedilol, she thought. She noticed her hands were flapping slightly, patting her knees as though she were keeping time. She consciously stilled them in her lap. Her whole life spent imitating the normals. "To get hold of that vine, not just the government has to sign off. The era is over in which we can make nice with a shaman for a few days in order to learn priceless botanical secrets. The shamans are onto us. The tribes have lawyers." No one who didn't know her well would detect excitement. In the field of science, the monotone of her voice helped her, sounding dispassionate. "Harvard's latest expedition is being sued by over fourteen different indigenous—"

"—No tribes are involved. No people at all," Roswell interrupted. "This vine, it grows several thousand feet up in the mountains, in a national park."

This caught her for a moment. She turned the fact over in her mind, examining it. "Where'd you . . . Who found the vine?"

"Gorillas."

"Excuse me?"

"Mountain gorillas."

"Look," said Stevens. "Jaguars were the ones to first use quinine, gnawing on bark from a cinchona tree whenever they had malaria. Pigeons discovered the power of coffee beans. For thousands of years humans have learned about drugs from watching other animals. Primates are especially sophisticated at botanical pharmacology. Female muriqui monkeys, for example, utilize over forty plants for everything from parasite control to contraceptives."

Max said, "Contraceptives?"

"During famines, the females consume a plant that's high in a progesterone-mimicking compound so they won't waste energy on pregnancy."

"Damn."

"Can we get back to the subject here?" Roswell used shorter sentences, a sort of staccato delivery. "Dubois is her name. The person who sent in the vine. She's French. A primatologist working with gorillas in the Rwandan mountains. She noticed the adult males would crush leaves of the vine in their mouths, then spit them out. Got curious about possible bioactive properties. Sent a sample to her college roommate who's a chemist."

"A chemist who happens to work for us," Stevens said.

Roswell continued, "We know gorillas are genetically prone to heart disease. Among the males in captivity, it's the biggest killer. Half the great apes you see at the zoo are on Lipitor."

Stevens held up one finger, waiting for the pause. He was proud of this next bit of information. "Contrast those gorillas with the ones in the mountains where this vine grows. The area happens to be where Dian Fossey set up her research station in the 1960s. For the decades since then, scientists have been doing postmortems on every dead gorilla they've found in the area, recording the results." He added, "No sign of heart disease. Ever. No myocardial infarctions, no dilated cardiomyopathy, nada. Even in the ones that die of old age."

Roswell said, each word slow and enunciated. "This vine might be why."

"Fuck." Fricatives so satisfying. "Fuck." On bad days she used to not be able to stop her swearing. Now she used it as a control valve, letting off steam when necessary. Done this way, it sounded almost the way others swore.

The men went still. They were surprised, but not necessarily displeased.

Max closed her eyes, breathing, concentrating on finding errors in their logic. "Gorillas are a different species. What works on them might not . . . "

"You ever talk to a vet specializing in great apes? They fill the prescriptions at CVS. The only difference is dosage."

Max said, "The primatologist? What about her?"

"Dubois?"

"Yes, she found it. She's got a prior claim."

"Well, about her, there are pluses and minuses." Stevens chose his words with care. "She did sign away her claim."

"A big plus," said Roswell.

"She signed in exchange for us paying for park guards to patrol the mountains for the next decade. I guess hunters in the area tend to kill the gorillas. She's a big softie about the apes."

Roswell said, "Paying for the guards works for us. We'll be protecting the world's remaining mountain gorillas. The advertising department will love it."

"And the minuses with her?" asked Max.

"She won't send us more of the vine or show us where she found it."

"Why not?"

"God knows," Stevens said. "She's weird."

"Dr. Tombay, listen." Roswell thumped his finger on the arm of his chair as methodically as a metronome, beating out a rhythm to his words. "Because we're paying for the guards," *thump*, "she'll let you stay at the research station." *Thump.* "You can search as long as you want." *Thump.* "She thinks no one can find the vine."

Max didn't worry about this part. She was good at finding plants. She had what might be called a single-minded focus.

"Look," said Stevens. "We're doing this right. Taking care of the gorillas, working with the government. This could be the role model for the future, the case that reopens ethnobotany for the 21st century."

Fuck the gorillas, she thought. It was the vine she wanted. Those beta-blockers.

So this was the point when she leaned forward in her chair, ready to bargain.

And at her movement, the men smiled, for the first time sincerely. They settled back, relaxing into their new position. The chairs squeaking, the audible shift of power.

She'd never studied matters of negotiation, never learned how to bargain. Perhaps like Rwanda and the primatologist, she didn't end up striking the best deal.

To her, it didn't matter. She was going to Africa.

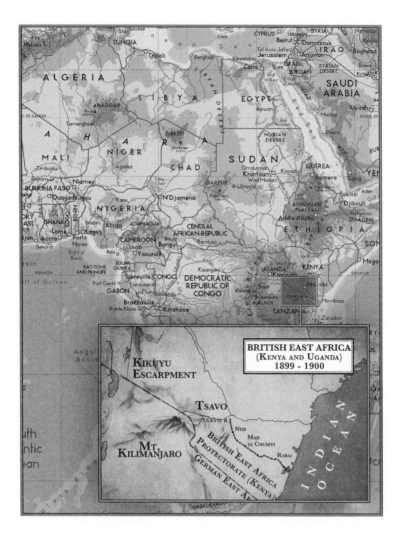

BRITISH EAST AFRICA
(KENYA AND UGANDA)
1899 - 1900

Near the Tsavo River, British East Africa
December 9, 1899

Stepping off the train, a few miles from Tsavo, Jeremy noticed twenty yards ahead of the engine, the railway simply ended. The rails stopped unevenly, the right rail a little longer than the left, a pile of sleepers next to it waiting to be placed, the recently raised embankment the red of a wound from the clay of the tropical soil. Fifty feet past the sleepers, the embankment trailed off, dead-ending in a scrubby forest. Stunted thorn trees as far as could be seen in every direction, the equatorial sun hanging low on the horizon. The only water available was imported one hundred miles down the railway from Mombasa. He had been told, with almost two thousand workers on the line now, the railway could not transport the water fast enough. It took time to load and unload, slowing down all the other supply trains in the process. And last week, the water had been halted entirely when a lioness decided to bask in the sun on top of the water tank and no one nearby had a gun. No matter how much noise the engineer and porter made, beating on jerricans with shovels and yelling, the animal had continued to sleep there for six hours. All the workers up the line near Tsavo, dehydrated already from their tight rations, simply lay down in the shade for the day, unwilling or unable to work until the water arrived.

Even those in command were issued only a small basin of water once a week to clean up in. Before today, Jeremy (who had always enjoyed his morning ablutions) had assumed this lack of bathing would bother him the most of all the deprivations of camp life. At the moment, however, standing in this ninety-degree temperature—wearing all appropriate layers of outer clothing and undergarments, with the added weight of the unfamiliar flannel spine protector pressing against his back—he began to glimpse for the first time that heat and thirst might take primacy.

Behind him, conscripted workers piled off the train, newly arrived from India, their term of contract three years. For the past twenty-four hours on the train, these Indians had eaten fruit he had never seen before, chattering loudly in languages he did not know, wearing a style of headdress he was not sure how they donned. Did a turban come pre-wrapped so one just tossed it onto one's head like a hat in the morning? Or did it take two men to get dressed, the first standing still, the other winding the material round and round his head? Coolies, these men were called, some of them as light-colored as a tan white person, others a saturated brown as dark as the natives here. In camp, there would be a scattering of Persian Mohammedans as well as a few tribesmen. The only other white man would be a British physician by the name of Alan Thornton. All of them would have to learn to work together.

Back in Maine, when acquaintances inquired why Jeremy had decided to travel all the way to British East Africa for employment, he had narrowed his eyes, looking off into the distance as though searching for the best way to explain. He started by mentioning that his Grandpapi had homesteaded in Maine, wresting an order from the wilderness, creating a large dairy farm from what had been simply a mass of trees. He described how much he admired that fact, as well as the honest and well-used nature of Grandpapi's hands. Even now that Grandpapi was in his sixties, those hands were muscled and tendoned, always cratered with working injuries, the pinky nail permanently missing from a long-ago mishap with a cow. Jeremy would admit he would be proud to have similar hands, to spend his life taming a land like his grandfather had.

Grandpapi was one of the pillars of the community, a loyal church member and town selectman. Most of the people listening to Jeremy's explanation would nod at his words, satisfied with his answer.

Sometimes however (mostly when he was talking with more distant farmers who had not caught up yet on recent gossip) the listeners would lean forward, awaiting additional reasons. After all, Africa was on the other side of the equator, weeks of travel away—a savage and unknown land. With these people, Jeremy inhaled and added that, since he wished to tame a wilderness, Africa was clearly the place to be. European countries had just divided the continent up into territories, were begging for settlers to homestead, handing the land away for free. His plan was to help for several years to build the railroad and then, from his firsthand knowledge of the area, pick some prime land to settle on.

Occasionally one of the listeners would mention the possibility of disease, but Jeremy would steer the conversation instead toward the vast profits to be made. The continent was rumored to have huge repositories of gold, diamonds, and copper, as well as untold tons of ivory, exotic furs, and rubber. How could a settlement placed in the midst of such wealth fail? He would ask the listeners to judge for themselves. Did they not believe it possible that the colonization of Africa could, as it had in America, result in the gradual unification of the territories? He would state there was no greater fulfillment he could wish for in life than to contribute to the birth of a nation, helping the continent to realize its power.

At this point, even the most distant acquaintances nodded, satisfied.

And the others, having heard the rumors, had already let the subject drop. They had reached their own conclusions long before.

Now, standing here in this foreign land, he felt gratitude that at least the railroad tracks were the same width and tolerances as the ones in America, the same materials. If the Indian workers had not been around, he might have reached a hand down to touch these familiar rails for reassurance, so straight and clean, what one of his engineering teachers used to call the iron rods of civilization. A few miles ahead lay the Tsavo River, over which he would have to build a bridge. He had been engaged here mostly on the strength of two facts. The first was that all his engineering projects so far—two railroad bridges in Maine—had been completed on schedule. The second was that no accidents had happened to his men, not even a crushed limb. He was proud of his record, had labored hard toward safe conditions, secretly terrified that a decision of his might result in another's death.

At a fundraiser for Rensselaer Polytechnic—the engineering school Jeremy had attended—he had once been briefly introduced to the elusive Washington Roebling. Impeccably dressed, the famous man picked his words with as much care as if they were bricks creating something permanent. He spoke this way even though the conversation concerned only the cheese-plate selection. Roebling's innovative Brooklyn Bridge had cost the lives of at least twenty workers. The bridge's feet, the caissons, had to be laboriously dug deep into the river's bottom, giving the men—when they returned to the river's surface—some type of previously unknown malady now being called "the bends." In the worst cases, the men's skin bubbled and they clutched their heads, shrieking into their deaths. And this was not the only type of danger associated with the bridge's construction. High above the water, the metal ropes Roebling had invented to hold the bridge up sometimes snapped and tossed workers hundreds of feet through the air.

Interrupting the discussion of the cheese plate, a woman had pressed in past Jeremy and taken Washington's arm. Ahh,

Jeremy realized, Emily Roebling, rumored to be as great an engineer as her husband, though she had never attended school for it. A thin woman with a lively face, she apologized to everyone and led Washington firmly away. The gossip was for years he had barely left his bedroom, pained with debilitating headaches and wavering sight, leaving Emily to oversee the work on the bridge. Perhaps these migraines came from his many hours down in the caissons. However Jeremy wondered if they could have been compounded by an unwillingness to witness any more deaths.

Unlike some of his classmates, Jeremy had never sought to have the primary value of his work come through its artistic merits or engineering feats. Instead he was content to have the worth of his bridges be equated with their usefulness, their ability to help people transport the food and materials they needed to survive. And this was a reason to work in Africa. While America was voracious at the turn of the century for bridges of technological wonder—longer and taller than any built before—Africa more closely matched his taste. It desired straightforward solutions.

He started to stroll down the embankment toward camp, following the Indians, gazing at the wilderness the railway cut its way through. This was the land where he would start his life afresh.

Unfortunately, at the moment, the land did not look like much. Back in Maine, he'd pictured trees hundreds of feet high, giant apes and elephants everywhere, the sounds of birds screeching and water dripping off leaves. Instead this area was semiarid, closer to a desert. The scrubby trees were not more than thirty feet tall, thickly entwined. Thorns several inches long grew everywhere on the branches and the trunks. Trying to walk through this forest without getting cut must be difficult. Nyika, he had been told the trees were called, Swahili for "barren land," because few people wished to live among them.

The trees were horrible to clear from the railway's path, slicing open the workers' hands and legs like teeth.

He had much to learn. On this continent, he could identify few of the foods or plants or animals, none of the poisonous snakes. He had no knowledge of the niceties of customs, nor the basics of any of the languages—not those of the African natives or the Indian workers. In this new land, the most he could hope for was to learn quickly. A man with the knowledge of a newborn, he would be in charge of over seven hundred men, the whole Tsavo River assignment.

Lost in these thoughts, following the Indians, gaping over his shoulder at the trees, he walked smack into a naked boy.

Jeremy's height of six foot one made him tall enough that his habitual stance was a touch hollow-shouldered, as though he were constantly in the midst of an apologetic shrug. This boy bounced off his elbow.

"Goddamn," he muttered at the sudden sharp jab, then turned with embarrassment at his oath. There stood a remarkably muscular child, now several feet back, balanced and unruffled as though he had never been touched, holding a branch in one hand. For an instant, Jeremy believed him to be a white boy with some manner of a terrifying full-body skin disease. Then he understood his mistake. The boy was covered with a thick white paste in which an elaborate pattern—or perhaps writing of some type—had been drawn, revealing his black skin. The thickset boy stood, head tilted, branch held out, muttering, concentrating, lines of writing running along each of his limbs and even down his male member. And as Jeremy's eyes rested there for a moment, he realized this was a full-grown man. A very short man, perhaps even a pygmy, but—considering the sagging scrotum and looser skin on the thighs—a man of advanced years.

Suddenly conscious of where his eyes were, he jerked his gaze up. The man watched without response, his stare locked on Jeremy, his lips still whispering. The end of the branch pointed at him, quivering as though in the lightest breeze. His mumbling was neither angry nor insane-sounding. Instead it had the same mechanical quality with which old women recite their rosaries.

"Terribly sorry," Jeremy said. "Excuse me." Although whether he was apologizing for bumping into the man or staring at his loins, he did not know.

The man whispered on.

At this point, Jeremy began to back away. Looking down the embankment, he noted all the Indians had come to a stop, were turned fully around, staring at him and the African. What had halted them at this distance, he wondered, what had made them turn? That small smack of flesh as he bumped into the man? His "excuse me?" The man's almost soundless whispering? There was something visually unnerving about hundreds of men standing still for no apparent reason, so motionless there was not even the rustle of cloth.

In the few minutes since the train's arrival, the sun had slid that final inch down behind the horizon. As Jeremy would learn over the next few weeks, here, there were no lingering sunsets. In the tropics, the sun did not arc diagonally across the sky to creep gradually behind the earth; instead it plummeted down. Hot shimmering day and then, with an almost audible snap, night. In the shadows, at this distance, the Indians' dark faces were already indistinct, their emotions hard to read. With the African's encrusted skin, it was difficult to discern with accuracy the edges of his eyes or mouth. His jaw moved on, as he mechanically mumbled. The branch shivered, pointed directly at Jeremy's heart.

Abruptly unnerved, Jeremy turned and walked away down the embankment, taking long purposeful steps, trying not to look as though he were fleeing. As he caught up with the Indians, stepping in among them in an attempt to lose himself in their ranks, he realized the branch had been nyika. Glancing down at his elbow, he saw the single drop of blood soaking through the white linen.

Jeremy had been hired for the railroad without ever visiting the newly named territory of British East Africa, without viewing the terrain he would be building on, without a single face-to-face interview. A simple correspondence of eleven letters sent back and forth: his resume and various recommendations, a few professional sketches of the Hadley bridge, a carefully phrased essay (in which Grandpapi's hands had featured prominently). In return he had received by post a technical description of the Tsavo River, a primer on the railway's political difficulties and urgency, a list of supplies and clothing recommended for his personal use, and the request for the transportation of certain engineering and medical goods from the States.

However, from those few letters, he had come to feel almost as though he knew this writer from Africa, his new employer. Ronald Preston—a methodical man, a driven one—was the top engineer responsible for building a railway across five hundred miles of extreme wilderness, cutting through swamps, jungles, and hills, leveling the ground and laying the tracks across every type of possible terrain, from a small coastal city to a point on the map chosen solely for its coordinates, not even a village there. The purpose of the railroad was not to transport African natives, but to claim the land, to attract European colonists and enable them to move any necessary building and farming supplies inland. The initial survey of this wilderness had barely been completed even before construction commenced. Many of the tribes had never seen a white person and some of those that had had sworn war on any additional whites they might encounter. The land was currently being ravaged by extreme drought and an ensuing famine, as well as by a continent-wide epidemic of rinderpest that was killing through its attendant ailments of diarrhea and pneumonia every kind of hoofed creature from the native Cape Buffalo to any imported cattle. Given rinderpest, the building of the railway would get no assistance from the labor of oxen, donkeys, or horses. No, this endeavor would be powered solely by train wheels and human muscle. This railway, this "lunatic line" as it had been nicknamed by the British press, was in a race with the German railroad in the neighboring colony as both imperial powers strove to tighten their claims on their disputed territories. When Jeremy contemplated Preston's responsibilities, he marveled at what must be the nearly insurmountable difficulty of simply transporting all the supplies necessary to keep up the pace of building half a mile of railway a day in such a foreign and immoderate land.

In spite of whatever pressures he was under, Preston seemed to have a certain kindness, a certain patience. He took a moment to cross each 't' with a careful swirled line (a line feminine enough to make Jeremy wonder why he had chosen engineering). And after the job had been proffered and accepted, Preston had taken the time to pen a last letter to him, a short but considerate warning that building a bridge and railroad in Africa would not be the same as in New England. Here the terrain and weather were more treacherous. Preston wrote that when trying to explain a task to the coolies, there were communication difficulties and, frequently, a lack of understanding of simple safety procedures. Here, human labor was cheaper and easier to procure than shipping in steam cranes from overseas, thus the larger and more dangerous operations were performed by large numbers of men attempting to act in concert.

Accidents happened here, Preston wrote. There was also malaria, blackwater fever, sleeping sickness, parasites, sepsis, and the way the smallest cut festered in the humidity of the rainy season. Even the wild animals would take their toll.

Here, Preston wrote, many would die.

FOUR

Bangor, Maine
December 7, 2000

W hy you?" asked her mom first thing.
"Mom." Max spoke as always in a monotone, but the speed of her words increased. "I'm a month from the end of my postdoc. I won the Ashe prize. I'm a . . . "

"Don't get upset. It's a genuine question. There must be a hundred established ethnobots in the area who'd leap at this chance."

"What do you mean by established and in the area?"

Her mom was accustomed to Max's need for terms to be defined. "They've discovered drugs which have reached the market and they live in New England."

Max's eyelids flickered once. Fast as a computer screen redrawing. "Sixty-seven," she said.

Numbers to her mom had never been that compelling. "Fine, there are sixty-seven other ethnobots in the area. Some of them are world-renowned experts. Why'd they choose you?"

"I'm cheaper." Max offered.

Her mom cocked her head at her. Her hands on her hips. Her freckled hands, her tired skin. "Something about this is fishy."

Researchers had many theories about the cause of Asperger's. One was that the cause in the brain at all, but in the gut. It was postulated that the intestines might be imperfect at breaking down food particles, that they might leak into the blood all sorts of things they shouldn't, including molecular compounds similar to opiates. The person's nerves jangling with a morphine-induced intensity.

Certainly for Max as a child, sensation seemed to pour in as an uncontrolled flood, shimmery and overpowering. Eyes averted, body rocking, she'd kept her hands curled tight all the time, protecting her fingers, all those tender nerve endings. She learned to pick things up by pinching them between her wrists. Glass was the worst to touch, like an eel shivering fast up her nerves, so cold. Visually, the worst were people's faces, chaotic and rubbery, their eyes strobing with intensity. She preferred to be alone, far from others, spinning the wheel of a toy, its spokes twinkling. Predictable. Controllable. She'd do this for hours.

As a child, she panicked when anyone got too close—the heavy flesh, a huffing presence overwhelming her. She'd wallop at the person with her fists. Wide-eyed panic.

She didn't talk at all until she was four, before that only squealed in inarticulate rage or laughter. Then in August just after her fourth birthday, she said her first words, strung together a whole sentence. "Mom smells nice." She was looking away of course, at the ground. Her mom whooped and grabbed her in a hug. Max flailed. There was a muffled crack. Her mom grabbing her nose, the blood spurting.

They'd taught each other compromise. The way they shared closeness was by sitting side by side on the couch, a foot of distance between them, hugging the other person's empty winter coat. Her mom's coat was corduroy and smelled like her: a sort of salty maple syrup. Max would press her face into it. She murmured, "Love love love."

And so her mom learned to sit beside her only child, not touching her or looking her in the eye. She tried very hard. However, sometimes she got a little hunched, holding her daughter's parka, hiding her face in the folds. Sometimes sitting there, she was silent for long enough that even Max would understand, get up and walk fast from the room.

"Look Mom, so far as I know this Rwandan expedition is the only one out there. Ethnobotany is dead. It's either this or I'm going to end up working for the fragrance industry. You want me to spend my life finding botanical sources for room deodorizers?" What she looked at was her mom's elbow. She worked to memorize the way the skin at the elbow—when the arm was held straight—folded into a sort of boneless nose. In Rwanda she might need to replay this image. "This is a heart med. It'll save lives."

Her father. Mostly what she remembered was that he had sat peacefully—so fundamentally different from every other human she knew—that she could ease her way into his lap. He didn't move much, certainly not unexpectedly, didn't seem to feel the need to talk. Never patted her on the back. Content to just hum to himself, something quiet and repeated, predictable, lost in his own thoughts. The research said her differences were probably inherited, popping up in the family for generations. It was possible he'd been like her, a trifle alien on this planet. For whatever reason, she could sprawl across him, relaxed, as she couldn't with other people. She used to rub the wood beads he wore round his neck. They were old and smooth to the touch. If she scratched at one with her nail and sniffed, she could catch the slightest scent of a spicy sweetness like cinnamon. She never asked to wear the beads; at that age she couldn't imagine the necklace could come off of him. That it could exist anywhere apart from his dark skin.

Her mom sat down at the computer. She didn't flinch from anything, not anymore. She was worn down as a rock pulled from the sea. All weaknesses battered away. "I don't like the way you described these men." She began to type. "Let's see what's going on here. Uganda, did you say?"

"Rwanda."

Her mom was inexact, emotional, no head for details. But when Max was young, she'd saved her: fighting with the school to get the best help and working with Max at home, sheer persistent effort. Max had told her that on six different occasions. Speaking in her flat voice. "Without you," Max had said, "I would have shot myself with Grampie's 45."

(Especially in high school she'd thought about the gun a lot. Loved the smell of its gun oil. The barrel tasted pretty good too. On her tongue it was unmoving.)

The first time she'd said this, her mom had reacted a bit like an aspie, turned her gaze away, face stiff. Then she'd locked herself in the bathroom.

Now her mom was clicking through web pages, head tilted back to see through her bifocals, scanning the words. Research was how she'd gotten assistance for Max in school, found treatments, an appropriate diet and meds. She put together the treatment plan herself. But right now she didn't have much time. The plane left tomorrow, the lab equipment was already packed.

Normally each morning at 6:58, Max would sit down in her cobalt chair at her cobalt kitchen table to take her first bite of oatmeal. She appreciated cobalt, the way it twinkled cool in the back of her eyes. She didn't add brown sugar or raisins to the oatmeal because they would taint the texture and color.

Tomorrow morning at 6:58 she would be sitting in an airplane—the only food offered: a tray of highly adulterated substances. She would be flying off to another continent for an undetermined amount of time, to live with strangers. Everything about this unsettled her, especially the speed with which it was happening. Still Roswell and Stevens had insisted on how quickly corporate espionage could outflank their lead. If that happened, she would spend her life researching deodorizers.

She noticed she was rocking slightly. She stopped. Inhaled, taking her time, filling her lungs from the bottom up, calming her body. In her life, she'd gone through a lot. She knew well how much she could deal with.

She started packing. Ten pairs of identical gray stretch pants, cotton and soft. Ten pairs identical gray T-shirts, form-fitting. It wasn't that she wished to reveal her body. No, if she could, she would erase her physical self from the vision of others entirely. Create some sort of stick-figure representation, a generic avatar holding a plant and a microscope. She preferred gray because it was the most unobtrusive. A cloudy haze, a fog. Because she wore the same near-uniform day after day, over time it stopped bothering her. Took up no part of her mind. The material was stretchy so the wind couldn't brush it against her skin, jarring her. When she was a child, her mom had to wash new clothes twenty times before Max would pull them on. As an adult, Max discovered eBay. Secondhand clothing came pre-softened. She just had to wash the scent of the previous owner out, pack it in a drawer with some fresh rosemary for two weeks and it was ready. In an essential way it ceased to exist.

Her mom was reading, intent. "There's a travel advisory for the northwest corner of Rwanda. Where are you going to be?"

"The closest town is Gisenyi. I'll be in the national park near there."

The clacking of keys.

When people met Max, she passed as normal, at least at first. More than passed. In Maine, she was exotic. Men's heads tended to track her on the street, until at times she worried she might be dressed or moving inappropriately. Even women refocused as she walked by, their bodies going still.

Of course once the men or women actually interacted with her, talked with her, their reaction changed. The flatness of her voice, the way she didn't look at them. The subtle social signals she missed. After a while the men stopped leaning in as close, their voices got less warm and confiding. It took differing amounts of time, depending on how much each had hoped. The women caught on more quickly. Their words would drag a bit as they puzzled it out. Then they'd spot the final clue. There'd be this pause. A silent adjustment.

Each year she got a little better at her imitation. Each year it took longer for strangers to figure out she was different. She found it easier, if she was going to have any sustained interaction with a person, to announce her difference in the same sentence as her name. It cut down on misunderstandings.

In high school, she spent a lot of her spare time reading biographies about early botanical researchers living among tribes, Schultes among the Kiowa, Spruce among the Yanomami. Working not to offend, the researchers sipped from a gourd of fermented saliva or tried to sit like the natives did, crouched on their heels for hours at a time. She pictured their struggles at mastering the social rules. She would flip to the pictures and stare at the photos of the white man wearing a grass skirt next to diminutive tribal folk. She was like them, a stranger in costume working to fit in.

She'd gone into ethnobotany because of these biographies.

"Gisenyi? I think that's in the area with the travel advisory," said her mom. "Did they mention there was trouble there?"

"Roswell and Stevens? No, they didn't."

Her mom was clicking through the BBC's archives. "I don't trust them."

Max packed her oatmeal and rice. She'd be able to get bananas there. Pale food calmed her. Pale food, only one ingredient, not even salt added.

"Well, it says here there's been some recent violence. Just across the border in the Democratic Republic of Congo. People attacked. A few deaths." Her mother peered closer at a photo, confused, then jerked back. "Jesus. How can they print pictures like that?" She held a palm against her chest. "OK, OK. Let me find a map."

Max counted the aseptic boxes of tofu. She didn't know how many weeks she'd be gone, how long it would take to find the vine. She could always have more tofu sent. The keyboard clicking in the background.

"Here we go," said her mom, peering at the map she'd found. "Your research station is in the Virunga mountains? Just north of Gisenyi?

Max nodded.

"Right. You're basically in the Congo."

Max stepped forward, surveyed the map, then the inset box about scale. "No, I'll be inside Rwanda's borders by 3.5 miles."

"That's what I said. Basically in the Congo."

"What were the incidences?"

"The articles don't say much. Nothing at all in the American press. The BBC has a few paragraphs. The Congo was recently in some civil war. There are UN soldiers stationed there now, but the peace is pretty fragile. There have been several separate attacks. They seem to be primarily directed against whites who live in the area."

On the map, Rwanda was such a tiny country. The Virunga mountains wedged in the corner under the looming monolith of the Congo.

"Any of these attacks in Rwanda itself?" Max asked.

"Not that I could find. But the embassy is clearly worried."

Her mom pushed back from the computer, staring at the screen. She was gnawing on a dry piece of skin on her thumb. When she was younger, working to raise Max on her own, she used to rip whole cuticles off. Ragged wounds along each fingernail. "The men you met with—" she trailed off.

"Roswell and Stevens. The company's called Panoply."

"They worry about legal stuff, don't they?"

"These days, what company doesn't?"

She tugged on the piece of skin with her teeth, her voice a bit muffled. "You know what I think? If the violence moves over the border, the two of them don't want to get sued for sending someone who's white into a situation where their skin color could put them in danger."

She turned toward her daughter. Max kept her eyes on the map.

"They chose you because they think in Rwanda you're going to blend in."

Neither of them commented on the likelihood of that.

FIVE

*Near the Tsavo River, British East Africa
December 16, 1899*

On the morning of his first hunt, when Jeremy pushed through the flap of his tent, a N'derobbo man stood outside ready to be his guide. Ungan Singh, Jeremy's head jemadar, had said he would arrange to hire all the men necessary for the sport. Here, Jeremy was led to understand, he would not hunt in the manner he was accustomed to, just whistling up a dog and slinging a gun over his shoulder to wander off into the forest. In Africa, whole parties accompanied each hunter: guides, trackers, gun boys, and bearers.

Jeremy did not know how long the N'derobbo had been waiting, but the tribesman stood there, balanced like a stork on one leg, leaning on his spear, the other foot pressed into the side of his knee, the stance of an African hunter. He might have been there for hours, standing with as much grace as though his goat-fur toga and shell necklace were the couture of a king. If Jeremy had to dress that way, his less wiry body would appear not nearly as decorous and he would never be able to arrange the robe's folds as elegantly nor be able to stand so still on one leg.

Instead of being a N'derobbo, Jeremy was referred to by the Indians as "Pukka Sahib." Straightening up outside of the tent flap, he felt—in comparison to this man's primitive clothing—uncomfortably cognizant of his crisply laundered safari suit and fine riding boots, his wide hat and gleaming gun belt. He didn't wish to appear conceited. Having mastered a few phrases of Swahili, he nodded, "Jambo, rafiki."

"Morning," the N'derobbo answered in a clear British accent, looking him straight in the eye, his gaze not wandering down to Jeremy's accessories of power. This was the manner in which the Africans tended to look at him. Unlike the Indians, they did not survey his clothes or guns, but searched his face instead for its strengths and weaknesses.

"I'm Otombe," the man said. "Pleased to meet you."

The hunting party broke out of the underbrush onto the savannah. After all the claustrophobic nyika, the vast stretch of the plain took a moment to adjust to, a shifting inside the mind as much as in the eye. The immense vista reminded Jeremy of the sea, the grass rolling in waves out to the horizon. Hunting here could not be the same as it was in Maine, a matter of stealth and cunning. Here, there were no forest paths to crouch beside in ambush, no trees to hide behind. In this thick grass, there could be no prints visible to trail. No, out on this plain, locating any prey must be a simple matter of wandering along until you spotted one, probably at a range of at least half a mile, and then shooting the creature down like target practice. Really, he was rather disappointed, surprised so many experts had made such a fuss over this pursuit in Africa. Assuming there was no further need to pay attention, that the trotting N'derobbo would guide the search, he loosened the reins, giving Patsy her head as he fell to daydreaming.

Preston, in one of his final letters, had warned him not to bring any animals with him from America. There was the rather exorbitant expense of the transport on a ship, especially a creature as large as a horse. Few animals adjusted gracefully to the difference in climate and, those that did, had to survive all the diseases of the tropics. However, if Jeremy had of one symbol of his adulthood, it was Patsy. Hers were the saddlebags he had packed to attend Rensselaer. She was the horse he had ridden to graduation, the one he had taken to his first job, as well as to pick up the mail on the day the job offer from Preston came. Although he'd said good-bye to everything else from his previous life in Maine, including his family, he was unable to imagine his future without her.

He'd had to pay dearly for a horse stall on the ship to be built and enough provisions for her to be stored, had to endure the captain grumbling. Still he judged it worth it. Patsy was only eight and had always exhibited a healthy constitution. Jeremy felt confident she would last many years here.

Among her many strengths, she was a good hunting horse, never spooking at a shot and when he jumped off to retrieve a kill, she drop-reined like a statue. Back in Maine, they had made a competent team, potted a fair number of animals: deer, fox, hare, and once a wolverine. These were the largest creatures one could find in the area because every farmer had a gun and the fervent desire to civilize the wilderness for both crops and people. Long before he had been born, the wolves had been exterminated, as well as almost all the bears. He had not heard tell of a moose in years.

Lazy from the heat, swaying in the saddle, he glanced back to see how far they'd come. Ten paces behind the last of his hunting party, two unfamiliar natives trotted along with spears the length of a man. They jogged patiently, utterly silent. The savannah had been deserted in every direction last time he'd looked. Startled by the appearance of the Africans as well as by the span of their spears, he remembered his mother predicting that the savages would be bloodthirsty. She had repeated this belief several times, maintaining that since the natives concentrated on the blood sport of hunting for the daily procurement of their food, instead of farming, the habit of violence must run in their blood. They would not be able to help it. While she spoke, his mother held up one thin finger, which looked even paler than it was from all the black crepe she wore.

Remember, she promised, no matter how they appear at the

beginning, you will see that those people are bloodied and violent, their true natures revealed. Do not trust them.

Unnerved, Jeremy asked Otombe, "Where did the two behind us come from?"

Otombe did not glance back at the hunters, his eyes continuing to study the rolling grass in front of them, in the manner with which a fisherman might examine the sea. "Always people around. Masai, Ogiek, WaKikuyu."

Jeremy searched the horizon, saw no one else for miles. How could a person hide out here? There was not a tree or big rock in sight. "Why do they follow?"

A short man, spare and tendoned as an antelope, Otombe's breath was not ragged even though he had been loping steadily along beside the horse for an hour since they had left camp. His goat-fur toga draped elegantly, leaving both arms bare but covering the torso down to the upper thighs like a furry dress, the bottom swaying back and forth as he ran. Regarding him from the side like this, Jeremy realized that the flapping item he glimpsed occasionally under the edge of the toga was not a loincloth or the end of a purse. Mortified, Jeremy jerked his eyes up. How was one supposed to maintain a proper decorum here if the people did not dress correctly?

"Where a white hunter is, soon there'll be meat," said Otombe. "They're hungry."

Jeremy tried to keep his gaze fixed on the horizon or on the hunter's face, but in the heat and boredom of the ride, he sometimes found his eyes drifted back down. Of course, he thought, the man must be cooler that way than if his clothing consisted of leather boots, woolen knee socks, linen underclothes, shorts, belt, spine protector, shirt, and thick hat. But, after all, a native could afford to wear less. Modern science knew that exposure to the tropical sun's radiation could waste a white man away—especially if the exposure was to the critical regions of head or spine. Thus the spine protector had been invented, a thick piece of flannel cloth running the length of the back held in place by rubberized straps over the shoulders. He had been assured by Dr. Thornton, the camp physician, that it would be close to suicide to remove his hat or spine protector for any length of time while outside, unless in complete shade. The corollary of all his protective clothing was that perspiration occasionally ran into his eyes, stinging.

"Otombe," Jeremy said, "I'm curious. Could you tell me how you came to learn English?"

Otombe looked at him, no change in his posture or the rhythm of his gait.

Where did this man get such self-possession, wondered Jeremy.

"A British missionary couple raised me as their own until I was six."

"What happened then?"

"They gave birth to their own child. Returned me to my tribe." He jogged on, his spear held loosely by his side.

Jeremy considered what that experience must have been like, the shift from a wood house to a wattle-and-daub hovel, from reading the Bible to hunting with a spear, from standing patiently in shoes to running in bare feet, from wearing restrictive clothing to near nudity. Aside from the painful shift in parents, he had to admit a touch of jealousy. After only a week, he found himself strangely at home here in Africa. He wondered if some relative of his could have resided here before, if something in him was meant to stand beneath this wide tropical sky. However, how was that possible when until a few years ago the only foreigners around were the Mohammedans, a few explorers and the Portuguese? Still, in the pre-dawn, he relished stepping out of his tent to hear the nervous cackle of the last of the night's hyenas and to smell the Indians' spices beginning to roast over the fires. Gazing out over the twisted thorn trees and the tents dusty with red dirt, he knew not a soul around him had heard a single rumor about his past, and in his chest he felt the rising flutter of love for this colony, this continent.

Most of the adult Africans he had encountered possessed willowy bodies and regal cheekbones. They stood with grace in the bright light of day, wearing only a few wavy lines of paint or some metal bangles, a leather loincloth or woven wraparound skirt.

Each day, the construction of the railroad plowed forward without him spotting a single African village in any direction, but still every morning, no matter what the weather, clusters of scrawny potbellied children would appear, to stare at the Indians and him with the same sober curiosity that he wished to turn on them but, out of propriety, could not. In fairly short order, the children learned to cluck their tongues and hold out their hands, begging. The men tossed bits of bread and rice, and the youths scrambled in the dirt for the scraps, an activity Jeremy believed no American would ever lower himself to.

And then there was the animal life. He had been informed that the drought that had ended five days ago had lasted two solid years and was the worst in living memory, yet to him the wildlife appeared to be flourishing. At night, the hoots and grunts, calls and shrieks were loud enough that on occasion one had to raise one's voice to be heard, as though this semi-desert were Eden. During the day Jeremy studied with amazement every creature he came upon, never having imagined such crazed coloring, varied sizes, or methods of movement. Red lizards bolted off in a blur of speed, giraffes lazily see-sawed away over the trees, a blue monkey small as a chipmunk plucked food off his table and leapt high into a tree. Before the rains he had seen vultures, awkward as crippled children, hopping toward the bodies of those animals that had died.

In the last few days since the drought had finally broken—with a torrential deluge of eight inches—the season of the monsoon had hit with a vengeance, making up for the years of dryness.

Yesterday, a rhino had clambered across a newly built railroad embankment and, afterward, the downpour had gradually eroded the plate-sized prints into one zigzagging fast-moving river, the erosion spreading until ten feet of railroad tracks had actually decoupled, sliding down with the washed-out mud into the swamped ditch. Surveying the mess, marveling at the destruction possible from something as simple as footprints and rain—something that Jeremy had always considered gentle and innocuous—he thought it was no wonder that modern civilization had developed in Europe instead.

Every day, before he rose, he reminded himself that here he was a complete neophyte, without the comprehension of half of what he needed to know to safely govern all these men he had been assigned. In this new geography he always tried to question his old assumptions, checking here that they sustained their accuracy. He felt he had been born anew in Africa, with the delight of an infant in each unfamiliar sight and with the same inability to recognize danger.

The second day here, he had learned this lesson well when he'd addressed his men for the first time, the Indians whose hands would assemble the geometric perfection of the railroad tracks—his Indians, all seven hundred thirty two of them. He watched the men convene, attired in puffy turbans and oversized white shirts hanging down to their knees. Still carrying the shovels and hoes they had been working with, they jostled closer to hear how he would address them, to see with their own eyes what kind of sahib he might make. So new here, he did not yet comprehend there were over forty different languages in camp, the only shared ones being English and Hindi. He did not understand the difference between the broad groupings of Buddhists, Hindus, and Mohammedans, much less those between Sikhs, Jainists, and Shiites. He had not learned that Mohammedans asked repeatedly not to work Friday afternoons while the Hindus would not touch beef if it were served. He did not know that the Mohammedans would stop work five times a day to bow down toward the North while the Hindus requested that, if they perished here, their remains be cremated. Instead, he mentally lumped all those dark attentive faces together into one homogenous group and labeled it *foreign*.

Before he could commence his address to the crowd—the Hindi translator waiting at his side—two of the men near the front began to push one other, other, no need for any greater complaint than physical proximity and religious distance. A few of the bystanders were hit by the scuffle and the fisticuffs began to spread. Jeremy froze, no idea of what to do. Five of the jemadars waded in, shoving and yelling, trying to separate the men even as more and more workers pressed forward into the knot of thrashing arms and yelling faces. Then he heard the first real scream and spotted the bloody edge of a hoe raised overhead.

Desperate, Jeremy discharged his firearm into the sky. The crowd froze, all their furious motion abruptly stopped, those brown faces staring up at him and his rifle.

This was not how he had imagined himself ruling. He had visualized his own enlightened kindness, their surprised devotion.

Instead, he found himself looking up at the gun as the rest of them did and noting how forceful it looked up there, against the bright equatorial sky.

Dr. Alan Thornton, the camp physician, was the one to explain to him why no Africans were being used to build the railroad. They refused to dig embankments for a full day in the tropical sun, not for money nor trade items. The only known way to motivate them was how the Belgians were rumored to do it in the Congo: mutilations, hostages, and wholesale slaughtering. Thornton explained that the prevailing view was that the Africans were a lazy lot, a work ethic atrophied by the torrid heat. Jeremy knew Thornton had much more experience with Africa and its natives than he did, but he was unsure how to jibe the man's statement with the fact that Otombe was continuing to trot on without stopping for what must be at least six miles.

The Indians who built the railroad were also an alien dark-complected lot, but they were much closer to the British in terms of common assumptions about the strictures and hierarchy of society. They knew how to read the details of Jeremy's clothing to discern his status and how to apply flattery when requesting a favor. From what he had observed so far, however, many of them seemed to get fulfillment, not from laboring hard for the British Empire as the English wished them to, but rather from attempting to outsmart the system.

The other day, he had ridden over the hill into the stone quarry perhaps an hour earlier than he normally did. Instead of hearing the busy ring of iron against stone, the entire quarry was silent, one hundred and seven masons stretched out in the little shade offered by the rocks, several men snoring. The three jemadars in charge were playing cards, their whips looped loosely beside them. As the rustling awareness of his arrival spread, men jumped to their feet and hammered away at the first available rock. In that instant, he could see the big-eyed fear of punishment battling with their pride at all they had gotten away with.

But even at times like this, it was clear they had learned the rules of the white man's system—were not standing apart, simply watching, like the Africans. Whenever his Indians requested an advance on their wages or a day off their eyes were lowered like women's.

So far he had continued to pay the railroad's standard wages out of fear of the men considering him weak, but at night he truly struggled with what fair pay should be for manual labor in this intemperate land where a simple scratch could lead to gangrene. Two days ago, he had examined the accounting books to get a sense of where the railroad's major expenditures lay. Checking the month's final totals, he had marveled at how cheaply so much labor could be engaged here on the dark continent. It was only after several minutes of study that he noted, underneath each man's name, a tidy column of negative numbers. After some inquiry, he learned that their wages were docked for the expenditure of shipping them here and then back to their native land, as well as for what they ate and drank and for any new clothing they acquired while here—all of this clothing purchased through the railroad's store. Glancing at these negative numbers, it was unclear how much might remain to send home to their families.

This arrangement bothered him. He had been raised to consider the responsibilities of class. He believed that those with affluence and power also inherited the onus to toil harder than anyone else, to be the last one in bed at night and the first one up, to make sure all was done for those who performed the more menial work. Thirty years ago, one of his Grandpapi's workers had gotten yanked halfway into the thresher by the edge of his sleeve. He had had four children under six. Of his own volition, Grandpapi sold a fifth of his farm to give the money to the widow. This was a tale frequently invoked by the family when discussing current events. Responsible leadership, his mother maintained, this was what the nation needed more of; then there would not be this unstated war between the Carnegies of the world and unionizers like Mother Jones. Responsible leadership—as was seen in her family, his mother believed—was what had made the Turnkeys all that they were.

Jeremy did not remember if she had talked this way, lionizing her family, before his father had disappeared. Of course there was not much he remembered from back then, before he was five, before they had moved in with Grandpapi—her father—on the dairy farm she had grown up on, before she had changed all their surnames back to her maiden name.

Since the start of the rains, more of the Indians' cuts were getting infected, fist-sized ulcers rising in a matter of hours, purplish and hot. Jungle sores, they were called. Already, the first cases of malaria had been reported. Yesterday, he had decided he would stroll through the hospital tent to visit the ailing men. He had pictured himself calling out words of good cheer to the three or four patients there, raising spirits, breaking the boredom of the sick bed, perhaps even sitting for a moment and chatting about the rapid progress the railroad was making, the service they were providing to this land.

Instead, as he stepped into the tent, he saw there were fifteen, maybe twenty, men. In the heat, the stench of vomit and putrefaction rose to his nose. Some of the men shivered in delirium. The male nurses moved between the beds, able to offer little aside from glasses of water, wet towels for fevers and, in the case of gangrene, speedy amputation.

Since Jeremy was a child, the physical processes of the body had made him light-headed. He could not even bandage his own cuts. The opened flesh and welling blood seemed so disturbing and *animal-like*, distinct from the human soul he recognized as the very essence of himself. His inability to help Grandpapi during calving season—the bawling bloody cows and mucus-covered newborns—had been a lot of his initial motivation for choosing engineering. Manufactured metal was clean, exact and durable, the apex of civilization, worthy of a lifetime's devotion.

Standing in the doorway of the hospital tent, he felt his face freeze in horror, an emotion he struggled to erase. These men— who labored hard under this tropical sun, who had traveled thousands of miles away from their families, risking death in a foreign land for the contracted period of three long years— deserved better. He created muscle by muscle the original smile of good cheer he'd had in mind, forced himself forward in a slow amble through the tent. To keep this expression affixed to his face, he made sure not to look directly at any blood-soaked bandages or open wounds, forcing his eyes instead just above the men's faces, while he nodded and called out words of encouragement. The overriding thought was this was his fault, each fever here, each missing limb, any deaths. He was the one responsible—as much as if he had injected each infection of malaria or inflicted each wound—him and the British, this railroad.

Just in time, he reached the far end of the tent, raising his hand in a casual salute good-bye. Three paces past the door flap, out of sight of the men, his left leg abruptly crumpled under him. He sat down hard, made no motion to get up, strangely content to listen to the rising static in his ears, while his vision tunneled in until all he could see was a single mango peel discarded in the dirt.

"Bwana," a man's voice said.

Startled from his memories, Jeremy looked up from his slouch in the saddle, recalling this hunt. Otombe was pointing to a large creature two hundred yards ahead in the midst of the grassy plain. "Eland," he said.

The animal stood as tall as Jeremy imagined a moose must, only it had spiral horns. It stared at the unfamiliar sight of a man astride a horse. He reined Patsy in hurriedly, although there was little possibility of escape for his prey. Its best hope would be to gallop—dewlaps flapping—for the crest of the hill half a mile away in an attempt to reach shelter on the far side. Wishing to forestall this option, Jeremy grabbed his 450 Express and raised it to his shoulder, ready to squeeze off the shot. For a moment he paused then, for the eland hadn't begun to run, but was still standing there, its deerlike eyes watching, filled with curiosity at his action. It had never seen a gun, he realized and this understanding spoiled a trifle the thrill of the hunt.

Still he pulled the trigger.

At the report, the huge animal simply disappeared, knocked backward into the grass. A moment later, even from two hundred paces, he heard the dull *whump* of it hitting the earth. With it standing like that, just waiting, a child could have killed it, but in the instant afterward he felt so much mightier than a child, so much bigger. The thump was as loud as when a ten-foot span of iron rail dropped into place at the head of the train tracks, such a sense of permanent change.

Galloping Patsy forward, he dismounted dangerously close to the twitching eland, amazed by its sheer girth and giant limbs. And yet he *had* dropped it, all this muscular mass. "Dropped" was the word, as though the only thing that had been holding this beast up before was his lack of desire to shoot it.

The bullet hole was obscured by the fur, so the dark stain spreading across its pelt did not appear to be blood, or even that visually interesting.

He noticed the way its shining eyes stared in single-minded concentration at the grass in front of its nose. Somewhere inside, it must know it would never run again, never stand. The life it had considered normal had ended. Still, it struggled to breathe, willing to settle for so much less than what it wanted in order to survive.

Jeremy knew just what that felt like.

Reaching out one finger, he tentatively stroked the fur on the half-ton of wilderness lying at his feet. At his touch, the animal exhaled and died.

When the rest of his hunting party reached him, he bade the Sikh gun boy to set up the camera and take a photo of him. He sat on the eland's shoulder, his rifle across his lap, his face impassive with his chin thrust forward, his best imitation of Grandpapi. He would mail the photo home. They could pull it out each time a guest inquired of him. In his correspondence, he would make sure to relate events backing up this image of him: successful hunts for large animals, observations of native customs, some of the technical difficulties with the railroad's construction. Every two weeks, he would ship home another envelope filled with a series of foreign and dusky adventures.

In his life, he had striven so earnestly not to disappoint them.

By the time the camera was set up and the exposure taken, the eyes of the eland had glazed over. Within the space of two minutes, the wild animal had turned into a furry mound of undressed meat. He reminded himself he had made this countryside a trifle safer for cattle and horses. The prevailing belief was that killing wild hoofed animals would decrease the speed with which rinderpest could spread. Although no one knew for sure which exact species the disease resided in, the theory was—when in doubt—shoot. The epidemic was so bad and the urge to help so strong, that across the continent, colonists hunted even from trains, resting the rifle in an open windowsill and blasting away at whatever they passed, shooting until the barrel burned with heat, the corpses rotting where they fell.

Perhaps it was partly the fault of the sheer size of the continent, bringing out such excess as this.

All this shooting, as well as the mounting toll from the rinderpest, was creating a scarcity of game that people were already noting. There was some talk of starting an animal preserve, as soon as the epidemic ended, perhaps around Tsavo, where no hunting would be allowed, not even by the tribes that resided there.

"Look," said the N'derobbo, "a lion."

Glancing up from the eland, Jeremy searched over the top of the rustling grass. Off his horse, the grass seemed surprisingly tall, the tips waving back and forth in the wind.

"Look," Otombe insisted, "look." He was pointing with his whole arm.

Newborn, Jeremy thought. I am a baby. He forced himself to survey the grass systematically in the area where the native pointed. He imagined the coup of posting home a photograph of himself sitting astride a dead lion.

"Sixty yards," said the N'derobbo. "Dark ears above the grass."

But Jeremy saw only grass, waving gently.

"Gone." Otombe let his arm fall while his eyes methodically searched. Standing now beside him, Jeremy realized this was the way the N'derobbo experienced the savannah, swimming through it, the grass up to his chest, holding only a single spear. The lion was somewhere out there. Jeremy understood now why he watched the grass around him with such care.

"Where did it go?"

Otombe shrugged.

The savannah ran uninterrupted up to this small trampled clearing where the eland had fallen. One of the bearers was kneeling down, gutting the animal. There was the coppery smell of blood. The organs were quickly scooped out and tossed onto the ground. Woozy at the sight, he turned away while the two unfamiliar natives who'd followed the hunting party stepped forward to claim the innards. Behind them the grass trembled. Was it only the breeze? Even holding his gun as he was, Jeremy found himself stepping closer to the N'derobbo.

Riding back from the hunt, Jeremy turned to see if any natives followed them now. The prairie behind them was empty, but he spotted the bundle of eland steaks balanced on the head of one of his WaKikuyu bearers. The bundle was tiny in comparison to the animal, fifty pounds taken from a half-ton creature. The meat was wrapped in the animal's own hide and, from a fold in the pelt, a little blood escaped, dripping down the WaKikuyu's neck. He remembered that moment while the creature had lain on its side, gasping for breath.

Turning away, he decided to leave these men for now. He should not have taken the day off, even if it was Sunday—too much depended on his leadership.

He sent the hunting party straight home while he journeyed back the longer way, following the railroad tracks, in order to check on the integrity of the newest section of embankment after last night's downpour.

Thus, when the sun set, he was riding Patsy along the tracks, getting close to camp, admiring the railroad's clean line. Although the tracks' final stop was supposed to be Lake Victoria, Jeremy had already figured out the lake would be merely an incidental layover to a much more important destination. This destination, the true purpose of the construction, had occurred to him as soon as he grasped the extent of the railroad's likely cost. The proposed budget was almost four million pounds, an imposing amount all on its own, but it seemed unlikely the total bill would come close to being that low. The surveying team had been too rushed to map the terrain in detail. Without a thorough assessment, any estimate of cost could be only a guess, and there were so many possible complications in this foreign clime: attacks by hostile tribes, the Indian workers going on strike, army ants devouring the wooden railway ties, the difficulties of engineering the railway up the two-thousand-foot-tall Kikuyu escarpment, the havoc caused by rhino footprints and rain. No, on this continent there was little chance that the railroad construction would proceed smoothly, that everything would play out according to a plan developed in a tidy, temperate country. The final price tag for this railroad would be staggering even to the British Empire.

And this was where the true destination or purpose became apparent. Once England had spent this much on a colony, it could not possibly let things continue as before, the tribes puttering around naked and hunting, the animals roaming free, the minerals lying untouched beneath the ground, the land unfarmed. No, long before this railway reached Lake Victoria, it would forcibly offload onto this land British values and lifestyles. Before this railway was finished, there would be cities built and English spoken, factories assembled and farms plowed, clothing worn and punctuality taught, the Christian god worshipped. Onto this wilderness would be mapped the straight and exacting lines of money and steel.

In a few years, he thought, little in this land would remain the same. He was glad to have the privilege of residing here now, experiencing it in all its beauty.

In the early darkness, he spotted something by the tracks. Seventy yards ahead, a tangled lump lay in the ditch at the bottom of the embankment, as though the passenger train were already running, and this was trash tossed from the window by some careless traveler.

As he approached, a creature slunk away from the debris, dragging a piece after it and wiggling effortlessly into the nyika. In the darkness it was hard to be sure of the animal's size: fox, hyena, or something larger.

As he halted Patsy, she shivered as though cold. Laying his hand against her neck, he could feel that her breathing seemed a trifle heavy from their walk. She must be acclimatizing to the heat here. He would give her an extra dose of oats tonight.

It was at this moment—his hand against his horse's neck, his thoughts on oats—that he registered the trash was actually a corpse.

From the way the Indian's body was tangled up in the sheet of the unraveled turban, it appeared it had been rolled down the escarpment into the ditch.

Five, perhaps six, seconds passed. Jeremy exhaled through his mouth.

Swinging an unwilling leg over the saddle, he dismounted.

His Grandpapi would do this without blinking, pick the corpse up, lay it across the pommel of the saddle, and ride back into camp with one hand grasping the seat of its pants, his jowled face revealing no emotion.

Standing here beside the body, Jeremy took a moment to look up at Patsy's familiar profile. In the darkness, the star on her forehead gleamed as clear as a light. To touch this body, pick it up, he would have to concentrate on something else, as he did at the dentist's while the man's pliers nosed about in his mouth searching for the rotten tooth. Numbers had always offered him a certain reassurance.

The Metric System, he recited from memory, *is derived from units of ten. Tera equals ten to the twelfth. Giga is ten to the ninth. Mega, ten to the sixth.*

Crouching down, reaching for the right arm, he noticed something was wrong with the face. He forced himself to breathe slowly. The skin was darker than normal above the mouth, stained perhaps by a birthmark or injury.

Deci, ten to the negative one. Centi, negative two. Milli, negative three.

He closed his hand on the bony wrist. Human flesh, chill to the touch. This close, he could see the mouth was propped open, something clasped between the teeth. For a moment he wondered if the man had choked on his dinner; that would explain the smell of cooking.

Micro, negative six. Nano, nine. Pico, twelve.

Reaching for the other wrist, he realized the object between the teeth was glowing. A live coal. The mouth charred. Sweet smell of meat.

Into his mind flashed an image of the accounting book, the neat row of negative numbers cribbed beneath each man's name. With an intuitive jump, he comprehended the railway's penny-pinching imitation of a Hindu cremation. He fell back on his buttocks.

The bush near him rustled. Perhaps the animal that had scurried away.

Scrambling backward up the embankment, he flailed, slipping onto his side, mud coating his hip. Fumbling upright, he scanned the brush near him, his rifle finally at the ready.

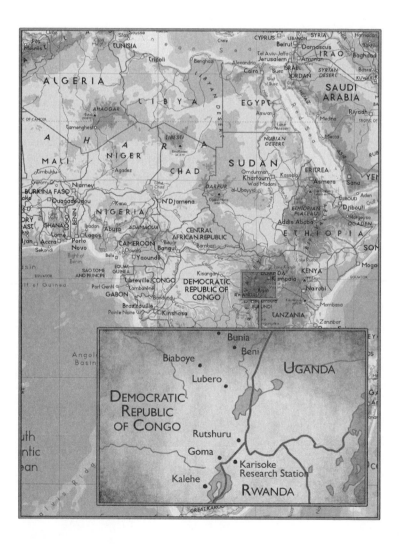

SIX
Kigali, Rwanda
December 9, 2000

As the airplane pulled into the Kigali terminal, an announcement was broadcast, requesting in three different languages that the passenger known as Dr. Max Tombay deplane first. The flight attendants herded her down the aisle. Stepping out the door, into the sunlight, she saw at the base of the airplane's stairs twelve officials in suits smiling up at her and holding up a banner that said "Welcome Panoply Pharmaceuticals." In smaller letters beneath, the banner added, "Rwanda: A Great Place for a Factory."

She held tight to the railing, blinking. The trip here had taken twenty-two hours, three different flights. All those fleshy breathing strangers packed in so close. The nubbly seats, the loud announcements, the mechanical air. She wasn't supposed to move, not pace, not flap her hands. For twenty-two hours, strapped into her chair, the roar of the engines had whined in her head like a noxious gas.

Now, exiting this plane, her feet were a little leaden from the tranquilizers. She stumbled slightly near the bottom of the stairs and four different arms in business suits were held out, wanting to assist. She stopped cold, out of reach, and waited there, eyes averted. After a pause, these hands were withdrawn. The flight attendants stood in the doorway behind her, whispering. A certain dry pressure in the back of her throat. She worked not to vomit.

She didn't address any one of the business suits around her, but instead talked in the direction of her left hand clinging to the railing. "I need a room to myself," she said, "for twenty minutes." She ignored the French phrase book in her bag over her shoulder; it was too far away. Instead, she just repeated her words more loudly. "I need a room to myself for twenty minutes."

One of the uniforms, maybe a translator, said something to the others about *nécessit*-a-something-or-other and *chambre*. Perhaps they assumed she had to make some phone calls, probably to heads of state, for they snapped into action, the whole crowd of them leading her into the airport, down a corridor and around a corner to an office that looked like it had been considered fancy in the 1950s.

They clustered in the hallway, one of them addressing her, probably the first sentence of a welcome speech, smiling, rolling his hands out in a wide gesture as though this hallway represented all that Rwanda could offer.

Before the translator could put these words into English, she closed the door in their faces.

Space without people. Something close to silence. Switching off the lights to stop the busy electric hum, she crawled under the desk, tight ball, tight ball, fists over her ears, rocking and moaning soft vowel sounds like a sick cow.

Later, she opened the door. She could at least function now. Five of the officials were still waiting, whispering among themselves. They turned, anxious and smiling. She announced she was ready and they led her back down the corridor. Not one of them asked a question. It was possible they'd heard her moaning.

The parade of them walked straight through immigration, followed by several porters wheeling her bags, the lab equipment and food. They cut through the crowds to the front of the line where a nervous immigration agent stamped her passport without saying a word.

She looked down to avoid the eyes of anyone who might be staring. All she saw were the hands and legs of the people she passed. Noted the median skin tone here was much darker than she was used to, close to the color of pumpernickel.

Her own color was an amber shade exactly halfway between her mom's ivory pinkness of a shaved mouse and her dad's reddish brown of cedar mulch. Still, in Maine, the combination of these colors had always seemed to confuse others. The first day of kindergarten, for example, her parents had walked in with her. The teacher had understood her dad was her dad. Had greeted him, exclaiming what a beautiful little girl he had.

And then hesitating, turned to her mom and asked, "Can I help you?"

On many subjects, neurotypicals were capable of deriving enormous information from minimal data points. Her mother, in a two-minute conversation with a neighbor, could deduce so much about the person's relationship, career and family life— information that Max would never have been able to infer. But on some subjects, normals seemed willfully thick.

Science was her respite, the exactness of vocabulary and measurement. Whenever she learned a new term, she could feel the frisson in her mind, the sparkle of connection. All sorts of examples would suddenly be illuminated. "Surface tension" and "crown shyness," they explained so much about the world, creating clarity where previously there'd been just a profusion of data.

So of course she found people's thinking and terminology about having darker skin confusing. It was so deliberately inexact, as though there were only two possible answers. At first sight, you either were black or you weren't.

Her mom said this toggle switch helped folks pretend the races were in separate encampments with walls built up between them. Max had difficulty with analogies, tended to take them literally. At her mom's words, she'd pictured the gap between East and West Berlin, on either side those vast concrete walls, barbed wire, and machine guns. For the next few years, she kept an eye out for walls like this somewhere around Bangor, assuming one day she'd be asked to move to the no-man's land between.

Upon meeting her, people tended to ask where she came from. When she was young she'd answer, "14 Pleasant Street, second floor." It wasn't until she was nine that her mother had told her this question was actually an inquiry about her racial background. From then on, when Max replied, she worked to be clear. After stating she'd been born in Bangor, she added she was a mulatto. If there was a pause afterward, she tried to be helpful, "Possibly even a quadroon." She assumed, in all situations, that specificity was good.

The airport lobby was filled with people and luggage. She spotted the main doors leading out of the building and strode fast toward them. She needed to get out. She had to keep juking—left, then right, then left again—to keep some space between her and everyone else, a very shy quarterback running down the field. The officials and porters trailed after her, zigzagging. The translator was half-running after her, talking loudly in English. His accent was hard to understand, the rhythm of his voice so different. Something about the tonnage of coffee beans and tin ore exports this year. She plowed on, desperate.

Pushing out through the doors, she walked straight into another crowd. She slammed to a halt, hands held up to protect her.

And half the men in this crowd, the second they saw her, stopped in the midst of whatever they were doing. There was a single quiet moment, then they all rushed her, yelling out "taxi, taxi," followed by prices in many languages and currencies. She went into a crouch, glancing around for some escape.

A stranger halted the stampede. He stepped in front of her, holding up his hands and yelling out something in French, a declarative statement. The men grunted, stopped and turned away.

"Dr. Tombay." The stranger said, "I am Mutara Gusana, head guide from Karisoke. Dr. Dubois send me. I drive you now." He held out his hand and she looked down at it. A calloused palm, dry skin. She was still breathing hard, couldn't deal with touching anyone.

"I don't shake hands," she said. "I have Asperger's."

After a confused pause, he withdrew his hand. It seemed likely his English didn't extend to the name of this syndrome. "Please to come with me." Any sort of warmth had disappeared from his voice.

The officials continued to follow her, the translator calling out information about the stability of their economy and friendliness of the people. The porters trailed behind with her luggage. The van was a beat-up Volkswagen from the 1970s, hand-lettered "Karisoke Research Station." The gorilla painted above the name looked a little like a hairy man with a bad back hunched over.

While her luggage was packed in, she glanced at Mutara and then away. This was the way she tended to get information about any person who stood close to her, a single fast stroboscopic picture of the person's expression and gesture. At this speed the person's face didn't overwhelm her. On the other hand, she didn't get all that much detail. He was a thin African wearing a blue shirt. She turned toward his shadow and asked, "The airport is full of people. How'd you know I was the one you were supposed to pick up?"

There was a pause. His shadow cocked its head. Then its arm gestured toward the airport. "But look. It is clear. You are the only . . . What is the word?"

She looked back at the crowds. She could do this since their faces were too far away to hurt her eyes. She saw, aside from being darker and half a head shorter than her, the Rwandan women wore designer jeans or ruffled skirts in vivid colors, high heels and large jewelry. A significant number of the men had on suits, some a little threadbare but all perfectly pressed. Most of them dressed as though they were about to interview for a job they really wanted. Max, on the other hand, wore gray stretchy sportswear. Her only jewelry was her dad's wooden beads strung round her neck on a simple string, her hair shaved as short as a Marine's. Nothing about her was designed to impress anyone with her social standing or fashion sense.

"American," she thought. From the distance of a hundred feet, anyone could pick her out as American.

"*Blanc*," said Mutara. "You are the only *blanc*."

The laugh burst out of her nose, a phlegmy sort of snort.

Her laughter was rare, but when it came, it geysered out. To fight it, she began to mentally recite the periodic table in alphabetical order, giving herself points for speed. "Aluminum, antimony, arsenic . . . ." Barium next? Her laughter faded as her eyes rolled upward, searching.

The tropical sky above, for a brief disorienting moment, looked so much like the sky over Maine.

The latch on the van's passenger-side door was broken and had been replaced by a thick braid of plastic bags that tied the door to the glove-compartment handle. Once Mutara got in, he retied her door shut, then bent briefly under the dashboard to touch two wires together. In the van with him, she could smell his scent of spices, mud, and soap. Coughing, the whole van began to rumble like an outboard motor. She winced and reached into her bag for her noise-canceling earphones.

"Money," he shouted over the noise. "Never enough, no? Please not to lean on your door."

As they drove away, the officials waved. Yelling good-bye with as much emotion as though she were their beloved.

She pulled on her earphones. From the edge of her eyes,

she saw Mutara shift his torso slightly to watch her do this, then turn away. For the rest of the drive, he didn't say another word. This was OK, preferable even.

She stared out the window. Not at all what she'd pictured. Way too many people bustling about, continuous stores and cement high-rises, palm trees and bougainvillea. Gradually the city was replaced by tiny farms, each an acre or less. The soil was the red of laterite, high in iron and aluminum hydroxides, a thin topsoil that washed away easily. It must be poor farming, but every inch of land was cultivated or built on, utilized in some way. Coffee, plantains, sweet potatoes. The entire country was crowded with people, working in the fields or by the houses, churning food in three-foot-tall mortars. Women strode along the roads with babies strapped on their backs. They walked the way she'd always dreamed of walking: perfect posture but not stiff, their hips and backs rolling and alive.

Although Mutara drove along a two-lane highway, it was nothing like the interstates she was used to. Here, it was startling how many people and belongings could fit on a moped. On the back of one were strapped two young goats, swaddled tightly as babies, eyes narrowed into the wind. Tied on another was an industrial-sized sink, a child peeking out of it forlornly.

Everyone wove from lane to lane, with little regard for the direction of traffic, unless the oncoming vehicle was bigger.

About an hour into the journey, an oil truck abruptly pulled onto their side of the road, roaring toward them. It was painted to look like a shark grinning. Tires squealing, Mutara swerved out of the way, rocketing now along the dirt of the shoulder, nearly sideswiping a family of four on a motorbike. For a moment it seemed the truck would still hit them, looming over them. Max could see jagged scratches in its paint.

There was a terrific clang as its side-view mirror broke off on the roof of their van and then the truck zoomed past, without having slowed at all.

Even through her headphones, Max could hear the way all the cars around tooted their horns, the honks somehow very third-world, not loud and outraged at someone else's transgression, but surprised and nearly joyful at survival.

Mutara glanced sideways at her, then did a double take. She was still grinning. When the side-view mirror had hit, pieces of glass had spun through the air. The shimmering beauty stunning. Like the sky itself was broken and spinning.

Death, to her, had never seemed that terrible.

Satisfied, she leaned back, closed her eyes, and just let the smells of the landscape waft over her. She sniffed at the air. Some days, she imagined herself as a mole: unreliable blinking eyes, hiding in her burrow, poking out just her twitching nose to experience the world that way. Unlike vision or touch, smell never betrayed her, never shivered or popped, electric and confusing. Instead it grounded her. She might not be able to hug her mom or more than glance at her face, but she could bury her nose in her mom's clothes all she wanted.

On the wind rushing in the window, she smelled wood smoke, rotting meat, cow manure, human feces, and something that kept reminding her of cough drops until she opened her eyes to identify a passing tree as eucalyptus.

In college she'd once met a woman who'd been born without a sense of smell. "Anosmia," the woman had declared matter-of-factly, the way one might say, "Parking ticket."

And Max jerked back from the word as fast as though she'd been slapped.

After three hours of driving, they parked in the lot of the Virunga National Park. Above them, the mountains loomed craggy and immense. Even here on the equator, two of the peaks had snow on them. Stepping out of the van, Max finally saw real jungle. Mile after mile of it swept up the steep sides of these mountains. No roads, no houses. Up there, the land would be empty of people except for a few researchers. Instead in every direction would be plants, massed thickly, rich and glossy. Waiting for her to study them.

Fifteen porters were in the parking lot waiting for them. They were not dressed as nicely as the people in the airport. These men wore the cast-off clothing of different countries and climates: a Manchester United T-shirt, a pair of ripped Brandeis sweatpants, a woman's cowl-neck sweater. All of the porters were barefoot except for one who wore ancient bowling shoes, the toes held together with duct tape. These men unloaded her bags out of the van and divvied them into approximately even allotments, then tied each pile up tightly in a sheet. Each man wove himself a padded crown of grass, hefted up his bundle and placed it on his head like some whimsical hat. Her Olympus microscope on top of two pieces of Samsonite luggage. Twenty boxes of tofu on her Plant Encyclopedia. Then, balancing these weights effortlessly, the men lit three cigarettes and passed them around, talking, while Mutara locked up the van. He pulled off his own clean and new-looking rubber boots to pack them away in his knapsack. Then standing in his bare feet, he neatly folded his pants up to his knees.

Max wondered how they would travel this last leg of the journey. From the map she'd looked at with her mom, she knew the research station was located high on the shoulder of these mountains, probably five miles and six thousand feet straight up. These mountains were supposed to be a major tourist destination, so she searched for a gondola or some all-terrain vehicles or at least a wide paved path. She could spot nothing along these lines.

Whatever language these men spoke, it wasn't French. Their words were all bounce and rounded vowels. When the last cigarette was smoked down to the filter, they turned and in a line, luggage swaying on their heads, walked into the jungle, heading up what she now saw was the narrowest of muddy trails.

Mutara followed.

Max stared. Roswell and Stevens hadn't mentioned this part of the itinerary. The slope was steep. The porters strode onward, making their ascent look easy. They began to disappear into the foliage, the bags waving good-bye from above the bushes. She glanced again up at the distant mountains peaks and then, having no choice, followed.

The mud on the path was slick. It felt as though it had been raining here continuously for weeks. Before she'd gone a hundred feet, she slipped and fell onto both knees and one hand. As with most aspies, physical agility was not one of her skills. At the best of times she walked flatfooted and unsteadiy. Right now, she hadn't slept in thirty-nine hours and the tranquilizers she'd taken on the airplanes seemed to have puddled in her feet. She stood back up, wiping the mud off her pants as best she could—mostly smearing it around—and then continued to climb.

Three times a week she jogged four miles, but only indoors on a track, an utterly flat surface. She enjoyed running round and round that perfect oval, keeping neatly between the lines. Years of this had helped her balance and stride appear slightly more natural.

But this path was definitely not flat.

Within the first half hour, she fell three more times and gave up trying to wipe herself off. Hoping her bare feet might get more traction, as it seemed to for the porters and Mutara, she pulled off her loafers and tied them to her knapsack.

With her toes, she could find a bit more purchase, but she was having difficulty now catching her breath, her ribs heaving. The van had climbed up the mountains a few thousand feet before it got to the parking lot. The air was getting thinner. The path went on and on.

Every half-mile or so Mutara waited for her, crouched on his heels at a turn in the path, smoking a cigarette. Perhaps he was embarrassed for her—huffing, smeared in mud, plodding up the path—for he looked at the jungle rather than her. She struggled on toward him, progress slow. Finally, the cigarette finished, he pressed it out in the mud, got to his feet and walked on. She was still 20 feet down the path. An awkward robot, her gears straining. She didn't complain or ask him to slow down.

Two hours into the climb, he waited at a turn in the path until she was close enough to hear his voice. Perhaps he'd gotten past his embarrassment for she could sense his head was pointed toward her, studying her.

"Do you wish the porters to carry you?" His voice puzzled.

She imagined the porters clustered tightly around her, carrying her in a litter, the occasional thoughtless hand laid on her arm or ankle. "No."

He paused, his head still angled to regard her. Then he turned and continued, moving up the path as smoothly as though this were a staircase, never seeming to consider where to place his feet or what to grab. He didn't breathe hard, must have lived at this altitude for years.

By the next time she caught up with him, even her hair was full of mud. She'd slid at one point nearly thirty feet before she managed to catch hold of a trunk and stop herself. Now, she came around a corner to find Mutara leaning against a tree, eyes closed, maybe napping. His clothing didn't have a fleck of dirt on it. When he heard her wheezing, he pulled his head up.

After a long moment, he said, "Feel for the tree roots with your toes. Use them like steps. Always hold onto a branch."

She followed the directions exactly, as she tended to do. They helped.

Throughout her life, she'd studied how neurotypicals reacted when faced with adversity. Some struggled valiantly, but the majority gave up once the situation got unpleasant. When it came to long swathes of her life, unpleasant wasn't a state she could discern. She'd been climbing for three hours. Her feet stumbled now from plain exhaustion. Each time she fell, she pushed herself back up and continued, working to step on the tree roots and hold onto branches.

Mutara began to climb again, but several times he paused to glance back.

At the next turn he waited until she reached him. It took her a long time. As she moved past him, her right foot slid out from under her.

He grabbed her elbow, caught her. That sharp electric flicker. Even now—on her meds, avoiding processed foods, no longer a confused child—that flicker cut at her. As soon as she got her balance, she pulled back from his touch.

"Please," he said, "let me help." No distance anymore in his voice.

She examined his feet. His toes were spread wide, the feet braced in a V. His balance certain. This was what her feet would have to master.

"Higher up where the gorillas live, it is sloped and muddy like this?" she asked.

"Yes," he said.

"Then don't help me. I need to learn how to do this."

T he railway reached the eastern bank of the river Tsavo. The tips of the steel tracks poked out over the edge of the riverbank, pointing to the other side a hundred feet away. From up the river, floated the distant bangs and shouts of the men assembling the camp in the wide shady clearing at the next bend. Jeremy figured they would reside here for at least three weeks, until the bridge was complete, then they could build the railroad across the river to continue on the other side. He had told the men they should take the time to set the camp up well because of the duration of their stay.

He stood now beside the tracks, examining the work site. In the shade of the lush trees along the bank, it felt ten degrees cooler than under the miserly thorn trees. Bending down to the river, he scooped water into his hat and clapped it purposefully onto his head. The water splashed down his neck and under his spine protector, shockingly cold. No more brackish drinking water imported from a hundred miles away. Also, for at least a month, the men would not have to hack through the razor-sharp nyika, clearing a path through the forest for the railway tracks. Instead, they could just build the bridge in this cooler shade, take dips in the river. Life would be easier on all of them.

Those first few days he had worked on the railroad, he had looked forward to the monsoons finally coming, believing they would cool things down, make the work easier on the men. In his mind he'd been imagining a temperate drizzle. Instead the sheets of solid rain made it hard to see and hear. Each shovelful of soggy mud was three times heavier than when it was dry. Even breathing in the downpour took some skill. Yesterday, he'd been called over to see, after an exceptional twelve-hour deluge, a brand-new embankment—previously as hard as baked clay—quivering with the consistency of pudding. Under the weight of a fully loaded train, it sprayed out ten-foot-long jets of mud, the train itself gently rocking from side to side like a boat on the sea. In the end, the engineer had been too fearful to come to a full stop for fear the embankment would cave in, so the train was unloaded while it chuffed slowly on.

Since the rains had commenced, the humidity had intensified. His clothes felt damp to the touch even before he pulled them on. His sweat never dried off; instead it dribbled slowly downward, gluing his underclothes to his skin, puddling along with the rain in his boots. Even without him performing any of the manual labor, he had started to develop heat rashes everywhere his body brushed against itself: under the arms, along the groin, even along the creases of his eyelids.

The rains had also brought out the insects: scorpions, ants, termites, and beetles. Did they need the humidity to hatch or had they been here the whole time and the waterlogged earth forced them out into view? Yesterday he had watched a glistening five-inch-long millipede undulate its furry borders straight up the path toward the cooking tent, as confident as though it were the camp's chef. The creature had weight and volume, its body thicker than his thumb. Eyeing its hard carapace, he was not certain he could crush it with his heel, even with all his weight behind it. Alan Thornton, the physician in camp, believed the bite of some millipedes poisonous. Jeremy let the insect go its own way.

He had bites of different kinds all over his skin, on the bottoms of his feet, between his fingers, and behind his ears. He knew the Indians, with their more bared flesh and lack of shoes, must be worse off.

Here, however, by the river, things would be different. Here they could bathe, clean their wounds, cool down. Everyone's spirits would be raised.

Glancing upriver, he saw, thirty yards away, a native sipping water from a cup made of a rolled leaf.

"Otombe," he yelled impulsively, then immediately worried he might be mistaken.

The man looked behind himself as though considering disappearing into the undergrowth, paused and stepped forward instead.

Once Otombe was closer, Jeremy called, "Will you go hunting with me again sometime?" He did not ask because he thought the N'derobbo had demonstrated great facility at the task. How difficult could it be to spot a tall animal out there on the savannah? No, this was just the first African he had met who could speak English with some ease. Jeremy wanted to know more about that moment he had sensed, standing out on the plains, grass up to his shoulders, wondering about the lion. Otombe's expression was alert, his eyes sharp. He resided in a hut with a spear, the nyika everywhere outside, this terrible heat for most of the year followed by months of torrential rain. What was it like to be human, obviously intelligent, but living under the conditions of an animal?

With his long gangly legs and bony arms, Jeremy knew he would not have survived childhood here. Sometimes, even now, long past the age where he could claim the excuse of growing limbs, when he tried for a burst of speed up the stairs or a fancy dismount off Patsy, his limbs twisted in some awkward way and he fell. If he had grown up here, he would have slipped into a ravine or tripped in front of a hippo, accomplishing something ungraceful and immutable.

Otombe stood in front of him, thin and still, balanced in his dark body. "What do you search for?" he asked, his voice quiet.

For a moment, Jeremy thought he was being asked about

the aims of his life and he opened his mouth fearful of what might emerge. Then recalling his original request, he played for time, glancing up and down the river as though searching for an animal right now. Actually, when he thought back to the hunt he felt a twinge of shame at the ease with which the eland had fallen and the paltry number of steaks they had cut from the giant body, leaving the rest for the two natives and the hyenas. He had given pounds of the meat away to each of his jemadars and still he was eating it, by now in stews and sundried as jerky. To Otombe, he had given only a large slab of steak as well as the single silver coin that Ungan Singh had said was more than enough.

At the time, taking the coin and the meat, Otombe's face had shown no emotion, neither gratitude nor disgust. Jeremy wondered what type of man Otombe saw before him. Someone spidery and pale, overdressed in the heat, heavy-footed. A creature so incapable he required a horse to carry him about, a servant to cook for him, a mechanical train to transport in the materials to meet all his needs. A fragile temperate-zone rose, transplanted and fussed around.

Jeremy rubbed his eyes. "What can be found here along the river?"

"Of the big game, you can find hippo, crocodile, elephant, and lion."

"Have you killed all those?"

Otombe looked down at the butt of his spear, twisting it in the dirt of the riverbank. "My tribe, we are not whites. We have no guns. We kill duiker, gazelle and dik-dik. Small animals."

There was a pause. The wind moved down the river, cool under the trees. Jeremy inhaled in pleasure. He had never realized before how much of his basic happiness depended on not being overheated, on not being thirsty or having sweat in his eyes. In this heat, how could you motivate yourself to go out and search for clean water, locate food? He found it hard to swing himself up onto Patsy, hard to pick up a spoonful of a meal already prepared and placed in front of him. He thought even Patsy felt this way. In Maine, she had always been frisky, kicking her heels up at the smallest excuse: a swaying branch, a flapping scarf. These last few days, she sighed instead when he mounted, picking her way forward only at a determined kick. In this heat, his hunger vanished. He was losing weight already and he did not have a lot to spare. Without the railroad shipping in his food and water, he did not believe he would have the will or skills to survive here more than a month.

As though he knew Jeremy would not be able to choose which animal to hunt, as though he knew his objective was primarily to converse, Otombe added, "This ford is where the slave caravans stop."

"Used to stop," Jeremy said, correcting his English.

"Excuse me?"

"This is where they used to stop. Slavery's now illegal."

"No. There was a caravan three days ago. Over there." He pointed across the river to an open spot under the trees. "Perhaps the Mohammedans will not bring them through while you camp here. They do not like the spot already because of the slaves that disappear."

"The slaves that disappear?" He thought even though both of them spoke English, so many other things separated them: knowledge, assumptions and stations in life. Him, the Africans, the Indians and Persians, even if they all used the same language, wore the same clothes, ate the same food, there would still be misunderstandings, confusions, and fights.

Otombe watched him. "A few disappear every night the caravans are here. Perhaps they run away or animals kill them. I do not know. Our priest, she says the spirit of the river takes them." He shrugged. "Tsavo, it's always been like that. The word means . . . " He rubbed his thumb along the shaft of his spear, thinking. "Death? Murder? It is hard to translate. Also, in the morning any slaves who cannot walk at the caravan's pace, they are left for the animals."

Jeremy looked across the river to the open spot under the trees. He tried to understand. "Left here? Isn't that good? Do they not escape then, head back to their villages?"

Otombe smiled—not that his lips moved, but his eyes, regarding Jeremy, seemed to hold slightly more warmth. "They are killed, as an example to the others. Their necks are cut. The animals here, the hyenas and lions, they are used to the taste of humans. They prefer it. The whites with guns, I have heard them say Tsavo lions are the best to hunt. The greatest challenge. They have no fear of people."

"In two nights," Otombe continued, "it will be the full moon. We can go hunting then, perhaps for hippo. After sunset, I will meet you at the path leading upriver from your camp."

That first day, the shade of the trees along the riverbank was wonderful to work beneath. The Indians began to dig a canal that would serve as a temporary detour for the river. Digging it would take them at least a week. Once the water flowing down the river was rerouted to the canal and the river bottom had a chance to dry out, they could sink the bridge's stone feet quickly and deeply into the ground. When the bridge was completed, they would reroute the river back into its original bed and start laying the railroad tracks on toward Lake Victoria.

It was a delight, while working, to be drinking as much water as desired, for here, boiled from the river, the water was so clear and fresh. Jeremy had gotten used to even his tea tasting of brine, mud, and creosote. The brine and mud came from the overworked water filtration system back in Mombasa. The creosote came from the railway ties that the Indians handled all day, the preservative rubbing itself deep into their hands and arms and legs from constant contact, then—as soon as the train's daily water car arrived—the men would jump headlong into the water to slake their thirst and fill the jerry cans of others.

"Indian tea," Alan Thornton called it.

That afternoon, after a full day of digging, the entire camp bathed in the cool river with riflemen posted along the shore, vigilant for crocodiles and hippos. In the water, the Indians sounded happy, calling out jokes, splashing water at each other, and scrubbing their laundry. During the workday, the simple act of watching a line of fifty or a hundred of these men swinging their shovels in the full sun exhausted Jeremy. He thought it possible, since they had never known life except in equatorial climes, that this work was easier for them than it would be for him. Still, he felt joy watching the Indians standing up to their chests in the river and dumping buckets of water over their heads. He hoped the bridge took months.

As the sun sank, the serenity of the moment vanished. The mosquitoes rose, creating a cloud so thick they nearly obscured the opposite bank of the river. Everyone quickly fled back into the tents, but even inside, the insects' buzzing was insistent enough to be heard clearly. Though Jeremy had worked to tie his tent flaps completely shut, a few mosquitoes managed to slip in. They flew frustrated outside the netting around his camp cot. As the night progressed, the buzzing became louder. He tried to lie in the exact center of his bed, keeping his limbs away from the netting.

Earlier that afternoon, drinking tea with Alan, watching the Indians hike back from the river carrying their tools, Jeremy had lightly sworn and got up to retrieve his grains of quinine. "Forgot this earlier."

Alan looked over.

How is it, Jeremy wondered, these British managed to convey such disapproval through the raising of a single eyebrow? Around people like Alan, so confident in their understanding of the world and their place in it, Jeremy tended to keep his eyes turned just a few degrees off, worried that if someone looked into them too deeply, the person might sense some of the more shocking images his mind had conceived.

"As your physician," Alan said, "I'd advise you not to make a practice of forgetting your quinine." He took a sip of the tea, his face permanently reddened from exposure to the sun. Before Africa, he had served in India. A single drop of sweat trickled down toward the end of his nose. "For the railroad, I've been logging the mortality of us Caucasians. The biggest killer isn't construction accidents, heatstroke, or animals. It's the tiny mosquito: malaria. First year here, 30 percent die." He raised his teacup and said, "Good luck."

Jeremy froze there for a moment. "Are you sure? That percentage seems terribly high."

Alan reached for another crumpet. The provisions for the railroad were shipped in from London: a preponderance of marmalade, tripe, and boiled beef. "Oh yes, quite. The figures are dreadful. I've checked them thoroughly."

Jeremy let his eyes slowly wander the landscape as he tried to think this through. He wondered if it were possible his mother and Grandpapi had known of this statistic when they had agreed to his traveling here. At the thought, he blinked and forced himself to look at the workers instead, walking up the road. "What about them?"

"Who?" Alan asked, spreading the quince jam.

"Them, the Indians. Do they catch the disease as quickly?"

"Oh." Alan paused, the crumpet held in front of his mouth, surveying the men. The only other white for twenty miles, Alan was not the kind of person Jeremy would naturally take to. "Rather interesting question." He took a slow bite and began to chew reflectively. "My first guess would be—without having the numbers to back it up—yes, they seem to contract it bloody easily."

Each night they spent by the river, the mosquitoes rose from the banks to cover the tents. The Indians' tents were not in very good repair, had divots and tears, many of the men had no mosquito netting round their beds. None could afford the quinine Jeremy took.

Three days from now, forty men would be shivering and delirious, the hospital tent beginning to reach capacity.

The day of the hunt with Otombe, Patsy began to wheeze even when standing motionless, her head lowered and ribs working. At sundown, Jeremy left her with the groom rubbing her down, a hot bran mash in her feedbag. He did not look back. She will be fine, he thought, fine. The symptoms of rinderpest were diarrhea and discharge from the eyes, not panting. It was not rinderpest, it was not.

Waiting at the edge of camp were the seven Indians he had arranged to help with the hunt. They stood restlessly in the dark, waving their arms at the mosquitoes and stamping their legs.

When Otombe stepped out of the jungle, he paused at the sight of all the men, then shook his head. "No, a night hunt must be quiet. Just us two."

Jeremy looked at him in surprise. In the moonlight, the man's dusky features were hard to read. He thought about walking through the jungle at night alone with this one African holding a spear, a man he barely knew. Violent, his mother had said, sooner or later you will see these savages bloody and violent.

Otombe took a step back, looking toward the path, ready to disappear. With every day Jeremy woke here in Africa, his desire to see more of it increased. At this moment, in the dark of the night, on the edge of this hunt, all its mystery seemed close enough he could almost wrap his arms around it. Here, it stood in front of him, backing up another step.

Jeremy said, "Alright."

Because Jeremy was not riding this time, Otombe walked rather than ran. To Jeremy, it felt very different this way, striding under the darkness of the trees. Trying not to slow Otombe up or look unfit, he hurried along, legs stretching out. At this speed, he was incapable of being quiet, his feet not so clever. Even with a full moon, under the trees it was close to pitch black, lumpy shapes leaning in on all sides. He had no idea how Otombe managed to decipher it all into bush or tree, rock or animal. Perhaps he did not. Occasionally some creature crashed away through the underbrush.

On his feet like this, without a horse's height for protection, Jeremy felt exposed. After a while, rather than have his rifle slung over his shoulder, he shifted it forward and kept both hands on it. Held this way, the strap occasionally snagged on passing branches, jerking him to a halt.

This hunt was also different because he was not wearing his flannel spine protector. He figured the sun was not out at night, the danger of radiation must be gone, so he had left the device lying on a chair in his tent like the discarded brace of a cripple, its elastic shoulder holders twisted and empty. Without it, he felt so much cooler. If it were not for the mosquitoes around at the moment he would be tempted to undo his shirt further than the top two buttons. He could comprehend how the Africans ended up nearly naked on this continent. Give him a few years here and he would find even Otombe's goat-skin cloak too confining.

After at least a mile, the path they were on joined another much larger one. From the width of the trail, he guessed elephants might come this way. He had heard that because of the elephants' thick skulls, they could not be killed if they charged you face on unless your bullet hit exactly the dollar-bill-sized weak spot above their eyes. Perhaps this was why the colonists brought many men on hunts, as a crowd to bolster their courage, as simple numbers to decrease their risk of being the one the elephant chose to crush.

The last time he had hunted, he had wished to stumble into

some large creature. Now in the dark, he found himself wishing the whole forest magically emptied of anything larger than a mouse.

After perhaps two miles, they reached a wide swampy bay in the river. Otombe slowed down, held a finger to his lips. Twenty feet from the water, he located a tree that hung out over the path and, with practiced ease, swung himself up into the branches. Jeremy waited below, surveying the limbs with dismay. When Otombe paused in his climb to look down at him, he handed his rifle up and then reached for a branch. Attempting a pull-up, he scrambled at the trunk with his toes. With a wheeze he managed to hook his knee over a branch. From here it was easier to ascend, climbing up the branches. Fifteen feet up, with a good view of the path and the river, they rested their backs against the trunk and waited. He tried to keep a certain amount of space between himself and Otombe. His mother, when considering his responsibilities in Africa, had never imagined him sitting in a tree at night next to a nearly naked native. This close to the river the mosquitoes immediately descended. Even in this heat, he rapidly buttoned his shirt all the way up, tucked his pants into his socks. The insects landed on his face and hands, wiggled their way up his sleeves and down his collar. In all the accounts he had read of the dangers of hunting in Africa—of rhinos charging, leopards clawing and elephants stomping—no trophy hunters had waxed eloquent on the dangers of mosquitoes biting. Otombe, beside him, pulled his cloak a little tighter and settled into stillness under the buzzing onslaught, watching the river. Jeremy tried to do the same. He thought the Africans must be more immune to malaria than other races or they would be long extinct from the number of mosquitoes and the length of their own exposed limbs.

Otombe leaned his mouth close to Jeremy's ear. "A hippo will walk up the path," he mouthed more than whispered, "probably within the hour." Jeremy could feel his breath against his cheek and backed away to create a more appropriate distance.

Struggling to ignore the mosquitoes wriggling into his hair, to stay motionless, he concentrated on listening to the jungle. Hundreds of frogs made pinging noises like rubber bands being plucked. An animal nearby chewed determinedly on wood; Jeremy hoped it was not at the base of this tree. Some creature to the left of him hooted.

"Is that noise an owl?" He tried to make his voice as quiet as Otombe's had been.

"What?" asked Otombe.

"Is that noise an owl?" he whispered, leaning closer but still maintaining what he felt was a proper six inches between him and the hunter.

"Civet," Otombe whispered back, his mouth nearly touching Jeremy's ear.

Jeremy backed away again. Africans seemed more comfortable with physical proximity than white men were. Several times, he had been surprised to see tribesmen casually holding hands as they watched the railroad crew work. "What is a civet?" he inquired.

Otombe thought for a moment. "Cat," he added, this time without leaning quite as close.

Jeremy imagined a cat, sitting high in a tree, pursing its hairy lips to let go a bird's sweet hoot.

A creature flapped by, the beating of wet sheets, wings wide enough to be prehistoric, a single sobbing laugh and the animal was gone.

Jeremy looked to him. "Bird," Otombe mouthed, less than helpfully.

Forty minutes later, something in the river moved. The water swirled, mud sucked at its feet as it clambered out. The night amplified every sound. Wet stones ground against one another. After a moment Jeremy understood this sound was the guts of the animal grumbling. The rising stench of mud and algae. The cracking of the brush. A dark hill appeared on the path, lumbering closer. Otombe held up his hand to wait. Perhaps he had doubts about Jeremy's ability as a marksman. Perhaps he worried a bullet-stung hippo could push down their tree, mangle them both. He waited until the shadow was fifteen feet away, wider than the single bed Jeremy slept in at home. Otombe let his hand fall. Jeremy's rifle cracked. Bright sparks from the barrel.

The hill fell down.

For a moment, he almost believed he had killed a hill, shot part of this landscape, pierced a hole in it for all this humid African air to whistle out of. Perhaps this was what the British were doing from the trains, not killing animals but slaying hill after ditch of Africa until the vibrant rolling landscape was deflated enough, dead enough, that England's neat hedges and tidy roads could be built over whatever remained.

He shook his head. The late hour and the heat were taking their toll on his thoughts.

"Shoot once more to make sure," Otombe said in a normal tone of voice, no need to whisper after the bark of the rifle. Jeremy acceded with a careful shot.

And as soon as the second shot stopped reverberating and the dying animal had grunted that one last time, he realized there was no way to carry the body back. It must weigh at least a thousand pounds: two miles, two men, no horses.

He whispered his worry to Otombe.

"I will come back with men for the meat tonight." Otombe said, continuing to speak in a normal voice. "No matter how quickly the crocodiles eat, there will be some left. It is too large even for them. I will drop the meat off for you at your camp."

"But I shot it for the head, the trophy." The head alone would weigh several hundred pounds; they had no way to cut it off. The skin would be mauled. He felt irritation at his own lack of foresight. "Fine. It is useless to me. Keep the meat for yourself and your village."

Otombe went still for a moment at this, seemingly surprised, then nodded and swung down from the tree, walking away. Reluctantly, Jeremy followed. Before they were sixty feet down the path, he heard the wet clap of teeth into meat. They walked on. Behind them came a scuffle and a roar as two crocodiles jousted over the remains.

It started to rain again. He was not sure what he thought of this role of white hunter that had developed for him, seemingly of its own power. He wanted to ask Otombe simply to take him for walks out here, to explain to him the ways of this wilderness, the people here and the animals. These talks did not have to be contingent on death. However, it seemed somehow unmanly to extend such a request.

On the way back, Otombe headed along what Jeremy believed was a different path, one not as close to the river. In the rain, he found it difficult to walk quickly, his wet clothes rubbing at his heat rashes, the mud sucking at his feet. The rain hissed harder all around, obscuring other sounds, limiting visibility. He followed with his head down, water running off his nose and brow. He did not bother to hold his rifle in front anymore; instead he entrusted himself to Otombe. After several turns and forks, the path gradually widened, the undergrowth receding. Through sheets of rain, Jeremy noticed the vegetation seemed different, more uniform, and he wondered if they could be proceeding through crops of some kind. Soon he could discern a large lump ahead, twelve or thirteen feet high, at least thirty feet long. He smelled wood smoke. A wall, he realized, a village inside. Lightning flashed and the many thorns on the wall glittered. He had heard these protective fences were called bomas, that the tribes wove them from the thorny nyika branches, built them around any place they camped, even if only for a night, a cheap version of barbed wire.

Otombe followed the path around the village. As they rounded the curve, an object appeared a few feet out from the wall. Too short for a tree, too tall for most animals, too wide for a human. Jeremy peered at it with some uncertainty, wiping rain from his eyes, noting Otombe was edging subtly aside without changing pace. When they were twenty feet away, lightning jagged the sky. A frozen diorama of wiry hair, solemn eyes, and sagging breasts. Only in the blinded aftermath did he comprehend this was not one creature, but three older women, shoulders touching. The glittering eyes of all three staring at him as though they had been waiting. In approaching the village, Otombe and he had not been making much noise, certainly not enough to rouse these women from their beds, to give them time to take their places outside, settling into a stillness as deep as if they had been waiting their whole lives for this moment.

From the little Jeremy had seen, the natives were generally deeply social, greeting each other elaborately. However neither the women nor Otombe spoke a word. In fact, if anything, Otombe sped up, head down. Acted as though he could not, or would not, see them. In response, Jeremy edged out even further. As he got parallel with the women, ten feet away, they swiveled their wet heads to watch him, smooth as ball bearings. Him, not Otombe. The center one parted her mouth to make a clicking noise with her tongue.

Repetitive, almost insectlike in its speed and precision. A twig caught in the spokes of a bike. The noise rising quickly in volume and speed. The whites of her eyes gleaming.

And strangely, the person he thought of was his mother in her immaculate Victorian crepe (wearing the black of mourning two decades after his father had run away, not died). He saw her sitting with her three closest friends, all the curtains pulled, holding each other's hands, calling the names of dead neighbors in quavering voices. The fashion of communicating with the Great Beyond had reached Maine: ectoplasm, spirit mediums, and tapping walls. Jeremy's mother and her friends held a séance every Tuesday afternoon, a time during which Jeremy quickly learned to stay away from home for the way the science of engineering seemed so utterly denied. While his Grandpapi made fun of the women's occupation, imitating their shivery high-pitched voices each night as he called in the dogs for dinner, Jeremy was affected differently. Simply glimpsing his mother at the table, eyes closed, chin tilted up in concentration, and hearing that earnestness in her voice, was enough to ensure he'd be jumpy that night when he hurried with the swaying lantern to the outhouse.

Jeremy was confused about exactly what occurred next, but the woman's clicking noise seemed to swell louder and louder, as though echoed by a hundred other voices, until the world was split with a lightning bolt close enough that he felt more than heard the crack of its impact in a tree perhaps twenty yards behind him. In a flash of light more brilliant than any he had seen before, the scene engraved on his pupils seemed to show the whole jungle leaning over him making the noise, the trees clicking their branches at him, birds clacking their beaks, animals snapping their teeth. In the darkness afterward, in the depths of this jungle, he needed no further encouragement.

He sprinted down the path, Otombe quick on his heels.

Jeremy ran on and on, his legs high and reaching until the village had long disappeared behind them, until the crops had faded back into the underbrush, until at least three hills were between them and the women. No one chased them, nothing bad happened. The rain ended as quickly as it had started. He gradually slowed, listening behind him. In the newfound silence, the frogs started up again and drops of water ticked off the leaves all around. Already he felt a distinct sense of mortification, Otombe must think him a coward. His Grandpapi would feel such shame. He leaned forward, hands on his knees, gasping. Rain dripped off his nose. Whispering, his breath was harsh. "What were they?"

Otombe shook his head, led him further down the path. Ten minutes later, they stepped out of the jungle at the base of the railroad's embankment, perhaps half a mile from camp. Out from under the shadowy trees, the landscape seemed abruptly so spacious and light. The sky was clearing, the moon scudding in and out of clouds. Climbing the embankment, Jeremy was able to see everything: the railroad tracks glittering into the distance, the small puddles of rain by his feet, even the muscles shifting in Otombe's lean legs. The visibility seemed miraculous. Here, the steel rails shone straight and plumb. Here, he understood things. Even with his eyes closed, he felt confident he could swing his foot forward with geometric exactness onto the next railway tie. This clarity, in comparison to those women and the rain, to that terrible clicking, reminded him why he had gone into the profession of engineering in the first place. Science, he thought, made the world so understandable.

"My tribe," Otombe said, "has a myth of a giant metal snake. Like the story of how the world started, it is one of common knowledge shared among the tribes. It is said, in a time of hunger, drought, and disease, the metal snake will arrive. It will stretch itself across the land to strangle the life from our tribes."

After a moment's thought, he added, "The women back there, they don't wish you to build your railroad."

Looking back at the forest, Jeremy could still almost hear that distant insectlike clicking.

Her Aunt Tilda was chasing her. Sweaty in a pink flowered dress, wide as a sumo wrestler, Tilda thundered
after Max, her breathing grunting in her throat. She
ran down the hall, grabbing at Max, deadly serious, demanding a hug.

Max jerked awake, standing across the cabin from the bed,
thrashing her arms through the air, defending herself.

She blinked around. The dream gradually faded.

It was morning. She was in Africa. She'd slept twelve hours.

Out on her cabin's porch, she ate oatmeal, gazing around at
the field dotted with the research station's cabins. Beyond the
field, in every direction, rose the jungle a hundred feet into the
air. Animals shrieked, birds called. She approved of the gorillas'
taste, far from the crowded lower elevations, among the plants.
Born anywhere in Rwanda, she would have moved up here too.

After breakfast, she did deep breathing meditation for eight
minutes, then walked twenty-nine times around the inside of
her cabin flapping her hands and shouting, "Fuckity fucking
fuck." Afterward, ready for the day, she walked across the field
to the cabin that Mutara had told her was Dubois'.

Standing at the door, she could hear voices inside, arguing.
As soon as she knocked, the voices stopped dead.

"*Entrez,*" called out a woman's voice.

Stepping inside she found three people standing quite still.
From long experience, she recognized the intensity of this
silence. They'd been talking about her.

One woman's toes in pink fluffy slippers. From her direction came the scent of coffee, acidic like espresso, no softening of milk. The woman probably held a cup in her hand.

The second person wore beat-up hiking boots and grungy athletic socks. Max assumed this was a man, until she noticed the calves were thin and hairless.

Mutara's feet Max could recognize, bare and dark and solid on the earth. She nodded at his toes. (Many times in the past she'd meet someone, converse for a while, but never more than shoot a single flash-glance at the face. The next time she bumped into the person, there'd be these unfamiliar shoes, different clothes, and she'd introduce herself all over again.)

"My name is Dr. Max Tombay. I'm the ethnobotanist that Panoply Pharmaceuticals sent."

"Oh, I think we figured that one out," said the woman in the hiking boots. Dry amusement. "We don't have a lot of visitors up here these days. I'm Kiyoko Matsuki. You can call me Yoko. I believe you've met Mutara. And this is the station's director, Geneviève Dubois."

There was a moment of silence. Perhaps Max was supposed to say something here. Before she could figure out what it was, Dubois spoke. "Are you sick?"

"Excuse me?"

"If you are sick, you can not go up to see the gorillas. Mutara tells us you have disease." A strong French accent.

Max was confused for a moment. Then said, "Oh. No, what I said was I have Asperger's."

Yoko's torso turned toward her. "Really?" At her movement, there wafted through the air the slightest odor of manure and straw, a stable ready to be mucked out.

Max examined Yoko's boots, scuffed and stained with red mud up to the ankles. The shorts she wore looked like they'd been intended for a linebacker and hung down past her knees. "Yes."

"Well, fucking shit," said Yoko.

Surprised by the swearing, Max looked fast at her face to see if she was an aspie. Saw rumpled hair, a blunt face filled with life and frank admiration. Max jerked her eyes away and stared at the wood floor.

"You're a brave one," added Yoko.

"Excuse me. What is this—euh—'Ass Burgers?'" asked Dubois.

Yoko said, "No. As-PER-ger's. Not a contagious disease. A mild version of autism."

"*Autisme*?" said Dubois. There was a silence while she took in this information. Perhaps an exchange of glances. When she spoke again, her voice was brusque. "Well, it matters not. She could still have another sickness. She can not see the gorillas for three days."

"Fine," said Yoko, "but after that she goes." Dubois and Yoko were talking to each other rapidly and under their breath. A continuation of some argument, probably the one Max had interrupted by knocking.

"If she has no fever."

"It's a deal. But, Dubois, get a hold of yourself. I don't want you screwing this up. You hear me?"

Exasperated, Dubois puffed air out her mouth in a very French way. *Pfff.*

"What's going on?" asked Max.

Yoko inhaled before she spoke. "There are only three hundred and fifty mountain gorillas left in the world. They haven't been exposed to human diseases. A simple flu could wipe out half of them. In the interest of safety, Dubois is being overly cautious."

"But after this period of three days I can see them as much as I want?"

"Yes," said Dubois. "But you keep the gorillas safe. Yoko tells you the rules. You break even one, you leave these mountains."

"Of course." Max was good at following rules.

Dubois took two steps closer, the pink slippers slapping along. Above them she wore Gumby pajamas. There was that cup of coffee in her hand, her fingers short as a child's, chewed nails. Her voice: no nonsense and low. "Understand well. You are here because Yoko persuades me. We do not trust that Roswell or . . . ahh . . . "

"Stevens," Max supplied.

"Yes, him. We think they cheat if they are able."

"But you have a contract with them, don't you?"

"Making a contract be respected across international borders, you know how difficult this is? *Non*, on that we cannot depend. They stop paying their money; we have no park guards. Without guards, the hunters come and kill gorillas. Yoko says so long as you are here, Roswell and Stevens hope for the vine and keep sending money. You search as long as you want, very long I hope, but I am not helping."

"And when I find the vine?" asked Max.

"Ahh, but these are big mountains, many many miles of land. I do not believe you find the vine." Her voice was full of her smile. "When you give up, they send others, and then others, and then again."

Max herself didn't smile or argue. She knew she would get the vine. "OK," she said and left the cabin. Closing the door behind her, she heard a different sort of silence from them.

At her cabin, she collected the necessary equipment and then walked twenty feet into the jungle. Not allowed to observe the gorillas yet, she could at least learn the local plants. Under the forest canopy, the air was heady with wet earth, rotting wood, and growing plants. She marked off a survey area of three square yards with stakes and then plucked the first plant from inside it. Using her botanical encyclopedia, she identified the specimen, then memorized its attributes: stamens lanceolate and homandrous, petiole incomplete, venation parallel.

With these details fresh in her mind, she scraped her thumbnail across its different components—the leaves, the roots, stem, fruit, and flower—and held it under her nose, inhaling small sniffs.

Most people believed their sense of smell to be vestigial, that once humans learned to walk around on hind legs, moving away from the odiferous earth, the olfactory sense began to atrophy. Max knew better. Research shows that four-legged creatures, so low to the ground, shoving their snouts regularly into decaying meat or feces, had to have nasal passages like mazes to stop dangerous bacteria from getting sucked into the lungs. Down those convoluted byways, their olfactory receptors needed to be magnified many times in order to catch any scent at all. Humans, on the other hand, with their noses up high, far from the bacteria, had passageways direct as arrows, could catch a smell from just a few errant molecules.

Unfortunately most people didn't understand this sense and didn't know how to use it, didn't get the nose close to the object and didn't take small sips of air. Whenever, for instance, her mom happened to catch the smell of something, she generally didn't pay much attention, didn't consider it long enough to analyze its various components. And in those unusual cases where she did linger on a scent, she had only a rudimentary vocabulary with which to describe it, words like "sweet," "sour" and "yucky." With such inexact terminology, it was hard to accurately label or file the scent. The memory of it so quickly fading.

Experiments have shown, with a little training and concentration, a quick primer in the vocabulary of common odor descriptors ("grassy," "citrusy," "woody," "urinous," etc.) humans could sense distinctions between, not dozens of scents or even hundreds, but millions. Many more than they could see of different colors or hear of different tones.

She crushed a leaf, then waved it under her nose, sniffed

lightly. A spicy vanilla with the overtones of a used Band-Aid. The roots of this plant had a different aroma, subtle, close to microwaved water. She opened her eyes and looked once more at the plant, memorizing it visually while she held the smells fresh in her mind. This way she never forgot a plant.

The aromas also gave her a lot of clues about internal chemistry. The next plant she plucked had a strong kerosene scent to its bark (behind that was the flavor of a rubber eraser). Terpins of some kind inside. The sweetness of the flower's aroma suggested an aldehyde compound. After all, what was scent but actual molecular compounds floating through the air? The olfactory bulb was a portable gas-chromatography lab, instantaneous and astonishingly accurate.

Methodically she examined each plant in the survey area. The only ones she didn't pluck were the trees and bushes that were too big for her to pull up. These, she walked around and visually noted their identifying characteristics, then scraped at different parts of them, sniffing. Remembering it all.

Her mom had once described a car accident she'd had at the age of twenty, the way her vision had tunneled down until the whole world consisted only of the wall she was skidding toward. The texture of its brick, its lines of mortar. No sound of the wheels squealing, no feel of her leg stomped on the brake. This story surprised Max, not because her mom had been in danger, but because the way she described that intensity of focus implicitly stated that kind of attention was unusual for her.

For Max, it happened several times a day. Her awareness closed down to encompass only the plant she held in her hand. When she was a child her focus had been more extreme. She used to spin, arms extended. Twirling like this, immersed in the swirling chaos, her normally jittery senses were so busy they didn't bother her. The only time she felt serene.

Her mother would have to push her to the ground to bring her out of it.

Even as an adult, when Max was working on an interesting problem, her lab mates sometimes had to tug on her sleeve before she'd hear their voices or see their hands waving.

Sitting on the jungle floor, crouched over a specimen, movement flickered through the trees. Monkeys screamed. Birds called. She didn't notice. Anyone watching her work would have a hard time reading her flat expression. Only her mom would have noticed the ease of her movements, seen how gently Max handled these plants, content.

For lunch, she opened a box of raw tofu and scooped the insides out with a spoon. Not only was it white and nutritious, she hardly had to chew to ingest it. The perfect food. While eating, she glanced back toward the research station and noticed a researcher—looked like Yoko—standing in a cabin door watching her. Max didn't wave or call hello, but continued to spoon the food into her mouth. Was back to work within three minutes.

After she'd finished examining every plant inside the first survey square, she pulled up the stakes and marked out a new area. This time she plucked only the plants she didn't recognize. After that square, she did another. By the end of the day, she was leaving almost every plant in the ground.

She worked until darkness, went back to her cabin and fell right to sleep.

The second day, at dawn, striding across the field to the jungle, she let her eyes range upward. About fifteen feet up the trunk of a massive *Hagenia abyssinica*, she spotted a nettle bush growing out of the crotch between several branches. Dirt, leaves, and water must have puddled in there, enough for the plant's roots.

She stopped dead. Of course, she should have thought of this possibility. She searched the trees, noted more and more plants growing up there, a long way from the ground. Conventional plants—bushes, small trees, and vines—were rooted in the dirt that collected in crevices and crannies. But there were also mosses hanging in long sheets off almost every branch, as well as epiphytic ferns, orchids, and bromeliads growing out of the bark of the trees, the plants needing nothing more than the nutrients and rain that fell from the air.

Gorillas were primates. They must climb. Because of their weight, they probably couldn't get much higher than thirty feet, but they would go that high. In order to learn all the plants they came in contact with, she would have to ascend the trees that far.

As with climbing mountains, scaling trees was not one of her skills. She found a trunk not more than a foot wide and, hugging it hard, tried to shimmy upward. After a minute of working hard at this, her feet were still on the ground, but her inner arms now had some significant abrasions. She searched for another way. In the end she found a fallen jungle giant, its root ball rising twelve feet into the air. Clambering to the top of the roots, she managed to pull herself up into the branch of a nearby *Pygeum*. She grunted with her movements, holding on tight and concentrated, her face pressed flat against the bark. The branch was slippery with moss. Finding a somewhat stable perch, she straightened to pluck the nearest plant. As soon as she'd finished examining that plant, she humped her way up a little higher.

Half an hour into this work, she leaned too far out reaching for a moss and fell, thudding down through the branches to land on her back. She lay there, flapping her mouth at the sky, eyes wide as a goldfish's, until her breath came back to her. Sitting up slowly, she tested her limbs for injury, held the heel of her hand against her forehead until it stopped bleeding and then she climbed back into the trees.

About halfway through the morning, someone called below her. "Tombayyyy. Where are you?" Perhaps the person had been calling for a while, for this yell was loud. A bellow.

Max startled, had to claw at a branch to catch her balance.

At the noise, Yoko swiveled to look up. She seemed as surprised as Max. "Shit. What're you doing up there?"

Max eased her way back into a sitting position. "A botanical survey. I need to learn the local plants."

"Hey, I don't want to teach you your profession, but the plants, they're down here." She patted a nearby blackberry bush as confirmation.

"A lot of them grow up on the trees." Max held out the fern in her hand.

There was a pause. "What happened to your forehead?"

"I fell."

Yoko stayed tilted back as she considered Max. Max crushed one of the fern's fronds and took a few sniffs of it.

"You should know," said Yoko, "the nearest hospital is three hours away by foot and I'll tell you frankly it's not the kind of hospital you want to visit."

"Acceptable risk." Max zipped the fern into a plastic bag and crotched her way unsteadily a little further up the branch, reaching for an unfamiliar monocot.

"If I asked you nicely, is there any chance you'd come down?" asked Yoko.

"No."

Since Yoko said nothing more, Max forgot about her. Later on, while she was eating lunch, she was surprised to see Mutara was down there also. They were watching her, talking quietly. She felt no need to converse. Her concession to the danger was to try to stay at least twenty-five feet up. From here she hoped she had a good chance of dying if she fell. Logically this seemed better than being permanently crippled.

Life, she figured, might be designed for neurotypicals, with all its social rules and expectations. But death . . . She pictured open space, soft gray fog in every direction, no bodies to jostle her or eyes to avoid. Peace of a permanent kind.

At some point Yoko and Mutara went away and came back with a long coil of rope.

"Yo-hooooo," called Yoko until she got Max's attention again. "If you're going to insist on being up there, we figure at least you can wear a safety rope."

Mutara climbed up to her, the rope over his shoulder. As when he walked up the mountain, he climbed smoothly and deliberately, no unnecessary effort.

Once he reached her branch, he stayed a yard back and didn't try to tie the rope on for her. Simply handed her it and described where to tie it and how. Perhaps Yoko had explained Asperger's to him. The rope where he'd touched it smelled of sweet potatoes and cooking oil. Once Max had the jerry-rigged safety harness on, he threw the end of the rope over a branch above her and then caught it and had her tie it back onto her harness.

"This way, you fall, you don't die," he said.

"You'll just swing around up there like Peter Pan in a grade-school play 'til we come back to rescue you," said Yoko.

Confused for a moment by the image, Max forgot to say thank you, but she did yank on the rope to make sure it was secure. Then turned back to her work.

At some point, she realized she was having difficulty seeing the plant in her hand. Wondering why, she glanced around and noticed the sun had set. Darkness seemed to have arrived with surprising speed. Or perhaps she'd been concentrating too hard to notice.

Using her harness, she lowered herself out of the tree. The rope was quite useful now, for in the growing gloom it was hard to judge the exact distance of any foothold. On the ground, it took her several minutes to untie the rope and pack up her equipment. Then, looking around, she understood she no longer had any idea in which direction the meadow lay.

Very slowly she swiveled about on one foot, peering between the trees, methodically angling her head this way and that, thorough as always. The noises of the jungle were starting to change into night sounds. The birds louder and more insistent. Animals coughing. Something roared, far away and enraged. She finally spotted a tiny flicker of light through the trunks. A lamp in one of the cabins. Walking in that direction, she stumbled a bit over branches and bushes, then felt space opening up around her as she reached the meadow. The light guided her forward. Walking through the field was easier than the jungle, although the ground was still uneven. She was carrying a fair amount of equipment and concentrated on stepping so she wouldn't stumble.

A sound came. A distinct grinding noise, closer to the jungle and off to her left. Probably two branches rubbing against each other in the wind.

For dinner, she'd have rice. Tomorrow she'd see about getting herself some bananas.

The grinding noise came again. The substance sounded harder than wood. More gritty, like rock or bone. The motion deliberate.

Teeth.

Teeth grinding together, large enough to be heard from twenty feet or so.

"Fuck," she said.

Mistake.

The animal snorted, surprised. A sound louder than a horse's snort, rougher, more cavernous.

There followed a short pause while the two of them stood there, considering each other's presence in the dark.

Then, with a grunt, it began to run. Hoof beats and a sloshing heavy stomach.

Charging toward her.

She paused. Not bravery. Disbelief.

Then bolted. Sprinting toward the light, toward human life.

The objects in her arms tumbling to the ground. She vaulted through the grass, stumbling over puddles. Her pale sneakers floating through the night. The light jouncing closer. A staticky roar in her ears. The hooves beat louder, the wheezing stomach, the huffing breath.

She caught its scent of grassy slobber and digestive juices.

Death she might not mind that much, but this . . . An image of its furry closeness, all that weight, the ultimate too-close hug, crushing her. Her nightmare.

She flailed up the cabin steps and through the door, slamming it shut behind her.

Outside came the sound of a grunt and then the hooves arcing away.

She slid to the ground, limbs sprawled. Her head flat on the floor. Her vision misty at the edges, but the center so crystal clear that—staring up at the corrugated metal ceiling—she could taste tin in the back of her throat. Her body vibrated like a hovercraft, some huge motor started inside her. Some energy she never knew she had. Holding her hand up in front of her, she saw her fingers shaky with that power.

Over her breath, she heard a noise inside the cabin and jerked around to face it. Dubois, Yoko, Mutara, and a woman she didn't know sat at the table with spoonfuls of stew halfway to their mouths, staring at her.

"What the hell just happened?" asked Yoko.

The demands of English seemed well beyond Max. Adrenalin, such a powerful drug, mobilizing the body's resources, flooding the muscles, shutting other systems down. Right now she could probably straight-arm Yoko over her head and carry her around, tendons creaking, like a Russian weightlifter.

And the strangest aspect of all this was she realized she was looking directly into Yoko's face (short disheveled hair, a smudge of mud on her cheek, a startled expression of straightforward interest). Max's vision didn't flicker, no cold metal shivered up her nerves. She didn't need to glance away, over-whelmed. She could just look, for as long as she wanted, like normal people did.

Stunned, she turned to the others. Taking in the essentials while she could.

Mutara's face was surprisingly round for how thin his body was: a chipmunk's head on a greyhound's body. Mid-twenties, emotions locked away inside, dark practical clothes. For the formality of dinner, he'd put on his boots.

Dubois was under five feet, blue eyes, wild hair, the upturned nose of an imp. (Reminded Max of a troll doll she'd loved as a child because it was motionless and its oversized head and dumpy limbs were so clearly not normal. However, in order to keep the doll in her room, she'd had to put duct tape over its big eyes.)

The other woman here, the one she hadn't met yet, had eyes sharp as a bird's and held her head canted a little back, like she might flutter off at any moment. The velour bathrobe she wore—with the name "Pip" written in script across the chest pocket—seemed incongruous in this remote cabin, wild animals with thundering hooves living just outside the door.

"Earth to Tombay." Yoko repeated, "What just happened?"

She turned back to Yoko. She couldn't seem to find any words so she settled for imitating hoofbeats instead. "TaDump taDump taDump."

"A forest buff," said the woman with the "Pip" bathrobe. She cocked her head to the side, just like a robin. "Getting chased by one through the dark's a bit dodgy, isn't it?" An Australian.

"The buffaloes come out of the jungle to graze at night on the field," said Yoko. "So long as you don't startle them, they'll leave you alone."

Max looked from one face to the other, intent as a child. She marveled at the color of their eyes, their straightforward gaze.

"If you go outside at night," said Mutara, "walk slow, wave a flashlight, make noise."

"After a few days, you are not even noticing," said Dubois. "You want some sweet-potato soup?"

Considering her answer, Max realized she was quite hungry. She got shakily to her feet and took a chair at the table. Yoko put a bowl in front of her. The soup was dark and in it floated many unnamed vegetables and spices. She forked out a single sweet potato chunk. The piece wasn't white and flecks of other food clung to it, adulterating it. Tentatively, she put it in her mouth, closed her teeth. Nothing happened. The different textures and tastes didn't jangle. Just warm soft food. She could smell meat and green peppers, sweet fat. Began to eat. Perhaps they asked her more questions about what happened, but she didn't listen, closing her eyes, concentrating on the food.

Within a few minutes, the hum of adrenalin began to fade. The shimmer in her vision crept back, the jumpy quality to sound. She tried to look at Yoko's face, then jerked her eyes away.

She put her spoon down and looked at her hands.

For dessert, there was a single chocolate bar and the others discussed for a while how to divide it. They brought out a knife and made marks before cutting. When a piece was placed in front of her, Max blinked at it, then shook her head. The others began a second conversation about how to divvy up this piece. From their seriousness it seemed they must be running low on desserts.

Yoko tapped the table in front of Max's fingers. "Hellooo, Tombay."

Max jerked her hand slightly back. The loneliness of her skin.

"You always been so brave?" asked Yoko.

For a moment Max wondered if she were making fun of her for flinching. "Brave?"

"Yeh, in coming here."

"What do you mean?"

"Well, you came here in spite of that stuff that happened with the doctors."

"What doctors?"

Yoko's head swiveled toward her. "The ones who got killed." She waited for some reaction, then said in a low voice. "Look, Roswell and Stevens told you about the Kutu, didn't they?"

Max felt the others shifting to look at her. "Kutu?" she asked. The room got quiet.

"Oh bloody hell," said Pip.

Dubois grunted and brought her hand up to her face, seemed to be pressing her knuckles into her eyes. "American companies are such pigs. A month ago, these four *Médecins sans Frontieres—*"

"Otherwise known as Doctors without Borders," said Pip. "Stop being so French all the time."

"And how about this French? Go fuck yourself."

"Hey, let's try to look like we get along, OK?" said Yoko. "Pip, be nice. She's got another migraine right now." She turned to Max. "The doctors were stationed in Lubero, a town near here in the Congo. They disappeared one day driving to the next village. A few days later some UN soldiers found the doctors' jeep in the hands of three Kutu."

"The name, 'Kutu,' is from the leader, this warlord, François Kutu," said Dubois.

"Warlord?" asked Max. She'd never thought the word would be used in any context having to do with her own life.

Yoko continued, "The Kutu are stolen children. Groups of them sweep through villages to capture more. If a group of kids is found, they're forced at gunpoint to kill one of their own with rocks. Growing up in the same village, they'll have known each other since birth. The child they kill might be their sister or best friend."

"After that they're a lot less likely to try to escape home, you know?" said Pip. "They feel too guilty."

"With rocks?" asked Max. None of them bothered to

answer. They were too involved in the story, the relief of telling someone new. They leaned forward, voices fast. Mutara was the only one who sat back, looking down at his hands.

"Afterward the captives are kept high chewing qat, forced to work as porters. They see a lot of violence, directed against them or the other kids," said Yoko. "After a few weeks, they're given Kalashnikovs. By then, they're different. They're Kutu."

"Qat's a plant around here. Heard of it?" asked Pip. She angled her head, shifted slightly in her seat. Small and nervous. At her movement, Max caught a whiff of a lab chemical, some preservative, like formalin.

"No," said Max. Laypeople always expected as an ethnobotanist she would know every plant in the world, be able to identify any specimen from ten paces. Having never paid attention to botany, they didn't understand there were over a quarter million different species, just counting the vascular plants.

"Truly?" Pip's voice held surprise. "Qat's used all over this bit of Africa. Like a mild cocaine. Chewing it makes you all trigger happy."

"When there is fighting . . . Euhh, a combat?" said Dubois, "All the older Kutu order the younger ones to attack. They, the elders, stay back and shoot anyone who tries to escape." She pointed her finger like a gun. Her nails short and rather ragged.

"But why . . . ?" Max trailed off. The term "child soldier" had never made sense to her. She pictured a Marine holding a gun, a large man with a crew cut, trained like a dog to attack. A kid struggling to lift that same gun would look silly. "If the Kutu have the choice, why don't they kidnap the parents instead, the dads?"

The others paused.

Mutara was the one who broke the silence. He used a gentle voice, as you would when talking to someone who should know better. "But rifles now are light. Made of plastic like toys. And—unlike parents—children have not much fear. Will run into anything, yelling and shooting their guns."

Dubois spoke. "You kidnap the dads, they try to escape, know how to find help. They have more . . . Euh . . . " She combed through the air with one hand, searching for the word.

"Life experience?" asked Yoko.

"Determination?" suggested Pip.

Dubois nodded and continued, "The dads hold onto their souls a long time, fighting back. Children, not so much."

Max considered this.

"When the doctors' jeep was found, a few Kutu were in it, trying to sell the medical supplies as well as some–" said Pip.

Yoko's head shook 'No.' Max glanced as far as her mouth and saw it was stretched into a tight line.

"I think she should—" asked Pip.

"No."

Since they'd started talking about the Kutu, none of them had taken a bite of their dessert. They were slightly hunched into the conversation. Pip had her arms wrapped around her waist.

"What?" Max asked. "What aren't you saying?"

Yoko turned to her. "The rest of the story is just . . . in Africa especially around a war, there's not much reliable news coverage. Instead information tends to travel from person to person."

"Radio Sidewalk is how it is called," said Mutara. He did not say much and, when he spoke, his voice was quiet.

"The information gets exaggerated." Yoko said, "We're scientists. We believe in facts, not gossip. We've heard many different versions of the story. The only confirmed facts are that the doctors disappeared and later on their jeep was found with some Kutu in it. The doctors haven't been seen since."

Into the silence Dubois said, "Since the doctors, there are other incidences. Belgian nuns in Beni. A boy from Peace Corps in Lubero. Three merchants of diamonds with their guards. The Kutu kill every white they come upon. It is difficult to know what they do to Africans. There are different stories. Some, they let go. Some . . . " She made a flicking motion. "Perhaps it depends on their mood."

"Don't forget that UN soldier," said Pip. "He stepped into the bush to take a pisser and the next people pass by found his head in the middle of the road." Max noticed Pip's fingers rubbing the edge of her robe rhythmically, like a child might with a security blanket.

"Radio Sidewalk," said Yoko.

"Whatever's in the road, it's dead."

"There are UN soldiers in the Congo. They try to keep the peace. War is there for years. Three times," said Dubois, "these soldiers come upon groups of Kutu. Does not matter how many soldiers there are, how many guns they have, the children attack."

"The soldiers," said Yoko, "are well disciplined, from Belgium and Ghana. They order the kids to stop, fire shots in the air. The Kutu keep charging forward anyway, chewing their qat, shooting their Kalashnikovs, crazy skinny little kids."

"They yell out they want a cuddle," said Pip.

"Radio Sidewalk."

"Whatever they yell, they keep running. The only thing that stops them is the soldiers shooting bullets into their hearts." Pip's fingers rubbed faster on her sleeve.

There was a silence. Max found her vision had settled on the door through which she'd entered the cabin. Plywood, a long smear of mud near the base. In some essential way it looked different than it had a few minutes ago. "How far away are these Kutu?"

"Probably fifty miles now, maybe forty," said Yoko.

Max looked right then left. In her life she'd come upon many situations she didn't know how to deal with—social difficulties or matters of etiquette. In these circumstances, she'd learned to locate the neurotypical she assumed had the most appropriate experience and ask that person for information and advice. "That's less than an hour's drive. Isn't this something we should be concerned about?"

Yoko said, "In the Congo there are no real roads left, not after decades of Mobutu and then the war. Nothing but dirt paths. Even with jeeps, it would take two days to travel here, maybe three."

"And they are on the other side of the border?" Max pictured the large stone buildings on the Canadian border at Interstate 89: officials and procedures, cameras and computers, gates that could be lowered. She could imagine these details much more easily than the scenes that had just been described.

"Well," said Pip. "Yes, but . . . "

"Then what are the chances we're in danger? Could you answer in terms of a percentage?" asked Max.

At this question the four of them went still. Perhaps there were looks exchanged.

"Too high for me," said Pip.

"Ah, it is not so much. Less than 10 percent," said Dubois.

"No real chance of danger at all," said Yoko.

They turned to Mutara for his answer and he paused, then began to lift his hands in the start of a gesture. Max noticed a long scar running diagonally across his left palm, pale against his skin. Looking at the scar, she realized he was old enough to have lived through the genocide here.

He said not a word, just shrugged, his palms cupped upward, as though to say it was in the hands of fate.

T he first murder occurred in the middle of the night.
Jeremy slept through the whole uproar and in the morning was told of all that had happened. Five men sleeping in a tent, their heads circled around the center pole, a ring of feet pointed out toward the wall. At some point, the story went, something reached under the canvas to snag one set of feet, sliding the screaming man out of the tent and dragging him away into the bush where his outcries abruptly ended. By the time the sun rose, the crowds of frightened men running around the tent waving firebrands at the darkness had erased any prints that could have told the tale.

The head jemadar, Ungan Singh, carried the remains over for Jeremy to examine while he ate breakfast. A man of great dignity, without experience in this sort of situation, Singh must have pondered the proper etiquette. In the end, he had proffered a small hand basin, the way a waiter might in a fancy restaurant, discretely flipping away the napkin that covered it. Unfortunately, having worried so much about the correct method, he had forgotten to announce the contents. Jeremy stared down into the basin for a moment, still chewing on an eggy bit of bacon, before he kicked violently away from the table.

Could not these people have any respect for their own physical remains? He did not know if the practice of stuffing a piece of coal into the mouth to represent Hindu cremation had been started by the railway out of expedience and continued by the Indians out of practicality, or if the reverse were true. Either way, the numbers of those with malaria were rising quickly now, men crumpling over on the job, the hospital full. Already Alan had informed him thus far five had died from fever, their bodies transported a few miles out of camp and abandoned along the railroad's shoulder. This, he had learned, was standard practice for Indian cadavers.

After Jeremy had backed away from Singh's basin and spat the piece of bacon out into his napkin, he asked, "Where is the rest of this man?"

Singh tilted his head slightly to one side. "The animals, sir." His white robe and turban were impeccably clean, his manners flawless. Several times Jeremy had sensed Singh's disappointment at having only an American to serve—not a nationality known for its appreciation of the finer points of social customs. Around Singh, whenever he remembered, he attempted better posture.

"Even the bones? The skull?" In Maine, there would have been more remains after a full year in the forest.

"Oh no, sir. There are bones." As proof, with two fingers, he delicately plucked something out of the basin. Jeremy turned away.

This was the day he had the men start the bonfire, ordered them to keep it burning day and night. With the wood so wet from the monsoons, it took a lot of kerosene to start and had to be periodically slaked with more. It popped from the moisture in the wood, tossing embers high into the air. From the fire sizzled a thick black smoke that quickly obscured any cadaver thrown on top.

He ordered them to burn all dead bodies from then on, no matter what their religion or burial preferences.

Before he had the pyre started, no Indian had mentioned to him any dismay at how the bodies of their comrades were treated. Of course, the bodies were abandoned a few miles from camp, where most workers would not see them, but yesterday riding in the train to Voi with one of the jemadars to pick up supplies, they had caught a momentary glimpse of a corpse. The limbs were twisted and splayed by predators, like a dancer in the midst of some complicated jump. Jeremy had flinched and then glanced at the jemadar who said nothing, no visible change in his expression. The man continued to stare stonily out at the rolling landscape as though the body of his countryman was nothing more than the meat of an animal lying there in the bush.

Jeremy had this funeral bonfire constructed in hopes it would stop all the nearby carnivores from learning to consider humans as food.

The assumption in camp seemed to be that a lion had killed the man last night, an assumption Jeremy doubted. Having heard a lot, back in Maine, about the king of the beasts, he longed to see one, but so far the only time he had actually spotted one was from seventy-five yards away. The distance was great enough that he would never have found the creature on his own. Standing on the top of the embankment, overseeing the progress of the workers, a jemadar had called his attention to the two small bumps above the tall grass of the riverbank. At that distance, they resembled the leaves of a bush. As though they knew they were under discussion, the ears swiveled toward his position, paused and then sank down slowly behind the grass.

Yesterday, spotting the cadaver from the train, he had noticed prints in the mud around the body. The prints were too large to be anything but a lion's pugmarks. He had also noticed pugmarks several times along the river near where the Indians washed their laundry, and twice there was a trail of them crossing the muddy earth by the newest section of train tracks. From how common these prints seemed to be, he assumed the creatures were everywhere in the area, but that when they sensed humans, they melted away into the brush to avoid being seen. These actions ruined his image of a ferocious hunter. He had begun to think of them as nothing more than tall hyenas, cowards who skulked away with a nervous giggle at the first sight of a human and a gun.

No, from what he had seen, he didn't believe a lion would walk into the settlement of several hundred men, even at night, to sneak its paw under the wall of a tent and calmly probe about, to drag away a grown man thrashing to his death.

For the perpetrator, Jeremy instead suspected the four survivors who had been in the tent. A week ago, two Shiites had ambushed a Sikh on the road coming back from the lunch tent and beat him unconscious. The man who had been dragged out of his tent last night and killed, supposedly by a lion, was a Mohammedan, a productive mason who had been paid well just two days before under Jeremy's newly instituted piecework wage. The other four men in the tent were Hindus who had signed up in India as masons, but Jeremy suspected, from the level of their output, that they were not sure of the working end of a chisel, and were simply trying to hoodwink the railroad into paying them higher wages. After realizing a full third of his masons fell into this category, he had instituted a wage based on the number of pieces completed. It was the only way he could think of to reward those who knew what they were doing while stopping the rest from stealing from the railroad.

However this morning, standing in front of the newly lit bonfire, its dark smoke curling up, hiding its recent load of corpses from the infirmary, he had abruptly realized his payment strategy could have caused the murder. Perhaps, the nonproductive and thus impoverished imposter masons had brained the Muslim where he lay sleeping, taken his money, and dragged his body into the bushes emitting their own screams the whole way. By morning, the thieves could be sure the animals would have destroyed any clue left on the body.

For a long moment, Jeremy remained there, utterly silent in front of the pyre, watching the dark smoke curl away across the river toward the other bank.

The Indians spent the morning recounting, for each other, stories of man-eating tigers in India, so many tales it began to sound like humans were the only food the tigers ever touched. The pall of fear that resulted from these tales meant that Jeremy was forced to lose the whole afternoon of work on the railroad as the men insisted on building bomas around their tents, cutting down nyika branches and weaving the thorny fences higher than a man's head.

To show how foolish they were, Jeremy spent that night as usual in his canvas tent out in the open, one flap pinned back for the slightest breeze. His gun propped up, as always by his bed.

That night he was irritated by the bad timing of some lions roaring in the brush. The creatures continued to call back and forth around the camp for at least two hours. He knew, at these sounds, the men's panic would worsen. Tomorrow they would be groggy from lack of sleep and they would probably insist upon putting up bomas around even the cooking tent and latrines.

The roars kept him awake until at least eleven, the noise of the beasts circling closer and louder, until, abruptly, they stopped. Afterward the silence seemed a bit unnerving, but he assumed the brutes had finally caught the scent of some prey— a kudu perhaps or eland—and commenced some serious hunting. He fell into a deep sleep.

Sometime, long after midnight, he woke. The tent flap waved gently, although from his cot he could feel no breeze. He considered the fact that at night, with him alone and sleeping, even a cowardly hyena could potentially be dangerous. Now that none of the men were around, he got up to tie the tent flaps. Outside he heard not a sound. Lying back down, he waited for sleep again, listening to the night sounds. The sawing cough of a leopard, the crazed xylophone of frogs. For a moment in the dark, lying in his fragile canvas home, he felt awe at how far he had traveled from all he held familiar.

Later, in the pitch dark, he awoke to screams.

Five of the Indians—confident in the height of the seven-foot-tall boma—had lay down outside their stifling tent, hoping for a breeze from the river. From the cities of Bombay and Calcutta, these men had no experience with large carnivores, believed the others' terror of lions overwrought. The night had been hot and still, the skies above shivering with stars. With sheets pulled even over their faces to keep the mosquitoes away, they had drifted off to sleep, each of their heads pillowed on another's belly or leg.

Two hours later, no one heard the soft *whump* of the lion's paws landing on the ground inside the boma. No one was awake to watch it cautiously circle the sheet-covered men, padding ever closer.

The killing was so fast and quiet, only one man awoke as his friend's leg was tugged out from under his head.

Jerking upright, still bemused by sleep, the man saw what he thought was a hunched-over giant dragging a bundle of laundry toward the fence. Then the sheet slid from the body and the lion raised its head toward him. The animal huge in comparison to the corpse. Picking the body up in its mouth, the creature turned and, with a grunt, awkwardly jumped the boma.

The man began screaming, waking the rest of camp.

This time, no one was brave enough to venture out, to wave torches and yell. Those few who had been sleeping on the ground outside quickly piled for protection until morning into whatever tent was nearest for protection until morning. Thus, the proof of the lion's visit remained intact in the mud.

In the morning light, the pugmarks appeared huge. Listening to Ungan Singh's translation of the man's story, Jeremy pressed his own hand into the dirt next to one of the paw prints. Although his outstretched fingers spanned a little further, the imprint he left was thin and spread out, some type of spindly heron or marsupial, whereas the lion's prints were solid with weight, the mark pressed as deeply into the ground as the wheel prints of a fully laden cart.

The Swifts, the next farm down from Grandpapi's in Maine, had a Newfoundland dog; it lumbered along at over one hundred pounds. Its prints, however, he had noted in the past, were comparatively dainty, nothing bigger than his closed fist. The pugmarks left by this lion were well more than three times that size, by far the largest tracks he had ever seen. If it were built on the same scale as the Newfoundland, this predator would weigh more than four hundred pounds: the heft of a small grizzly, the speed of a cat.

The man who had woken and seen the lion, said the animal had been without a mane. If this lion were a female, Jeremy could not imagine how large the males must be.

The imprints of the toes and claws were deep where the animal had landed inside the boma. Her prints then walked cautiously in toward the sleeping men. She had circled them, two feet away. After nearly a full circle, the prints stopped. Who knew why she had chosen the man she did or how she had killed him, but the death must have been instantaneous, for there was remarkably little blood. Afterward, the pugmarks trotted directly to the fence, the prints partially erased by the drag marks of the victim's toes and the backs of his hands.

In preparation for jumping the boma, the creature's prints had not changed in any way, not lengthening their pace or leaving a visible kick-off. On the far side, it had landed three yards in, then trotted off into the scrub. Certainly the Indian workers were not a large or fleshy people, but to jump over a seven-foot barrier carrying that weight must take immense strength.

He remembered once seeing a farm cat leap onto a windowsill carrying a squirrel a third its size. The grace of its leap had been marred only by the fact that its head was canted up to keep the squirrel's body out of the way of its legs.

Following the pugmarks, four hundred yards from the boma, Jeremy found the scene of the man's corpse. There was no longer any single object that could be referred to as a body. The skin gone, the contents scattered, even the bones cracked and eaten by hyenas. All that remained was a darker stain to the soil, the stain wiped liberally around a thirty-foot-wide clearing, small gritty pieces overlooked in the dirt, a two-inch flap of hairy scalp somehow impaled a yard up on a thorn.

For once, it was not raining. Jeremy wished that it had been raining all night so the scene would have been at least partially cleaned up, so he would not have to stand here beside Singh, looking over the stain of the remains. Or to state it more truthfully, he wished, with Singh watching him, he would not have to stand here, *pretending* to look over the remains. After that first horrifying impression, he kept his eyes trained just above the ground, on the mostly clean branches, while he struggled with his nausea.

From the moment he had spotted the lion's tracks, he had known what would be expected of him as Pukka Sahib, the top representative of the railway here. He was helpless to stop the mosquitoes from biting the Indians or the fever from building in their blood. None of the Indians assumed he would even attempt to deliver safe working conditions or high-quality medical care. Instead, aside from their nominal salaries, in return for risking their lives here in Africa, the Indians expected him—in the tradition of the great British rajahs—to exterminate any threatening large animals. He was the white man in charge, the one with the guns. The least he could do in front of Singh was act confident.

The wind came fitfully from the south where the bonfire

was. Alan had told him two more men had died from malaria during the night. Drifting through the tree branches came a wisp of black smoke and the stench of burning hair.

By this point in his investigation of the murder, over fifty Indians clustered behind him, waiting to see what his next move would be. They did not say a word, standing silently around the edges of the clearing and back along the path, watching him. He assumed some of them were the friends and relatives of the dead man.

In a deep and—he hoped—confident voice, he called for his 450 Express and his gunbearers and trackers. He on announced he would follow the lion's tracks into the nyika. The rifle arrived, but, one by one, all of the men who had gone on the hunt for the eland refused to accompany him now. One man threw himself to the ground, his hands clasped, pleading he had four children. Jeremy let them refuse. It seemed to him theirs was the preeminently logical choice. He could not imagine why the British disparaged the intelligence of other races when over the last century they had proudly pioneered the role of wandering into thick brush after large carnivores, a role which he now felt forced to take on.

With Singh and the others watching, he searched the ground for any signs of where the lion might have exited the clearing. He tried to step as lightly as he could on the stained dirt, but still felt as though he were desecrating a body. Crouching down, holding his rifle, he spotted a tunnel in the nyika, the pugmarks going in. He did not know how tall a four-hundred-pound lion would be, but he imagined the beast must have had a hard time fitting down this passageway, especially with a fully gorged belly. Either she had wiggled ignominiously forward on her elbows or she had pushed bravely through, ignoring any knifelike punctures of the thorns through her skin. The lion could be sleeping off her meal in the brush fifty feet in or she might have wandered miles away.

Glancing over his shoulder, he saw the Indians watching. They stood so close together, their white shirts and turbans glimmered like a single object. He turned back to slash roughly at the undergrowth with his machete. The entwined branches were hard wood, the machete an instrument unfamiliar to him. Within a minute, he had ascertained he would need an axe and an hour to chop open a path ten feet long. Any animal within half a mile would hear him and easily escape.

For a brief moment he thought of Otombe, wishing he were here to offer him advice on what to do. Without any better idea, he impulsively got down on his hands and knees, swung his rifle behind his back and crawled into the tunnel after the lion.

Inside of fifteen feet, the tunnel narrowed. He had to crouch low even in his crawling position, his head tucked down, his rapid breathing echoing off the ground. In here, under the tangled brush, the shade was thick. His eyes blinked, working hard to adjust. Because of the way the tunnel curved, he could not see more than four or five yards ahead. There was the smell of earth and leaves. In this position, in an enclosed space, he was not entirely sure he could reach his rifle where it lay against his back. Still, he crawled on, pushing the machete in front of him, knowing the camp might mutiny if they saw his legs squirming immediately back out of the nyika. He imagined trying to explain to Preston why he had given up the hunt after half a minute. Preston had worked in Africa for years, Brazil and Australia before that. He would listen to Jeremy's stuttered excuses with amazement.

He did not think his Grandpapi would ever get himself into this situation. He would have a much better plan than this ineffectual creeping forward into what might be the animal's lair. However, if it came down to it, if he felt there was no better choice, Grandpapi would certainly crawl forward.

While he was trying to peer ahead, a sweat bee landed on his cheek. Buzzing, it began to sip at a drop of perspiration near his ear. The nyika around him was tight with thorns; he would not be able to easily reach up to slap it. The sting of these bees was, if anything, worse than that of wasps at home. Pausing in its drink, it spotted a bigger pool of liquid and strode confidently across his face in the direction of his eye.

When he slapped roughly at the bee, the strap of his rifle caught on the thorns above. While trying to rub his now-stung cheek, his right arm got snagged in two places. In trying to free that arm, he got his left shoulder caught.

He fought the thorns for three endless minutes, getting progressively more entangled, before he started bellowing for help.

If the lion were sleeping her meal off nearby, if she ambled over to see what all the hubbub was about, he knew he would be able to do nothing more in self-defense than swing the machete about in a mild limp-wristed manner.

He waited for the men to cut their way through the undergrowth to him. His scrawny ankles were found first, twisted in their safari linen, helplessly kicking at the red laterite dirt.

I'm concerned about the Kutu," Max said, but halfway through the sentence, the satellite phone spat static back at her, then cleared again.

"What?" Stevens half yelled over the phone. In a lower voice, talking to someone on his side of the line, he said, "Do you know how to work this thing? The signal's breaking up."

The station was running low on diesel, so the generator had been on for only two hours last night. Perhaps the phone hadn't had time to charge fully.

Stevens spoke loudly. "The reception's bad, Max. I don't know if you can hear me, but if you can, keep talking and we'll do what we can on this side." Near the end of this, the static flared, but—other than that—the signal was clear on her side. He added in an aside to someone there, "Is there a way to switch channels on this? You know, like on a cordless?"

She spoke as clearly as she could, popping her consonants. "If you hear me, please say so. I can hear you. It is unknown how much of an imminent danger the Kutu represent, but I believe it would be wise to have an exit strategy prepared just in case."

"I tell you, Fred, all I'm getting is static." His voice sounded muffled now and there was a rustling noise. Perhaps he held the receiver against his chest.

"Stevens," she half-yelled, "Get . . . me . . . an . . . open-ended . . . ticket . . . back . . . just . . . in . . . case."

"What do you think this button does?" he asked.

The certainty struck her he was pretending not to hear, trying to keep her at the research station.

"Sure," he said. "Try it."

And the phone went dead.

In order to get her here, he hadn't told her about the Kutu, was willing to risk her life in hopes of getting the drug.

She snorted. He didn't know whom he was dealing with. To get a chance at finding this vine, she would have come anyway.

Yoko, Mutara, and Max hiked up the mountain to find the gorilla group, T2, the one habituated to Yoko's work. The three days of Max's quarantine had passed. The trees loomed above. The humans were tiny ants climbing near their base, swimming waist-high through bushes and ferns.

Max's lungs were getting more acclimatized to this atmosphere, and she didn't lose her footing as often. She knew now to climb without shoes, to feel with her toes for tree roots and always to hold onto one branch or another. She was still slower than the others, however, and sometimes slipped and fell onto her knees.

After half an hour her breathing was ragged and hard, her vision getting blotchy at the edges. Still she kept forcing her feet forward, head down in concentration.

Somewhere ahead of her, Yoko called out, "Hey Mutara, let's take a break."

"What?" he said, surprised. He was in the front, his voice faint with distance.

Perhaps he turned around and saw Max. When he spoke again his voice sounded different. "Yes, good idea."

Yoko and he leaned against a tree, chatting about when the research station might get their overdue supplies. They breathed easily. In her rain gear, Max flopped down on her back in the mud, her feet propped up against a trunk so she wouldn't bobsled down the mountain. Every part of her—mouth, shoulders, back, and ribs—was deeply involved in the action of sucking as much air as possible into her lungs.

Meanwhile, she stared up at the tree her feet were braced against. A distant part of her mind identified it. *Hypericum lanceolatum*, a tree-sized version of Saint John's Wart. Hanging off the branches was the mistletoe, *Loranthus luteo-aurantiacus*. If its leaves were crushed in the hand, they had the scent of bell pepper with an overtone of fresh-cut grass. Probably some type of pyrazine inside.

She moved her eyes from plant to plant—recalling names, remembering smells. She already could identify almost all of them. Her preliminary work had been done well.

Her love of plants came from three ways in which they differed from animals and, most importantly, from humans. First off, on a purely olfactory level, they were more pleasing. They never farted methane from the inefficiencies of digestion, never reeked of bacterial effluvium if they hadn't showered. Even when dead and decomposing, plants didn't stink of protein breakdown like rotting meat did. No, the scent of an old log or a large pile of leaves came from their decaying carbon bonds: a fragrance sweet and vaguely nostalgic.

Plants were also much more interesting chemically. Rooted in one spot throughout life, a plant had no need to lighten its load by regularly discarding its byproducts. What an animal piddled away carelessly upon the ground, a plant instead treasured and experimented with. If you ground up one specimen of every animal species and chemically compared the remains, the variation would be nearly nonexistent. Various proteins and lipids rearranged as either massive rhino or microscopic rotifer. This bland sameness was not true of plants. Even the most primitive could borrow any of the intermediate chemicals involved in the fifty steps of the Krebs cycle. They used these to manufacture other compounds and then returned the chemicals like a borrowed cup of sugar. Plants had to be master chemists, for they weren't able to yank up their roots to flee from predators or chase after mates. Instead they issued commands to animals in a terse chemical voice, using fragrances, colors, tastes, or poisons. "Rub against my stamens." "Eat my fruit, then poop out my seeds in a steaming pile of compost." "Don't touch my leaves." Even today, half of the medicines sold in drug stores were directly made from extracts of pharmaceutically active plants. The concept behind many other drugs had been cribbed from the original inspiration of a plant.

Her third, and perhaps most important, reason for loving plants was that their movements never scared her.

Most people didn't understand; they considered plants as static as a bureau or a shoe. When Max was focused on a problem, she could be *still*, concentrated and barely breathing. An hour passing, two. Most humans in comparison were jittery squirrels, shifting this way and that, crossing and recrossing their legs, jumping up within fifteen minutes to use the phone or get a glass of water. This difference between her and others allowed her to understand there wasn't just one speed in the world; other organisms could have a different meter to their movements. When she looked at a tree, she saw not a stationary object, but a photo of a dancer in mid-motion, the gesture of its branches describing its battle for food or love.

She'd always wanted to set up a tripod and camera to take a photo once a minute of a tree—for instance this *Hypericum* her feet were propped against. After a week's worth of timed exposures, she could play the images together as a film. Immediately, any animal life would transform into a fuzzy mist at the base of the tree, insubstantial and irritating, obscuring a true clarity of vision. Having stepped into the botanical scale of time, what would reveal itself as truly alive would be the plants, a vine twisting up the *Hypericum* trunk like a snake, its branches spreading their fingers and its leaves turning their faces to follow the sun's progress.

If she slowed down her camera even more, taking a photo only once an hour, the narratives of the plants would be revealed, their individual struggles for life, their strategies and stealthy attacks. At this speed, flowering wouldn't be seen in terms of individual blossoms, but more as an event that swept across the organism, a shimmer of the skin, the blush of a shy mate. Against this painterly exhale of sex, this colorful beat of time, the *Hypericum* would stretch its limbs high into the canopy, ruffle its plumage out into maturity, and then fall over. Two saplings below would race for the sunlit hole, twisting and arching over each other as canny as basketball players. Meanwhile, a few feet down-hill, a strangler fig growing out of the fork of that *Pygeum* tree would lob its roots like ropes down into the ground, more and more roots until they encircled the *Pygeum*, thickened and then merged, the fig swallowing its host alive, voracious as a boa.

Max didn't fit in with the restless timescale of her own species. At the same time, she was exiled from the life of plants, left examining only a still frame of their struggles. But from that photo, she conjectured what had come before and might come afterward. In her mind, she imagined living long enough, stand-ing motionless enough, to see the graceful dance of a tree.

"Hellooo," said Yoko, waving her hand in front of Max's face. "Time to get going."

She jerked back, startled. She breathed for a moment, then got to her feet and climbed again, following Yoko and Mutara.

The two of them kept their heads up now as they climbed, watching the jungle. Perhaps they were getting close to the gorillas' territory. No one talked.

In childhood, one of the few people she'd felt comfortable with was her dad. A mathematician at the university, he could be still, contemplating the permutations of a theorem for most of an afternoon. She'd lean against him, confident there would be no movement other than his breathing and perhaps a slight vibration in his chest as he hummed. She could depend on him. Her mom tried so hard to stay still for Max, but the feeling was different, concentrated and stiff. Within ten minutes she would inadvertently shift her weight or check her watch or try to pat Max's hair, her touch frittery and jarring. By the time she was three, Max wouldn't sit in her lap anymore.

"Asparagus" was one of the code words that aspies used to discuss their syndrome in public, as in "Do you think Sam might have a bit of asparagus?" Max found this botanical term so appropriate. When her dad was sitting, his stillness had an almost Zen feel to it, calm and engaged. For a plant, each motion was energy-intensive and final, the direction in which it would grow. A plant considered its actions carefully. Her dad sat, thinking. Asparagus.

Her dad. The day she was six years old, two months and twenty-four days. A Tuesday in November. She wasn't making the most graceful transition to school. She'd watched the others enough to know everyone else in her class played together. That day, she tried playing trucks with Ricky Draegor. Well, not so much playing "with" as "next to." He insisted on driving the trucks all around, making *vroom-vroom* noises, rather than lining them up on their sides and spinning the wheels, staring at their metal spokes. So she clonked him on the head hard with a Tonka dumpster. The principal called her parents. Her dad picked her up at school early, brought her home and fed her lunch. Afterward she sat in his lap for a long time, needing the comfort, playing with his wooden necklace.

At 1:43 (still in his lap, she was staring at the oven clock, watching the way the minute dial twisted, rolling the new digit into view. For a distinct portion of each minute, there would be no number there at all. A very literal person, she wondered what time it was when it was '1:4 ') he abruptly jerked to his feet. She was thrown to the floor.

He made noises, garbled words she didn't know. One arm flapped.

Alarmed, she shot a glance at his face. His features twisted and unreadable.

She scuttled into a corner and began to rock. The noises behind her got louder. She began to knock her forehead into the wall. With each hit, there was a *clunk* inside her skull and a flash of light.

Something fell over behind her.

She hit her head into the wall harder, staring at the light. She hummed loudly. Time went away.

By the time her mom got home, he'd been lying half turned on his belly for a long time, motionless. Max, in the corner, slamming her head against the wall, her forehead dripping blood.

At the funeral, her Aunt Tilda had forced her to wear a dress. The air moving past her bare legs jingled along her nerves, making her jumpy. The bandage on her forehead crinkled with every movement, the sound inside her skull. She had a hard time keeping herself calm. When the normals began to lower her dad inside of the box into the ground, she began to slap her chest, moaning. Had to look away.

Her vision moved past the people and the intoned words, past everything happening here. She saw the tree at the edge of the clearing. An enormous oak. Her eyes rolled up it, rising into its branches, its presence expanding inside her. So vast and patient. Motionless and dependable. Her slapping slowed. She took a step closer, then another. Drifting forward bit by bit, staring, until she leaned against its trunk. Letting her face rest against its rough skin. Wrapping her arms around its solidity. The wind moved through its branches, creating a noise a little like an inhalation. When she stopped moaning, she could hear these breaths better.

The trunk smelled like the wooden beads around his neck. The beads she now wore.

She rested against the tree, eyes closed.

Throughout the funeral, no one came over to talk to her, to touch her or try to move her away from the tree. Since his death, now it was others now who wouldn't look at her.

When she finally stepped back from the trunk, she was calmer. She blinked around at the world.

The sun had moved to an entirely different side of the sky. Her mom was the only one remaining, sitting on a tombstone a few feet away. Max glanced; her mom's body was concentrated, sitting still, her face pointed toward her. Who knew what thoughts she had, watching Max on this day?

After a moment her mom pushed herself heavily to her feet and the two of them turned and headed home.

Max bumped into Mutara's back. Stepped away fast. She saw now he had his hand up, calling for a halt. He was examining the mountainside, listening.

"Keep your eyes open, Tombay." Yoko whispered. "We're near where they bedded down last night."

In the silence Max heard some bird make a call that sounded remarkably like a Ping-Pong ball dropped from a height, bouncing and bouncing and finally coming to a halt.

She searched the slope above, saw mossy trees vast and secretive in the curling mist. A flock of birds, long tails of cobalt and vermillion, ribboned through the air above.

Jesus, she thought, *Africa*.

Mutara gestured them forward, moving slower now and looking all around.

Two decades ago, when Max was growing up, not much was known about Asperger's. Confused with psychosis, it had yet to be officially classified as a condition in the United States, much less have a standard treatment. Still her mother fought to help Max, her will unshakable. Using research, she battled with the school system for the best services and teachers.

In return, Max worked as hard as she could at her lessons, with all her focus. And every once in a while, she'd bring home something for her mom that had caught her eye. She handed the gift over, careful not to touch her mom's skin: a shiny spoon or crumpled blue napkin or a tiny disco ball she'd found half-crushed in the trash. Her mom took the gift, whatever it was, examining it. In lieu of her daughter's hand, she held the gift for a long time.

Afterward she placed it on a shelf by her bed, lined up with the other gifts, where she could look at them first thing when she woke up, while she gathered the energy to get out of bed.

The year before Max went to college, she happened one day to notice these gifts afresh. Stopped on the way to the bathroom to stare at the group of them there on her mother's shelf. Broken bits of glittery trash.

After that, she bought her mom socks instead, on the appropriate days of her mom's birthday and Christmas. Brown knee-highs. She would take an old pair to the store each time to match the size, kind and color exactly. Bought six pairs every time. In spite of the lack of surprise about the contents, Max had the gift wrapped. Humans had their customs and she tried hard to follow them.

Unwrapping the socks, her mother understood the effort. She always said, "Thank you, Max, this will be of use. I love you." And she wore a pair of them every day.

Still her mom continued to keep the childhood gifts, dusted them and left them lined up right beside her bed.

Her mom's older sister, Aunt Tilda, had had children who were all smiley and cuddly. Growing up, they had many playdates and sleepovers with friends and classmates. The youngest, Nina, for a while was on the state gymnastics team. After college, she and Sarah got jobs as salespeople; Robert became a psychologist. On Christmas cards, they grinned into the camera, blond hair, arms linked around each other. Their bodies fitting together as tightly as a puzzle.

Talking on the phone with Tilda, Max's mom said mostly, "Congratulations," and "Well, that's great." When she did discuss Max, she tried to emphasize the gains.

Max imagined returning with the vine she searched for. It could be a blockbuster drug, saving the lives of thousands of people. The vine's discovery would allow her mom to talk to her sister in something other than that small voice.

It would help make up for how Max had sat rocking in a corner while her dad's brain—a major vein to it blocked off—suffocated and then died.

The three of them stepped into a clearing, the underbrush trampled down. They stopped at the edge.

Mutara sniffed the air.

Max copied him. The sweet decay of forest litter, the green oxygen of thick foliage, the thin tropical dirt. And in the background was the slightest hint of something animal.

Yoko leaned close, about to whisper something.

Max moved back.

Yoko blinked, then remembered. "Around the gorillas, no matter what happens, don't run away, because they'll chase you like a cat would. And you *really* don't want to be caught."

Max remembered the forest buff charging her. She tried to imagine standing still while a gorilla rushed her.

Yoko noticed something and she pointed with her chin. "Look." A pile of manure lay there.

Max tried to picture a primate big enough to make that. It was as large as a horse's dump and smelled similar: grassy and sweet. From the scent, she understood two things. One, gorillas were absolute vegetarians and, two, Yoko always smelled a bit of this manure.

"What do you research?" Max asked.

"Parasites," Yoko said. "Poopies are my profession."

Mutara began to cluck his tongue against the roof of his mouth, the sound a farmer might make to warn a large barnyard creature he was approaching. Mutara watched the foliage around them. The three of them moved forward.

Yoko whispered, "Titus is the silverback for this family, weighs about four-hundred pounds. He's basically a gentle soul, but he's seen a lot of violence in his life. His uncle and father were killed by humans in front of him. Don't ever do anything he might consider a threat. I once saw him attack a researcher. This guy, Matt Rupert, a bit of a hotshot, was getting too close to a newborn, wanted to figure out the gender. Titus rushed him like, I don't know, a furry train, bit him in the neck and tossed him thirty feet. We all helped Matt walk down into town for medical help."

"He could walk?"

"No choice. He had to." Yoko ripped a stalk off some wild celery and handed it back to her. "When we spot them, munch on this. Keep crouched down, on all fours. *Never* stand upright. Move slowly. Act like a harmless ape."

Max looked at the celery in her hand. "They fall for the act?"

"What the hell." Yoko turned. On the slope above, she loomed over Max. Her feet planted wide, her short hair standing up, a few stray leaves caught in it. A forest nymph in a rain slicker. "Recognize your phylogeny. You are a Great Ape. We're more related to gorillas than most warblers are to each other."

She turned back and continued to climb, clucking.

Max searched for movement or dark fur anywhere above them. To her right, she spotted an imprint in the mud. After a moment of considering it—some kind of footprint or part of a face?— she understood it came from four knuckles. Taken together they were the width of a boxing glove.

When she was a child, whenever Aunt Tilda visited, she demanded a hug, would chase Max around the house to get one. Loud and extroverted, she believed Max just had to get used to the experience. "Regular hugs every day and she'll settle right down," Tilda used to say, "Look at my children." She was the least Asparagus-like person Max knew. Whenever she caught Max, she'd crush her to her bosom, the scent of armpits and floral perfume, the rigid structure of undergarments.

Max's whole adult life, she'd had nightmares of this, her panicked fleeing, her lumbering aunt, the inevitable capture, herself pressed into the heavy body so hard. She knew her aunt wanted to shove Max right through her body to come out the other side draped in normal flesh.

Max imagined all the worst parts of humans in a four-hundred-pound body with sharp teeth.

She was getting whiffs now of something in the air. Wet dog combined with sweaty teenager. The scent came and went with the breeze.

Her face felt hot. She forced herself to keep climbing. Her fear wasn't at all like that shot of adrenalin she'd got after being chased by the buff. This wasn't exhilarating or transformative. More insistent and unpleasant. Her stomach felt nauseous. Her breath came too fast.

She climbed, digging her toes into the mud for traction.

A startled chuff. Maybe twenty feet to her right.

The branches there shook.

She stopped, kept her head rigidly down, looking at nothing directly, sucking air in through her teeth.

The bushes exploded with dark objects popping up for a look. A moment passed while she steeled herself for the attack. Do *not* run, she thought. Do *not*.

Then, as she feared, came the loud crashing of foliage, a pell-mell flailing of limbs and leaves and mammoth hairy bodies.

All of it, however, scrambling uphill and away. Fleeing. Startled screams, the thick musk of fear and diarrheic dung.

Within seconds, the gorillas were gone, the jungle stunned into stillness.

A last distant shriek. The pock-pock of a chest being beat.

"Huh." Yoko said into the silence afterward, "Guess they're not so used to newcomers anymore."

S hame was something Jeremy had dealt with before. He had a complete lack of ability with the cattle on the farm, a deep unease around blood and, in social chatter with the women of his social milieu, a certain persistent awkwardness.

The skills he did possess were mostly those of a type unappreciated by his mother and Grandpapi: a general excellence with numbers, a clean execution of design drawings, and a methodical care when ordering supplies. He did not know how much of their unwillingness to admit his strengths was exacerbated by the more profound difference they increasingly sensed within him since he had reached adolescence.

Once he reached twenty-two years of age, his mother took him to the family physician. Red-faced Patterson had the habit of breathing through his mouth in a way that did not advertise good health, decreasing the gravity with which Jeremy was wont to listen to his advice. Jeremy's mother and the doctor closeted themselves away in his office for a few minutes to discuss the reason for the visit. Then, while she waited outside, the doctor had Jeremy undress and sit on the leather examination couch. The moment he took out his stethoscope, Jeremy could tell his mother's good manners had impeded her clarity. Patterson listened to his heart, palpated his belly, and asked him about aches and bowel movements just as he always did. While he was peering into Jeremy's ears he finally inquired what his mother believed was wrong with a young buck like him. On the doctor's breath was the smell of the pork he had had for lunch.

Jeremy cleared his throat. He had agreed to go to the doctor's only on the assumption his mother would do the talking. Sitting here, on the leather table in his undergarments, staring at a glass cabinet full of medicines that would never help him, the shame of his position overwhelmed him. "A man of my years," he said, borrowing one of his mother's phrases, "should be more rowdy and disobedient."

In his ear, Patterson's raspy breath paused. "That is not something most mothers complain of."

Looking down at his spidery body, a thin fold of belly pressing against the linen of his underclothes, he felt much more naked than he would if he were completely unclothed. He used more of his mother's words. "I do not display any great interest in marriage."

"Of course, that's natural. You are still a young man. You have got a few years before you settle down. Believe me, you'll meet the right woman, feel differently."

Exhaling through his nose, Jeremy closed his eyes. He tried to imagine describing the visions his dreams were full of, the desires seemingly built into his loins. Through sheer frustration, he allowed his voice to take on some of its real emotion. "I won't feel different." He turned to face the doctor, his expression bare. "I am *different*."

The doctor stared at him, comprehension erasing his smile. He stepped back, fumbled with his instruments, putting them away. "You may get dressed."

Patterson's instructions to his mother included the advice he exercise regularly and vigorously, perhaps pulling stumps or pounding fences in. He might spend more time with older married men on whom he could model his behavior. He should not drink hot liquids but try to sit out in the sun a little bit each day.

Perhaps the rumor started with Patterson, or maybe just an observant neighbor. Soon afterward Jeremy noticed that fewer people asked him which girl he had set his cap on. At social events, he felt the eyes of others on him. He went into town less and less.

By the time he was twenty-four, Burt Donahue was one of the few people he still saw. His mother was not encouraging of a friendship with a papist, but, given that he was the town priest, at least she could not impugn his reputation. Most times the two men would play an aggressive game of horseshoes or go duck shooting. Wearing normal clothing instead of his vestments, Burt showed himself to be adept with a rifle. In a way their friendship was an alliance. Whenever they saw a courting couple riding by in a buggy, holding hands, both the young men shifted their eyes away. And at the kinds of subjects that other men around them were wont to bring up upon occasion, Jeremy and the priest would both tighten their mouths, sometimes their throats working involuntarily. Jeremy never knew what desires exactly Burt fought against (there were those clothes he had to wear on Sundays, so confusing, his male legs slapping impatiently with each stride against the confines of his skirt). Whatever the reason, being around Burt was enough for Jeremy to feel a trifle less alone, less different. He looked forward to each visit.

It was not as though Jeremy thought it out, would ever have planned it this way, when one hot day they went for a swim in the pond. The air so stifling and motionless, the water such a cool relief. Surfacing, they howled and splashed about like any youths, but as Burt started sloshing out to shore, the wet wool of his bathing suit began to cling to the outlines of his body. Jeremy waded slower, hanging back a bit, his expression frozen. Glancing back, sensing something, Burt was unwilling to give up his lightheartedness. He stepped forward to grab Jeremy's shoulders, attempting to toss him back into the water. Both of them wrestling intently, struggling for purchase in the mud and silt.

And, feeling his balance beginning to give, his toes starting to slide, Jeremy planted a rough and wet kiss on Bert's lips.

Even as he pulled away—before Burt wound back his arm to punch him with a force and skill startling in a priest—Jeremy registered for a moment the joy in the man's face, the gloating that in the end the weakness had been Jeremy's.

The requirement of the church to keep a secret, such as one divulged in the confessional, evidently did not extend to what happened at a waterhole. Within a few days the rumor had reached his mother. She began suffering from a tightness in her breath, sometimes had migraines that lasted for days. She gave up her position in the church knitting circle and as secretary for the whist association. His whole family became nearly cloistered in their house. Each time he walked into the kitchen where his family sat, their harsh silence rang in his ear. He began to retreat even further, into the solitude of his room. Looking around at the four walls, he saw the confines of his future if he stayed in town.

Within weeks, he happened to read a pamphlet on the many opportunities available in Africa.

Jeremy had a hunting blind built for himself next to where the lion had leaped over the boma, figuring the animal might return to a spot where she had obtained food. Other than the sound of the hammers pounding together the blind, the camp was comparatively quiet. The workers were not laboring on the railway, filling the air with the clangs of shovels and picks. Instead they built and rebuilt the thorn fence around their tents, making the boma walls higher and thicker. They worked faster and more intently than he had ever seen them. The only sounds were those of the branches being stacked and restacked and the men hollering out instructions. This morning, he had observed that when they were off duty, they no longer sat outside their tents, playing cards, laughing, and singing their strangely nasal songs. Instead they came out of their tents only to get their food, peering around intently for lions and then scuttling back inside to eat, the flaps jerked shut.

Today, when the Indians walked by him, they no longer smiled or called good morning. The story of his aborted hunt for the lion, the way he had been found snagged in the nyika, had quickly traveled around camp. The feeling of isolation seemed uncomfortably familiar.

A little after ten in the morning, while he was overseeing the camouflaging of the hunting blind, using bundles of branches to make it look like a bush, he turned to see Patsy's groom running toward him.

"Your horse," the man called. "She fell."

Jeremy sprinted across the camp, the mud splashing under his feet. Vaulting over the paddock fence, he found Patsy gasping on her side. Sprawled this way, her legs appeared implausibly delicate for the round heft of her belly. He threw himself down beside her, lifting her head onto his lap, brushing her neck and talking softly. Her eye rolled to look at him, a clean white froth bubbling from her mouth and nose. Her head rocked with each labored breath.

"I'm sorry," he kept whispering. "So sorry I brought you to this." Gradually her eye moved past him to regard the sky. He heard a faint ticking noise deep inside her. Over the next half an hour, the ticking gradually slowed.

In the silence afterward, he thought of the tribal woman clicking in the forest.

Until now, when Jeremy considered the many men who died during their first year here, he had had faith he would not end up that way. He had believed he could not die.

Alan proclaimed it African Horse Sickness. Standing over the body, tamping the tobacco into his pipe with his thumb, he pointed out the froth and the way her head and neck were bloated, especially the hollow above her eyes. Her lungs, he said, were full of liquid. She had drowned on dry land.

"Bloody shame," he said. "Right nice horse." He spun his flint lighter a few times before the wick caught, then he lit the pipe and puffed hard on it, the wet smack of his lips audible.

Jeremy had always tried to be as stoic, a man of few words—the way his mother said the male Turnkeys always were—but for him there had been times when he could not stand the tension anymore. Those times, back in Maine, he had gone riding long and hard on Patsy. Deep in the forest, he had whispered quietly into her ear, bowed his face onto her hot working shoulder.

There was the question of what to do with her remains. Jeremy could not stand the idea of throwing her into the bushes, hyenas cackling over the feast, a fox perhaps running between the tents with her ear.

He started the Indians working on a grave immediately, but within twenty minutes mountainous black clouds rolled in from the east and the wind picked up, scattering twigs and dirt across the ground. Flocks of small birds zigzagged confused from bush to bush, riding the gusts. When the rain came, everything further than fifteen feet away was grayed out from the ferocity. Even after two weeks here, he still expected the rain to feel cool against his face, a refreshing summer shower. Instead the rain hammered the earth and his body, warm as sweat. It went on and on, the air more humid, the spray kicking up off the dirt. He bid the men to keep digging.

Utterly soaked by the downpour, he paced the camp, waiting for the grave to be completed. He spied a coolie in a tree up ahead, his oversized Indian shirt matted against his body, tying several jerry cans together to a branch. With some curiosity, Jeremy approached. When the Indian had finished trying the cans, an askari standing on the ground experimented with yanking on the attached rope. The cans clanked together loudly. The askari backed into the nearby tent and, closing the flaps, tried yanking the rope again. The askaris were responsible for watching over the camp at night. This one hoped to scare away any lion without leaving the safety of his tent.

Jeremy found himself trying to recreate the exact rhythm Patsy's hooves had made at a walk. Such a sassy walk she'd had, her ribcage rolling from side to side. Dup dup da dup, he said to himself. Dupup da dup.

He had already given one of his extra guns to an askari in each of the three main boma encampments, retaining only one for himself for his evening wait in the hunting blind.

The lion, so far, took one man per night. On the other hand, two to four Indians tended to die from malaria in that same time frame. The engineer inside of Jeremy could not help calculating, if the lion continued to kill at this rate—keeping the terrified Indians in their tents slightly more protected from mosquitoes—a considerable number of lives might be saved overall.

Coming back to the grave, he found the pit's sides had collapsed in the downpour. The body, covered by several sodden blankets, lay on the ground nearby, hooves peeking out. She would need to be buried at least six feet down to keep the animals away. So far the hole was not deeper than two feet. He told the men to hurry, to shovel the water out first, put some muscle into it. If anything, the rain was coming down faster.

Alan arrived under an umbrella, a tight snare drum of rain. A careful man, he wore his Wellingtons even in this heat. Somehow the toes of them gleamed, clean of mud. He stood there for a moment, surveying the work. The pit looked like a pond with the men standing up to their calves in it.

Raising his voice over the rain, Alan said, "If the lion is still in the neighborhood, it would be good to dispose of the body before nightfall. We don't want the smell of carrion in camp, now do we?"

At four, Jeremy ordered her remains soaked with kerosene and thrown on the bonfire with the rest of the day's cadavers.

Her ashes would be mixed in with humans'. He did not know if the workers minded. At the moment, he did not care.

About an hour after dusk, Jeremy heard a lion roar. The sound echoed through the trees, the call of dominance, of health and raspy strength and speed. No human could make such a noise, lacking a ribcage big enough, a throat long enough to growl out such a deep sound.

Once riding back from Rensselaer Polytechnic for summer break, Jeremy had crossed a noisy river and ascended the far bank slowly, the day hot and gusty. Climbing over a ridge, he had halted in the face of an immense crackle and heat, a monstrous shimmering light in the trees not a hundred yards hence, the crack of branches and the roar of destruction. The sound so overwhelming, it filled his eyes and mouth and lungs; it vibrated in his muscles. There was no conscious thought to his reaction or to Patsy's assent to his request. They had wheeled and were galloping back across the river before he could recognize what he had seen, give it the name "forest fire."

The lion's roar created some of the same physical reaction inside. The sound shivered up his back and vibrated even in the air that he drew into his lungs. It brought forth a straightforward primal reaction. Run, said his feet, run. Instead sitting in the small room of the hunting blind, he shifted on his stool and held tighter to his rifle.

The hunting blind that had seemed so clever in the light of day abruptly looked different. He had had the Indians build a four-sided version of the kind from which he commonly hunted ducks and only now did he question the wisdom of his design. The foot-tall gun slot running the width of each of the four sides, he saw, was a potential window for the lion's paw to reach through; none of the sides were reinforced enough to take a direct charge. And then there was the lack of a roof.

A second lion answered to the south maybe half a mile, later another responded from the east. Jeremy concentrated, trying to guess the animals' locations and number. Perhaps there were fifteen lions out there, most of them silent, or maybe there were only two noisy ones, circling the camp. He did not know if any of them were the man-eater.

Sitting on his stool, the rifle pointing out the gun-slot, he noted the thorn fence that surrounded these tents appeared shorter than it had in daylight. He knew this fence to be ten feet tall, but in the darkness, with the rumbling calls of lions in the background, it appeared so much shorter.

The rain started again, slowly at first. The drops tapped out their beat on the brim of his hat. Da dapdap dap, he said. At a canter she had rocked like a chair, her belly sometimes wheezing. The storm began to gather strength, the rain drumming straight down. After a while it was hard to see the walls of the tent nearest him, much less keep watch for anything that might jump over the boma ten yards away. He hunkered over in the torrent, the water streaming down his back.

At some point, the lions' roaring stopped. He dozed lightly on his stool, dreaming of Patsy's labored breathing, the weight of her head in his lap. The gun was hugged tight to his chest, the strap wrapped twice round his arm for security. He told her again of his sickness. In the dream, she whispered back.

He jerked awake. The rain had stopped, the camp quiet around him. Had that rough breathing come from his dream or somewhere nearby? In the dark he could see no movement, could barely make out the ground four yards away. How well could a lion see anyway? The animal hunted at night the way a house cat did. Probably it had better night vision than he did, as well as a good sense of smell. He squinted through the gun slot at all the dark lumps around, half of which he was not sure he remembered seeing earlier in the evening. Rice sacks? The trailing edges of tents? Every breath he took echoed inside the blind. Was that dark shape over there a stack of lumber?

He remembered the way the clearing had looked after the lion had eaten, covered with blood and small gritty pieces.

As the minutes passed, he spotted nothing moving. Perhaps if something had been nearby, it went away. Perhaps it just stayed and watched. Each time he turned his head to look behind him, his hair rustled audibly on his collar.

It was strange how alone he felt in here now. He told himself he was within calling distance of several dozen men. He had people around him all day long; more than seven hundred lived in camp; during the day he was always giving them orders, surveying their work, constantly interacting. Yet this was not the first time he had felt alone in camp. He was the leader, the only American, a white man surrounded almost entirely by brown.

Dawn finally came, grainy and yellow. Throughout the night, he had heard no screams from anywhere in camp. Even through his tiredness, he felt such relief. Perhaps things would get better with time.

It was perhaps an hour after lunch—hunched into his fatigue, overseeing the digging of the canal that would reroute the river out of the way while they built the bridge—that he heard the outcry from camp. "*Sher, sher,*" came the screams of many men. For a moment in his exhaustion, he thought they were yelling, "Share, share." Did they want more water, more pay, his quinine? Then he comprehended his mistake and, before the first runners reached him, he was sprinting back. The simple act of conveying himself from one spot to another took so long without Patsy, his breath high in his throat. His pith helmet kept flopping forward obscuring his sight.

Alan had told him that lions tended to nap during the day's heat, preferring the mask of darkness for their hunting. In the bright light of day, they were more cautious of humans, would never approach a large group. However, their lion did not seem to be aware of this, for a little after two in the afternoon she wandered in through the gate of a boma that had been propped open first thing in the morning. By this point, the hospital was overflowing with patients laying on cots in the shadow of the gate. The two men who had their eyes open must have believed the lion walking by them was a fever-induced hallucination. They had watched with interest, turning their heads to follow her. It was not until one of the hospital staff strode around the corner of a tent that anyone started screaming.

In their confusion and fear, the men afterward could not come to agreement about her exact size, certain only of tawny weight and rawboned grace and that she was bigger than they had imagined any lion could be. She had ignored all the yelling to stroll into the tent from which, three nights ago, she had dragged her first victim. When she came out, she held the victim's leather satchel in her mouth. With the healthy men screaming "*Sher*" at her—"tiger" in Hindustani—and banging jerry cans from their hiding spots behind tents and up in trees, the malaria patients too sick to even roll under their beds for protection, she wandered by them all, out through the gates, stopping occasionally to shake the satchel from side to side, like a kitten with a play-toy.

By the time Jeremy arrived, she had disappeared without a trace into the nyika.

During that night, three men died of malaria and one of yellow fever. As though the satchel was entertainment enough for the lion for now, she did not roar or reappear all night.

After breakfast, Jeremy ordered the men to pack up their tents and bomas. They moved a mile back from the river, back under the paltry shade of the nyika. This retreat Jeremy ordered to protect them from the river's clouds of mosquitoes and the attendant malaria. A fifth of the Indians had contracted it now.

Many of the Indians refused to walk to the latrine forty paces from each boma unless someone with a gun accompanied them. They believed Jeremy was moving the camp to get away from the lion.

Having spent another near-sleepless night in a hunting blind (this time, one with a sturdy roof), Jeremy asked Ungan Singh to find Otombe.

Aunt Tilda was chasing her, her arms out for a hug, her wide body filling the hall. Max fleeing silent and deadly serious. Her mother strangely just stood there, smiling at the scene.

Tilda cornered Max and stepped forward, hands out. Her odor of floral perfume and sweaty intimate areas. She grabbed Max and, in the ensuing struggle, ripped a chunk of skin off the girl's arm. The flesh coming off not bloody and ragged, but all of one color, like a chunk of play dough. Her aunt pressed the flesh into her chest, patting it down until it merged in seamlessly. Then she tore off another chunk. Each piece of flesh became her own, part of her determined normality, fused into her body permanently. Max understood her aunt had done this to other children, many of them, those who were different, erasing them entirely. This was why she weighed so much.

Max shuddered awake, gasping.

Unlike other kids, she had never screamed at nightmares. Just woke up gasping and rigid in her bed. Then she would roll out of the blankets and run to her mom's bed to stand beside it. Not touching, not speaking. Standing a foot back, breathing hard and staring at her mom's hands and their tired freckles, concentrating on her smell until, calmer, she could lie down, not on the bed beside her mom, but on the hard predictable floor. There she could finally sleep.

Jerking awake that night in the darkness of her African

cabin, she breathed for a while, then climbed out of bed with her blankets to sleep on the floor.

The next morning they set off again to search for the gorillas. About a half a mile up the mountain, Mutara, Yoko, and Max moved off the game path they'd been climbing, onto the gorillas' trail. This was not like following a deer, a spread-out series of subtle clues: a hoof print here, a twig turned there. No, the trail of each gorilla looked like a giant bowling ball had been rolled through the jungle. Broken branches and crushed vegetation, each individual shoving and munching through the underbrush.

At first Max followed directly behind Yoko on the same trail, but branches occasionally slapped back into her face as Yoko let go of them, so she copied Mutara's strategy and walked up a different trail. All the paths interwove, the gorillas heading in the same direction. Bushes snagged on her clothing. Ferns and grasses brushed against her, soaking her clothes from the shoulders down. She was huffing, head down, concentrating on keeping up with the others.

As her hormone levels had begun to change with adolescence, Max's startle reflex got more extreme. A few of the kids in school noticed and occasionally screamed just behind her or clapped their hands in her face. High school filled with such casual cruelty. Within sight of her own adulthood, she understood for the first time she was likely to be alone throughout her life.

And so, eight times during high school, she brought different boys back home to have sex with her. It was her best guess at a solution. She hoped the boy would sit with her afterward for a few minutes. Maybe he'd talk to her at school sometimes. It seemed to work for other girls. As the kids streamed out of school at the end of the day, she would walk up to a boy she selected for the color of his shirt or the shine of his belt, and ask him if he were willing.

In order to endure the act, she had requirements. In her house with the boy, she stated them clearly, ticking them off on her fingers. The boy's weight could not rest on her at any time. There could be no kissing. His hands could not touch her.

Having listed her requirements, she shucked her pants off and got down on her hands and legs, waiting for him to kneel and start.

Even under these conditions, she vacated her body as best she could. She was proud of herself for this new ability, busied her mind reconstructing favorite smells.

Throughout the act she knelt there as unmoving as furniture.

As soon as he was finished, the boy would stand up, move back fast. He'd pull his pants up, averting his eyes, his actions uneasy. He'd leave without a word.

There was the silence afterward, the room alone.

After a bit, she'd wiggle her way between her two futon mattresses, so one was on top, one beneath. She lay there for hours with her head sticking out the far side, a human sandwich. The hug of the mattresses comforted her, dependable and utterly still.

And her mind would begin to work—at first occasionally, and then unceasingly—on the problem of imagining some kind of adulthood for herself, any kind of adulthood, that she would consider worth enduring.

The ninth time she tried sex, the man pulled out halfway through, began to punch her and then to kick.

He made guttural noises in the back of his throat, spit came from his lips. She'd met him an hour earlier on the way back from school. He'd appeared physically healthy, had asked her name, been polite. Having given up on the boys from school, she'd wondered if an adult might be more ready for a relationship. Had decided to test the theory.

One of his work boots caught her in the mouth. She heard something crunch inside, wet sticks breaking.

The pain and anger overwhelming—an entire lifetime of trying very hard.

She moved faster than she knew she could. She grabbed the back of his boot at the top of his swing. Yanked hard. With his pants around his knees, he fell badly. His head hit. She was already on him, jabbing her thumbs into his eyes, all her weight, all her might. She was screaming, "Fuckity fucking fuck."

He twisted out from under her and ran.

After two blocks, she gave up chasing him. Stood there on the street corner, wearing nothing from the waist down except a pair of gray kneesocks, watching until he disappeared from view. Then she walked home and called her mom at work. On the phone, even while she explained that she needed to be taken to the emergency room, she kept her lips pursed so the pieces of her teeth wouldn't fall out. Sitting down ever so gently, she worked on breathing, waiting for help.

Three birds exploded out of a tree above. Max jumped at the movement, caught a glimpse of large mascaraed eyes in faces of raw skin. She looked away. The birds' laugh was shrill, the beat of their wings prehistoric.

"What were those?" Max asked.

"Hornbills," said Yoko.

A few minutes later, a tiny deer burst from the bushes by Mutara's feet and galloped off through the underbrush. Not much taller than his knee.

"Duiker," said Mutara.

It began to rain. They pulled up their hoods. A persistent patter fell on their raincoats and the leaves. In the wet, the scent of earth and rotting wood rose in the air. They pushed on, following the gorillas' trails.

Three weeks after the man attacked her, she'd gone to Gramps' home. Had thought it all out. Gramps was at church, the side window didn't have a lock. Her mom believed she was doing homework at the library.

She wiggled through the window. From his bedside table, she fetched the key and a bullet and went downstairs to unlock the gun cabinet. She pulled out his .45. Used to being thorough, she'd researched at the library how handguns work, had thought each motion through. She had no hesitation in loading the bullet. She knew she would not need more than one; she would not flinch.

Her decision about what method to use had come to her during the root canal to repair her teeth. The dentist had hairy fingers. He leaned his hip against her shoulder, put his hands in her mouth, breathed on her with his minty breath. She'd taken three Klonopin before this appointment, had been taking one every four hours since the man kicked her. The panic was so much worse now. A person passing within three feet filled her body with the white-eyed fear of a fawn. At the dentist's, in spite of the tranquilizers, in spite of her willing herself still with all her considerable determination, her body squirmed away from his touch, wiggling back in the chair.

The dentist told her to stay still, his tone irritated. He didn't know anything about her except the two missing teeth. He told her not to be a wimp.

With the metal of his retractor in her mouth she decided on the gun. She was sixteen years old.

To avoid a stain on Gramps's furniture or floor, she walked outside to her favorite tree in the backyard, a shaggy willow. She ducked under the circle of its branches and sat down inside its green and secret room, leaning back against the trunk. She pointed the gun upward. Such a purposeful weight. A coiled steel muscle.

Putting the barrel in her mouth, she closed her lips around it, like suckling from a baby bottle.

It was early fall. A few leaves fluttered down. The piles of leaves smelled of sweet decay. In the distance she could hear a neighbor mowing, the aroma of fresh-cut grass.

She clicked back the gun's safety. Paused. Finally here.

While she waited in this moment, other smells began to float up in her mind, unbidden and whole. Smells are processed in the brain right next to the limbic system, the site of emotions. This proximity is why smell—more than any other sense—can sweep an attendant emotion right in with it. The scent of a pencil—wood and lead—clenched in her sweaty child fingers in first grade. The smell of a copper penny held just under the nose during recess while all the others played.

The gun was warmer by now in her mouth, the barrel slightly wet from her lips.

The warm fragrance of her mom's glass of red wine as she helped Max with her homework. In the backyard, by herself and relaxed, pine needles crushed in the hand. Fresh-picked mint from near the shed. Crawling under the porch, hidden and safe, the earthy aroma of secret mushrooms. On the wind, the salt of the sea. Caramel candy. Watery paint. Her nose pressed against her arm, the sweet saltiness of her own child's body.

And then an image came to her and it stayed. Her mother's chair, the green one where she sat each night to read books and articles about what was beginning to be known as Asperger's. Worn into its velour was the outline of her mom's buttocks, the silhouette of her spine, the imprint of her sheer determination.

Max remembered her mom after her dad's funeral, the way she used to stare at a wall for the longest time. Whenever Max flash-glanced at her, her mouth was slack, her face empty.

Max weighed this memory against the hum of silence around herself in the crowded high-school halls.

The understanding struck her that simply the fact that she was sitting here, a gun in her mouth, meant she had given up all hope of a normal life, had let go of it fully.

For a long time she considered the space where the hope had been, turning the lack of it over in her mind.

When she finally took the gun out of her mouth, she had changed.

From that day on, she no longer tried to copy the ways others made friends or boyfriends, instead immersed herself in whatever really interested her. Plants. Smells. Chemistry. She read her first ethnobotany book, about a researcher among the Kiowas in the 1930s. She stared at the photos. A tall man with glasses perched neatly on his nose, his clothes crisp, he posed beside nearly naked Kiowas who stood so solidly there. A clear case of which object doesn't belong. Still he was with them—the distance between his body and theirs the same as the distance between each of their bodies. He was part of the group because he knew about something they all considered important. Plants were the language he'd used.

The ascent up the mountainside got steeper. The rain fell harder. Max couldn't see much with her hood on, her head tucked down as she worked to keep her balance.

No one was talking. Glancing over, she saw Mutara's mouth was open with the effort of the climb.

She leaned into her movements, huffing.

A few months after the man had attacked her, she asked her mom to help her learn how to read human expression. She needed to be able to understand neurotypicals better, not be so surprised by their actions. She was still taking four Klonopin a day.

Together they learned that researchers had broken down facial expressions into individual muscular actions and given each of those actions a code. Contraction of nostril wings—E7. Chin boss protruding—G3. The scientists hoped that one day, using a system like this, computers might be able to read human emotion. As though she were a computer, she had to memorize these codes and their attendant movements. Then she and her mom worked their way through every Disney movie. They freeze-framed every facial close-up in order to code the muscle movements—B3, H4, C1, and F2—then correlated the codes to name the emotion.

As she got better at literally decoding the facial component of a conversation, she got better at predicting the words and actions that would follow. Less surprised by humans, she became less stiff in her interactions and people began to respond to that. She eased back to two Klonopin a day.

In college she discovered email. In written communication, her strengths of logic and sheer factual knowledge came to the fore. Her flat tone of voice and averted gaze didn't matter.

She majored in botany, minored in chemistry. Senior year, she won the Ashe prize. Other students, and then professors, began to ask her opinion. In grad school, she found herself around researchers with obsessive interests and, occasionally, poor social skills. A world in which she could find a home.

Then the year she started her postdoc (at a farmers' market one Saturday) she noticed cucumbers. She already loved plants, so in a way the idea seemed only natural. Cucumbers had no confusing social rules, no expectations, no demand for conversation. Once a week she would go to the market, sorting through the different options, considering texture and size, until the farmer behind the table began to stare.

If she couldn't find an organic one, then back at home she rolled a condom over the cucumber to avoid possible pesticides.

Sometimes she talked to the vegetable. Told it about her day and her work and what she was learning. She relayed the information the way she needed to, going into the details, no matter how minute, not explaining any vocab or research, not stopping herself every few minutes to inquire about the other's life, simply following her thought process with enthusiasm. Letting the words tumble out. The way she'd always wanted to.

So much less lonely than those times she'd tried this act with humans.

Maybe from above, the crackle and thud of the humans had sounded like a few more gorillas approaching. Or it could be the apes were all crunching through too much celery to hear the people, the rain thundering down on the leaves all around.

Breathing hard, the rain on her hood, Max certainly heard nothing of the gorillas.

And so, she and the others simply stepped into the midst of the group. No time to give warning by clucking, no time to knucklewalk gradually in, no time for the apes to get used to the idea of the humans or for the humans to get used to the apes.

Max ducked under the branch of a bush, straightened up and saw beside her a large furry bureau. Her head swiveled.

She stood as close as in a cocktail party, as though she might be about to pass this silverback—Titus—the salmon croquettes.

Even as she jerked her gaze away, his eyes were widening. Time telescoped out.

Staring down at the ground now, she could feel him begin to straighten up, rising on his hind legs, all this width and heat and smell and sculpted black leather skin, all of his wet hair ruffling up like the fur on a dog when it's angry, making him bigger and bigger.

And seared into her memory was his face. Such a sense of presence, that he was *there*, staring back. Two dark shining eyes, thin chapped lips, a complex combination of emotion and soul. An immense face furrowing into fury.

He screamed with anger and, grabbing hold of a three-inch-wide branch, ripped it off a tree as easily as Max could tear paper.

From somewhere in the distance, Yoko's voice hissed, "Get *down*."

But Max stood frozen, breathing through her mouth.

He slashed the branch through the air a foot from her head.

The breeze rushed past her face, startling her. She threw herself to the ground, as though before an emperor or God.

The speed angered him. The branch swished by twice more, just above, his screams cutting the air, more furious by the second.

He roared, galloped away and then back, a bristling blur of hair and mass. She clenched every muscle in her body. Yoko had said she could not run, not run. He slid to a halt a few feet away, as he threw his arms up and up, the branch in his hands. Then it began to come down. His massive shoulders behind its weight, his back, his legs. The wood whistling through the air. She knew she'd never even make it to her feet. Don't move, don't move. Closing her eyes, forcing herself motionless, concentrating with all her strength.

The wood punched the earth a yard from her head. Through the ground, she heard the dull *whhmp*, like some far-off explosion. The branch shattered into a thousand pieces. Shreds of bark pattered down on her cheek.

Her breath sighed out her nose. She lay on the ground, slack as a wet towel.

As had happened after the buff had charged her, her jittery nerves realigned.

Complete silence. All the humans and gorillas motionless. After thirty seconds, maybe longer, he sidled a half step closer. One of his hands cautiously touched the ground a foot from her face. His fingers up close were leathery cigars, the dry skin so scuffed it was a light gray. Filled with a feeling of calm like cool water, she eyed his knuckles and fingernails.

An animal with cuticles, she thought.

She heard him sniff. His bristly chin lowered further.

And strangely enough, *she* glanced up.

Looked him in the eye. Not a flash-glance, a real look.

His brown eyes widened.

She didn't see his arm move, it was too fast, didn't feel his hand hit, her body simply became airborne, flying backward, the wind in her ears, then a loud *thwack* as she hit a tree— somehow the sound outside her body. She slid down the trunk to the ground. Lay there on her side, breathing.

Her eyes pointed ever so obediently now away from him. The shock focusing her mind.

Having shown his mastery of her, he coughed twice and moved off.

The idea of movement wasn't even a possibility in her head. Her heart *ba-bumped* rhythmically in her chest. Everything she saw appeared crisply luminous, as though lit from within. Three feet from her nose, along the underside of a fern's frond, she could pick out its granular dots of sporangia. The patterned precision mesmerized her.

She pictured herself gently nipping the sporangia off the frond like candy buttons from a strip of paper. She inhaled the scent of the grass near her cheek. Only gradually did the numbness of her body begin to shift to a throbbing along her ribs where she'd hit the tree.

Looking cautiously around, she found the gorillas were sixty feet uphill from her, throwing her occasional spooked looks. Yoko was sitting fifteen feet to her left and Mutara crouched a little past that. Both of them eating wild celery, putting on busy displays of being harmless primates while they stared at her. Her ribs now pulsing solidly with pain. She pushed herself up in stages into a sitting position, trying to look small. Something that shouldn't move grated together in her chest. Sparkling lights appeared in the periphery of her vision. At least one rib was fractured. She focused on the lights.

She ran one hand slowly over her side, testing for other injuries. She waited for the pasty taste of pain to retreat. Titus had only cuffed her with the back of one hand, the way one might discipline a dog.

The gorillas were clustered together, trying not to look nervous. They crunched and rustled through the underbrush, shooting glances at her from the corners of their eyes. Titus sat with his back turned to her, loudly uninterested, chomping on a bamboo shoot.

Yoko knucklewalked over on her hands and knees, imitating as best she could the way the gorillas moved, munching on celery, stopping occasionally to check if any of them were bothered by her movement.

Three feet from Max she stopped and whispered, "You OK?"

Max didn't nod because that might make her rib grate again. She kept her head very still and whispered, "Yes." She tried to breathe moving only her belly, not her ribs.

"Don't ever look them in the eyes again, especially not Titus."

"OK."

"Gorillas consider staring aggressive. They tend to hit."

"Yep." As a child, hitting was how she'd instinctively reacted to staring also, until her mom made her stop.

"Also, don't get too close to them," said Yoko. "They don't like it. Never touch them."

"Alrightie."

"Jesus, that was scary. You sure you're OK?"

And for a second time Max said, "Yes." She did not like doctors with all their prodding and poking. She didn't want to go to the hospital at the base of these mountains, the one Yoko had said was bad. She would tightly wrap the rib tonight. That was probably all any doctor would do anyway.

"Well, stay fairly still today. Just let them get used to your presence. Be quiet and keep at least fifty feet away." Yoko snuck a clipboard out of her knapsack. "Tell me if you need anything. OK?" She crawled over to a pile of poop and began to make notes.

Max's rib had changed from a throbbing to something close

to a high-pitched humming, a white heat. She kept her body as still as she could. In an effort to distract herself, she watched the gorillas, willed herself into studying them. If at any point they looked at her, she darted her eyes away to make sure they didn't get angry.

They sat on their heels, hairy Buddhists monks, jutting vegetarian bellies. Combing their way through the foliage, they focused on plants, absorbed in their task. From sixty feet away, she tried to figure out what they were eating. Bamboo shoots, wild celery. One gorilla was plucking some type of berries off a bush. She couldn't identify the species of bush from here. Sometimes they tugged a plant or two out of the ground and chewed on roots, or reached up and yanked down moss or vines hanging from branches. The crunching and rustling sounds like a herd of moose rummaging. Occasionally there was a loud crack when a branch was broken.

A young gorilla the size of a five-year-old child glanced at her from around its mother's hip. Its face was as wrinkled as an old person's face, but with these shiny eyes. It glanced fast, then ducked back behind its mom.

When the other gorillas looked at Max, Yoko, or Mutara, it was with the same type of shy glance, and then they'd look away. At first she assumed this was from fear of the humans, but after a while, she noticed that this was how they looked at each other too, a short flick of a glance. Also when two or more of them ate off the same bush, they didn't seem to interact much. They gave each other room and waited their turn, eyes averted. They acted a bit like strangers in a cafeteria collecting their lunch, striving not to invade anyone else's personal space. This confused her because, from what Yoko had said, this was basically a family: Titus the father, the females the mothers. Yoko had told her this group of seventeen had been together for years, most of them born into it.

Puzzling this over, she noticed that, although they treated

each other like strangers, they never wandered more than twenty feet from the group. As they moved through the jungle, they stayed clustered together, wanting this closeness.

The young gorilla she'd spotted before had wandered about seven feet away from its mom. It looked back at its mom, glancing fast, as though they'd never been introduced. Then it began a seemingly casual knucklewalk closer, strolling circuitously, until it was near enough to sit down with its back to the mother. A precise gap of twelve inches between their bodies.

Instantly recognizable to Max. Her mom and her on the couch.

Quickly she looked around, searching for other clues and spotted a female sitting in a beam of sunlight, eyes closed, no movement at all except for breathing.

Motionless and concentrated. Max's dad.

Surprised, she whispered, "Asparagus."

U ngan Singh found a N'derobbo to lead Jeremy to Otombe's village. Without Patsy, Jeremy was forced to walk everywhere, feeling the labor of travel, time dribbling by. Moving slower, he could notice more, found himself studying the river, the jungle, the grace of the N'derobbo's body and walk. The man had outlined ribs, while the joint of his knees bulged wider than his thighs. Not a fleshy people, Jeremy thought. They must run so much, chasing food and escaping danger.

At first he did not recognize the village as a village. The open gate, woven from nyika, merged seamlessly with the forest. The walls of the round huts were fashioned from cattle feces and mud, the roofs of woven grass—from a distance they had the appearance of small hillocks. Abruptly they snapped into focus as human habitation. He walked in through the gate, staring.

His guide led him to one hut, pounded the butt of his spear three times onto the ground, and called out a greeting. Otombe gracefully stooped out of a doorway that was no taller than Jeremy's hip. Inexplicably, Jeremy felt mortified, as though he had come upon Otombe snarling over a piece of meat. Through the door, the floor was visible, simple beaten earth. Looking around, almost everything he could see was made of grass, manure, animal skins, or mud.

"Otombe," he said, inclining his head. "I hope your family is well." Etiquette had always been his first recourse.

Otombe nodded, replied he hoped the same was true for

him, no surprise visible in his face at Jeremy being here. He added nothing more to the conversation. A group of villagers began to form, staring at Jeremy.

He smiled uncomfortably. He was the only one he could see wearing anything he would refer to as trousers.

"I have come to request your help," Jeremy said. "A lion has killed two men in camp. No one there is brave enough to help me hunt it."

"It is not one lion," said Otombe, "but two who work together."

He was startled, not used to being contradicted. "How would you know?"

"They have been killing the N'derobbo, WaKikuyu, and Masai for months. The people track them, chase them. The lions always get away, always kill again. Never have there been such creatures." After a short pause, he added, "They took my younger brother, not yet ten summers old."

"Was he . . . Did he . . . survive?"

Otombe stared at him.

Jeremy blushed at his own North American innocence. "Why didn't you tell me what was happening?" By this time the crowd around them was large. He thought possibly every man, woman, and child in the village was standing within fifteen feet of him.

"Would you have done anything?" His eyes glittered. The interview was not going well.

Then a small child stepped forward, latched her fingers onto Jeremy's belt and started scrambling upwards.

"What does she want?" Jeremy asked, his hands held out, not sure if he were allowed to touch her, if her parents might react badly. Her tiny feet kicked for purchase on his calf, her arms straining, trying to scale him. She wore no clothes, only a necklace made of shells and a leather thong around her waist.

"To touch your hair," Otombe spoke without emotion. "She has never seen anything like it."

Jeremy looked down at her big eyes, bony legs and arms. She weighed no more than twenty pounds, yet—from the shape of her face and her facility of movement—seemed to be at least four years old.

He remembered once when his sister's child, Beatrice, was about this age, he had lifted her in his arms to feed Patsy a carrot. He had been surprised by the compact weight of her body, her strength as she strained upward with the carrot. There was no fear, not of the giant Patsy or himself. She had propped one hand back against his face for balance, using him without thought. His family had recently begun to withdraw from him, conversation stopped when he entered the room. Physical touch was a surprise. Her tiny hand had felt hot against his skin, her fingers pressed tight against his cheek. Ever since that day, he had loved her utterly.

For two nights in a row now, the only sleep he had gotten was dozing in the hunting blind. He was tired; this morning he had nodded off in a chair waiting for Singh to bring his breakfast. Whenever he could, he leaned his weight against a tree or a post, found himself blinking around at the sights as though he had imbibed a glass or two of wine. Perhaps he was not thinking with his usual restraint.

He forgot about this child's skin color, her nudity, the diseases Alan had warned him any of them might carry. He simply bent down on one knee, took off his hat and lowered his head. The girl's hand fluttered nervously over his hair three times, light as a wing, and then she laughed. A laugh sounding to his ears remarkably American, no accent here, no foreign trait, a child's straightforward delight.

And then, before he could arise, the other children rushed in, touching his hair and face, one running a finger over his pale lips, one tugging on his ear, all of their faces filled with surprise. The touches gentle. In the three weeks since he had moved here, to a construction camp of men, this was the first time he had been touched on purpose. For a moment, closing his eyes for a toddler to pat his eyelids, he felt such gratitude to be here, the strangeness of this Africa.

One of the adults clapped and called and, fast as that, the children were gone, running behind legs and up into arms, a cloud of red dust raised in their wake.

He got to his feet, busily brushing off his knees, hoping he had not offended anyone. Otombe was staring at him.

He tried to get back on track, sound businesslike. "Will you help me hunt the lions? I have some guns. They should help. We might be able to stop them from killing more."

Otombe blinked surprised down at where the children had been a moment ago. "Yes," he said. "Yes."

Back in the railroad camp, Jeremy showed Otombe the hunting blind first, proud of it. Otombe walked slowly around it. Watching him closely for his approval, Jeremy realized he moved in a different fashion from the N'derobbo guide who had led him to Otombe's village. The other man had walked so smoothly, his head high, limbs relaxed, clearly part of a group whose only transportation was their own feet. Otombe instead walked with a slight waddle, his feet angled out a fraction, his back stiff. His eyebrows cocked artificially high. At first considering some mild birth defect or muscular inability, it took Jeremy a long moment to recognize—in this nearly naked man of a nilotic tribe—the English gait and facial expression. This was the inheritance his missionary foster parents had left him with.

There must be other changes in his mind and habits, in his desires and fears. Leaning down to the river for a drink, was Otombe surprised to see his own dark face reflected? Halfway between the cultures, was he at home in his village, or did he sometimes feel as isolated as Jeremy had been on his family farm?

On the walk to camp, Jeremy asked what recompense he wished for hunting the lions. Otombe was silent for a moment, then asked not for money but for food, five pounds of rice a day and ten pounds of meat, a forty-pound bonus of both for any lion they killed.

At this request, Jeremy reconsidered Otombe's stripped-down body, every tendon visible along his bony legs, the skin tight across his cheekbones. He had assumed this was simply the way these people were built, streamlined as antelope.

For the first time, he remembered the two-year-long drought that had just ended, no new crops yet able to mature.

Shamed, he nodded acquiescence to Otombe's request, tried to picture how many children he had seen in the village, how far ten pounds of meat would go.

Otombe stood looking in the window of Jeremy's hunting blind, shaking his head. "The lions have good vision. At night, they see you through this window." He sniffed at the branches Jeremy had had tied to the blind as camouflage. "They can smell you. You forget. These creatures are different. They will not run away like duiker or gazelle. They are smart and very hungry. If they sense you in any way, they will hunt you."

In the afternoon, Otombe led him to where the lions had killed two nights ago, a WaKikuyu village three miles distant along a game trail. Since he was a child, Jeremy had been riding in a carriage or on a horse. He had never realized how much energy walking could take, how much time. The prickly heat rash under his arms had spread across his chest and back, as well as in areas more private. His linen underclothes scraped against the rash with every step. Sticky with sweat, the spine protector gradually rumpled as he walked, climbing up his back, seemingly determined to crawl out his collar. Sweat bees dive-bombed his face and armpits. Jeremy nervously flapped his hands at them. Otombe, on the other hand, walked calmly on, hands at his sides, bees crawling across his face and arms.

"A sickness has killed off many of the Cape Buffalo," said Otombe, his eyes as always scanning the nyika around them. The path was only two paces wide, the branches entwined thickly all around, even above. Jeremy kept his rifle in his hands. He imagined the lions dropping down on them from above, or springing on them from the side. Even if he saw them before they jumped, the distance would be so short, little more than the length of the rifle.

"Rinderpest," said Jeremy, trying to concentrate on the conversation, rather than his fear. "That is the name of the disease. The physician at camp told me it was imported with European cattle." A large dragonfly whizzed by his nose, making him jump.

Otombe shot his eyes at him. "There are many new diseases your people have brought, for both the humans and the animals. Fevers, measles, mumps, sores that come with intercourse."

Jeremy stared at him, jarred by the word "intercourse."

Otombe added, "Half of my people are dead."

He was not sure how to respond. He had been told native people did not have a strong grasp of mathematical concepts. Otombe must be overestimating the impact.

Seeing his expression, Otombe looked away into the nyika. He turned the conversation back to the subject of the lions. "The Cape Buffalo are what the lions prefer to eat. There used to be herds of hundreds. Now not many remain. This land is dry, high up, few other animals live here. The drought and rinderpest have killed most of these."

"So two of the lions have switched to humans instead," Jeremy said.

Otombe nodded. "For the last few months, these lions have eaten a few from this village, a few from that. Then you arrived. The railroad. Hundreds of men, not many guns and no spears. At first you did not even build bomas."

They emerged onto the savannah, the grass green and full from the recent rain. In places it had grown as tall as Jeremy's forehead. The blades swayed in the wind, brushing his face. Pausing for a moment, amazed at this ocean of grass viewed from the level of someone drowning in it, Jeremy lost sight of the shorter Otombe. He half-ran to catch up, the grass rustling loudly with his movements. If any animal stalked him here, he would never hear it over the noise of his own progress.

Fighting claustrophobia, he asked the first question he could think of. "Are both the lions female?"

"Excuse me?" Otombe stopped in the hallway of his passage, looking back at him.

"Are both of them female? The men in camp, the time they spotted one, it was maneless but apparently huge. I wondered if the second lion were female too."

"Oh," Otombe walked on, the panting laugh in his throat soundless. "These are Tsavo lions. For other lions, the ones down on the plains, life is easy, plenty of water, less heat. They sleep a lot, kill zebra and antelope, smaller animals. For Tsavo lions, not much lives up here worth eating except buffalo, two or three times the size of a zebra, sharp horns, dangerous. The lions here, they are bigger, stronger. Some stand this tall." He held his hand out, four feet from the ground. Jeremy stared into the space under his hand, trying to fill it with a head, chest, legs and paws. He tried to imagine this creature padding forward through the grass, its face appearing at his elbow. "The males, from the heat and maybe the thorns, many times they have no manes."

Jeremy absorbed this. "You think they are both males?"

"From the size of the paw prints, yes." After a moment, he continued. "Some people, they say Tsavo lions are more aggressive. In comparison to a buffalo, a human without a gun is simple to kill."

"Have you ever hunted a Tsavo lion?"

For the second time Otombe stopped, facing Jeremy directly, the grass waving in front of his face. "I told you before. I am not a white. I am not tall with a loud voice and a gun. My tribe and I, we survive by keeping away from danger."

The wind blew, the grass swayed forward, hiding all of Otombe's face but part of his forehead and one eye. "But do not worry. To avoid a lion, I have to be able to think like the lion, where he will be, what he wants. We have a gun now and a need. I will think like these lions and I will find them."

His eye watched Jeremy. "Then you, you have to shoot fast and well."

T he next morning, the humans approached the gorillas, slowly foraging and knucklewalking, eyes obediently down. When the family spotted Max, they stopped eating to cluster together on the far side of Titus, watching her with great attention. A few of them coughed at her, loud aggressive barks that echoed through the trees. Titus stood squared off on all fours, vast and impassive, considering.

Forty feet down the slope, Max waited, head down, her breath rasping in her throat, riffling her fingers through some grasses in front of her. Before getting dressed this morning, she'd ripped up a sheet and wrapped it tightly around her ribs. Climbing the mountain to the gorillas, she'd worked hard to move somewhat normally, to hide the pain of her fractured rib. She had to search for the vine. And she wanted to see the gorillas.

Somehow overnight she'd forgotten how big they looked, a sense of immense furry weight and those shiny eyes. And they weren't like a school of fish or a herd of deer, where she knew without doubt exactly what the reaction would be at her approach, all of them wheeling to flee as a single body. These primates instead examined her, evaluating their options. She plucked some of the grass and chewed on the ends, trying to make her movements appear slow and relaxed. Her heart thumped in her chest.

Rising on his hind legs, Titus beat his chest in a rapidly escalating tattoo. She could see a bit of his movement from the corner of her eyes. The sound wasn't the deadened *thud-thud* of knuckles pounding flesh as in King Kong movies. No, this was a much louder sound, a popping noise. Must come from him clapping his cupped palms hard against his bare skin.

He screamed down at her. Somehow her actions—keeping her head down and pawing half-heartedly through the grass—weren't reassuring enough. He was warming himself up toward real anger. He began to pace back and forth, agitated.

On impulse, considering how aspie-like they'd seemed yesterday, she experimented. Shot one flash-glance directly at them, then away.

She heard a fast inhale from Yoko.

From the gorillas, on the other hand, there was a silence. She could feel them considering her. Titus paused in mid-motion, head cocked to one side.

As a child, when she'd been introduced to a stranger, she'd tried to circle round to the person's back or sides, some place where it felt less likely the person's eyes might suddenly snap up and stare at her. Allowing her to slowly get used to the person, without worrying about that confrontational stare.

So now, she casually shouldered her way up onto her knuckles, shifting herself six inches to the left to face a wild ginger plant, settling back down with her side to the gorillas. She tugged at the plant, busily. Happy unto herself.

The gorillas were utterly still.

She dusted the plant's roots off, then sniffed them. The spicy ginger scent. She took an exploratory bite of the crisp root and chewed. The white flesh inside tinged green. She kept her hands out where the gorillas could see them.

Normals met each other face on, shaking hands in a vestigial gesture developed long ago to reassure the other they clasped no small weapons.

The aspie version of a handshake would be parallel play, shoulders turned.

After watching her for a long moment, Titus made his decision.

He yawned. Angling her head just a little, she could see the edge of him. His massive stagy gesture—head thrown back, wide gaping mouth, loud groan of an exhale—demonstrated his utter boredom with her, while also elaborately displaying the length of his yellow fangs.

Then he sat down and stared off in another direction, mirroring her own turned-away posture.

Given this all-clear signal, within a few minutes the family started eating again, tossing an occasional glance at her, but no longer acting as alarmed.

Yoko knuckled over. "I *told* you not to look at them."

"I remember."

"Then why'd you do that? Listen to me. If I believe you're acting unsafe with them at any time, that you're endangering yourself or them, I will kick you off this mountain."

Max was still watching the gorillas from the edges of her eyes, listening to them. She stated, "Don't worry. I'll be fine."

Yoko grunted, sounding like Titus. "You're lucky they calmed down so fast. That was weird." Then she moved off, heading toward a steaming stool sample.

That whole morning, Max kept at least thirty feet from the apes, allowing them time and space to get used to her, and her to them. From the edges of her eyes, or with fast glances, she watched their posture, gestures, and what they were eating.

While the gorillas moved through the jungle, she followed leisurely behind them, picking up the half-eaten pieces of plants they'd dropped and examining each. Identifying the plant and the part eaten. *Galium ruwenzoriense*—they pulled the whole vine down, eating the leaves, stem, berries and flowers. With their huge fingers, they neatly picked blackberries off the bushes and popped them into their mouths, smacking their lips with satisfaction. They plucked leaves off nettle bushes and balled them up so the spines wouldn't jab them in the mouths, rolling each leaf up as carefully as a spitball before swallowing it. Like horses, they ate continuously, but unlike horses, they didn't rip mouthfuls off the landscape indiscriminately. Instead they considered each possible bite: giant gastronomic vegetarians picking through the countryside.

Every piece of chewed-up foliage that she found discarded on the ground, she sniffed intently for what chemicals might be inside. She closed her eyes and sucked in the smell in short bursts, concentrating. She took no notes. She had no need. She remembered everything.

About halfway through the morning, she noticed when they moved toward a new plant or spot, they didn't walk directly, but more eased up on their goal, wandering in slightly roundabout, as though they didn't want to startle the plant. Yoko and Mutara didn't seem to have noticed this because each time they headed for something, they knucklewalked forward in a line as straight as an arrow. Their actions determined and fast. Like a tone-deaf person humming, they could purse their lips and make noise but not get the tune. Each time, the gorillas glanced at them, their eyes glittering.

The next time she moved to a new spot, Max tried easing up sideways on the locale. At her movement, the apes kept eating, not bothering to look.

She foraged like they did, her head down and focused on the plants.

On the other hand, Mutara just leaned against a tree, off to the side, his hands empty, directly facing the apes. Yoko also sat still, unoccupied, waiting on the outskirts of the group until one of them crouched for a moment and pooped. As soon as the gorilla had moved away, she knuckled forward in a straight line, bug-eyed in her safety goggles, to burrow through the soft glop, looking for parasites. The family watched her from the edges of their eyes.

As Max worked, she listened to the gorillas' sounds, not just the noises of them munching through the foliage, but their vocalizations: loud smacks of enjoyment, a few satisfied grunts and chuckles, some cavernous burps.

About halfway through the morning, the sun broke out from behind the clouds, changing the jungle light from a gloomy underwater feel, to the flickering light of a disco. One of the females (Max knew the gender from the lack of a silvered fur across the back as well as the lack of swaggering muscles) stopped in a shaft of light and tilted her leather face to the sun. Steam rose from her fur. She let out a grumbly purr of contentment. It came out in two syllables, "Ra-oohm, ra-oohm." A meditative chant mixed with a rumbling sound suggestive of digestion. Her eyes were closed, a chunk of juicy *Galium* vine clutched in her hand. Her voice low in the gut.

The family considered her statement, then a gorilla to her left chipped in to agree. "Ra-oohm, ra-oohm," the gorilla answered. And one by one, like a role call of happiness, all the other family members responded with a chant-purr, each voice so distinct and emotive it clearly offered the speaker's identity, location, and mood.

The last one to respond was the baby gorilla—Yoko had said her name was Asante. After she chant-purred, she stood up on her tiny bowed legs to beat her cupped hands against her chest for a muffled patter. Unlike a horse or dog, she didn't prick her ears forward or wag her tail. Instead she showed her emotion the way a human would. She smiled, lips closed, her chin tilted proudly.

At midday each family member wove a giant bird's nest on the ground for their nap, padding the inside with soft grass and ferns. They lay down with loud sighs, staring up at the jungle canopy and lazily making popping noises with their lips. Ready to fall asleep, they flash-glance repeatedly at the humans until Yoko signaled to the other two they should leave.

The humans retreated a few hundred feet down the mountain so the gorillas could nap in peace. There, they ate their lunch and Yoko began to write up her notes from the morning, yawning, clearly needing a nap herself. Mutara leaned against a giant *Hagenia* trunk and closed his eyes. Max flipped rapidly through her plant encyclopedia, double-checking each of the plants she'd seen today. The vine Panoply had sent her to find was rolled in the mouth and then spat out, its bioactive properties too strong to ingest. By finding out what the gorillas chewed and swallowed, she was creating a list of what could not be the vine. By the time she finished her task, the others were asleep.

Although only a minor percentage of humans were diagnosed with Asperger's, everyone was really "on the spectrum," ranging from the most outgoing glad-handing salesperson to a hunched and rocking autistic. The lightest sprinkle and you got an unusual ability to focus and be introspective, to follow an idea to its logical conclusion. You got Picasso and Cassatt, Einstein and Curie.

A bit too much of a sprinkle and you got Max, unable to control her focus, to pull herself out of her work. Her condition might be the price paid so the species could have diversity in tasks and abilities.

Half an hour later, Yoko and Mutara woke up, and the three of them wandered slowly up the hill, listening for clues that the gorillas were done with their siesta. Hearing the snapping and crunching of foraging, they approached.

Titus rose onto all fours to look them over, then grunted and sat back down. This time, accepting Max's presence that easily.

The other gorillas cast a few shy glances, then turned back to the business of eating. Max wandered slightly sideways to within twenty feet of them, then sat down, searching through the plant bits they'd dropped. Near them again, she was at peace. Flash-glancing at them, she felt she was finally communicating in something close to her own language.

Overwhelmed with the moment, she rumbled at them, "Ra-oom ra-oom," grumbling the noise up from her belly.

Yoko and Mutara turned to her, eyes wide.

From the gorillas, there came a pause. A little surprised perhaps that she'd addressed them.

Then, lipping in a long string of hanging moss like an errant spaghetti strand, the mother of the baby gorilla agreed. "Ra-oom ra-oom."

And one by one they chipped in their response.

Crossing the meadow that night to Pip's cabin for dinner, belting out "Row, row, row your boat" and swinging the flashlight around—trying in every way she could think of to warn any nearby forest buff that she was walking by, don't be alarmed—she heard a sound directly ahead of her. Her feet swiveled to run even as she pointed the flashlight toward the sound.

Yoko stood on Pip's porch, laughing. "Hey Tombay, the buffs aren't hard of hearing. You don't have to be *that* loud."

She waited while Max climbed the stairs. Through the door came the sound of voices arguing.

"What's going on in there?" asked Max.

Yoko didn't respond.

So Max walked in and Yoko unwillingly followed.

Pip was flipping through the Rwandan phonebook. "No, I tell you that's it. The last straw."

"*Vous êtes trop émotionelle*," said Dubois. "Go to sleep. Tomorrow, you wake up. You see it is not so bad."

There was the bitter smell of fear in the room.

"Look, do what you want with your life," Pip said as she dialed. "I'm getting out of here."

Max asked, "What's bothering her?"

Yoko said, "The Kutu, what else?"

"Scientists. They're offing scientists now," said Pip, and then added, "Oh hullo, I'd like to book a flight."

Dubois snorted. "She speaks English to them."

"What happened?" Max asked, flash-glancing at them. Mutara was standing by the window looking out into the dark, away from all of them, rubbing the scar on his palm.

Yoko said, "Some geologists were killed by the Kutu. You don't need to know the details."

"I don't agree," said Pip.

Yoko's torso turned toward Pip. "You talking on the phone or to us?"

"They put me on hold. Max has to hear the story." Saying these words her voice was pitched lower than normal, serious.

"She doesn't have experience here. She can't judge how places like the Congo work, what's dangerous and what's not."

"Doesn't matter. It's her life." Max stood still, not fidgeting, her body squared off toward them. If Pip talked this way normally, stood calm and certain, perhaps the others would listen to her more.

"If she gets scared off because of this, her company will stop paying the park guards. Without guards, hunters will climb the mountains looking for bushmeat." Yoko turned to Dubois and said, "Hellooo. We're talking about your beloved gorillas here."

Dubois' hands were stuffed into her pockets, her fingers nervously fiddling with change or an old house key. "I know. I know. But I think I have agreement with Pip."

Yoko's torso turned toward Max. "Look, have you ever lived outside the US or even Maine?"

"No."

She hesitated. "Excuse me for saying this, but you have Asperger's. You're not going to be good at judging violent interpersonal conflict between groups of people. Making decisions about what to do will not be one of your strengths."

"You're right."

There was a pause from all of them.

Nodding down at the floor, Max added, "But there are lots of things that I am not especially good at that I still have to do as best I can. Just as there are tasks in your life I could accomplish better than you, but you get to do them."

There was silence from the others.

She said, "I promise I will ask for your advice before I make any decisions. Tell me what happened."

Dubois cleared her throat. "Yesterday three men from a mining camp in the Congo drive near Kirumba to look for coltan."

"Coltan?"

Yoko said, "It's the material that cell phones need in order to work. The area of the Congo on the other side of these mountains is one of the few places in the world that has it. Worth boodles per ounce."

"Greedy idjuts," said Pip.

Yoko interrupted, "Yo, some of them are dead. Let's not call them names. And if she's going to hear the story, at least let me tell it. I'll stick to the facts. You'll put in crap just to scare her so you won't feel like a coward when you leave here."

"That was mean," said Pip. When she spoke again it was in her lower serious voice. "I have a child. I can't risk my life for your gorillas."

"Please," said Mutara, almost in a whisper. He didn't turn away from the window. "Please do not fight. There is enough fighting out there."

There was a rustle of cloth as the others looked at him.

After a moment, Yoko spoke in a quieter voice. "Coltan, gold, and diamonds are what pays for all the guns the warlords have around here. Part of the reason the Congo's so screwed is cause it's got resources. Everyone wants to control it. Geologists, they don't bring a lot of good to the area."

"Kirumba is more south than the Kutu tend to go," added Dubois. "These geologists, yesterday, must believe it is safe."

"Safe," snorted Pip.

While they talked, Max turned her head further away from them, watching their reflection in the window that Mutara stood looking out of. Their faces there in the candlelight didn't overwhelm her, hazy circles transposed on dark glass. Although Mutara was the closest to the window, because of the color of his skin, he was the hardest to see.

"The survivor—what was his name? Patson? Patterson?" Yoko asked. "He said he and the two other geologists were still setting up their equipment when some kids with Kalashnikovs stepped out of the bushes. Ten, maybe twelve years old. They seemed pretty jumpy."

"Qat," Max said, remembering.

Yoko nodded. "Yeh, they were high from chewing qat. The Kutu pushed the geologists back into their jeep and drove them to a spot where there were at least eighty other Kutu milling through the trees, a few cooking fires burning. The geologists were told to kneel on the ground and lace their fingers together on top of their heads. Some of the kids hung out near them, playing a game with shells. A few stood guard. Others lay down and slept."

"At one point," Pip interrupted and Yoko snorted irritated, but didn't stop her, "one of the kids got up to get some food. Walking by, he touched the barrel of his rifle to the back of Patterson's neck. Left it there for a tic, then walked on."

Max remembered sitting under the willow tree with her Grampie's gun in her mouth. She imagined how different it would be if the gun were pointed at her against her will, if it was an assault rifle and a child's finger was on the trigger.

Yoko continued, "Patterson didn't know how long they knelt there, but the kids finished several games and his hands had been laced on top of his head for so long his shoulders were trembling."

"Hullo?" Pip said into the phone, "Yes, I'd like a ticket to Australia? Ticket?"

"And then this man comes by," Dubois said.

Max noticed a strange eagerness in their voices in telling this story, the way their words rushed in one after another. She'd heard this tone before when people talked about car accidents, robberies or childbirth. The need to divulge details, the relief that came from describing trauma.

"We assume it's François Kutu, the warlord, 'cause he's the only adult there," said Yoko. "Approaching, he didn't seem especially scary. He was on the short side and had a sort of mincing walk, might have come from his outfit that was a little tight around the ankles. The outfit was so ripped and stained, Patterson couldn't figure out what it was, thought maybe something ceremonial or a frilly bed sheet."

"Hullo?" called Pip into the phone. "Hullo? Am I on hold? Anyone there?"

"François stands there. He says nothing," said Dubois.

"Stop interrupting, alright? If anything, I'm telling more than I should," said Yoko. "It seemed understandable he could control the kids. He was the only adult and he never seemed to blink. This was the point that Patterson noticed the beading on the outfit. It was a woman's wedding dress, the train all ripped and dirty. He had the longest eyelashes Patterson had ever seen. François looked the prisoners over and then pointed at the geologist to the left of Patterson. A guy named Stan Mukowski."

"*Rat-a-tat* goes the guard's rifle," said Pip. "That fast."

"Hey, fuck off. I mean it." Yoko said, "Three Kutu grabbed the body by the collar and dragged it away behind some trees. One of Stan's shoes came off along the way and, later, a kid came back to pick it up. Patterson kept staring at the drag marks all afternoon."

Max continued to watch them in the window. She examined their reflected gestures and stance. She could see her own body was very still. "How do you know all this?"

"Pip was schtupping a Reuters photographer."

Dubois said, "You Americans are children about sex."

"Reuters came here to do a story on us a few months ago. This photographer was with them. He didn't end up taking so many photos."

"When we heard the news, I rang him up," Pip said. "He got the story straight from the fella who interviewed Patterson." She was pacing back and forth as she waited on the phone, three steps one way, then three steps back.

Yoko said, "Patterson said the Kutu were mostly boys, some girls. All of them emaciated. There was no uniform. Some of the older soldiers wore weird stuff, seriously mis-sized: a man's jacket, a woman's shirt, or a girl's dress. Like they were playing dress-up. He saw one boy had on a sequined prom dress, another had on a blond wig and carried a monogrammed purse. One dragged along a teddy bear. Everything was stained and ripped.

"When François came back, he was wearing the vest of the first geologist over his wedding dress. Again he stood in front of the remaining two men. Just as he's raising his finger to point, Patterson saw his eyelashes weren't real, but those fake glue-on ones. One edge of the eyelashes had come unstuck and was uncurling from his eyelid."

"He points. *Rat-a-tat*," said Pip. "The other geologist is dragged away."

"Jesus," said Max. In the glass she watched the women, noticing how the story affected them. Pip continued to pace, occasionally glancing at the door, as though expecting Kutu to come crashing in at any moment. Dubois sat there compact, like some tiny fierce dog, a Jack Russell terrier ready to spring into action.

Mutara stood in the same room with them, but he sat so still she nearly forgot about him, the hand with the scar on it resting in his other hand. He stared out the window into a distance she could not imagine. He must have been in his teens during the genocide here. She did not know which role he'd been born into: killer or killed.

Yoko stood still, straight and tight as a solider. When she spoke, her voice was flat. "François walks away. Patterson can smell lunch cooking, and some of the kids walk by eating from bowls. He's left there alone for the longest time, with his fingers laced on top of his head, listening to his own breath and the sounds of the kids playing. François comes back a final time. Stands in front of him. And Patterson, he must have gone a little crazy. He can't explain it other than that. He gets to his feet and with all his strength he screams his college-rugby attack-cry right in Francois's face. 'Yur-*AWWWP*.'

"Standing, he finds he's a foot taller than everyone but this man. From his yell, some of his spit hits the man's lips. François begins to smile, real wide. He has a bit of meat stuck between his front teeth."

"He didn't point," said Pip.

Yoko spoke over her, "When nothing happened, Patterson stepped backwards, moving away. He didn't mean to look brave, but his legs wouldn't run, so he walked. François watched, grinning. The children didn't raise their rifles. Once Patterson rounded the corner in the road he managed to shuffle forward into a half-jog. Before nightfall he'd hitched a ride out of the area."

"See," said Pip. "I told you . . . . Ah, hullo. Ticket? Airplane?"

Dubois shrugged a very French shrug, her whole body involved, her lips pursed as she blew a little air out. "*Bof*," was the sound she made, accepting the full mystery of life.

"How long have you been in this country?" Max asked Dubois.

"Three years."

In the background Pip was saying into the phone, "Australia? Perth?"

"And you?" she asked Yoko.

"Five months."

"And Pip?"

"Ten weeks."

Max tried to think of herself as the new assistant in the lab. Yoko and Dubois could tell her what not to touch, where the dangers lay. She lowered her voice to talk to them, while Pip spoke into the phone. "So I said I'd ask your advice. Do you want to leave?"

"Ahh," said Dubois. "But no. This story is terrible. Terrible. The man is lucky to be alive. But this happens far away."

"How far?"

"Almost thirty-five miles," said Yoko. "That's like being in Connecticut while a gang shooting happens in the Bronx. It doesn't concern us."

"The Kutu were fifty miles away before."

"Yeh, they're a little closer now. But they're still on the other side of the mountains. They're still across the border," said Yoko. "Pip, she doesn't understand. You should hear some of the crazy stuff that's happened in South Africa or Somalia . . . "

"In Sudan or Burundi," added Dubois.

"Or here," said Mutara. "Here in Rwanda."

There was a silence after his words. Pip was the one to break it. She was repeating the words "Perth" and "Australia" with varying emphasis into the receiver.

Max asked, "Mutara, where were you during the genocide?"

"Gisenyi. The town down there." In the reflection in the window, she saw him gesture with his chin.

"So you've seen what can happen?"

He didn't speak, but his head nodded once.

She thought this over. "At what point would you be alarmed by the Kutu? At what point would you leave?"

Mutara didn't answer quickly, so Yoko spoke instead. "If they got closer than fifteen miles."

"*Oui*," agreed Dubois. "Otherwise, it is just a bad thing that happens somewhere else. Like a train accident or explosion in another country."

"Think of all the people there are to murder and pillage between Kirumba and here," said Yoko.

Not knowing the distance to Kirumba or how populated the countryside was, Max continued to await Mutara's advice.

Into the silence, Mutara spoke, answering Max's question. He said, almost to himself, "Where is there to go?"

Pip's voice got louder. "Planes? Vroom, vroom?" She took the phone away from her ear to stare at it in amazement, then hung up. "The phone charge is gone." Her voice was tight. "God, I hate this."

"We charge the phone tonight. Wait for tomorrow. Call the airlines again. Ask Mutara to speak for you in Kinyarwanda." Dubois spoke soothingly, stepping over to pull Pip close. "You must not worry. You will be with your daughter again. *Tout va bien se passer.*"

Pip pressed in against her, hiding her face.

Late that night, Max lay in bed, wondering what to do, thinking over the responses of the others. They were neurotypicals. She normally relied on them for what to do. Unfortunately they didn't all agree on one course of action.

She imagined not going back up the mountains tomorrow, not seeing the gorillas again. Not finding the vine. She imagined returning to Maine now, to live back among the humans.

Yoko had the flattest, least emotional voice. A voice Max associated with being scientific and objective. A voice similar to her own.

She decided to go with Yoko's estimate.

Otombe led Jeremy to the WaKikuyu village where the lions had recently killed. Standing on the riverbank, Otombe pointed out where the lion had ambushed a woman when she was washing clothes at sunset, dragged her under the nearby tree to eat her, with her five-year-old watching. Now, no one went out at any time close to sunset, did not step outside of their bomas until well into the next morning when the lions would probably be sleeping.

The tree was a huge baobab, the trunk twenty feet in diameter, the limbs clenched and twisted. Beneath, the shade was cool and the grass rich, a strangely beautiful site for a murder. By the time they arrived, there was nothing more incriminating remaining than some slightly trampled grass, not even a stain. Morning doves called, grasshoppers whined. After the long walk, Jeremy felt the need to lie down here in this cool shade, on the matted grass and nap. Instead he studied the branches above for lions.

Catching him at this, Otombe said, "Lions are poor climbers, too heavy. People can go higher, faster. If you need to flee, always run up a tree. Climb more than the height of two men. They can jump that high."

Run up a tree, Jeremy thought. *Run?* He remembered his awkwardness in scaling the tree when they were hunting the hippo.

From the WaKikuyu village, a crowd shuffled toward them. The children were bony and naked like the N'derobbo children.

A few of them had strangely distended bellies as though they had just consumed the meal of their lives, but even these ones moved as slowly as the old people, barely lifting their feet. These WaKikuyu, he saw, were not faring as well as the N'derobbo.

"The more you know about lions," Otombe said, "the better you will hunt them, the more likely you will survive. I will teach you. Any boma must be very tight to stop them. The lions are used to thorns. They have to push their way through the nyika all day long. They can force themselves through tiny holes."

He thought of the small nyika tunnel he had attempted to crawl through a few days ago, in order to trail the lion.

"If a lion catches you, he will kill in one of three ways. Sometimes he stops your breath with his mouth over your face." Otombe opened his mouth wide and fit it over his fist, kept it there for a long moment. Jeremy found that his breathing became a little labored at the thought. "Sometimes, instead, he pokes his teeth through your temples. That is the best way. Death is like that then." He clapped his hands. The children turned their slow eyes to him, not able to comprehend even a word of English. "Sometimes, with his hind claws, he kicks out the belly of you, the entrails. That is not so good. Most times you are not dead before he starts to eat."

Jeremy felt no desire to know how Otombe learned these details.

"First thing," he continued, "lions like to lick the skin off your body, especially the thighs and haunches. They lap the blood up for their thirst. They eat the muscles after that, some of the innards. Most times, they do not touch a human's head or face. My people think it is because the lions are spiritual, believe it a sin. The head and the bones they leave to the hyenas. Hyenas are not like lions. They will eat anything."

The hunter continued, "Lions do not like to go into enclosed places they cannot see into. They do not know if there might be danger in there. You are safer in a tent than in the open, even though they could easily rip through the canvas.

"Whatever happens, never run unless you can get up a tree. They are cats and will chase whatever flees, and we are not fast like gazelles. If you cannot escape up a tree, better to stand quite still."

Momentarily Jeremy attempted to picture this, staring at a lion from a few feet away, a cat weighing over four hundred pounds, standing four feet tall. He imagined trying to stand still without his legs crumpling underneath him from the fear.

To distract himself from the image of what would happen next, he took his lunch out of his satchel for the WaKikuyu children. After hearing how the lions ate, he had lost all hunger. He held the sandwich for a moment in his hand, uncertain how to divvy this tidbit up for so many. Before he could arrive at a solution, the children leapt forward, adults slapping them out of the way, everyone grabbing. He was squeezed out of the crowd by the frenzy. Afterward, as he remembered it, the detail that frightened him the most was the utter silence of the fight; not a single child cried out in pain.

While the village battled over the scraps, Otombe led him away, walking fast, not saying a word in praise or rebuke.

Late that afternoon, they trailed the day-old prints of the lion that had walked out of the railroad camp carrying the dead man's bag. They followed the pugmarks for half a mile before they found the strap of the satchel. It lay at the bottom of the river detour that Jeremy's men had been digging for days. The strap lay torn and chewed, marks in the dirt where the lions had rolled on their backs and played with it like kittens. Crumpled up on the dirt nearby, the leather satchel itself was wet with their saliva. They must have come back here recently.

Otombe crouched down to examine the prints up close, but Jeremy noticed he touched nothing.

He does not want the lions to get a clear whiff of him, Jeremy thought with sudden certainty. He does not wish for them to know who in particular hunts them. Jeremy became aware, after walking all day in the heat, he was rather fragrant himself. He eased away from the nearby bushes that might brush against him in the breeze.

"They've been at this spot more than once," said Otombe, hunching down to look at a pugmark so clean Jeremy could see the imprint of hair between the toes. "They like this place, this man's things. Do you have any sheep in camp?"

Jeremy blinked at the change in subject. "Some goats I believe."

The man nodded. "Have three tied up here to an object so heavy the lions cannot drag it away. Use chains, not rope, nothing the lions can bite through. Tonight, we will wait with your gun in a nearby tree, at the very top. See if the lions return. Now, we must bathe. Scrub with herbs at the armpits and groin. Tonight we must have no scent."

For their bath in the river, Jeremy summoned two askaris with rifles to stand on vantage points upon the riverbank above, watching for crocodiles and hippos. He had been around Otombe all day long, with him wearing only his goat-skin toga and choker, yet when the man dropped his robe to the ground to step into the water, Jeremy turned away, trying to erase from his mind the image of his slender body.

Involuntarily he remembered Bert at the watering hole, his drooping bathing suit, the look of triumph he gave Jeremy just before punching him.

His own clothes were much more difficult to remove, unbuttoning and tugging, him hopping about on one foot trying to pull off his drawers. He did not look at Otombe, did not want to see any amusement at the complexity of his layers. Finally naked, he hurried into the river.

In the water it was different. After the heat of the day, the water felt delicious against his body, cooling him off, easing the tightness of a headache. He wondered what the askaris saw looking at the two of them in the water. Without guns or clothing to differentiate who had the power of the railroad behind him, they simply became two men, one short and sure in his body, the other not.

He kept his back turned to the men as he scrubbed himself awkwardly with the plants Otombe had given him. They smelled of mint and something medicinal. Even though the water felt cool, he stayed in it not one extra second, sloshing quickly out to hide in his towel.

Otombe stayed longer, floating on his back, breathing gently out his nose, his chest bobbing at the surface, his face quiet. Whatever he felt about the upcoming night's hunt was not obvious.

When they returned to the site of the satchel, the goats were securely chained to a railroad sleeper, a trunk of creosoted wood weighing almost three hundred pounds. The goats' vibrating *maah-ahhs* of confusion traveled far through the forest. Otombe requested that a ladder be propped up against the side of the nearest tall tree and, once it was there, the two of them climbed it, neither them nor the ladder touching the trunk of the tree anywhere below fifteen feet. Twenty feet up in the tree, they nailed boards into the branches, one for a seat, the other for a seatback, and then settled down to wait. Carrying the ladder, the Indians who had helped them hurried back toward the safety of the boma.

"Down there, will the lions not smell us? On the goats and the sleeper, on the ground?" Jeremy found he was beginning to talk like Otombe, his sentences shorter and rhythmic.

"They can smell humans, yes, but the smell will be hours old. With luck, they will not scent us now in this tree. Not on the trunk or on the breeze." Otombe looked at him. "No more talking. If you have to, make hand signals. Move as little as possible. They will start hunting soon."

The sun set within minutes, the night calls of the riverbank began, the groans and splashes of the hippos, the yips of the jackals, the *woo-oop* of the hyenas. The mosquitoes rose as a low cloud. Otombe sat motionless, his arms tucked into his cloak, not slapping at the insects. Jeremy draped some mosquito netting over his hat, tucking its ends deep into his collar to keep the bugs off his face and neck. He hid his hands in his armpits and attempted to sit still.

Within half an hour the first of the lions roared, perhaps a mile to the west. The noise rough and full, echoing through the night. The sound and the distance it traveled clearly signaled the power of the animal.

Nervous, Jeremy started to pack a pipe with tobacco. Otombe closed his hand round Jeremy's fingers on the pipe and shook his head. Jeremy looked down at their hands together. Otombe did not make the gesture brief, did not withdraw from the contact as a European would. Jeremy waited long enough to feel the warmth, the firmness of the man's grip, then he broke the contact, putting his pipe away.

He assumed at no point during the long night ahead would he be allowed to sip from his flask of fragrant coffee either. Even his water, he realized, must be rationed, because urine would smell.

The second lion answered from the southeast, some trailing grumbles at the end of his call. He could imagine the brute standing there, his paws spread, head back, the roar rumbling through his chest. His golden eyes half-closed as he sampled the breeze all around.

Below the tree, the goats bleated uneasily and their wood bells thunked. The chains tying them to the sleeper clanked. After a minute, one of the goats tore at the grass and began to chew.

The moon rose above them, an orange orb low on the horizon, lighting the ground below them surprisingly well. Otombe mimed sleeping, then he pointed to Jeremy and a spot in the sky the moon would reach in about three hours. Nodding, Jeremy wrapped the rifle's strap several times around his forearm, leaned back, and was asleep almost instantly.

He awoke when a bird flapped by his face close enough he could hear the waxy whisper of its pinions. He startled up, even in his alarm remembering to be silent. Otombe sat motionless beside him, his eyes fixed on a spot off to the right, somewhere past the nearest trees.

Below them, the bell of a goat thunked. One of the goats shifted its footing. Looking down, Jeremy realized the night was strangely quiet. Not a hippo chuffed, not a leopard rasped. He could just make out the goats below, standing at attention, all looking in the same direction as Otombe. Jeremy ran his eyes over the trees where they looked, a few low bushes, tiny pinpricks of fireflies signaling intermittently. He wondered if the goats' strange yellow eyes had good night vision, if Otombe's dark irises worked better in the darkness than did his green ones. Perhaps, while he had slept, there had been some noise. At the moment, the silence was so crisp he could hear it ringing in his head.

Then the screaming started, the gunshots and the clanking of pans. Camp.

At this distance, all the fear and frenzy was stripped from the noise, just faint clanks and pops and squeals, the pathos of bugs. Above the other noises, one man's voice cut through, a single word called again and again, crying out the name of his lost friend.

Y oko and Max lay on the mountainside, staring up at the trees, waiting out the gorillas' afternoon nap. Mutara sat a little back from them. He had a radio he was listening to with earplugs. He stayed very still, his head cocked to one side, moving only when he needed to wind up the radio. Perhaps he was listening to news about the Kutu. His intensity made Max nervous.

"Why doesn't Dubois want me to find the vine?" she asked.

Yoko was lying on her back, facing the jungle canopy. Up there, the sun shivered through storey after storey of leaves, a twinkling of green. The dry leaves below her rustled as she rolled her head to face Max. "There are two reasons. If you find the vine, then you're going to leave and, at that point, your company will have gotten what they need from us. Roswell can stop paying for the park guards if he wants to. Without guards, the hunters will come and the gorillas start dying."

Max pictured the family as they lay at the moment, napping in their giant bird's nests, hairy and snoring.

"Why would anyone want to kill them?" It couldn't be very challenging to track them. A child could follow their bulldozed paths. Once a hunter reached them, of course the silverback would charge the intruder, hoping to buy his family a few seconds to escape, offering his chest for target practice. "Trophies?"

"They eat them."

"Eat?" In her mouth, the word felt foreign. It made her see again the gulf between her and most other humans. She, who ate primarily tofu, oatmeal, and bananas, tried to imagine sinking her teeth into a gorilla's dark arm.

She remembered her recurrent nightmare of Aunt Tilda chasing her, wanting to take over her flesh. She could imagine how a gorilla might feel, understanding it was to be eaten, its body transformed into jumpy human flesh.

"Look, for the last fifty years, the developed world has given this country vaccinations without following up with enough condoms. There are over eight hundred people now per square mile. Surviving off the land. They desperately need some source of protein. If they come upon a gorilla and they have five children at home screaming with hunger . . . " Yoko shrugged.

"And the second reason?"

"Reason?"

"The second reason Dubois doesn't want me finding the vine."

"Oh yeah. Sorry," she said. "If you find the vine, it'll take a while before your company is able to molecularly manufacture the active compound. Until that can be managed, Roswell will need lots of the plant to experiment with and to make into medicine for the clinical trials, lots of it. If he offered enough perks to Rwanda, the government would allow people up here, hunting through the jungle for the vine, harassing the gorillas and driving them further up the mountains."

Max looked at the distant peaks above. "Well, there's still more land up there for them, isn't there?"

Yoko scrubbed her eyes so hard there was an audible squishy noise. "The gorillas aren't meant to live this far up the mountains. At this altitude, there are fewer of the plants they eat and the temps are colder. They're at their limit. Still, the people down there need firewood and arable land. Every year they push the gorillas a little higher. Edge them out of existence foot-by-foot. Most research predicts the gorillas will be gone within twenty years."

Max picked up a stick and turned it over in her hands. Even without leaves or much bark, she could identify it as *Hagenia*.

"That baby up there," said Yoko, "Asante, she's part of the last generation. The least we can do is let her live out some of her life in relative peace. Keep the hunters away. Stop crowds of people from tramping all over the mountains."

Max, thinking this through, noticed her body was rocking slightly back and forth. She forced herself still. "Can't some of the gorillas be kept alive in zoos?"

"You'll find lowland gorillas in zoos, but not mountain gorillas. Back in the 60s and 70s, a few zoos tried kidnapping a baby or two, but a whole family will die fighting to stop that. Not just the mother and the silverback, but every adult and juvenile will run screaming straight into gunfire in an attempt to protect a baby. The baby, having seen its whole family slaughtered in front of it, won't eat, won't drink, and shortly thereafter dies from grief."

Max's hands were clenched into balls now.

Yoko inhaled. "You know, when they're really sad, they sing. I heard it once. After a baby died. It was the most . . . "

There was a distant crack. It could have been a branch breaking or gunfire far down the mountains. They both turned to look in that direction.

"No," Yoko said. "They will live on these mountains. Or they will die."

"Fuckity fuck," Max said. "Isn't it time to go up?"

She climbed upward as quickly as she could, leading the others. Even with her fractured rib, she was climbing a little faster each day. She'd always been able to manage pain well. Among all her fairly extreme sensations, pain had never seemed all that interesting. By now her lungs were more accustomed to the altitude, her balance was better, and she was learning strategies to keep her traction on the muddy slope. Today she managed to stay in the lead, rushing upward until she heard the gorillas again, the distant crunching and cracking of their foraging. They'd finished their siesta.

She paused, breathing hard. The pain of her rib was a hot yellow shimmer in the back of her head. She consciously turned her attention to the smell of the gorillas drifting by. That living scent of moose-like flatulence and crushed vegetation, of furry heat and adolescent sweat.

Gradually she wandered closer, knucklewalking in roundabout until she sat down on the outskirts of the group. Close to them again, she felt her muscles ease, her shoulders relax. The gorillas ambled about in their sideways navigation around one another, eyes politely on the plants, their dance of distant affection. The color of the earth and the bark, the tangled intensity of the jungle. She observed their movements with glances, using all her considerable attention, memorizing every detail. A headache was blooming up the back of her skull.

Several of the females were harvesting moss off a *Hagenia*. From the coloration, it looked to be at least two different kinds of *Sphagnum*. They stuffed masses of it in their mouths, then sucked the trailing ends in with loud kissing noises. Further up the slope was Rafiki, the mother of Asante. She was easy to recognize because her right arm ended in a stump. Yoko said she'd lost it in a hunter's trap. Rafiki half-stood to reach one of the lower branches of a *Vernonia adolfi-friderici*, wide leaves, clusters of lavender-tipped buds. Levering the branch down to her height, the wood whining, she held it using the stump of her right arm while she tugged off bunches of its buds with her left hand. When she let go, the branch shot back up with the *kunkh* of an arrow hitting. She settled herself beneath the tree and began popping buds into her mouth with little smacks of satisfaction.

Uncle, the other silverback, circled the *Vernonia* trunk until he found a spot where the wood was a bit rotten. Uncle was older than Titus and tended to startle quite easily, sometimes jumping a foot into the air at a sudden noise, not a great attribute in a male gorilla responsible for defending the others. At the moment, he gnawed on the trunk, staring off into the distance with a reflective expression, his teeth rasping against the wood.

Max plucked blackberries off a nearby bush. She crouched on her heels, munching on the berries, arms draped forward. She didn't have to remind herself anymore to sit like a gorilla. During the day, in the jungle, when she moved forward, it was automatically on her knuckles, lumbering along with her shoulders. In the evening, down at the research station, she sat straight up in a chair and ate with utensils. The results of a lifetime spent imitating the social norms of others.

As she ate the berries, a few family members in their foraging moved closer to her, one sat down within six feet, solid and relaxed. No more distance between them and her than there was between each other. She'd noticed recently Yoko could knucklewalk into the group to examine a poop—the family would let her—but the circle of them would never repair itself around her.

Now the three-year-old Asante approached her, roundabout, her eyes directed toward anything but Max, the very soul of misdirection. The style of the gorillas had begun to seem almost Japanese to Max, with their lowered eyes and clear rules of propriety.

Even after a week, Asante still seemed curious about Max and got at times quite close, trying to peek inside her knapsack or run off with her notebook.

Today Max listened to her rustle through the blackberry bush beside her. From the edge of her eyes, she could see her fingers picking berries. Her fingers weren't large and fleshy like an adult gorilla's, but narrow as a human child's. Yoko said she was only three years old, but her fingers moved quite deftly. It seemed impossible to picture her grown up and searching for food on the rocky mountaintops above, chronically undernourished in the cold, her family dying one by one around her.

Five feet behind her sat Rafiki, shooting a glance over at any sharp noise. She didn't like her child being this close to a human.

Within an hour though, Rafiki finally relaxed enough to move ten feet off, was harvesting some *Galium* vine, faced away and yanking the plant down.

This was when Max glanced over and saw Asante's hands harvesting red berries. She was plucking the berries from a plant that looked a lot like wild ginger, but the leaves were clustered in groups of three instead of two. The stamens a purplish color. *Solanaceae benutis*. Nightshade family. Deadly.

Max slapped Asante's hands, knocking the berries out. The slap made an audible *thwap* and Asante squealed. Both noises echoed, as loud as in a library.

Every gorilla turning. Time telescoping out.

Titus rising to his feet, mammoth and bristling.

But Rafiki was moving faster, bolting toward Max and screaming. Her charge like a speeding car—the rushing forward of wind and impending weight.

Max yanked the *benutis* out of the ground and held it up. She tucked her head down, bracing for impact. As hard as she could, she crushed the roots in her fist, digging her nails in to release its bitter vinegar scent.

This small plant her only noun, verb, and plea. This plant her shield.

Rafiki barreled into her, full on.

Perhaps Max had a momentary blackout because, later on, she couldn't remember getting hit. She only had an image of the moment afterward, lying on the ground, no pain, not from her rib or shoulder. Her heart beating a loud *wa-shunk wa-shunk*; Rafiki crouched over her. From underneath, the girth of a gorilla was immense. Max's hand still clutched the *benutis*. Her fist with the tattered plant jammed against Rafiki's chin.

And Rafiki was motionless. Face averted.

Beneath her like this, Max could feel each raspy inhale of air into her huge lungs. One inhale. Two.

Then Rafiki tucked her chin in to look at the plant, its distinctive triad leaf pattern. Its purple stamens. Her large eyes refocused on Max—not flash-glanced, but looked-looked. What is white in a human's eye, is dark brown in a gorilla's eye. Maybe this was what made her eyes so emotive.

Every other gorilla stood motionless, awaiting her verdict.

Then Rafiki grabbed the plant from Max, spun on her heels and bolted toward Asante, running in a totally different way now, not all bristly and roaring, but floppy and fast, scooping her child up and sniffing her hands and face, prying her mouth open and smelling in there too, pushing her fingers in, checking for any of the bloody red pulp.

Max lay very still. She rewound her memory to examine the *benutis* as she'd held it against Rafiki's chin. She could picture only three empty stems where berries had been. Probably those were the berries she'd knocked out of Asante's hand. She moved her memory further back to scan the ground near where Asante had been. Couldn't remember seeing any other *benutis*. She waited, listening. After a few moments, Rafiki seemed to arrive at the same conclusion. There was a slap of flesh and Asante squealed, much louder than before. Rafiki roared. Max shot a glance. Rafiki was waving the plant in her three-year-old's face. Then she swiveled and roared her challenge at the entire jungle, daring any of it to hurt her child.

Titus bellowed, backing her up, and then there came the *pop-pop-pop* of him slapping his chest. The loud crack of a branch or small tree being pulled down. He barked and threw leaves in the air.

Yoko and Mutara sat as small and still as rocks. Max lay where she was, eyes closed, just breathing. She became aware of pain now in her left shoulder, rising in a throbbing hum. She didn't move.

The gorillas were restless for a long time afterward, coming one by one to sniff the *benutis* where it lay on the ground. They would jerk back and snort. Then move over to inspect Asante, sniffing loudly. Only gradually did they settle down enough to feed again.

When Max finally felt it was safe enough to sit up, she found her left arm hung in front of her body, limp and foreign, the lump of her shoulder all different. Cautiously, she flexed her fingers and found they still responded.

The three humans moved a hundred yards from the gorillas, far enough away to stand up and discuss how to pop her shoulder back into its socket, pooling what scant knowledge they had. Mutara was elected to do it. Yoko would hold onto Max to help her brace herself.

Yoko said, "Max, I hate to state the obvious, but we're going to have to touch you to do this. You OK with that?"

"No choice," Max said.

"You ready?"

Max held up one finger while she searched for something to concentrate on. A place for her mind to go. As she had done with those boys in high school, she recreated smells, evoked them in her mind, vivid and layered.

A linen closet smelling of dust and cedar.

Hot, sweet pee tinkling into the toilet.

She let her finger drop.

Dimly she was aware of Yoko behind her, wrapping her arms around Max's waist and across her chest, her whole body tight against Max's. Mutara took hold of her upper arm with both hands.

"One," he said.

The times those boys had been with her, there was a lot less surface area involved than this. Still she found being held by these two was easier.

A pile of autumn leaves: airy and rich decay.

"Two," he said.

Cold white wine, like sharp metallic sunshine.

She was older. She'd worked hard on changing, acting more neurotypical.

Also, she trusted these two.

"Three."

His yank was firm and clean. He twisted the arm, angling it, and then pushed it back toward the socket. There was the grinding of bone against bone, pain poured a searing liquid across her chest, and her arm grated sideways, all wrong.

He let go and stepped away for a moment, breathing, before trying again.

She closed her eyes now and worked on finding something *much* more interesting to focus on.

Yoko swore, holding her from behind, her mouth against Max's ear, her voice flat and mechanical. "Shit shit shit."

Between each try he would wipe his hands several times off on his pants. Each time when he pushed, trying to pop the bone into place, Max let no noise escape her lips, while he grunted low in his chest as though he'd been cut.

The fifth time—both Mutara and Yoko half-panting by now from their effort—he spat out something angry in another language, then slammed her arm hard, shoving it home with a force that made both Yoko and her half-stumble backward. The shoulder clicking into its socket. The pain shrieking like metal.

Mutara sat down at the base of a tree, breathing through his teeth. Yoko stepped away and walked around and around, slapping her arms forward and back, a swimmer just before a race. "*Fuck* that shit," she said.

Max though stayed still. She had finally found her focus. That moment Rafiki crouched over her, her rough hair, her raspy inhale, the vinegar scent of the *benutis*. That moment they'd communicated.

Max stood there, her head tilted. Not even moving.

After that day, Asante wouldn't get very close to her again, unnerved by the slap and the scene that had followed. Max didn't mind all that much. Now she didn't have to look at Asante's tiny hands and contemplate their future.

Instead, over the next few days, she found Rafiki began to take Asante's place at her side. Rafiki would wander gradually in until she foraged three or four feet away, studiously ignoring Max the whole time, as though this proximity was pure accident.

She wondered if Rafiki came closer partly because Max's arm was in a sling now, forcing her to forage with one hand also.

Since Asante now always stayed on the far side of her mother, Rafiki didn't seem as anxious anymore. The times she looked at Max, it was at her hand, perhaps to check her picking technique or to see if she'd found something especially good to eat.

Max didn't mind her being close. She remembered that moment of Rafiki standing over her, her head turned away as she smelled the *benutis*. She felt no fear of her.

Because of her missing right hand, Rafiki moved through the jungle in a different way than the other gorillas. Putting weight on her stump seemed to hurt, so she didn't knucklewalk very often. Instead when she needed to move a few feet, she would heave herself up onto two legs and walk. The transformation was startling. Upright, she became human: her head, her shoulders, her posture. The main difference was her legs, half the length of a person's. However this difference seemed more like a birth defect than the design decisions of a different species. Faced away and in a dress, she could have walked through any mall and people would throw her glances of pity, not alarm. Massive and muscular, her torso rolled from side to side over her hips, the way dwarves with congenitally short legs moved.

And when Max moved forward, she still tried to knucklewalk. Because of the sling, she could only use one hand, so she half-crawled along, on that one hand and her knees, awkward and breathing hard since this position put pressure on the bandages round her fractured rib. She labored forward in limping impersonation of a gorilla.

The pair of them wandering this way through the jungle.

Yoko had said Rafiki had lost her hand as a child, when the silverback Uncle had ruled the group. Her right hand must have gotten caught in a hunter's wire trap, a noose meant for much smaller prey. Of course with her hand snagged, first thing she would have done was jerk her arm back, trying to free herself. This would have ripped the trap loose from its anchor in the ground, but also tightened the noose, cutting the wire in through her flesh to the bone. Now the wire became impossible to pull off, not with fingers, no matter how frantic they were. Tugging on the end of the noose just pulled it tighter.

Yoko explained that every few years a gorilla would get caught in one of these wire traps. If the noose wasn't loosened, then the hand slowly died from lack of blood and over the next few weeks it rotted and fell off. If the gorilla was young and strong, sometimes she survived this.

Three times, researchers had witnessed different silverbacks successfully help the wounded ape. Right after the noose had tightened and the snared gorilla had yanked backward, jerking the wire deep into the flesh, the silverback would begin to scream and display and bark. He would act more terrifying and out of control than ever before, throwing small trees around and slapping the ground and making short furious charges at the injured one, until she lay there utterly still, so terrified she was barely breathing. Then the silverback would step in close, lean down and bite her wrist. Sink his incisors into the flesh far enough to wedge at least one tooth under the wire and tug up, then bite again and again in different spots, prying upward until the noose was loose enough to come off.

When Rafiki was a juvenile and her hand had gotten caught, Uncle had ruled the group. She'd been too young to understand what he was trying to do. And even in his prime, he'd been a bit jumpy and hesitant. He hadn't been able to terrify her into submission, to let him bite her wrist. And so she'd lost her hand.

She'd learned to cope. Her left hand could pluck food surprisingly quickly, much faster than Max could with her one hand. Sometimes when working on an exceptionally bounteous harvest, Rafiki would roll back onto her tailbone and use one foot as well as her left hand, balanced there in what looked like a yoga pose.

She seemed interested in Max's clumsy foraging, as well as in the plant samples she collected. She glanced sideways each time Max pulled out a sample bag, watching from the edge of her eyes as Max tucked edible plants away into her knapsack.

Once, when Max left one of the sample bags on the ground for a moment, Rafiki reached forward to prod it with a single knuckle. At the light crinkle of the plastic, she pulled her hand back to her chest. Max continued to examine the *Pygeum* leaves in her hand, trying to look busy. Rafiki leaned down close to sniff the bag, then backed up, tucking her chin in.

Max didn't want her putting the bag in her mouth to taste it or perhaps try to swallow it, so she casually picked it up, opened it and slid in the plant sample, then put it away in her backpack. Rafiki watched this from the edge of her vision, considering it all.

The next morning on the mountain, within the first hour of being with the gorillas, Max came upon five nettle leaves, all balled up on the ground beside each other, ready to be swallowed. She glanced around, unsure of which gorilla had gone to the trouble of rolling the leaves up, then forgotten to eat them. Rafiki was the closest. Perhaps Asante had distracted her just before she'd swallowed the leaves. Max unrolled each one, smelled and examined it to make sure there wasn't something different about these leaves that a gorilla might have detected just before eating them. Rafiki glanced at her twice while she did this.

An hour later, she found another pile of food, this time of *Loranthus luteo-aurantiacus*, the mistletoe mounded on the ground as neatly as if it had been patted down by a spoon. Again Max took the pile apart, examining the specimens.

She caught Rafiki in the midst of assembling the third offering, trying to get a blackberry to balance on top of the others. It kept rolling off. After the third try, she snorted, popped the berry in her mouth and stalked off on two legs to a thick cluster of ferns. Max sidled over to the berry pile and contemplated it. What use could this abandoned food serve? She glanced at Rafiki and caught her watching, sideways, but with interest.

Considering the neat pile of berries, on impulse she pulled out a sample bag and dropped the blackberries one by one away in it, the bag open on the ground where it could be seen. Then she tucked the bag away in her knapsack, buttoning the flap afterward.

Rafiki watched, motionless, then roused herself and went back to foraging.

After that, when she left the piles, they were closer to Max, sometimes right beside her, two to three a day. Each time Max would elaborately accept them.

And of course, at no point during this, did either of them look directly at each other.

Max and Yoko walked through the darkness to Pip's cabin for dinner, waving their flashlights and calling out, "Hee yaw." Max imagined the forest buffs standing in the darkness of the meadow all around them, their massive heads turning to track the women, the swaying flashlights reflected in their eyes.

To distract herself from this image, Max asked, "How come Pip and Dubois don't go up to see the gorillas?"

"Dubois, she runs the station, the administration and stuff. She spends her days pleading with the government for more money or help. Pip, she works on the gorilla's phylogeography using samples of their DNA. She's trying to figure out when the mountain gorillas split off evolutionarily from the lowland ones, and how much diversity remains in the survivors. You know, at what point the inbreeding will get so bad they'll all be hemophiliacs or something, unable to reproduce viable offspring. The last few weeks she's been working like mad to make sure she's got all the data she needs. She *really* doesn't want to have to come back here later for more."

"She said she had a kid. How old?"

"Eight, named Annie. She's staying with the dad right now. If Pip finishes the research, she can publish. Get a better job."

"Hey, I forgot. When's she flying out?"

A beat of time passed before Yoko answered. "It turns out all the flights leaving the country this week were booked. But she's got a reservation for next Tuesday."

Max considered the way Yoko had said that. She asked, "Were all the flights *into* the country booked?"

"No, they were empty." Yoko opened the door to Pip's cabin and rather busily stepped away from Max to get herself a bowl of soup.

Max sat down next to Mutara, thinking about this while she awkwardly tried to saw open a box of tofu with a knife, her left hand cradled against her in the sling.

Mutara gently took the box from her, cut it open and put it back in front of her. He asked, "Excuse me, but has it truth that the Madonna likes women?"

"I'm sorry?"

"Women. The Madonna, she likes them? I hear this and always wonder."

"Oh." She understood abruptly. "Oh, you mean the singer. Yes, I guess that's the rumor."

He shook his head. "Beautiful woman."

"Can I ask you a question?" The others were busy debating whether to save the last few bottles of beer for Christmas dinner or drink them now. "Can you tell me about the Kutu?"

Mutara turned away from her to rub at a smudge on his spoon with his napkin, considering her request. "What is it you are wishing to know?"

"Anything, everything."

He was silent for a moment, then seemed to come to a decision. When he spoke, his voice was much quieter. "The Kutu, they like things of the dead, like to hold them. Play with their toys, put on their clothes." His words came out quickly as though they'd been in him for a while, waiting to get out.

"Why?"

"They think this way they have power of the dead person. Their favorite is, ahh, how you say? *Une mariée*? A woman who joins with a man."

Max cocked her head. "A wife? A bride?"

"Ahh yes. A bride." He repeated the word to make sure he remembered it. "Brides of Affonso, this is what they call themselves."

"Who's Affonso?"

"Long ago Affonso is the last true king of Kongo, back when the country is powerful, before the whites start wanting slaves. The Kutu love Affonso and the Kongo back then." He actually whispered now. "It is said the Kutu hate Rwanda, you know, for the invasion." He spoke these words with weight.

Unsure of which part of this information to ask about first, she said, "More than everyone else they hate?"

Before he could respond, Yoko interrupted. "It's just a rumor."

The rest of the room was silent in a charged way. Max glanced. Yoko and Dubois were watching Mutara with narrowed eyes. Pip was looking down at her napkin, folding it into squares. The napkin wasn't a face, so Max studied it, watching it get folded into smaller and smaller squares.

"There are plenty of rumors," Yoko said. "You can't look to the Kutu for accurate predictions of what they'll do next, attack Rwanda or Uganda. They want to freak the crap out of as many people as possible. That way everyone's too scared to fight them. Rumors work even better for them than killing people."

Mutara was rubbing his napkin against the spoon, busy with the dirty spot. His posture turned away. She realized he'd been told not to tell her this.

Yoko continued, "During every war in Africa, it seems someone somewhere starts a rumor. People repeat it and repeat it until it becomes fact. Radio Sidewalk reaches far more listeners than any actual radio broadcast."

"You remember the doctors who disappear a few weeks ago in the Congo?" asked Dubois. "There is a detail we are not telling you. When the soldiers of the UN find the jeep of the doctors, there is a Kutu in the back selling *meat*."

At this word, Pip stood up and went to the fridge. No one objected at the sound of her popping open one of the last of the beers. They all listened to her take a long swallow.

Max thought this through. "Meat?" She felt ever since she entered this country all she did was ask questions, unable to make the associations everyone else seemed to consider obvious.

Yoko cleared her throat. She wasn't pleased at the turn the conversation had taken. "The rumors abound. There's no one central story, but hundreds of variations for each incident. That's why I don't believe them. In the version I heard, the boy in the jeep was laughing and chewing on what the soldiers assumed at first was a gorilla's foot."

Max noticed no one was touching the soup. Yoko and Dubois had both put down their spoons, placed their hands on the table. She thought she could look at thousands of hands and be able to pick out theirs, they were so familiar. She felt disoriented, as though she'd been here on these mountains for months instead of nine days.

Then Max said, "Oh." For a moment, she couldn't think of the word. "Jesus, you don't mean . . . " Autotrophism, saprophagous? "Come on, no one still does that." She felt a visceral upward shrinking of her flesh, a pursing of her nether regions. That image of her aunt chasing her, grabbing her, wanting to rip her flesh off her bones.

"Ha," said Dubois, expelling disgust through her teeth. "Do not be so naive. Jeffrey Dahmer was but a few years ago. Humans always have this possibility inside of them. It never goes away."

There are many famous people rumored to be aspie: Bill Gates, Nicholas Tesla, Alan Turing. Jeffrey Dahmer was one of them. The theory went he was confused about how to give affection, wanting someone he liked permanently still before he could sit nearby. After the first murder or two, he came up with his famous twist on the act of love. Perhaps he thought it might diminish his loneliness, for there would be two of them inside his skin, permanently. When Max first heard of what he'd done, she remembered that sexual reproduction had evolved billions of years ago from a microbe attempting to consume a similar microbe and botching it, the two nuclei fusing instead: cannibalizer and cannibalized. Jeffrey's actions harkened back to the very roots of love.

Her mom had reacted to the news stories of Dahmer with fascinated disgust. Max had just felt tired, so tired. Had slept ten hours or more each night for the weeks Jeffrey was on the news.

Dahmer had begun to appear in her nightmares instead of her aunt, his canny sideways glance. Herself frozen in horror. He stepped forward in her aunt's oversized dress, knife in hand.

At night, for at least a year, her nightmares had been intense.

Yoko said, "François Kutu is not from a tribe with a tradition of such things. He could just be spreading these stories, trying to keep the international peacekeepers away. He might be betting the UN council wouldn't want the scandal that would result if any of the soldiers lent to them got eaten."

"Or maybe it is true." Dubois said quietly, "Once you eat a gorilla, how difficult is it to eat a human?"

Max still stared at their hands. Yoko's lay on the table, clasped into fists, the knuckles a trifle white. Dubois' were loose and open palmed. Mutara was tracing the scar on his palm. She remembered Asante's hands again—the fingers, the knuckles, the nails. The main difference was the skin was darker than Mutara's.

Behind them, Pip's hands pressed the cold beer against her forehead and rolled it back and forth.

At dawn, walking back from spending the night in Otombe's hunting perch, Jeremy discovered the men had begun to build their beds into the trees in the hope of staying above the lions' reach during the night. Everywhere he looked in camp, there were men hanging from branches, wielding hammers, and nailing boards together. On top of the water tower stood seven bickering men, each attempting to claim enough room on which to sleep.

Looking up at the tower, Jeremy felt a sudden sense of vertigo and placed his hand on a tent wall for balance. Three nights straight he had spent waiting for the man-eaters, holding tightly to his rifle, the little sleep he had gotten fractured and uneasy. His eyes felt so very dry.

We are being stalked by cats, the thought struck him, so we take to the trees like birds.

The progress of the railroad was already two days behind schedule, falling further behind every hour. A quarter of the men were down with malaria. Of those who still retained a healthy constitution, one in five were posted as lookouts for the lions while the others worked. And every moment they were free from work—or at any time that Jeremy turned his attention away—the men desperately wove the bomas higher and thicker, or hammered more beds into trees, taking any boards or nails they needed from the railroad. Whenever he caught them at this, they kept their gaze focused on their work. No one looked at him, no one asked his permission for these materials.

Alan and Jeremy sat in front of the tent, the table between them spread with cucumber sandwiches and tea. The WaKikiyu woman Singh had hired carried a bowl of sugar toward them, her robe rustling. Like Otombe, she wore a toga-style skin knotted over one shoulder, covering her chest and body down to her mid-thighs. Her robe however had had the goat hair scraped off it, making it seem more like cloth, more like a civilized—if inadequate—dress. Round her neck hung long strings of white shells and her head was shaved bald except for a tuft in the back.

"Ahh," said Alan. "The sugar. Good." As she walked away, his eyes trailed her.

Following Alan's gaze, Jeremy saw, without the fur on it, the robe hugged her closely, affording the men in camp a better guess at her body.

"So bony." Alan said and spooned some sugar into his cup.

Wanting to forestall Alan from pursuing this subject, Jeremy asked the question he had been mulling over. "Why is it the Indians stay?"

The doctor turned to him, his eyebrows raised. "Stay?"

"Yes. Working for the railroad does seem rather brutal from their perspective. The malaria, the heat, the hard labor, the low pay, and now these man-eating beasts. Frankly, I wonder why they do not just head back home."

Alan busied himself biting into his sandwich, but could not hide his amusement. "My dear man, how would India be any different?" He looked up at the sky for a moment, chewing. "Did you hear about Taylor?"

"Taylor?" Over Alan's shoulder Jeremy could see the workers working on the boma near them, weaving more branches through it.

"The new Englishman, Rupert Taylor. He was to take over the coordination of the second more intensive land survey."

Jeremy nodded, sipping the hot tea. He was on his third

cup. He hoped it would keep him awake for tonight's watch. "Haven't met him yet."

"Well, you won't now. This afternoon, I chatted with the conductor of the supply train. Evidently Taylor brought his wife and children along for a brief vacation here, before his family headed back to England. They were camped at Voi. What's that, fifteen miles back?"

"Oh, I think twenty at least."

"Last night, his wife, getting up to check on one of their children, who had a fever, requested that Taylor check on a noise outside. He stepped out, saw nothing, and called to the askari keeping watch ten paces away. The man also spied nothing. Reassured, the family fell back to sleep, Taylor and wife sleeping together in their cot. Later, she was woken by a sound she thought was her child breathing thickly from his sickness. Sitting up, she noticed her husband was gone. She stepped outside to find his corpse on the ground, not a mark on him. As she leaned over to touch his face, she felt a presence. A lion stood a pace away, looming over her. She screamed and the startled askari shot into the air. The lion bolted.

"The people in camp dragged Taylor's body into the tent. All twelve people ended up huddled in that single tent, listening to the lions circling outside, sighing with hunger. The askari had to keep firing at random through the walls to keep the animals from claiming the body."

"Oh my lord, the poor children," Jeremy said.

Alan nodded, "In this heat, the body will never make it home, has to be buried here in British East Africa. They have lost their father in more than one way."

Whereas the coolies each seemed to have several lion stories by this point—where they had been standing when the lion walked into camp, or how they had been only one tent over from where the creatures had taken their last victim—this was the first one Jeremy had heard Alan tell. His voice had real pain in it, for the woman and her children.

It was the first one to involve Europeans.

Otombe let his cloak drop to the ground and stood there, waiting for Jeremy to get undressed before he stepped into the river. "This bathing in the water, it is a time to prepare yourself for the hunt."

"What do you mean?" Jeremy directed his eyes down at the buttons of his shirt. Normally, he believed it polite to look at a man when he talked, but not now. He simply hurried to strip. Struck with the impropriety of both his front and back, he turned to the side and hunched slightly. His fingers were clumsy from fatigue. He worked hard to pretend that the askaris who watched the river a few paces away did not exist.

"Men in my tribe, even if it is only with a wet cloth, cleanse ourselves before we hunt. Let our thoughts fall away, concentrate on the animal's mind."

"Concentrate on its mind?" Surprised, Jeremy glanced up. Flustered with what he saw, he looked right back down. The spareness of Otombe's body reminded him of his engineering instruments, everything of a purpose. He wondered what the man looked like when there was not famine, what he acted like when there were not man-eating predators around. Did he talk more, did he laugh easily?

"Think like the lions. The more we can do that—see what they see, smell what they smell—the better we will know where these lions will hunt next. The better we will be at killing them."

Nodding, Jeremy dropped his last wool sock onto his pile of discarded clothing and quickly waded into the river. In spite of his nudity, he felt the pleasure of the water this time. The humidity today had been so intense it had seemed at times hard to breathe. A headache had pulsed up the back of his head, sounds seemed close, colors bright. He pushed deep into the river, until he stood up to his neck in water, his body concealed. There he stilled, his eyes closed, concentrating on the coolness, the lack of sweat-dampened scratchy clothing. In front of the men, all day, he'd had to hold up his rifle, try to look tough. The water was such a relief. He let his head roll back, closing his eyes. With his ears underwater, all sound was gone except for the rasp of his breathing and the distant underwater clink of a pebble. He felt he could let his feet float up, his whole body letting go, falling asleep on the bed of this river even as he drifted quietly away.

When he climbed out, he dried off and pulled on all his clothing except for the spine protector. He simply felt too much fatigue to deal with untangling its elastic shoulder bands. Instead, he left the device lying in the grass like some discarded snakeskin. He imagined it would not take long for mold to grow on it in this monsoon season, the rain-soaked flannel absorbing the red of the dirt. A seedling or two of grass would take hold, a colony of mice nesting underneath, the proud label of the Culpepper Mills fading. Gradually, it would become one with this land.

Jeremy had ordered the goats chained up to the railroad sleeper again, twenty feet from where the satchel still hung from its bush. For their roost, Otombe chose a tree a little further from the goats than last time, downwind perhaps sixty feet. He wanted to ensure the lions would catch no hint of the presence of the men. Taking his seat on their hammered-in bench high in the tree, Jeremy felt uneasy without a boma around him, even with his rifle cradled in his arms. He sat a few inches closer to Otombe than he had the previous night. Though the man did not hold a gun, Jeremy felt safer this way.

The sun hung for a single moment above the rim of the forest, then disappeared. Somewhere far to the west came the first rumble from a lion.

Jeremy said quietly, "They killed another person last night.

Not just the man in camp, but also a railroad surveyor twenty miles away."

"Twenty miles?" Otombe raised his eyebrows.

Jeremy nodded.

The hunter looked in the direction of the last roar, sitting very still. For a moment, it seemed he would not respond. When he spoke, it was in a whisper. "It is unusual, but there are two lions. Not much meat on a man once you subtract bones, entrails, and head. Each lion requires thirty to forty pounds of meat a night. If they can, they will kill more than once."

Jeremy asked, "But why would they travel so far to find another? There are many men in camp, people in villages all along the way from here to there. Why would they walk twenty miles to eat a surveyor?" Searching Otombe's face for the answer, he realized a few days ago he did not know these wide cheekbones, these dark eyes. Now, up in this tree, the face of this man seemed as familiar as someone he had grown up with. And at night, in the darkness, Jeremy was hardly conscious anymore of the color of his skin, only that Otombe was a person he trusted.

"This is why we must learn to think like lions. Especially with these two. They are different. If we do not think like them, become them, we will never catch them."

Through the trees came the sound of jerry cans being clanked together in camp a mile away. They heard the single report of a gun. Jeremy caught his breath, waiting for more shots, for screaming, but all was silent. After a few moments, he figured a guard, jumpy from the lions' roaring, had shot his gun off at some unexpected movement or sound. Before the long night had ended, they would hear eight more shots issued at random, never any commotion afterward. In the morning, he would learn one of the askaris had been hit in the arm by gunfire when he approached a guard for his turn at watch.

"Unless your shot is sure," Otombe warned, "do not use

your gun. We cannot let the lions know we are hiding up in trees waiting for them. They are smart. They will learn quickly. After they know where we are, they will start to hunt us."

Another lion answered, seeming closer than before, although perhaps that was Jeremy's imagination. It was now completely dark.

"It is the lions' time now," said Otombe. "No more talking." From near the river a leopard's two-toned rasp came, like a saw being drawn forward through wood, then back.

Jeremy fell into a kind of trance, not asleep, but not entirely awake, his eyes open, his breath coming slowly and deeply. Otombe beside him made not a single sound. The lions roared closer and closer. The sky clouded over. Without the moon, he had no way to tell how much time passed.

In the night, he found it surprisingly hard to judge how far away a sound was. Everything seemed so close. He persuaded himself the last roar came from a hundred yards away, then decided it was more like half a mile. He felt certain only that the lions were moving in this direction.

When the creatures finally fell silent, he felt relief. His knuckles ached from the tightness of his grip on the rifle. Relaxing his fingers consciously, he leaned back a little in the wood seat.

Otombe sat tall, every muscle solid with concentration.

Otombe touched one cautious finger to the rifle barrel, ticking his head side to side in the smallest *no*. Only then did Jeremy understand the danger.

The moon was gone behind clouds, soon it would rain. Below, the three goats were barely visible in the darkness, mostly a sense of occasional movement, the sound of cropping grass and shifting feet, the occasional clank of a chain. He stared down, scanning the underbrush. Somewhere below were two killers, each half the size of a horse, creeping closer step-by-step through the nyika.

He waited so long, holding the gun. He began to feel certain the cats had moved away or Otombe was wrong to think they had ever been nearby.

Something below thrashed hard. A goat's scream was cut off abruptly, a wood bell clacked hard twice.

All was silent except some sort of rhythmic rasping. Perhaps a goat's labored breath, perhaps a lion panting. Then the breathing stopped.

Jeremy stared, his fingers sweaty, looking, looking. He could see nothing. None of the goats made a noise. Could they all be dead so quickly? Where they had been tied, something large shifted, something rustled through the underbrush. Jerking his rifle to his shoulder, he aimed at the sound, ready to fire, before he realized the noise was the railroad sleeper being stealthily dragged away. After it, at the end of their clanking chains, rustled the corpses of the goats. Jeremy aimed ahead of the railroad sleeper, watched and watched, but he could make out no movement more than a bush shifting here, a branch there. Not even a shadow underneath. Logically he realized, in the dark, in the underbrush, the difference between tawny fur and reddish soil would be nearly impossible to distinguish. As though the man-eaters were not there, did not exist at all, as though instead it were the wilderness itself dragging away its sacrifice.

As when he was in the river with his ears underwater, his own breath echoed noisily. The whole time Otombe sat motionless beside him.

Still Jeremy kept the rifle at his shoulder, waiting for a shot, waiting until long after the rustling had faded and he knew the lions were gone.

Rafiki continued to leave little piles of food for Max, the food prepped for eating, stripped of twigs or rolled into balls. Max accepted the gifts, putting them away in sample bags, while she continued to search for the vine. Every once in a while she would grunt lightly to reassure the family with noise. A few of the others would grunt back absentmindedly.

She'd always been conscious of how much space there was around her, worried other people might bump into her, that jittery electric shock skating up her nerves. So her mind habitually mapped out the locations of herself and others, a bird's-eye view, calculating distances. Being with the gorillas, that worry gradually went away. They stayed a few feet back, circling politely around her and each other in a wandering waltz. She found this distance deeply relaxing. That part of her mind, so used to monitoring proximity, loosened bit by bit like a muscle that had been tight way too long.

Occasionally, when out of sheer habit her mind considered the space around her, she noticed the distance between herself and the gorillas was the same as the distance between each of the gorillas. One morning Rafiki stood up next to Max, to lever a *Vernonia* branch down to pluck bunches of its buds. After she'd picked several bunches, she continued to stand there, holding the branch down with her stump, looking away, waiting. Max watched her, uncertain of what she was waiting for. Yoko had said that standing upright was uncomfortable for the gorillas, the same as knucklewalking was uncomfortable for humans. Also, the branch was a good size. It must be hard to hold down like that.

Max wondered if this might be a different type of food offering.

She cautiously raised herself up, moving slowly, watching for a single flash-glance reprimand from Rafiki or the others. No one looked over except Yoko and Mutara, but up here on this mountain, the censure of humans did not count.

So she got to her feet beside Rafiki. Being so used to crouching down, in the shadow of Rafiki's large body, it seemed strange to discover that when they were both standing upright, she was the taller one. For a moment the two of them paused there—one slender and hairless, the other muscular and short. The feeling was not like being next to a dog or horse. It was more like standing beside a weighty and hunched aunt. Max plucked a few clumps of buds, while Rafiki waited, face averted, her own harvest held to her chest.

As Max sank slowly back into her normal crouched position, she looked down. Their feet were side by side. The length of Rafiki's feet was close to that of her own. The width, however, was utterly different, because—while Rafiki's heel and instep were like a human's—the front of her feet spread out into four short fingers and an opposable thumb. A child's hand sewn onto the front of a foot.

In high school, she'd had a biology teacher, Mr. Denni, who'd emphasized the importance of thumbs. He tended to speak in a booming voice suited for a much bigger audience than a few bored eleventh-graders, as though he'd never gotten used to the idea he wasn't lecturing in a large college auditorium. At least once a semester he let drop the fact that he was a member of MENSA and that his wife's uncle had invented the flame-thrower. Discussing evolution, he called out his belief that opposable thumbs equaled manipulation of the environment

and, thus, must be followed by brain development. Thumbs—
he said—were the reason humans were the dominant species on
Earth. He held up his own thumbs and wiggled them around.

Gorillas had four of them.

Rafiki released the branch and sank back down to eat her
buds, chomping through them as methodically as a person eating popcorn.

A few months ago, Max had read a study that disproved the
idea that Neanderthals died out because they were dumb.
Instead, the study demonstrated they had a significantly bigger
braincase than even modern humans. It was possible that, half
a million years ago, the Neanderthals had been capable of
higher order thoughts than anyone living today.

Still the archeological record showed that soon after *Homo
sapiens* arrived in any area where Neanderthals lived—even
large groups of them—all traces of the Neanderthals disappeared.

She wondered if, like the gorillas, they'd been a gentle people.

Someone touched her on the shoulder and she swiveled fast.

"Lunchtime," whispered Yoko. "Let's go."

After a morning with the gorillas, her hairless skin and confrontational stare seemed shocking, such a foreign species.

Late that afternoon, the temperature began to drop suddenly, wind moving through the jungle, the branches creaking
and groaning. Titus rose majestically on his hind legs, peering
at the sky, sniffing. With an authoritative grunt, he led his family up the mountain.

Mutara led the humans in the opposite direction. They'd
barely descended a hundred yards before the rain started. Within
a minute it was lashing down so hard the spray rebounded several feet into the air, the lightning almost continuous. Waterfalls
of red earth gushed down the slope, the trail turning into a rushing river. For the first time Max began to glimpse the scope of the
word, "monsoon."

They half-walked, half-slid down the mountain, over the plants and mud. All of them so fighting for their balance, they didn't say a word until they came in sight of the dark research cabins. The rain beginning to slow, night was falling. By this point, the generator had gotten so low on fuel that they didn't turn it on any more, saving its power in case they needed to phone out for an emergency. They now lived and cooked and worked with candles and fires, as though they'd gone back in time.

They headed straight to Pip's cabin for dinner. After eating, they would return to their cabins to do what work was possible without computers or other electrical equipment.

Just before they got to the cabin, a scream rang off the roof above them. Max took a fast step forward, running straight into Mutara's back.

"What?" He turned around. "Ahh, the sound. It is a hyrax. Little animal." He cupped his hands to show how big it was. "Makes much noise, yes?"

In Pip's cabin, the only illumination was a single candle in the center of the table. In the light from it, Pip and Dubois were sitting by the radio, not saying a word. They made no move at the entrance of the others.

"The radio . . . the radio just now." Pip's voice wavered. "They announced . . . "

Dubois continued, "This morning a UN plane is flying near Rutshuru, forty-two soldiers on board." She wrapped her arms tightly round her ribs. "Nigerians and Belgians. Soldiers to keep the peace in the Congo. The people on the ground, they say they are seeing the plane in the air, then something flies up to hit it. Then it catches fire. And falls into the jungle."

In the meadow outside, a forest buff moaned, hoarse and surprisingly cow-like.

"A missile?" Max said. "What a minute. The Kutu have missiles?"

"Hey, we don't know the Kutu did this," said Yoko.

All of them, even Max, turned to stare at her. After a day in the jungle, Yoko's hair was standing straight up, a little like a cockatiel's feathers.

"What?" Yoko said, "It *could* be someone else."

There was a pause, then Dubois continued. "They do not know yet if the soldiers live. If any are captured."

"Rutshuru, how far away is it?" Max asked.

"Thirty miles," said Yoko. "Two days of travel on the jungle paths they call roads around here."

Max could imagine the UN soldiers who survived the crash limping out of the plane, dragging those who were wounded to safety. Crouched over the bodies, trying to stem the flow of blood, these men would look up when the children stepped out of the jungle, what appeared to be toy rifles looped over their shoulders.

"Little wankers." Pip's voice was almost without emotion. "Are the planes going to be flying on Tuesday? I want to go home."

Yoko stepped forward to get them soup. They sat down, listening to the clacking of the ladle. On the table, she placed the bowls and, since they'd run out of sweets, a small bag of Doritos for dessert. The four of them took slow bites of the soup. Max ate her tofu, no one saying anything while they listened to the rest of the BBC news hour. She was getting much better at eating with just her right hand, her other hand in the sling. She'd learned to wedge the box of tofu between several bowls so it didn't fall over when her spoon scraped at the corners.

Whenever the radio's volume got too low, one of the others would pick the radio up to crank it back to full power. There was a story about the brokering of a cease-fire in the Chechen Republic and another about five fans trampled at an Italian soccer match. Nothing more about the UN soldiers.

After the end of the show Dubois leaned forward and clicked the radio off.

In the silence, with just one lit candle, with no phone or light bulb working in camp and the Kutu getting closer, the precariousness of their situation seemed clear.

Yoko was the one to break the silence. Her voice was quiet. "Maybe it's time we abandoned the station."

There was a rustle of surprise at her words. In the light from the candle, the parts of her most visible were her hands lying pale and thin on the table. Having stared at chapped gorilla hands all day, Max noted the smoothness of these narrow fingers. This was not someone who'd lived outside, struggling with the elements. These were the hands of a researcher, a bookish academic. Examining the hands of the others, she understood none of them had much practice in recognizing physical danger, in delineating the exact point when their previous methods of coping should be abandoned and new rules adopted. For each of them (except Pip), one of their biggest fears seemed to be overreacting and looking like a fool.

Yoko addressed Dubois. "Without electricity, we can't get much work done."

"We go to town soon and get fuel," answered Dubois. She picked her hands up, seemed to be rubbing her temples. Her voice was tense. Possibly another migraine was starting. She'd been getting more of them recently.

"We won't be able to afford that for long. The black market's too expensive."

"We can pay for a while."

"Soon we'll run out of paper and even potato soup. Soon we'll have to leave."

"If we go," said Dubois, "our stipends stop, no? Then no more patrols. Without us and the patrols, the hunters come."

Into the pause afterward—that pause while they all considered what their response might be—Pip spoke. "Please, you have to leave. I don't want you to die. You've no guns. You can't stop anyone, Kutu or poachers." Her voice was loud and pleading.

Yoko grimaced in irritation and the moment was lost.

Max noticed Mutara. He'd finished his soup, wiped his mouth, and pushed back from the table. He did not add anything to either side of the debate. He kept his head down. His hands, she saw now, were much rougher than the researchers'. She remembered the way he'd grunted with pain each time he'd tried to jam her shoulder back into the socket, a private sound. That final time, he'd jammed it in hard, filled with sudden fury.

Sitting here, he didn't offer his opinion on what they should do.

Back from the night in the hunting perch, Jeremy napped in his tent before commencing the day's work on the railroad. He slept now whenever he had a moment, fast as a rock falling, instantly unconscious.

He dreamed he had somehow become Taylor, the railroad survey coordinator. He lay on Taylor's bed in his tent near Voi. The unlikely perfection of the moment overwhelmed him: to be here if only for a little while, listening to the breathing of sleeping children, feeling the warm weight of a wife beside him. His gratitude was intense. He relaxed enough to feel the extent of his exhaustion, all those years of pretending. He had hopes if he made no noise, drew no attention to himself, he could sleep here a little while, just until he was less tired.

Then the lion cupped his mouth over Jeremy's face.

Warm darkness, saliva dripped onto his cheeks, the rough tongue rested on his nose, the jowls forming a tight seal. There was the stench of decomposing meat bits wedged between the animal's teeth. Jeremy gasped at the lack of air, suffocating.

Even in this moment he did not thrash or kick once. He would endure so much in order to lie beside someone for a while.

It was only as the lion began to tug him from the bed that he woke.

Opening his eyes, he stared at the woman's face above him. It took him a moment to recognize his WaKikiyu cook pulling on his shoulder, sent to rouse him for work.

He and Otombe walked three miles to a Masai village. The village had been attacked twice in the last few weeks, and Otombe wished to learn what the Masai knew.

Jeremy was limping from three insect bites on the soles of his feet. The circumference of each bite was swollen red. In the center was a visible puncture with flesh missing. Palpating each, he could feel something hard and lumpy beneath. The infection, he wondered, or some type of burrowing beetle? Each time he took a step, pain shot upward. He marveled that he had not noticed the bites when they occurred.

Hoping to distract himself, he asked, "Last night, how did you know the lions were nearby?" At least without his spine protector, these long walks were easier. His back perspired less, his movements were less restricted. He could only hope his spinal column was protected enough from the sun's radiation by his hat and shirt alone.

Otombe said, "Lions roar in the beginning of a hunt while they are figuring out their plan. Come this way, one says. No, this way, the other answers. Once they go silent, they have agreed on a target. Last night, they went silent around the time they could hear and smell the goats."

Outside the boma of the Masai village, twelve men waited in a line for them. They stood almost at attention, their robes, hair and skin smeared with red dye.

"Feel honored," said Otombe. "They have put on their finery for you."

No, Jeremy thought, they did so for my rifle.

As he got closer to the men, he was taken aback to see they wore necklaces, headbands and, even many earrings—tawdry and layered as a little girl's attempt at dress up. Still they were clearly men. Their height rivaled his own, a few were distinctly taller. None suffered from his poor posture. Instead, they stood with their heads high, backs straight, male hips squared inside their skirts.

"Are these hunters?" Jeremy tried to concentrate on the way each held his spear as confidently as though it were another limb.

"No," said Otombe, smiling. "These are shepherds. They don't even kill their cows, just bleed them a little, drink that and the milk."

Otombe and the men greeted each other in Swahili. An old Masai began to talk, his chest sunken and voice quavering. Jeremy surveyed the men for signs of the famine. They wore robes that looped across their chests, covering their torsos and upper thighs. Their limbs were bony but he had gotten so accustomed to slender Africans that he could no longer tell what was normal.

The older Masai led them around the village's boma, stopping after a time to point at the thorn wall. Jeremy assumed the man was explaining the details of the fortifications, the width of the wall or the technique with which the branches had been woven.

"Last time the lions killed one of their people was a week ago," Otombe told him in English. "They do not know how the lion got into the boma. No lion had ever tried before. It was night. The animal just appeared, grabbed a woman from her hut and dragged her away. She was screaming. Her husband chased after her with his spear, but was not fast enough. He watched the lion tug her right through the wall here."

"What?" asked Jeremy. "Where?" He squatted down and tried to peer through the thorn wall. Angling his head from side to side, he could see only the smallest pinpricks of light.

"Here," Otombe said.

Looking closer, still unable to find any sign of a tunnel or even a thinning in the woven wall, Jeremy noticed on some thorns a few tatters of hair and a wrinkled flap of what might be skin. "But that is impossible. The wall must be two feet thick."

"Three feet," Otombe nodded. "The husband says he has

never seen another animal do such a thing. It was as though the lion was not made of flesh. The animal tucked his head down and just backed through. The wife, as she was pulled through, tried to grab hold of even the thorns."

Otombe added, "Some of the people believe these lions are not physical beings. They think if we do shoot them, the bullets will pass right through, in the same way the lion passed through this wall."

On the walk back through the savannah, Otombe said, "You are limping, you have been all morning."

Jeremy admitted, "A few insects appear to have bitten the soles of my feet."

Otombe asked, "Is there a lump left within each bite?"

"Yes," said Jeremy.

"They are worms who lay eggs. You must get the eggs out before they hatch. Take off your shoes and socks. I will cut them out."

"Cut?"

"Shallow cuts. Just enough to scoop out the eggs."

Jeremy looked down at his feet. They were the least favorite part of his anatomy, pale and spindly as the appendages of some cave creature. He explained with embarrassment, "In the heat my feet are rather fragrant."

"Because you make them swelter in tight leather. Take off your shoes." He waited for Jeremy to respond. "The worms, when they hatch, they burrow through the body, eating. Their favorite organ is the brain."

Jeremy sat right down in the dirt to tug off his shoes and socks.

Squatting down and cupping Jeremy's ankle in his hand, Otombe made no face at the smell. His fingers were hard with calluses. He pulled his knife from his leg sheath; the blade was beaten steel, three inches long and glittering. Jeremy did not wish to appear a coward in front of this man. He closed his eyes, forced his attention on the sounds around him, breathed deeply. A bird's trill, the wind rustling through the grass. From somewhere behind him he heard the lightest *tap-tap*, like salt being shaken over a leaf. Glancing that way, he saw an eight-foot-tall termite mound. Inside, the tiny insects drummed busily.

The knife cut so fast he felt the pain only afterward. He jerked back to face Otombe. He was alone in the forest with a near-naked savage, his knife scooping a parasite's eggs from his flesh, the man's fingers wrapped tenderly round his heel. This was not, he thought, the life his mother had imagined for him. He stared hard at Otombe's face, those cheekbones outlined by famine, the man's concentration.

The knife sliced a second time. Its searing pain almost a relief.

He wished so much he were fashioned in some other way.

"Tonight," Jeremy said, "I have to sleep in my own bed. This is all too much for me."

Head down, Otombe nodded.

During tea, in front of his tent, Jeremy found Alan unusually reticent. After a minute or two of silence punctuated only by the clink of spoons on teacups, Jeremy said, "It is strange, is it not, that everyone assumes an engineer like me should be the one to hunt the lions. You know, crawl into the bushes after the creatures and all." Alan nodded, but seemed uninterested in responding further. Jeremy added, "It was not exactly the subject of my schooling."

The WaKikiyu cook brought sandwiches over and placed them on the table. Aside from the scent of the fresh bread, there came with her the smell of the cooking fire and the goat grease she used on her hands. She headed back toward her fire without once having glanced at the men. Jeremy did not know her name and had yet to hear her voice.

Alan grunted and announced, "I know I'll have been here too long when she begins to appear attractive to me."

Jeremy glanced after her, not knowing how much English she might comprehend. Her pace did not falter. Personally, he did not understand why Alan would say this. Yes, her head was shaved and her race Nilotic, but her body was young and strong and she carried herself with some grace. From what he had observed of the tendencies of other men, this seemed to be all that was required to regard a woman with interest.

"About the lions," Alan said, "Shooting a few pesky predators is an integral component of the colonization process. I have seen it work time and again. The tribes immediately become more pacified, convinced we whites offer certain benefits." He bit into a watercress sandwich. "Since these lions have plagued so many tribes in such a large area, if you successfully shoot them, it will do more to tame this colony than years of our railroad running through its heart."

Jeremy heard a loud crack from somewhere in the forest outside the boma, like the smack of a hammer on rock.

A new silence fell between the men. Normally Alan chatted about all the hunting he had done. Today, however, he seemed to have little to say and his eyes kept returning to Jeremy, something in his expression puzzled.

He heard the sharp crack again. It came from the direction of the bonfire, its dark smoke rising in the air.

"What was that sound?" Jeremy asked. He stirred his tea, conscious of Alan's eyes following his hands, watching the way he handled the spoon, the way he picked up his cup. Jeremy began to feel a distinct unease.

"That sound like snooker balls hitting?"

"Yes." In Jeremy's late teens and early twenties, one by one his family had begun to study him, appearing a trifle confused as Alan did now. Each person would stare, examining the way he walked, as well as his expression when he looked at the farm hands, observing him whenever they thought he might not notice.

"Three patients died last night. I had the remains tossed on the fire. During the cremation process, there's a point when the skull cracks open, from the heat." Alan took another bite of the sandwich, his teeth white against the blistered red of his face. "The coolies believe it a good sound, the soul released to heaven."

Trying to move his mind away from that information, Jeremy said, "I visited a Masai village today."

"Really?" Already Alan sat with his chair pushed farther back from Jeremy, his legs angled away. "I've just been reading an article about that tribe. A missionary who has lived among them for two decades has data to suggest the rate of births is decreasing, as well as the number of marriages and their overall health. It started years before this recent famine. The man suggests this decline might be endemic to many of the less-civilized tribes."

Jeremy remembered Otombe saying half of his tribe had died. "Why would that happen?"

Alan served himself another sandwich. "Well, first off, let us be objective about this. You have to question if it's true. The man is no scientist. The data is far from ironclad. It covers such a short period, just a few villages, primarily one tribe. Still, it piques the interest. Before now, no one has bothered to survey these people."

Jeremy nodded, not trying to make his gesture overly firm or masculine. He knew acting would never work in the long run, not with someone who was around him extensively and who already had suspicions. Instead, he kept his eyes on the smoke of the bonfire, endured Alan's gaze, waited for the man to be sure.

Alan continued, "If it is true, you must wonder at the timing of the Masai. We are here bringing technology, religion, and modern comforts. Things are finally looking up for this bloody continent. Why would they decide to exit now?"

Jeremy knew he and Alan would not be having tea together for much longer.

For the first time in four nights, he lay down to spend the night in his tent. Rolling the mosquito netting down around his bed, he was surprised at how uneasy he felt to be here. Laying down on a cot, even in the center of a boma, now seemed like an unnatural act, attempting to sleep at the level of the lions, thin canvas walls between him and the night. He placed his rifle across his chest and felt utterly defenseless. The Masai's boma had stood at least fourteen feet high, its walls three feet thick. At each sound, he startled slightly. He craved the safety of a bench high in a tree and the solid darkness of Otombe by his side.

In spite of his misgivings, he must have fallen asleep because he was jarred awake by the first of the lions' roars. He blinked around confused, not sure how much time had passed. Five minutes? Five hours?

The answering roar came from a mile to the south, some-where around the nearly completed canal. The lions seemed to regard all the torn-up earth as their playground. He looked at the bright flame of the kerosene lamp by his side. With it lit, the lions would be able to see shadows through the tent walls, have a better idea of what lay inside, where to attack. He blew it out, then—shocked at the absolute darkness—hurriedly lit it again.

The lions roared intermittently, gradually getting closer. Around the time they reached the railroad tracks, their roaring stopped. He waited, counting, forcing himself not to hurry. One Mississippi, two Mississippi. A fox yipped by the far end of camp. Three Mississippi, four. Not a sound from the lions. He reached twenty Mississippi and blew out the wick again. The darkness around him was complete. He lay on his cot in it, staring up at the ceiling and attempting to control the slight hiss of his breath. The waiting began. For the first time he began to comprehend the depth of the Indians' terror.

The men's voices, tight with fear, soared from boma to boma throughout the camp. Some yelled in English; the rest yelled foreign words he did not know. Jerry cans clanked and rattled. Slowly his eyes grew accustomed to the darkness. He shifted his grip on his rifle. A faint illumination came from one of the askari's bonfires twenty paces away, the glow flickering across the roof and walls of his tent. He watched for the shadow of anything moving.

Lying here, Jeremy considered all the children in the villages nearby, attempting to sleep curled tight against the sides of their parents, the thin doors of their huts barricaded as well as possible. He imagined in the morning all those mothers lugging their laundry down to the river, uneasily watching the bushes lining the sides of the path. He pitied the fathers stepping out of their bomas to hunt, holding tightly to their spears.

As time passed—twenty minutes, half an hour—numb with the monotony of fear and from four nights with little sleep, he found himself drifting into a state he had never experienced before. Each sound struck him strongly and clearly. He could identify each and even locate it in space. The frightened squeal of a hyena near the quarry, the chuff of a hippo on the river, the low whispers of the men who had bedded down for safety on top of the water tower. Meanwhile, his breath deepened, his eyes closed.

His viewpoint gradually floated up in the air, rising slowly to a point far above his body. Spread out below him, he saw the landscape of Tsavo, the trees and animals and Indians and Africans, rocks and river and the railroad. And beneath all this, the skin of the continent oozed its red mud, the laterite dirt binding it all together, discoloring clothing, coating tents, dyeing any hand that touched it with a bloody stain.

In this half-conscious state, floating gently above camp,

Jeremy could feel the animals out there, probing the base of the bomas, sniffing, seeking weaknesses with those huge tawny eyes, testing each possibility. Determined and smart, nature's perfect hunters, in the wide curve of their skulls they had capabilities he could not even imagine.

Hour after hour passed. Strangely, the lack of any sudden screaming did not reassure him. He could almost see the animals tucking their heads down and pressing forward into a subtle weakness in a boma. They had no long manes to get snagged. The thorns jabbed and sliced, but sinuous as snakes, the lions twisted through.

Silently appearing in the firelight beside a tent full of Indians.

Soon men would bellow and die once again, shots would be fired and pans clanked. In the pandemonium, the lions would vanish into the darkness all around. And tomorrow evening he would climb into a hunting perch, forced up there by the Indians' expectations and his own emotions.

Until this was all over, he would spend his nights in the trees, beside Otombe. He could not stand it any other way.

I n her nightmare, she saw her aunt's pale dress walking toward her through the darkness of the cabin, the floral pattern as oversized as on upholstery.

Frozen with fear, she lay in bed, her limbs heavy and unmoving.

Then, as the dress moved into the light of the window, four feet away, she saw it hung loose on a man's skinny body.

Dahmer took a step forward, pushing his glasses up on his nose with one finger. Good-looking and blond, his thin lips holding tight to all his secrets, he stood as close as she'd always imagined the right man might be able to do. He leaned tenderly down over her bed, bit into her cheek and began to chew.

In the afternoon Titus climbed a tree. Generally the gorillas stayed on the ground or on the branches only a few feet up. Like humans, they were heavy and ponderous, not aerial long-limbed monkeys meant to fly from tree to tree. The branches rustled and creaked as he pulled his four-hundred-odd pounds gingerly upward, ten feet, then twenty, his expression concentrated.

Max moved back to survey the tree. It was vaguely oak-like, the leaves cordate and serrate, intermittent clusters of small blue fruit. Thirty feet up, Titus stopped and began to pluck at something she couldn't see from down here, half of his body obscured by leaves. She couldn't tell if he were eating part of the tree—the leaves or berries.

Or perhaps some vine growing on it.

This was the only time she'd seen Titus climb a tree to eat something. The other gorillas waited patiently below, as though they'd been through this routine before. None of them made a move toward this food source he'd found. She remembered Stevens telling her that only silverbacks touched the beta-blocker vine, the vine they used as medicine.

She knuckle-walked to the trunk and looked up. If she got a large sample now, she could do a crude extract tonight. Assuming the results demonstrated enough beta-blockers—proving this was the vine—she could leave with the remaining sample tomorrow, hire a car in town, wait in the capital until a flight out was available. It would be safer there. Once home, she could work on transforming this plant into a medicine to save lives.

The first branch arched off the trunk just three feet from the ground. She put one foot on it.

"Hey," whispered Yoko from a few feet away. "What are you doing?"

Max didn't answer. She began to climb the staircase of branches around the trunk, concentrating on the placement of her feet, the grip of her hand. She slid her dislocated arm out of the sling in order to use it, but it felt weak. Her hand didn't want to reach any higher than her shoulder and she didn't trust its grip. Within a few feet, the climbing got more difficult, the branches uneven. Her hands were too small to span the branches. She understood why humans exited the trees.

"You are a Great Ape," she thought to herself. Changing the inflection, she repeated, "*Great* ape."

"Pssst, Tombay," whispered Yoko from down on the ground. "Get the fuck down here." Uncle, the second silverback, coughed at her for talking, and she didn't say anything more.

Max held as tightly to each branch as she could, picking each step with care. In the tree, she found her boots a hindrance. In them, her feet were unable to grip the branches or feel for traction. She figured she only had to climb high enough to see what Titus was putting in his mouth. Probably twenty feet up, maybe twenty-five.

One of her feet slipped. She threw her good arm round a branch to catch her balance.

Holding tight, she kicked off her left boot and let it fall, then her right. The distance she'd climbed was all too clear from the many thuds the boots made hitting branches on the way down. Titus jerked around. He was only ten feet above her now and a few feet to the side. She sensed him staring in the direction of his family for a moment, listening intently. When nothing else happened, his head swiveled toward her.

If he wanted to, he could move through these branches much faster than she could. He could push her out of the tree, no matter how tightly she tried to hold on.

When his head turned away, she flash-glanced at him. He was looking off in the distance, chewing mechanically. She tugged off a chunk of nearby *Sphagnum* and pretended to eat it, for the slow count of thirty. Then she eased herself up onto the next branch.

She looked down. It was clear what a fall from this height would mean. Her body a fleshy water balloon.

She imagined death. It would be gray and spacious. No bodies to touch, no faces to avoid. She climbed up to the next branch.

From this angle below, Titus's hip blocked the view of whatever plant was in his hands. She was close enough now that tiny chunks of leaves and stems were pattering onto her head, too small and chewed up to tell what kind of plant they came from. With Titus, she didn't normally get closer than ten feet.

Still, he continued to eat, didn't act particularly bothered by her proximity. Perhaps, with his family at the base of the tree, further away, he had no need to act the tough guy, no need to scare anyone. Or maybe he'd just grown accustomed to her as the others had.

He glanced down at her again, yet made no aggressive motion or sound. Perhaps he was curious to see her in a tree, the way she eased herself so gingerly upward. He turned back to grab more of whatever he was eating. She could hear his lips making the rubbery slaps of a horse mouthing grass. Below him like this, it was obvious he was more than three times her size. The furry span of his rump eclipsed much of the sky.

If she did bring back the vine, it was possible she would have leverage. She could try demanding Roswell keep paying the park guards. She could work with the Rwandan government to manage the influx of people harvesting the plant. She could attempt to set some rules up.

In any case, the harvesting wouldn't continue more than a year or two. Probably.

Pulling herself up to within six feet now, she kept her weight back a bit, ready to retreat if needed. He turned toward her. She glanced. He was pursing his lips as though considering the situation. Some type of foliose lichen hung from his mouth, long strands of it, hairy and fine.

It would be easy for the chemist who analyzed this plant to have misidentified it as a vine. Not a true plant at all, lichen was a symbiosis of both fungus and algae, capable of surviving everything from extreme drought to life in the Arctic. Some specimens lived for hundreds of years in areas where no conventional plant could last an hour. Lichens were ancient and canny, could definitely have evolved a chemical that strongly affected the heart.

Four feet up and to her right, a clump of the same lichen was growing in a big pad of moss, and she reached for it. Slowly, slowly. So close to Titus—her body stretching forward into his shadow, not even a branch between them. Her hands sweaty. She could feel him watching her intently, lips still pursed, making no sound but that of his breathing. She tugged a chunk of lichen off and, in an effort to reassure him, stuffed some of it into her mouth.

Busy doing that, her left foot slipped.

For a long moment, her body twisted, her balance off, her damp fingers scrambling, unable to hold.

She began to slide.

A hand clamped down on her arm, the fingers iron strong.

Her dislocated arm. Her weight jerked the shoulder clear out of the socket again.

The pain exploded, all encompassing, a bright light in a new room she'd entered. High in the tree, she swung in his grip, bumping twice against the trunk, her breath loud as a furnace. Her tendons creaking.

In this drama, she thought, *I am not playing the role of the good guy.*

His nails up close were not animal claws at all but flat nails, with a pale rim that looked almost manicured. The width of his grip covered her forearm.

Roswell, she remembered, had never even shaken her hand.

Belatedly, she kicked her feet about for purchase, her other hand grabbed a branch. When she was standing again, Titus let go. Her arm flopped down against her side. The imprint of his five fingers remained on her skin, her arm changed.

She flash-glanced at Titus's face. His startling dark eyes, thin-lipped surprise at his own action.

Turning politely away, without any other method of communicating her thanks, she nodded once, a short but serious motion. Then, double-checking her traction at every step, one arm slack at her side, she climbed down. The pain was strobing in the periphery of her vision. She breathed through her teeth and worked on not fainting before she got out of the tree.

"What the hell were you doing?" whispered Yoko as she reached the ground. "Fuck. Your arm again? How'd you do that? Mutara is *not* going to be happy."

Max sat down fast on the ground, leaning back against the trunk. "I'b god it," she mumbled around the lichen in her mouth. She tried to muster up some sense of giddy discovery. She didn't look at Rafiki or Asante. She didn't glance up to where Titus sat in the tree still eating, blissfully unaware his life had changed. She didn't look at any of the gorillas she was betraying.

Her trembling hands pulled the lichen out, held it up and she said more clearly, "I've got the plant I came here for." On the ground, she had no desire—and no words with which—to describe the moment hanging from his hand.

A laugh burst out of Yoko. "Are you kidding?" Her laugh was close to a cough, involuntary, no enjoyment in it. "That's not it. You think we could let it be that easy?"

Looking at the lichen, Max understood afresh how badly suited she was to her own species.

An askari tried to shake Jeremy awake in the predawn dusk. At first he thought the rough handling was the lions mauling him. Still, he tried to sleep on, so exhausted. When he finally sat up, his face felt slack as dough and a pulsing headache made him touch his fingers to his forehead. Dehydration, he thought, happened quickly here.

"Pukka sahib, hurry," said the askari. "They pulled down a tent. The lions. Come, come. Men are inside."

Barefoot in his bathrobe, Jeremy started running, chasing the askari between the tents. His head throbbed with each jolt of his wounded feet on the path.

From a distance the tent looked like a crumpled jacket tossed on the ground. Sprinting closer he saw the gaping rips in the fabric, the feeble movements of the men underneath, wrapped in ropes and bloody canvas. In the dirt, leading away from the tent, was the bloody trail of something dragged toward the wall of the boma. The lions were gone.

"Why has no one helped these men?" yelled Jeremy. "Get Dr. Thornton, get help."

"He is here," said the askari quietly and Jeremy turned around to see Alan standing a few feet back, fully dressed and methodically packing tobacco into his pipe with the ball of his thumb.

Alan said, "I assumed you would like to see the unaltered clues." The distance in his watery eyes could be disturbing.

Later, the survivors told their story. An hour before dawn,

a lion jumped onto the roof of the tent. The tent collapsed onto the sleeping men, ropes and tent poles falling. The Indians thrashed blindly around beneath the heavy canvas, seeking a way out. The lions, being cats, attacked the muffled movements, biting and clawing. The resulting screams made all the men flail harder while the snarling lions hopped from one squirming bump to another.

It took perhaps five minutes before they had sliced a hole in the canvas large enough for them to drag one of the victims away. Seven men were left behind, severely mauled.

After the survivors' stories, Jeremy summoned up an image of his Grandpapi, the way he would talk, chin jutting forward, eyes stern. Jeremy addressed the men in a carefully deep voice, ordering the bomas be thickened yet again.

Several nearby Indians turned to look at him, their faces expressionless.

After breakfast, a hundred men filed out to cut down more thorn trees for the walls. Guarded by askaris with guns, the men were divided into three different crews: one to cut the trees down, another to chop the branches off, and the last to drag the branches back to camp. Every chance the different crews got—waiting for another tree to fall or a fresh pile of branches to be cut—they squatted on their heels in the shade and stared at the ground.

Singh stood with his perfect posture beside Jeremy, his silk vest neatly buttoned in this heat.

"Singh," he asked. "Do the men seem to be working slowly today?"

"Sahib?"

"The men, Singh. It seems to me they are working slower than a few days ago. Do they not seek to make the camp safer?"

Singh's eyes moved to the work crew, then back to Jeremy. A moment passed. His irises were such a dark brown they seemed black, designed for protection against the equatorial sun. It was at this point that Jeremy wondered if eye coloration could create subtle differences in vision. Perhaps his own pale eyes had to close down so much in this blinding light that they missed out on details the Indians could easily see. And maybe, in anything close to shade or darkness, Singh's eyes were not able to discern subtleties that jumped out to Jeremy. Perhaps during the dazzling day gazing at the stacks of railroad ties left to be laid, and during the dark night examining the jungle surrounding them, and at any time in between looking at the differences in hue between Singh's and Jeremy's skin, their two sets of eyes beheld completely different worlds.

The man replied. "They are dispirited."

"In what way?"

"The lions, sahib. No matter what the askaris do, no matter how tall the bomas are, no matter how many trees you hunt from, the lions still get into the camp and kill."

"They do have damnable luck."

"That is just it, sahib. Some of the men believe the creatures have more than luck."

"What do you mean?"

A nyika tree shrieked and fell crashing to the ground. The coolies stared at it for a moment before a jemadar yelled at them to chop it up. Several walked slowly over.

"Some of the men," Singh said, "believe the lions are not strictly lions. These men believe no matter what we do, each night the beings will appear to take their victim, seeking to kill all those connected with the railroad."

"Many of the men down there," Singh continued, "the only thing they spend energy on now is prayer. Praying to be spared, or at least to be at peace with their God when it happens."

Walking down the lane between the tents, Jeremy spotted an African boy with an Indian worker. This boy was perhaps seventeen and slender as a woman, dressed in a cobalt blue shirt and calf-tight Indian leggings. None of the men looked twice at the coolie and the boy walking hand in hand. Instead, they turned toward Jeremy, at his expression as he stopped dead, staring.

He made himself shut his mouth and walk on, tried to piece his normal expression back together. These days, people figured him out faster than when he was younger. His tendencies must be more transparent, betraying themselves though his gaze, through his gestures.

As recently as seven years ago, his mother had hoped his friendship with Sarah Madison might turn out to be more than it was. Of the women who used to come calling occasionally in hopes of bumping into him, Sarah was not from the wealthiest or most respected family, but she was clearly the only one he willingly took on walks. She was unfashionably wide in the waist, and he felt a sympathy for her labored breath in the cinched-tight corset, as well as for the way her eyes jumped about from some inner shame that was about more than just the width of her middle. In the interest of good manners, he never inquired into the origins of this shame. For a while he tried to believe they might marry their awkwardnesses together, decrease the pain of it all through a public pretense at pairing.

In the end, though, he had decided his mother would never be fooled. She had such sharp eyes and a clenched mouth. Since his father had left, she had always been tight as a post with vigilance. Before she entered a room, the noise of her bereavement preceded her, the black crepe rustling around her, the clinking of her jet beads. Her clothing was made of a matte darkness like the pure absence of light.

In spite of her public mourning, he knew hidden away in her desk lay the letters his father sent each year for Christmas from a different area of the world. Jeremy had discovered them when he was twelve and missing the concept of a father deeply. Each time she left the house for town or to visit a neighbor, he would systematically search her room for clues about his father until he had found this correspondence, bound unceremoniously in white twine. In three short minutes he had read through all seven of the missives, each of which contained only a few chatty sentences. The contents were what you might send a family friend or elderly neighbor, concerning the weather or a play just seen, hopes for good health to all. No word of a possible return, no address to reach him, no mention of money enclosed.

Sometimes from the tightness of her jaw and the look she turned on Jeremy—the only male of his father's issue—he thought the many years of her mourning were more than a deliberate pretense about his father's fate.

Directed at his father, it was a deep wish that the pretense come violently true.

At lunch, as the WaKikiyu woman bent over to put down the gazelle chops and potatoes, Jeremy blinked. With her face turned away like this, for a moment there was a resemblance to Otombe, her slender brown body, her goat-skin robe and sinewy arms. Jeremy was beginning to see him everywhere, walking away around the corner of a tent wearing a turban or glimpsed in the posture of an askari at the edge of camp scanning the forest all around.

Pouring water into his glass, she caught him staring at her. Like Singh, her eyes were a dark brown.

"Excuse me, what is your name?" he inquired.

Her expression assessed him, warily. She responded with a phrase that had several *t*'s in it.

"Can you say again?" he asked and she repeated the phrase. Her name, he wondered, or was she announcing she could not understand him? She straightened up slowly, to her full height. Like so many of them, she had admirable posture, as though she were wearing a corset and had been trained in the finest of schools.

He said, "How about the name Sarah then?"

She nodded, perhaps understanding or maybe simply wanting an end to the exchange. There was the chance the nod did not signify "yes." The Indians, he had found, signaled "yes" with a diagonal waggle of the head (to him the gesture looked more like confusion, or the way a dog angled its head from side to side to focus on a tidbit of food held in the hand).

When she walked away, her shaved scalp shone in the sun around the tiny patch of hair at the back of her skull, like a handle to hold her with.

While he stood by the new canal, overseeing the digging men, a lone coolie came running from the station, the tail of his oversized Indian shirt flapping behind him. Collapsing at Jeremy's feet, it took him half a minute before he was able to speak around his ragged breathing.

"Lions at the station. Three men trapped within. No gun."

If anything, Jeremy was irritated. This was the fifth time this had happened. The men were so spooked, they made the glimpse of the tiny back of a dik-dik into a sleeping lion, or the foraging head of a gnu fifty yards away into a near-death stalking. Each incident meant he had to waste time checking out the possibility. He had tried to persuade them the lions were primarily nocturnal, that during daylight hours they were almost certainly safe. Most of the men wouldn't look him in the eye while he made these statements.

This Indian, trembling from his run, flat out refused to accompany him back to the station. Thus, Jeremy paced out the half mile on his own, carrying his rifle under his arm, thinking about how best to word his letter to Preston about the setbacks in schedule. In this heat, Jeremy could not sprint madly about, especially not the way he felt today, clammy and overheated, a tight pain pulsing in his temples. Maybe the lack of sleep was getting to him, his body having a harder time coping with its combined stresses. All day, no matter how much he drank, he had felt parched.

Thus he walked on, the rifle's safety on, his head down, until at a turn in the road, no more than a hundred yards from the station, he came upon a large pile of droppings, fresh enough that only one dung beetle had discovered it. Passing by, Jeremy surveyed it with mild interest. If it were from an oryx or bongo, he should tell Thornton, who had yet to pot one of these on his hunts. Then he noticed the dark clump of fabric sticking out, a fragment of someone's clothing.

A distinct lion print no more than a pace away.

For a single moment, he paused in his walk, one foot still dangling forward, while his eyes slid over the bushes on both sides of the road. He forced himself to walk on, trying to look natural while being silent, pulling the rifle up to the level of his chest, cradling it in both hands as he eased the safety back. His breathing so scratchy and loud.

Circling cautiously round the bend in the road, he could see the station now, the window on this side unbroken, the nearby embankment empty. As he moved up the gentle rise, an Indian's face appeared in the window. Behind the glass, his mouth began soundlessly to shout.

"Where," Jeremy silently mouthed back, "Where?" His eyes ran along the brush all around, the leaves glittering in the sun. No wind, nothing moved. A drop of sweat rolled into his eye, making him blink. In this instant, he found what he desired most was a glass of cool water. For once, he was not thinking of how his Grandpapi would handle the situation.

Now all three men stood in the window, pointing to the left side of the station, far left corner. Their arms jabbed wildly, their mouths yelling. Flee that way, he wondered, or was that where the danger lay? There was a high ringing in his ears. Standing here, scenting the wind like an animal, he realized what Africa smelled like to him: wood smoke and raw onions, human sweat and the Indians' curries, the sun-baked earth and creosote from the railway sleepers. Such a wonderfully smelly place, he thought.

In his mind, he pictured the topology of the land around the left corner of the station. The railroad tracks ran parallel to the building, both the tracks and the station elevated on their barren manmade embankment, a few water barrels under the eaves, the forest fifty feet beyond. He prayed no spare sleepers had been offloaded from the last train, casually piled about to give the animals cover.

Readjusting his hold on the rifle, he used his shoulder to wipe his cheek free of sweat as he began to pace to the left, slowly circling the station, keeping thirty feet out from the wall. How fast could a lion charge? Would he have time to get off one shot? From the corner of his eye, he tried to suss out from the men's expressions if he were taking the correct action. Their gestures got more vehement, less clear. One man kept pointing up at the roof, another curled his fingers like claws by his face.

In this moment, easing forward, eyeing the corner, he felt so vividly the sensations of his body. The shirt rasping across his chest with each motion of his arms, the pain of the worm cuts jabbing his feet, his ribs rising and falling in the continuing work of his breath. He realized his body, which he had always disliked, was doing all it could, as well as it could. He felt terribly alive, sensitive to the slightest sensation.

He stepped around the corner. The red dust of the ground lay bare in all directions. No sleepers, no lions. He looked up on the roof. The only signs left anywhere were their prints on the ground and the sharp stink of cat piss.

He sat down hard in the dirt, his hands slack on the rifle. That high whine in his ears. Behind him the door opened and the Indians came piling out, calling out their gratitude for scaring the beasts away.

For the rest of that day he felt flushed and overly aware of his body, its discomforts and wants. Just before sunset, standing waist deep in the river, watching Otombe scoop water up and across his gleaming chest, Jeremy felt the heat in his head like a pressure. He took a half-step toward Otombe, almost reached out to touch him, even with the two askaris watching. Then stopped.

Glancing down at his own body through the distortion of the dark water, it no longer appeared gawky and reprehensible. Perhaps it had a purpose.

He touched his fevered brow. In the cool of the river, he was still sweaty. He had never been this sleep-deprived, this thirsty, this hot.

He had never felt so at home in a land or with another person.

Otombe turned into his stare. He must have sensed by now the difference between Jeremy and other men. Still he did not move away or cover his body up. He returned his gaze levelly.

Jeremy stared, his mouth open. This tension could not last.

That afternoon, Otombe had found the satchel again along the empty riverbed, this time in a spot closer to camp. As the sun descended, he and Jeremy climbed up a ladder into a tree about sixty feet from the satchel. Before they were even settled, the askaris below were hurrying back to camp with the ladder, casting fearful looks all about. Every day, Jeremy found the coolies were a little more terrified and less obedient. Occasionally he caught them staring at him, their dark eyes filled with thoughts he could not read.

He believed one day soon they would stampede en masse to a departing train to climb on, clinging to its side and roof, fleeing this murderous river and area. After that, the building of the railroad would cease. The rails would be left just as they were, the project abandoned, the army ants and termites gradually chewing through the ties, the embankments caving in one by one.

If the railroad project were stopped, what would he feel? Failure, regret? Relief?

Up in the tree, hammering the bottom board of the seat into place, he searched for conversation, nervous about the long night alone with Otombe. "You mentioned before your younger brother was killed by the lions. May I inquire how it happened?"

Otombe kept his head down for a moment, while he held his side of the board. "He was ten summers old."

"If you wish, please continue." Jeremy passed him the hammer.

"The lions had killed twice, perhaps twelve miles away. We were not scared yet, not careful. That night my brother stepped out of his hut to make water. Our mother slept inside. She was awoken by his body hitting the hut. She heard the lion roaring, Ituma's struggle. She had three other children with her, could not open the door to fight for him." Otombe stood there for a moment looking toward the sun, then bent down to hammer the board into place.

At that moment the sun dipped below the horizon and from the point where it had been, a momentary green flash lit the trees. Alan had described to Jeremy these tropical sunset flashes: some strange artifact of refraction and humidity.

"He is not the only child of my tribe to die." Otombe turned to face him, his gaze intent. Was he focused on Jeremy or on the memory of his brother?

"I would die to kill these lions." Otombe said this not as an empty turn of phrase, but as a simple statement of fact. "It is dark now. No more talking."

Jeremy took his seat beside Otombe, allowing himself to sit closer than he ever had before. Quickly he found himself beginning to tremble with what he labeled at first as excitement. Then the shivering got worse, every muscle in his body vibrating with an electric ferocity. Only once his teeth began to chatter did he understand he was medically ill. Hunched over, he clenched his teeth into silence, wrapped his fingers tight round the edge of the seat and settled down to wait out the attack. In the darkness, there was no safe way back to the camp and the doctor, to his quinine.

Otombe touched his shoulder lightly to ascertain the source of the vibration, then reached down to undo Jeremy's belt. Staring at his dark fingers tugging the leather out of the first few loops, Jeremy was unable to piece together the entirety of his emotion. Then Otombe fastened the end of the belt round the board of their seatback, making sure during the night Jeremy would not fall from the tree in his delirium.

Exhaling, Jeremy closed his eyes and leaned back. A headache began to press itself into his temples, as sharp as fangs.

To the east, the first lion roared.

Rubbing his temples as best he could with his trembling fingers, he forced his thoughts away from Otombe, and to the animals instead. It was not the sheer number of people the lions killed that produced the men's terror of them. The mosquitoes killed more, as did the parasites in the river's water. However, no one screamed at the sight of a mosquito or at a glass of water, for neither type of bug sought human flesh in particular. Dying that way seemed more like pure chance, as impersonal as getting struck by lightning.

But, with the lions, what elicited the men's terror was the predators' intelligence and free will. From near the quarry, he heard a raspy grunt. This lion, able to manage the complex strategy of stalking prey in coordination with another, surely had the capacity to think ahead to the likely result of the hunt. At the moment, having just awoken, smacking his jowls sleepily, the creature was probably considering what he wanted to eat tonight (a gazelle, a wildebeest, a person), considering his options the way a child standing at an ice cream counter might pick a flavor. Then, rising to his feet, he sauntered toward the railroad camp.

And later tonight, once the lions had stalked and caught a human, their prey would shriek, through sheer volume struggling to explain how much more important he was than the taste of his flesh.

In response, one of the lions would kick out his bowels.

Jeremy's teeth were now distinctly chattering no matter how hard he attempted to clench them together. With his knife, Otombe cut off a bit of his own robe and gently pushed the piece between Jeremy's lips, using it as a cushion to silence the chattering. He closed his eyes and let his mouth fill with the flavor of goatskin, fire, crushed grass, fresh earth, and sweat. He sucked on the leather, tasting Otombe's skin.

In the night's slow wait that followed, he felt the fevered distortion of time. It seemed he had been perched precariously up here above the half-completed canal for several months, near the chewed-up satchel, craving sleep, waiting for the lions to show themselves. He felt he had been born sitting near Otombe.

The lions stopped roaring. He nodded off into the new silence, his shivering worse, his teeth vibrating against the goatskin. In the distance the men's voices in camp called out from boma to boma, warning each other. He saw his mother pacing slowly round the house in her nightgown, checking all the locks as she did every night, the metal snick of each bolt sliding home. Outside, the snow fell lazily, the bright twinkle of stars in a cold winter sky. In the barn, his Grandpapi eased his large hand between a birthing cow's legs, his head resting companionably on her rump, eyes closed and the steam of his breath rising. He tugged the calf's thin fetlocks partway out, holding them together in his hand like some type of mucus-covered bouquet.

Trembling with exhaustion and cold, Jeremy lay back on his narrow bed in Grandpapi's house, tugging his childhood duvet up to his shoulders. Abruptly, the canvas of a tent slapped down across his face. He stiffened in the utter darkness, the weight of poles and ropes across his limbs, knowing his only hope lay in staying completely still. In the room next to him, he heard his sister cry out and beat at the canvas, then the hard *thwap* of the lion's pounce and her scream. Before she had stopped moaning, the lion paused, then stepped through the doorway. Jeremy felt a heavy paw tread on his leg. Breathing against the canvas, he tried so hard to quell his shivers. Still, the lion's claws begin to tighten into the meat of his leg, the animal's weight shifting forward as he lowered his giant head.

As the lion closed his teeth around Jeremy's skull, the animal transformed into the three African women who had stared at him in the forest. They were pressing the points of their machetes slowly into his temples.

His mother in the hall screaming.

Gasping, he forced open his eyes, blinking around at the night. The moon was full, a pale orb starting to set. The silhouettes of bats swooped through the night sky. The screams came from camp half a mile away, rifles shooting wildly. Beside him, Otombe sat still as a statue, no emotion visible.

After the camp's uproar faded, Otombe shifted in his seat for a more comfortable position, readying himself for sleep now that the lions had completed their hunt. Exhausted, Jeremy leaned his head back against a tree branch.

He had just begun to drift off when he became aware of a distant rustling. Whatever was moving, shoved its way through the bushes near the half-dug canal, breaking branches and crunching through the undergrowth. He and Otombe sat up. Something heavy dragging and bumping along the earth, coming closer.

The dragging stopped on the other side of a giant baobab tree fifty feet away. The first growl rumbled out, low and raspy.

And then every noise rang clear in the silence. The lap-ping and chewing, the crunching and wet smacks. The occasional thud of a limb dropped or the snap of a tendon. The animals purred under their breath as content as two housecats at their meal.

Horrified, Jeremy took Otombe's hand. He cared not a whit anymore about respectability. He clung to the hand as hard as a child to his father's, a man to his lover's, a boy to his mother. He rubbed his fingers over the back of the hand, the palm, the soft skin between the fingers. He moved over it knuckle by knuckle like a rosary for at least a full minute listening to the lions eat, until he realized in all that time Otombe had not tried to wrest his hand away, nor let his fingers go limp in silent protest. Instead, Otombe held him firmly back.

For a single instant, Jeremy believed it possible that from his sickness not just evil could come.

And drunk from elation, feverish from malaria, jumpy with fatigue, he jerked his rifle to his shoulder and shot in the general direction of the baobab tree without a chance of hitting the lions, simply unwilling to listen to those grisly noises for a moment longer.

Even as the rifle jerked with the shot, he realized what he had done. In the terrible silence following, as clearly as if he could see it, he felt the two lions raise their bloody mouths, lifting their yellow gaze toward the sound, their cat eyes cutting easily through the darkness until they spotted him and Otombe in the tree.

From now on the lions would know how to find them.

C hristmas had never been a day Max cared much about, but that morning, before she started climbing up with Yoko and Mutara, she gathered a gift for the gorillas. She harvested a large bunch of baby bamboo shoots, a tender treat the gorillas loved that was hard to find higher up on the mountains. She tied the bunch together with the cobalt silk ribbon she'd had since she was a child. Whenever she was anxious she used to rub the ribbon between her fingers, its softness and color so calming. The last few years she hadn't needed the ribbon that much. Perhaps they would enjoy it.

The bamboo bundle barely fit in her knapsack. Hefting the bag up, she used only her right arm. Even though Mutara had popped her left shoulder back in its socket again, the whole joint was swollen to twice its size and the throbbing of blood through the area was so insistent she hadn't been able to swallow any food this morning.

This relentless distraction irritated her, getting in the way of how she functioned. She alternated ibuprofen and aspirin every other hour and worked to focus elsewhere.

She pulled the knapsack onto her good shoulder, tying the other strap tightly across her waist to hold the bag somewhat in place and set off after Yoko and Mutara. Although it wasn't easy to hike with this weight balanced only on one side, she managed to climb the whole way to the gorillas without falling.

There, she knucklewalked gradually in among the family,

placed the bundle of bamboo on the ground and backed off a few yards to watch.

Rafiki was the first to wander over to it, followed by Asante and the others. They all crowded around to consider the food, their heads tilted. None of them tried to grab the whole bundle and run.

Titus reached out and, with two fingers, delicately tugged a single shoot from the bunch.

His teeth made a crisp crunch biting into the bamboo. Several of the others grunted, low in their throats.

Still they each waited for a turn to pull out a shoot and gravely bite into the food.

With them all crowded together like this, Max was struck by the sheer size of them, a bunch of linebackers, a wall of vast shoulders and backs. Or perhaps, given their gentle nature, more like cows crowded round a trough. For a moment she saw them the way people at the base of this mountain might (starving on their tiny farms, their children screaming for food). Titus's body alone would feed a village for a week.

Uncle, the second silverback, was the one to pick up the ribbon, while the others chewed through the bamboo. He sniffed the material, then rubbed the smooth silk between his calloused fingertips. Startled at the sensation, he cocked his head for a moment before he raised it to his face to brush across his eyelids, where the skin was most tender.

Asante grabbed the ribbon from him and ran with it through the jungle, waving it as a blue trail through the air. Another juvenile chased her, and for twenty minutes they played furiously as puppies until it caught on a thorn five feet up and tore, hanging there sad and ripped.

The family sat around and watched the ribbon—a bit like a TV—as it swayed and twisted in the wind, while they chewed on the last of the bamboo.

Scratching under his chin, Titus eyed the ground around him for any last bits of food. "Ra-ooom," he grunt-chanted, low in his gut.

One by one, they answered, purring their contentment back. "Ra-ooom," "Ra-ooom." Grave jungle souls.

During the gorillas' siesta, the humans retreated as usual two hundred feet downhill, to give them some peace. Lying down on a thick bed of ferns, Max fell asleep for a few minutes, worn out from the pain in her shoulder.

When she woke, the sun had appeared from behind the clouds. The last two weeks on these mountains, she'd been surprised by how much the light could change along the jungle floor. At times it was as gloomy as a basement, at other points it gleamed otherworldly with mist. Sometimes it dazzled the eyes, as brazen as a spotlight.

Right now, a thick beam of dusty light poured down through a hole in the canopy. In the brightness of this luminance, everything shone as though lit from within, the stained-glass of the flickering leaves, the brilliant red of a parrot flying by, the hewed columns of the giant trunks. The cathedral of the trees. This must be where humans came up with the architecture of churches—the vaulted spaces and filtered light imprinted in the genes as the original holy place.

By now climbing these mountains had become as natural to her as climbing stairs. The jungle comfortable. The plants, the smells. The gorillas.

Her good hand was resting against her sling, touching her forearm where Titus had held her. When she noticed, she pulled her hand away.

Late that afternoon, they hurried down from the mountains to listen to the BBC broadcast, wanting to hear about the downed UN flight. In Pip's cabin, huddled around the hand-cranked radio, they ate their soup while the announcers discussed the exploits of Manchester United and then the recent downturn of the Venezuelan economy. Max ate tofu out of its aseptic container and the others chewed mechanically through their potato soup. The soup was what they ate now three times a day, all the other food consumed. Their diet as repetitive as an aspie's.

She accepted by this point that the other four knew where the vine was and weren't telling her, even though that meant keeping her here in danger. She didn't blame them, because she figured she was doing the same thing—choosing to keep herself in danger. And their motivation was more pure, had nothing to do with their careers, or even their species. It would be hypocritical to feel anger.

In the last week, they'd begun to ask her opinion on different aspects of the gorillas. Dubois had asked her if she thought any of the females might be pregnant—were any of them eating or acting differently? Yoko wanted to know if they might be using some of the plants they consumed to remove intestinal parasites: maybe through a bioactive ingredient or simply from the exfoliating property of the nettles passing through the intestines. They listened to her observations carefully and posed follow-up questions. Only afterward did she marvel at the fact that she was being asked to interpret the actions of others.

Halfway through BBC news hour, the announcers hadn't mentioned the Kutu and their hostages. Perhaps discussion of them had been eased out by that morning's suicide bombing in the Middle East.

Then the announcer said, "And now to Julian Turner in the Democratic Republic of Congo where a United Nations airplane full of peacekeepers was shot from the sky two days ago by a surface-to-air missile. Julian, any word on the survivors?"

"Why, yes, Robin. Yesterday morning, a rebel group, the

Kutu, claimed responsibility for the downing of the flight, saying they now had possession of both the airplane and the twenty-four soldiers."

"Twenty-four? Weren't there more?"

"Yes, evidently eighteen died in the crash. The Kutu say they have the surviving twenty-four and will trade them for concessions of territory from the UN. Then, just an hour ago, François Kutu, the militia's leader who the group was named after, announced the UN wasn't acting quickly enough so he'd had three of the soldiers killed and eaten."

"I'm sorry," said Robin. "Can you say again?"

"Mr. Kutu claimed three of the soldiers have been killed and, although neither fact can be verified at this point, he maintained his army had consumed the remains."

"Oh." Such a crisp British "Oh." "Is this common?"

"It's unclear. These so-called 'Brides of Affonso' have been rumored to engage in some fairly brutal incidences, including unconfirmed reports of cannibalism. It does seem fairly certain they've killed most Caucasians they come upon, as well as any Africans who disobey them."

"And the captured soldiers? What is their racial makeup?"

"Of the original forty-two soldiers, twenty-nine are from Belgium and thirteen from Nigeria. We don't know how many of each group survived the landing."

"Exactly how many Kutu are there?"

"Between ten and twenty thousand. Mr. Kutu's promise to bring back the ancient glory of the Kingdom of the Kongo, as well as rid it of all Caucasians, is a powerful one in this region. He has been winning many converts and forcibly enlisting more at gunpoint."

"Any guesses, Julian, as to what the UN's reaction will be?"

"Their lead negotiators are talking to Mr. Kutu. No one's making any statements yet. We'll just have to wait and see."

"Well, thank you, Julian. Let's keep our fingers crossed for the remaining soldiers. And now to a report on the homeless in Devon."

The four women sat there in silence, no one looking at each other. Pip turned down the radio. Somewhere on the meadow outside, a forest buffalo moaned.

"OK, OK. Let me think," Dubois said, scrubbing back her hair with both hands. "I must go to town and talk with our embassies and the government. Find out the news. The timing is good, no? We need more fuel and food. I take with me Max and Mutara. We leave tomorrow as soon as there is light."

Mutara nodded, but Max stared down at the table, confused.

"But . . . we don't have to worry that much, right?" she asked. "The Kutu are still more than a day's travel from here. They're busy with the soldiers."

"We are six kilometers from the Congo, in a famous research station known to be full of whites, in a country that is hated by everyone in the Congo. The Kutu are being crazy now. We need to tell again the government we are here, that the gorillas are here." The tone of Dubois' voice suggested she believed she was being comforting. "That way, if the situation goes bad, they rescue us."

"What about the gorillas?" Max asked.

For a moment there was silence.

"Hey, they survived the last war," said Yoko in a forced cheerful voice.

"Why do you want me along?" Max asked.

Dubois said, "Because I need help to bring fuel and food up the mountain and your work is not so important."

"Not so important? The plant I'm searching for could save thousands of—" The tension of the last few days was audible in Max's voice. "You know my mother always warned me about people who had tendencies toward racism, but you, you're something more. You're a . . . " She searched for the right word and in the end had to coin one, "gorilla-ist."

For a moment none of them moved.

Then Dubois spoke, surprised. "*Oui,* I am a gorilla-ist." She sounded proud as a child.

A noise came from Yoko's direction. Max flash-glanced to see her pressing her fingers into the bridge of her nose. Her face was clenched, her shoulders hunched.

"You OK?" asked Dubois.

Yoko's attempts to muffle her laugh sounded a bit as if she were blowing her nose. She waved her hand in front of her face, trying to direct their attention away. "I just . . . I got this image of you in a white hooded sheet." Laughter can be so close to crying. "Burning giant *g*'s in the lawns of humans."

"*Pardon?*"

Yoko sighed, and as fast as that, the laughter was gone. "Forget it."

Dubois looked around at all of them. Taking her time. When she spoke again her voice was gentle. "Look, all of us worry. *C'est normal.* We need a change. I turn on the generator. Tonight, let us put on the lights, talk and think of nice things. It is Christmas after all."

"Nice things?" asked Yoko.

"I have two bottles of wine I save for my birthday, but now is better. We drink them. Tomorrow we get fuel and life is more easy."

"What kind of wine?" asked Pip.

"Sancerre."

"Oh lovely."

"We can turn on the lights?" said Yoko.

"Yes."

Yoko inhaled then said, "I'll get some music."

And the party was on. With the generator humming again in the background, they turned on every light in the cabin, even the ones in the bathroom when no one was in there. Yoko offered up her last Toblerone bar. They each ate their piece of chocolate with great happiness except for Max, who simply sniffed hers, deep whuffling inhales, her eyes closed, and then she passed it back. Yoko, watching, said she thought Max had enjoyed her sniffs more than any of them had enjoyed the actual eating.

They played music—Etta James, the Gipsy Kings, and Midnight Oil. Mutara, surprisingly, turned out to know all the words to "Bem Bem Maria." The volume of the music drowned out the noise of the animal calls outside.

Sometime around 11 P.M., the generator coughed once, then worked for three more minutes. It coughed again and died. The music went, the lights clicked off. They stumbled around in the dark room until they found their flashlights, bid each other goodnight and walked back to their own cabins to sleep. Although the party had seemed a good idea, now the silence and darkness seemed much deeper than before.

It was certainly easier going down the mountains than climbing up. Max strode quickly, moving with what was for her a fair amount of agility. Dubois and Mutara followed behind. She wanted to get to town to hear the news firsthand. She wanted to be further from the Congo for a few hours.

As she descended, the air got thicker. The increasing amount of oxygen filled her veins, making her feel strong as a super-hero and a little giddy. After a while she was nearly running. The vegetation around her changed with the decreasing altitude: the trees getting taller, the variety of plants increasing, the bamboo stands becoming thicker. Down here, she noticed more of the plants that the gorillas preferred to eat: *Vernonia*, *Galium*, wild celery, and blackberries. This altitude was probably the gorillas' natural habitat, but now it was too close to humans.

After an hour, she turned a corner and came upon the lot where the research station's van was parked. The asphalt took her by surprise. After over two weeks in the jungle, the perfect flatness of its surface looked unnatural, the lack of vegetation bizarre. Stepping out from under the trees, she felt exposed. Her eyes blinked in the sun. She had assumed near civilization she would feel safer.

Two steps onto the pavement she spotted a parked jeep with a three-foot-long gun mounted where its back seats should be. She backed up quickly into the jungle. Only once she was behind a bush did she stop and examine the jeep as well as search the surroundings for its owners. The rifle gleamed, large and metal, some sort of submachine gun.

There were no soldiers in sight, only two Rwandan women and their children squatting on their heels on the far side of the parking lot, bags of food and clothing stacked up all around. The women and children stared straight at her. From the fact that they didn't call out any greeting, it was clear even the children recognized her as a foreigner. Her lighter skin, her fancy knapsack, her gray athletic clothing.

Dubois and Mutara stepped off the trail onto the tarmac beside her to stop dead at the sight of the jeep. Dubois muttered, "*Pourquoi êtes-vous ici?*"

Mutara called over in Kinyarwanda to the women squatting on the embankment. They responded, their language filled with consonants in unexpected places. Meanwhile Dubois walked around the jeep, keeping a few feet back as though it might jump at her if she got too close.

Glancing again at the Rwandan women, Max wondered why it was she'd never understood her dad's genetics were not purely African. In Maine, his skin had always appeared so very dark.

After a few minutes of talking with Mutara, one of the women eased her hand into a baby-sling wrapped around her chest. She adjusted the baby inside, then she and the others began to get to their feet, gathering the bags.

Mutara turned back to Dubois and Max. "These are women from up the road. They think it is good we move our van. The soldiers who were here before say the army will take over the parking lot later today."

"Because of the Kutu?" Dubois asked.

"This is what they say."

With the women standing now, it was possible to see that both of them had several chickens hanging down their backs. The chickens were alive and surprisingly calm, dangling by their feet from a rope, wings slack. They snaked their heads from side to the side, their lizard eyes blinking.

Mutara called goodbye to the women, then said, "They leave the area. One of their sisters lives fifteen kilometers from here. They think with God's will, after things quiet down, they get their home back."

"Aren't they overreacting?" Max asked.

Dubois shrugged. "Radio Sidewalk. Who knows what they hear?"

Silently, they watched the family walk away, down the road, away from the border, all of them barefoot. The chickens swayed back and forth, limp and clucking. A three-year-old lagged after the rest of her family, dragging a rope bag full of potatoes. Her wails were heard long after they rounded the corner in the road.

Driving in the van down into town, Dubois, Mutara, and Max were silent. Twice they saw an army jeep rush by, filled with men and weapons. Both times, they turned to watch the other vehicle as it drove up the road.

On the outskirts of town, Dubois pulled the van over in front of a large white church. "OK, both of you get out. I drive to the town hall to talk to the officials. I use the phone. Try to hear the news." She paused while another army jeep roared by. "Here is some cash. You and Mutara find food that is fresh, candles and lots of fuel. Buy all you can. Do not approach the soldiers, no? Meet me in front of this church at noon."

She drove off in the van, the rattle of its broken muffler audible for a long time.

Max looked around at the buildings, the sharp angles and flat surfaces so alien from the jungle. The part of her mind that constantly monitored proximity began to tighten up again, even now, with no humans visible other than Mutara. Following him down the street, she noticed the town seemed strangely deserted, of both people and vehicles. After a few minutes, two cars drove past them and squealed off around the corner, both full of soldiers. The first car was an aging Volkswagen with its front bumper held on with rope and the second was a Citroën hand-painted a Day-Glo orange. The Citroën's missing head-light had been replaced by a lamp glued onto the hood (a porcelain woman proudly thrusting her bare light bulb aloft). The soldiers inside were packed together. They sat on each other's laps, rifles up, faces set, looking even more dangerous somehow in this undignified condition.

She repeatedly flash-glanced at Mutara for how to respond to all of this. At first, he seemed bewildered. He kept search-ing up and down the street as though expecting hidden town-folk to come running out at any moment, laughing at their elaborate joke. After a few minutes his reaction began to shift. He started walking faster. When a goat bolted out of an alley next to them, he jerked back. Max felt increasingly uneasy.

After fifteen minutes of searching, Mutara and Max found only one person, an old man carrying something small in a bag that squirmed and cried—it didn't sound like a chicken. Mutara questioned him. The old man's replies were terse and he never stopped walking. From the tone of Mutara's voice as he asked follow-up questions, Max didn't think he liked the information he was getting. She eyed the wiggling bag. The old man disappeared around the corner, calling some answer over his shoulder. Mutara scanned the street for more people. Then he announced he and Max should split up.

"You search for food," he said. "You find a market, you point at what you want and pull out money. People understand. I find friends, learn what is happening and get fuel. We need to go fast-fast. We meet at the church. OK?"

She didn't like this, but figured he knew how to manage this situation better than she did. He handed her some of Dubois's money and jogged away around a corner. Wandering on alone, she continued to find street after street deserted. She looked behind her frequently. Finally she turned down a wider boulevard and found a small crowd bargaining over a few fruits and cans displayed on blankets on the ground. She walked over, for once happy to be among humans. They glanced at her, but seemed too intent on their own business to be very curious. She pointed to some mangos and pulled out a single bill. The money was a bright red color and said 1000. It caught the eye of the woman selling the fruit. Max made a scooping motion as though to take all the mangos, then held out the bill. The woman snorted through her nose. She pointed to the money, held up three fingers, then pointed to a single mango. Max didn't know the exchange rate or how much the day's emergency might have driven up the prices. She didn't know if the woman might be trying to hoodwink a foreigner. She remembered that moment with Rafiki, holding the *benutis* plant against her chin. She trusted that communication more.

In the end, Max managed to buy five pounds of mangoes and twenty cans of something she hoped was edible because on the label was a picture of what looked like soup steaming in a bowl. Even though this wasn't half as much food as the station needed, it was most of the food in the market and she was inordinately proud at having completed the transaction. She packed the cans awkwardly away in her knapsack and the seller handed her the mangoes in two tired-looking plastic Home Depot bags. How, Max wondered, had these bags ended up in Rwanda?

After this, she headed back toward the church. Everywhere, the streets were empty. Turning a corner she came upon a pack of wild dogs quartering the ground, sniffing for scraps. Their hides were laced with old scars, their stride effortless and feral. They came to a halt at the sight of her, heads cocked, considering the possibilities. Her right hand holding the bags, she eased her left arm out of its sling to pick up a nearby stick. She hadn't tried to use her arm since Titus had caught her in the tree. Her shoulder still looked all wrong—pudgy and reddened—no longer clearly identifiable as a shoulder. She felt pity for it as though for some broken machinery.

In forcing her fingers to tighten around the stick, the pain didn't bother her as much as the fact that her mouth began to salivate. There was a chance she would vomit. Her throat worked up and down, fighting the need. Slowly she eased forward, moving past the dogs. Their heads turned to track her. The only sound was the rustling of her plastic bags and their panting. She held the stick up in a way she hoped looked determined. Some decision passed through them. They turned as one, like a school of fish, and arced away down an alley.

After they were gone, she put the stick and the bags down and, using her other hand, eased her arm gently back into its sling.

Everywhere were signs that people had recently been here. Clothes flapped on laundry lines above the street. A bucket lay tipped over, the earth beneath it damp. By this point, she glanced down each street before crossing it—searching for townspeople, dogs, or Kutu, she wasn't sure. In a doorway, she noticed a child's toy, a foot-long racing car ingeniously modeled from a single long piece of copper wire, the number 52 traced on the hood, the metal tires made from beer cans. Clearly a labor of love, it lay on its side, abandoned.

Staring at this toy, she understood how far she'd traveled from any situation she had experience with. Glancing all around, she began to stride fast in the direction of the meeting spot.

As she turned a corner, she came upon Mutara stepping out of a door.

He flinched at her arrival, his motions stiff. He didn't say a word. It seemed likely he'd heard some news about why most of the townspeople were gone. Standing alone on this empty street, his hands limp at his side, he looked younger than before, perhaps only early twenties. Maybe he normally seemed older because of his serious voice and the confidence he showed in the jungle. During the genocide he must have been just a child.

Searching for some way to break the stillness, she held out her Home Depot bags. Worried he might bolt at any loud noise, she whispered. "Hey, look what I got."

She could feel his eyes on her. He stared for a long moment at this American holding up mangoes for appreciation on a dirt street from which all the residents had fled.

"Christ," he murmured. He looked up and down the street. "Maybe the *féticheuse* helps you." He jerked into action, leading the way, his steps a little uneven. Perhaps his awkward walk came from the shock of whatever he'd learned or maybe he'd taken a drink to bolster his nerve.

He turned down an alleyway no wider than his shoulders. Following, Max had to twist sideways to squeeze past some stacked jerricans.

She asked, "What's a *féticheuse*?"

Mutara struggled for a translation. "She has much power, might help keep you safe. Come, fast fast. We don't meet Dubois for twenty minutes. It is better you are off the street."

The door consisted of a gray plastic tarp hung across an entrance. It crinkled noisily as Mutara pushed it out of the way. Inside, the room was dark, no windows, no lights. Blinking, she halted. Something dripped; there was the smell of rotting meat and, behind that, the musk of drying plants. By scent she recognized tobacco leaves, mint, datura, and what she thought might be belladonna. She sucked in these smells. At least here was something she understood.

In the muted light of the tarp, a yellow ruffled dress rustled toward them, the only thing gleaming in the room. For one terrifying moment she thought "Kutu," then saw instead this was an old woman, canted to one side by age.

The *féticheuse* stepped in nearer to Max than any American would. Unnerved by the proximity, Max glanced at her while starting to back up. The woman's eyes were smoky blue with cataracts. In the light through the tarp, they gleamed like cloudy marbles. Max could stare right into them, her nerves jangling no more than when she looked at an elbow. She stopped, fascinated.

"Ask her where the townspeople went," Max whispered, glancing over her shoulder for Mutara.

It took her a moment to spot him, standing motionless in a dark corner by the door. "Shh," he said.

The woman's eyes were pointed off to the side, looking nowhere, her head cocked. She seemed to be listening to Max even though Max wasn't speaking. She seemed to be listening to something quite complex. Her concentration was somehow familiar, the depth of her stillness.

The woman inhaled and placed her hand on Max's face, covering her eyes. Waiting. The feel of a calloused palm.

And Max stayed still for this. The *féticheuse* didn't move her hand—the touch as calm as her dad's.

Or maybe the gorillas were changing Max.

When Max opened her eyes, the woman had moved away. She asked Mutara a question and he answered, the *click-clack* of those consonants. Nodding, the woman took a rolled-up leather mat from a plastic bag and knelt painfully down to unwind it.

Whatever was inside the mat, the old woman scooped into her hands to shake like dice and then drop. White toothpicks scattered across the leather. Max leaned closer, saw these were some type of bones. Behind her, the kerosene fridge grumbled.

A fortune-teller, she understood. Her eyes were adjusting to the light. The hacked-off leg of an animal hung from the wall dripping blood into a bucket. Clusters of drying leaves and roots dangled from nails in the ceiling. A basin of laundry sat on the beaten earth floor. Several bags lay scattered around, half packed with food and clothes.

The *féticheuse* patted the bones with her fingertips, so gently not one of them moved. She spoke and Mutara translated. Her eyes pointed off toward the wall, as emotive as knees. "No husband. No father. No children."

Her concentration was complete, her body motionless except for her fingertips, listening to the universe spin. If she wasn't an aspie, she'd somehow earned this stillness.

"Trouble. Death. A body on the ground."

"A human body?" asked Max.

The woman made no response.

Max found herself staring at the *féticheuse*'s dress, ruffled and frivolous as a Barbie's. Because of her tilted body, the low V-neck hung slightly off center, revealing the crease of one withered dug.

Muttering, the woman pushed herself laboriously up onto her feet. Whatever she was saying Mutara didn't translate. She tugged part of a root off a plant on the ceiling, three leaves off another, pulled an item out of a box, pushed everything she gathered into a tiny purse. It was clear she was in a hurry.

Some part of Max's mind automatically noted that none of these plants was a vine.

The woman pressed into Max's hand the purse, the neck knotted. The bag was made of fur. Distantly she wondered what kind of animal it came from. The woman's fingers were leathery and thick.

The *féticheuse* spoke in that beaten language. Behind her, hiding in the shadows, Mutara translated. "You find soon what you seek. Then you must decide what to do." In the dark, his voice became the woman's echo, became her voice. "Keep this with you. Perhaps it can help."

The woman's pupils glimmered, cloudy, massively enlarged in an attempt to adjust to the permanent darkness of her cataracts. "You have strength," she spoke through Mutara's soft voice. "Use it." The hacked-off leg dripped, the fridge gleamed with moisture. Underneath the table something rustled around on a chain.

"What's in here?" Max whispered. "What's this thing supposed to do?"

"It has power," the *féticheuse* said. "It helps you. Do not look." Losing interest, she waved them away, no payment requested. She went back to packing, an old woman putting her life away in plastic shopping bags, waiting for what would come.

S tepping out of his tent in the morning after a desperately deep two-hour nap, Jeremy's foot stumbled over something soft and feathery. Looking down, he discovered discarded on the dirt the body of a headless chicken. He stared at it for a moment without comprehension, his face as heavy as a wet blanket, before he noticed blood had been splashed in lacy fountains across the door of his tent. The chicken had been beheaded right here, the body aimed like a champagne bottle with the cork removed. He focused on the lack of the head, as though finding it would explain the existence of the body and blood. Circling the tent, he kicked through the nearby grass, but was unable to locate the head anywhere.

In his tent, in the depths of his sleep, he had heard nothing. He wondered if the Africans had done this in a protest against the railroad? Or was it the Indians, angered that he had not killed the lions yet? Or was it Alan?

Deep in his chest, the shivers commenced once again. His fingers, he noted, had blood upon them from undoing the buttons of the tent flaps, his flesh stained and sticky. Each time the malaria hit, the chills jarred him afresh. His vision blurred, while all the sounds and smells around him swelled, washing over him in waves. Each sensation struck him as vividly as though he had been born new to this world. In the distance a hammer clanged and he closed his eyes, the noise lingering like metal in his mouth. *Hammer*, he thought, marveling at the concept.

The sensory wealth of this colony, all these laboring unwashed men, all these uncovered latrines and burning corpses. The yells of many languages, the ululating call to prayer, and the clanks of tools and machinery.

The blood shone so red across the white of the tent; the liquid had not had time to dry. In the doorway of the cooking tent, he spotted Sarah watching him. She was standing the way Otombe did when he waited, like a heron on one leg, the other foot pressed against the side of the standing leg. She regarded him without expression.

Spooked, he backed slowly away.

Jeremy oversaw the men as they dug out more of the canal, shoveling the dirt into large baskets. As soon as each basket was full, it was hefted up onto a worker's head. The Indian, balancing the basket, would pace regally up the side of the canal to toss the dirt onto the top of the bank. They only had a few more feet to dig before they would open a channel to the old river, the water beginning to pour for the first time into this detour. The river would rise smoothly to fill the gulley between these new banks, churning red-brown and muddied. At that point, Jeremy thought, he would feel as though he were making real progress. The water would wash away the lions' pugmarks, removing their favored play area. And perhaps the satchel lay somewhere along its length, ready to be washed away, rolled along in the muddied water toward the sea, its curse rinsed like a stain from this area.

Within a day of the river starting to flow down this new branch, the workers should have the original branch dammed up. After that, they could start digging the feet of the bridge into the newly dry riverbed. Under such conditions, they could complete the bridge with relative dispatch, then redirect the water flow back into its original bed and leave this accursed area far behind.

Above, the clouds hung thick and waiting, a grayish-yellow,

the air motionless before the storm. It was possible the upcoming downpour might collapse part of the canal's sides. Turning his head to survey these clouds, Jeremy spotted Otombe picking his way down the banks toward him. He twisted quickly away. He believed Otombe would be disgusted with him for his behavior last night, for holding his hand, as well as for discharging his rifle at the lions, letting them know that they were being hunted and in what manner. With the workers, he bellowed out in a loud voice, clearly an important man with responsibilities. Only after a full minute did he casually glance behind him and blink, as though startled to see the hunter.

Otombe inclined his head in greeting. "I wish to find the satchel again. We need to learn more about the lions. We need to create a new way to hunt them. It will be more dangerous today, for they know now we seek them. Do you wish to come?"

He found no censure in Otombe's expression, no anger or disgust in his tone or attitude. This lack surprised him at a fundamental level.

"Yes," Jeremy said, "yes."

He signaled to Singh to take over the management of the Indians for him, then he and Otombe set out. Once they had scrambled up the riverbank and started into the nyika, Otombe moved more slowly than usual. He made no noise, his concentration focused on the brush around them. This felt different from the walks they had taken previously. For Jeremy, the shift in mood seemed sudden, moving from the clamor of men yelling and shovels clanking to this silent attentive stalk through the jungle. He felt instead as though he were the primitive in a situation of unspeakable complexity. Leaves rustled, birds called, grass swayed. He had no knowledge of where to look, what sounds to listen to, how to scan for danger. Much of his attention was simply taken up with navigating his large leather-bound feet through the undergrowth in relative silence. At work as an engineer, he could let his attention stray for minutes at a time without any toll being taken. Here, that same laziness could potentially cost Otombe and him their lives.

He held his rifle across his chest, at the ready. The birds seemed quieter than normal, perhaps because of the impending storm, the sky looming above so dark. From the tension of this walk, he broke into a slow malarial sweat, the heat prickling along the base of his hair and beading up on his face. To maintain a tight grip on his rifle, he kept wiping his palms off on the sides of his shorts.

After half a mile, they stepped into a small clearing along the top of the canal's bank and Otombe stopped without warning, so Jeremy bumped right into his back. Alarmed by the hunter's attitude, Jeremy followed his gaze to see the satchel on the canal bed below them. Even from a hundred feet, it was easy to spot. The neat man-made square of it, the leather dark against the red dirt. Deep pugmarks everywhere around.

Only then did the smell rise to his nose—faint but distinct—of cat pee and rotting meat.

The lions were nearby.

The men stood there, utterly still. Around them the birds continued to call lazily, the wind to blow. Pressed up against Otombe's back, a significant section of Jeremy's vision was taken up by the curve of the man's ear, the wiry ends of his hair. Through his chest, he could feel the heat of his body and the silent swell of each breath. A drop of sweat ran into the corner of Jeremy's eye, making him blink from the sting.

They stood there, feeling the continuing beat of their hearts, as close as scared children.

And the rain began, drops falling large as grapes. The loud patter everywhere around them, a resonant roar on the canopy above. Jeremy was instantly soaked, his hair hanging forward into his eyes. Objects more than thirty feet away began to gray out in the downpour.

Otombe started swiveling his head, so slowly it was hard to see the actual movement. The only way to tell he was moving was that, over time, more of his cheek became visible. His skin looked darker in the rain, black as a stone, smooth as a carving. His gaze was unfocused, trying to catch movement anywhere around them. Delicately scenting the air, his nostrils widened for the dissipating smell of lion. Perhaps, disliking rain like all cats, the creatures had headed for cover moments before the men entered the clearing. Or maybe the rain was merely flattening their scent, obscuring their nearby presence.

Jeremy eased one foot backward, hoping there was no stick behind him ready to break. He did not bother to watch around them, staring only at Otombe's face for clues as to where the danger might lie. There was the slightest crackle of a leaf beneath his leather sole. Before taking a second step, he wiggled his other foot out of its shoe. His sock-encased toes were able to feel about more delicately for twigs or leaves and thus able to shift his weight more quietly. He slid out of his other shoe. Otombe backed up after him, step by step. Five feet, ten, fifteen. The satchel eased out of sight, the clearing disappearing from view. Otombe turned slightly sideways as he moved down the path, watching behind him as much as he did ahead.

Jeremy imagined, after the storm had passed, the lions yawning and stretching, stepping out from the tree they had taken refuge under, hunching down to shake themselves dry, jowls flapping, their joints as loose as any dog's. Then they narrowed their eyes and ambled forward with curiosity to his abandoned shoes, lowering their massive heads, nostrils widening over the wet leather. Learning about him and his acrid fear, what he had for breakfast, and the particular scent of his shaving lotion, memorizing his smell so as to be able to track him down.

As the two men got further from the clearing, Otombe did not lead them straight back to camp through the nyika, but took a roundabout route. After fifteen minutes, the rain stopped and they reached the edge of the savannah, began pushing through the long grass. The soles of Jeremy's feet began to ache from the lengthy walk in wet socks. It felt like the wounds from the worms' eggs might have opened up. Perhaps he was bleeding. Still, Otombe kept extending their walk through the savannah; much of the time he paced backwards in order to watch the grass behind them.

"What are you looking for?" Jeremy asked in a normal tone of voice.

Otombe whispered, "If the lions follow, their path will be marked by moving grass. Look for breaks in the normal pattern."

Jeremy had assumed any danger of the lions was long gone. Startled, he glanced back over the grass. After the rain, uneven gusts of wind fingered it in different directions. The whole plain moved and shivered unpredictably.

A bird about a hundred feet back called out a warning and flew straight up. Otombe's face became so concentrated he looked like a stranger. The men continued to ease themselves silently backward, Jeremy watching the sea of grass with all the care he was capable of.

An object to their right banged straight up.

Both men jerked around to see a gazelle hanging in the air, looking around for the humans it had scented. All around them now, gazelles spronged upward out of the grass, living popcorn, legs ramrod straight beneath, their tails swishing behind their tight white buttocks. Moving so quietly, the men had snuck into a herd of Thomson's gazelles, the tall grass hiding the animals from the humans and visa versa.

My God, were the only words in Jeremy's head. His gratitude so intense to be here, in Africa.

The gazelles bounded away in the direction the men had come from, their bodies arcing over the top of the grass like dolphins over the sea. Otombe began to relax. He kept an eye on the area where the herd had disappeared. "If the lions come this way," he whispered, "the gazelles will jump again. Will give us warning."

In this hour after the rain, the air was slack and clean. From a termite mound nearby, hundreds of newly hatched insects launched themselves into the air, their shiny carapaces catching the light. Some landed on the men, their arms and faces. Jeremy stared at the translucent wings sparkling in Otombe's hair. He looked down at his own arms covered with faceted insects, vibrating from the effort of their transformation.

Half a mile later, three Africans stood up out of the grass, nodding solemnly in greeting. Their hair was shaved short; thick necklaces hung upon their bony chests. The rest of their bodies were obscured by the thick grass.

"*Jambo*," Otombe called.

"*Jambo, rafiki*," they responded.

Otombe conversed with them for a moment in Swahili. Jeremy caught the word, "*Simba*." They turned to examine the direction Otombe and he had just come from. Their eyes lay sunken in the narrow bones of their faces.

Bidding goodbye, Otombe walked on, saying to Jeremy. "These are WaJamousi. They asked if you are hunting."

The men watched them go; Jeremy felt the power of their stares. There was no animal in sight to shoot to give them food. He fingered his rifle and raised the palm of one hand in farewell as he followed Otombe. "How many people do they hunt for?"

"Their whole village. Africans share their food."

"Even if they catch but a dik-dik?"

"Yes."

To distract himself from their plight, he asked Otombe the first questions he could think of. "Are famines like this common? How do the people survive?"

"Many are not surviving."

"But famines must have occurred in the past."

Otombe nodded.

Jeremy pressed his point. "How did they survive before?"

"This famine is worse than most. Also, it is possible in the past the tribes used to be different."

"Different how?"

"In the time of my grandfather's grandfather, the stories say, some tribes nearby had silversmiths, stone buildings, something you might call a postal system. In case of famine, my grandfather says, the people in neighboring areas helped each other survive."

The man glanced back over his shoulder. To look at the WaJamousi or check for lions, Jeremy did not know. "And then came guns. Any tribe without guns fell to the first army that had some, whether it was European or African. The way to get guns was to trade slaves for them. Slaves were the only money the whites would accept. Many kings started wars with their neighbors to capture people and trade them for guns."

"The more wars that were started," Otombe continued, "the more need there was for guns. Many many people were sold. Kingdoms were splintered. Tribes disappeared. Much knowledge was lost. People do not trust each other, do not care for each other the way they used to. There is less law."

"According to the stories," he gestured back in the direction of the WaJamousi, "this is new."

Teatime took place during the height of the day's heat while the Indians napped, dark bodies lying prone in the shade of the tents.

Jeremy turned around from his desk to watch Sarah set out the tea. From behind, she was so thin she almost appeared to be a boy. As she straightened up, he noted the silver bangles on her biceps. They glinted in the sun, catching the light as she walked away. He was still watching when she looked over her shoulder and caught his stare. She paused for a moment, neither smiled nor looked away, then stooped into the cooking tent.

Waiting for Alan before he started the tea, Jeremy began to shiver, his teeth chattering, his vision trembling. Even in this temperature, he found it necessary to wrap two blankets around himself. When Alan still had not appeared after a few minutes, he began to gulp down the hot tea in hopes it would warm him up.

Yesterday at dawn, when Alan had done nothing at first for the mauled men lying under the slashed tent, Jeremy had spoken strongly to him. He stated that Alan should help these men. When Alan continued to stand still, startled by the harshness of the words, Jeremy had responded by bellowing, loud enough to make all the nearby Indians turn around, regardless of whether or not they understood English.

"You are a goddamn physician." The curse kicked out of his mouth, satisfying in its hard anger.

Alan had paused before stepping toward the wounded men. Yelling at him was bad enough, but doing it in front of the coolies compounded the insult. His eyes had been slightly hooded, glittering.

Since yesterday, Jeremy felt he could not show weakness of any type around Alan. Thus far, his malaria seemed remained relatively mild. He was still able to talk, to walk around. He knew the majority of the Indians who contracted the disease lived. His chances, he assumed, were better than most from the quality of the food he ate and the quinine he took. As a precautionary measure, he began doubling his daily dosage. He did not know if there was any level at which the medicine became toxic.

Taking a night off to sleep from hunting the lions, even when this ill, was unthinkable. He could not let Otombe face the creatures alone. All day, he kept remembering the quiet way in which Otombe had said he would die to kill them.

When he was back overseeing the work in the canal, Jeremy

held himself rigidly straight in front of his men, trying to quell his shivering. What he wanted above all was to see this canal completed, these last ten feet dug, the muddy water spilling along this detour, destroying the lions' favored playground.

The men seemed to feel none of his urgency. They dug leisurely, long pauses stretching out between each rasp of a shovel into the earth. Each man waited a moment before hefting up his full basket of dirt, moving just fast enough to not attract a jemadar's wrath. Like Jeremy, the men must not have slept well since the night the lions took that first victim. They moved so slowly as to appear to be sleepwalking.

After an hour of work, with only two feet of progress made, Jeremy lost his temper.

"Move men, move," he yelled. They turned to him, surprised, unused to this tone from him.

He searched for the right words. "Do you not understand? The faster we complete this bridge, the sooner we are away from these foul lions?" His voice spiraled louder with each word, audibly trembling from the shivering in his chest. "The quicker we work, the sooner we are away from this river's malaria." Listening to the volume of his voice, its vehemence, he seemed to float a little above himself. He could see his body swaying on its feet, red in the face. In this heat, people with his skin coloration did not look their best. "The faster you build this, the more of you will live." His neck swelled with his words, spit flew from his lips. "So work, damn you, work."

The men's dusky faces were closed. Some of them did not understand English. Singh, standing beside him, stared, not translating.

Exhausted, he plopped down into his canvas chair, blinking up at the sky. After the storm this afternoon, it had turned a delft blue. He made himself inhale deeply while he watched the lilting path of a swallow chasing insects overhead. With every day that the lions slowed the coolies in their work, the railroad's final bill mounted higher. The British Parliament had already vigorously debated whether they needed this colony at all, much less this expensive railroad which ran straight to a lake hundreds of miles from the nearest European settlement. If the lions stalled the railroad's progress long enough, the price tag might grow so large Parliament would order a halt to the work.

Jeremy found this thought was not entirely unappealing. Yes, it would mean his job here would terminate early and the railroad that he had worked to build would end up helping no one. However, on the other hand, without the railroad, this land would stay a little longer the way it was. This red dust, the leaping gazelles, these nearly naked people. Otombe's tribe. He had not forgotten the manner in which some of his neighbors in Maine had regarded him. Once this railroad was built and more settlers arrived, he could well imagine how Otombe would be treated.

Of course modern life must come to this area at some point. But perhaps if this railroad were not built, if this land were not transformed now, during these years of Europe's scramble for African territory, then at whatever point the change did happen, in a decade or two, it might be managed in a slightly different manner.

He was lying back in the chair now, shivering, phrases rolling through his head, *overseeing my men, seeing over my men*. Opening his eyes for a second, he saw Singh watching him. Jeremy tried to smile back. Only after he closed his eyes, did he realize Singh was not smiling.

That night sitting in a tree again above the satchel—the goats below chained up to several railway sleepers, their tentative *maa-maas* echoing through the forest—sweat began to bead up on Jeremy's face. Otombe had not yet thought of a new way to hunt the lions, one the beasts would not expect. The only idea Jeremy could come up with was to release the goats and chain themselves up instead. The smell of two humans seemed much more certain to attract the lions. Even feverish, he knew enough not to suggest this idea.

Tonight was New Year's Eve. Back in Bangor, his family would be having a dinner party to celebrate the turning of the century and all they believed the next hundred years would bring: modern technology sweeping poverty away around the globe, the regular use of soap even by the lower classes, the spread of the Christian faith, and a modest style of dress to all swarthy peoples. Even his Grandpapi must be staying up late to raise a glass of port to the glories of the future.

At some point, delirious, Jeremy began to mumble to himself and felt Otombe clasp his hand across his mouth. He quieted under the hand, reached up to trace each of the fingers. He was getting sicker, his temperature fluctuations more intense, the times between the deliriums shorter.

He had begun to notice that even when he faced away from Otombe, or, like now, when he closed his eyes, he could sense the precise shape of the space between them like an object. He knew the distance from his shoulder to Otombe's, from his face to the other's, the gap between their hips. Through this new sixth sense, he knew how the hunter was sitting, down to how his left hand lay on his knee with the thumb slightly bent. Still holding the man's palm over his mouth, eyes closed, touching the streamlined beauty of his hand, the heat of the fever swelled in his chest and somehow he understood the encounter with the lions would come within a few days.

He could almost see the beasts, too, with all they now knew of him, their giant heads lowered, tracking through the grass the familiar scent of his trail, moving silently through the underbrush until they could raise their yellow eyes toward his tree, pricking their ears forward intently. Soon they would meet.

Then, either the lions or he and Otombe would die.

Either way, the end of his hunting with Otombe would come, their connection and mission, their time together at night. As it was now, their differences were what brought them together in this tree—Otombe's knowledge and Jeremy's rifle.

If the lions were the ones to die, then afterward a certain awkwardness would result. No longer would there exist a clear subject to discuss or tasks to accomplish. Greeting one another, after the first few sentences, the silence would swell. Their differences would seem more apparent, the disparity in culture, wealth, and expectations. Confusion filling them, each would shift his gaze away.

And in any case, with the lions dead, the railway bridge would soon be built, the construction of the tracks moving on again, past the river, a half-mile further each day. Jeremy would surge ahead with the railroad, tightening its hold across the land, leaving Otombe and his tribe behind.

Startled, Jeremy let the man's hand fall.

In the first light of dawn, after an eventless night, the two men slithered down the tree, the cloth of Jeremy's pants rasping loudly against the bark. The sun was starting to peek through the nyika, the birds chattering. Jumping to the ground, Otombe paused to stretch out after the night's cramped waiting. Jeremy half-stumbled as he landed, but straightening up, he watched Otombe. His arms reaching up, spine arching, his head rolling back. The skin tightened across his neck and, for a moment, the beat of his jugular was apparent. Mesmerized, Jeremy took a half step forward, perhaps to trace this delicate pulse with one finger, perhaps to pull this man's whole body against his chest. If he did not arrive at some sort of new understanding with Otombe within the next few days, he would lose him.

But even as his weight shifted forward toward the hunter,

he imagined what the crack of Otombe's fist would feel like against his jaw, the punch so hard his head would twist and his body follow, the slow-motion stumble and fall, his face bouncing in the dust.

Mid-step, Jeremy stopped. Loneliness did not frighten him; he had borne it one way or another for most of his life, but if Otombe's gentle eyes regarded him with disgust, if he hit him . . .

The engineer stood there, frozen.

When it came to this area of his life, he was used to surviving on so much less than he desired. Thus, in this moment, unsure of what to do, the question he asked himself was not what he wanted. The question he asked was what he required for survival.

And the answer appeared to him so quickly it was as though it had been prepared long ago, only waiting for him to ask. He thought the minimum he needed was to hold on to his memories of the past few days: walking with Otombe through the nyika, the nights in the trees, bathing in the river naked, all the while feeling himself understood and accepted. In many ways this was more than he had ever believed he could possess. As mechanically as though he were turning the crank to shift the weight on some vast fulcrum, he forced himself to twist his face away, to turn from the man who was just easing out of his stretch.

Thus, Jeremy was the first to spot the pugmarks. The prints pressed deeply into the mud beside a puddle, six feet from the tree. The wide pads of each paw, the crisp indents of the claws. Looking around, he found the prints everywhere. The lions had not touched the goats, but spent their night quartering the ground around the tree, staring hungrily upward.

Otombe followed his stare. For the first time, Jeremy saw his expression fill with something he would call fear.

A s Dubois drove the van into the parking lot, they saw it was now full of the army. Jeeps and trucks and cars were parked everywhere; soldiers leaned against the doors, smoking cigarettes. There seemed to be no uniform. Instead there was a hodgepodge of jogging pants, T-shirts, and sneakers mixed with a scattering of as much camouflage as could be afforded. Mounted on the back of many of the jeeps and trucks were large guns. The sheer number and size of these riveted Max's attention. Before today she'd never seen any gun bigger than a policeman's neatly sheathed handgun.

On the drive here, Dubois had told Max the news she'd learned, that yesterday an American spy plane had flown over the known Kutu encampment. Beamed back to Washington, the aerial photos had shown an empty clearing, no people visible, only the cindery remains of three large bonfires.

The Kutu were on the move.

In the parking lot, two soldiers signaled to Mutara to stop the van. One walked around to lean in the driver's window, examining the passengers. He spoke a fast command.

"We get out of the car," said Mutara. "The army takes it."

"Tell him we are from the research station," said Dubois. "They do not take it."

Mutara paused for a moment, looking at Dubois, before he turned to the soldier and translated the statement. The man didn't bother to reply. He simply nodded and the soldier on the other side of the van clicked back the safety on his rifle.

The three of them piled out of the van with laudable efficiency.

As Max stepped from the vehicle with her bags of food, she realized she was losing the van's ability to speed her away from here, away from this situation. Everything around her clicked into sharper focus. The guns, the soldiers, the jungle behind. Up until now, this region had been one she simply voyaged through, surprised at its conditions, while her mental viewpoint remained anchored in Bangor. Standing on the asphalt now, her perspective shifted dramatically. This country became her country in the critical terms that this was the place in which her body currently resided, her particular pocket of flesh sucking in its measure of air.

While one soldier rummaged through the van searching for anything of use, the other told Mutara if they wanted to dispute the loss of the van, they should talk to the Colonel over by the yellow Honda.

The Colonel was speaking on a cell phone in Kinyarwanda. He was easy to pick, out for he wore a real uniform. He had only one hand, his right arm ending in a beige nub where the wrist would normally be.

Max wondered how many more right hands were missing in this country than in the States. She imagined Rafiki and him meeting each other, reaching forward to clasp invisible right hands together in a hearty handshake—sharing so much.

When the Colonel hung up, Mutara addressed him in Kinyarwanda, his voice clear but respectful.

The man paused, probably while he examined them, then replied, "I grew up in Uganda. You can speak English."

"Sir, we are researchers from the Karisoke Station." Dubois said, "Your soldiers take our van. I ask you to give it back." "Mandative" was the word that came to Max. It was clear Dubois had dealt with government officials before.

"We require its services for now."

Dubois took half a step forward as she pressed their case. "Perhaps you appreciate to know your Minister of Environment is my employer. If you like, I ask him to call you." She sounded collected and confident. Max's eyes drifted over to the nearest jeep and the three-foot-long gun mounted in the back. She stuffed her hands in her pockets and worked on not rocking back and forth.

His voice tightened at her persistence. "It's possible you haven't heard the latest news. A convoy of several hundred jeeps has been reported headed in this direction from Rutshuru."

Max glanced at Dubois to see how to take this. Her expression revealed no emotion, but her eyes moved fast to look up at the mountains.

"So far this story comes only through secondhand accounts," said the Colonel. "I have also heard stories of trucks heading away from us toward Kinshasa. I've even had an eyewitness describe a hijacked plane leaving for Florida." A soldier appeared and saluted, awaiting his attention. The colonel held up one finger to the man to wait. He was working hard to be patient with them. "What am I to believe? Perhaps none of these rumors are true. Or maybe, as we speak, all twenty thousand of them are hiking up the other side of these mountains."

At this image, Max's fingers clenched and touched something hairy in her pocket. Already on edge, she jerked her hand out in a big motion as though she'd been burned. Then remembered the *féticheuse's* pouch. Everyone, including the waiting soldier, turned to stare at her. "Fuckity fucking fuck," she said, flapping her hand.

There was a pause while they absorbed that.

Dubois spoke first, "Some researchers are still at the station up there." She motioned toward the mountains.

The Colonel said, "Use my cell phone. Get them down now." There were two soldiers lined up now, awaiting his attention. A third was striding briskly toward them.

"The phone up there is not working. We no longer have electricity. Listen, you keep the van. In exchange, you give us twenty men to protect us. We go up to bring the others down." Dubois spoke quickly, bargaining for all she could get. "Also, when we get back, you transport us away from here."

The Colonel paused, probably he was staring at her. "Perhaps you haven't noticed, but I don't have a lot of men here." He gestured with the nub of his arm around at the soldiers. They seemed to number in the hundreds rather than thousands. "We do not have people to spare."

"I call our embassies," said Dubois.

"Good. Have them send a car and get you out of my way."

"Sir," said Mutara. "If researchers die up there, it makes trouble for Rwanda. Maybe we get four men. We are off the mountains by nine in the morning."

His torso turned toward Mutara, considering.

"Remember," Mutara said, "that journalist during the genocide, how angry the Americans get?"

The Colonel was silent for a moment. "Two men. Be off the mountains by seven."

As they turned to go, he held up the nub of his wrist. Maybe he had a clear image of the motion he was making with his missing hand. In his mind he might have been holding his hand up in a policeman's gesture to stop, or pointing his index finger authoritatively at the mountains. Or perhaps his palm was simply cupped, to catch whatever fate was thrown their way. "Understand. I cannot begin to guarantee your safety."

Within five minutes, the two soldiers were ready, and Dubois stood at the base of the path with them, tightening her backpack. She seemed to feel no doubt about this mission, and assumed Max would come along. Max watched her, unable to decide. She imagined the first Kutu just reaching the top of the mountains, peering down toward the clearing where the research station lay. She did not want in any way to climb these mountains. If Dubois, Mutara, and these boys went, was her presence really necessary?

The soldiers the Colonel had lent them were definitely not his most valuable men. They looked no older than fourteen. The oversized rifles and ammunition seemed unfair burdens on their gangly frames. The officer who had brought them over talked to them first in a loud voice, pointing up at the mountains and then at their chests, jabbing his fingertip into their sternums. Although Max couldn't understand what he was saying, she did see Mutara's head turn fast toward the boys, startled. In spite of their youth, their breath in the breeze had a rotting scent to it— the breakdown of protein—like someone with a wasting disease or bad dental hygiene. When the older boy responded, his voice sounded like he might cry. The younger one kept his head down, but his voice, when he talked, held no shame in it.

"It is one-thirty," Dubois said over her shoulder to Max. "If we climb to the station in three hours, we can descend before dark." In French, she repeated her statement to the soldiers, then had to say it again slower and with some illustrative pantomiming before they nodded. Their French seemed far from fluent.

Dubois started to climb, leaving Max at the base of the path, frozen with indecision. Then Mutara spoke from behind them. "Dubois."

Turning, they saw him still standing down on the asphalt, his arms at his sides. Dubois came to a halt.

He talked to her, not Max. "You understand. I cannot go with you."

"What?" said Max.

"Oh," said Dubois. "Your family. You must care for them. Get them away from here?"

He nodded.

"Family?" asked Max.

Dubois ignored whatever fear she might have held for herself. "I thank you for helping us. For taking the time."

"I am sorry I am not able to do more." His neck turned so his head faced in the direction of the two soldiers then turned back to Dubois. The shadows of the afternoon had already started. His voice when he spoke was not happy. "Climb down tonight. Get off the mountains fast."

Dubois said, "Next time we meet, we have a big meal and tell stories of this day. Good luck to you and your family. For now, let us hurry." She turned and started climbing.

Max forced herself to look into Mutara's face, into his eyes. "Thank you," she said. She noticed for the first time he had a small sty on the bottom of his right eyelid. His jaw was tight with worry.

Holding his gaze, she nodded once as she had with Titus, a short and serious nod.

Then she turned her eyes to Dubois, who was moving upward, low and purposeful, planting each foot firmly and grabbing onto what branches she could. She had her hair pinned up, out of the way for the hike. This hairstyle revealed the back of her neck, the tendons so narrow and exposed. For a moment, Max could picture exactly what the end of a rifle barrel would look like, nestled there between those tendons, aimed at the spinal cord.

The world creaking on its fulcrum.

This tiny woman climbing up, all alone except for two boys.

So Max followed. Not so much a decision as an unavoidable response given the circumstances. Perhaps her lifetime of forcing herself to do things she didn't want to somehow made this choice easier.

She concentrated on simply moving, finding handholds, and not slipping. She imagined herself running back down this slope at sunset to be driven away from here in a military car— Yoko, Dubois and Pip sitting giggly and exhausted beside her.

When she reached the first turn in the path, she glanced down one last time to the parking lot and the safety of the army. Beyond them, she glimpsed Mutara running along the road toward town, head down and serious.

For a moment, standing there, she could smell again that dank room full of datura and tobacco hung up to dry, could hear the *féticheuse's* voice rumble in her ancient language, "You have strength. Use it." Jerking away from the sight of the road, she continued to climb. At least up here among the trees, she felt less exposed.

Hiking up, they were all a little nervous, but the soldiers seemed the most twitchy. They held their rifles in front of them at the ready, even though that made climbing more difficult, and they jerked toward every loud birdcall, pointing their guns. This slowed their climbing down. Within a few minutes, she caught up with the younger soldier on the trail. Climbing past him, she noticed out of the edge of her eyes a wad of food or tobacco bulging in his cheek. His jaws worked on the wad nervously, his hands tight on his rifle. It was possible these boys had never been in a jungle like this before.

Twenty minutes up the trail, a nearby hyrax screamed, and the younger boy panicked, shot a short round in that direction. The noise was explosively loud in the jungle, the violent chatter of a jackhammer. Where the bullets hit a *Vernonia* tree, wood chips flew out, a canyon created big enough for Max's foot to fit inside. The white center of the trunk was revealed, seeping slow sap.

At the gunfire, the older boy threw himself to the ground, while Dubois and Max, inexperienced with flying bullets, stood there tall as patient targets, gaping shocked at all the damage visible in a being as large and solid as a tree. Max knew she could have chopped at the *Vernonia* with a hatchet for ten minutes before she could create that much damage. Luckily, a tree could survive a wound as deep as this, for its large body was based on the concept of multiple redundancies: many leaves, many roots, many veins filled with sap. Nowhere was there the soft lump of a fragile and irreplaceable organ.

Standing there, her ears echoing with the noise, she knew that her body, on the other hand, was a pulpy bag.

Her eyes turned to the rifle the boy carried. Her wariness of it had intensified exponentially. The other soldier lay on the ground, cradling his hands over his head. She had never imagined she would live—even for a few hours—in this sort of world. She glanced at Dubois, who was gaping at the tree, mouth ajar. Max would have to learn on her own how to navigate this.

Lesson number one, she thought. Next time bullets flew, she'd be the first to throw herself to the ground, hug it for safety. Around guns, she could not afford many lessons.

After Dubois had explained to the boys in French that the sound that had scared them had come from a tiny animal, the group began to climb again. The soldiers tired quickly at this altitude, huffing like Max had her first day up here. Within half an hour, they were stumbling along the trail, heaving for breath and pleading, "*Arrêt, arrêt.*" It was clear at this speed the group wasn't going to reach the research station soon enough to get back down the mountains during daylight.

Half a mile from the station, the women hurried ahead of the soldiers, to warn Pip and Yoko. They got seventy-five feet ahead, then maybe a hundred. The yells from the soldiers got more emphatic. "*Arrêt,*" yelled one of them, "*arrêt.*" Dubois ignored this, but the shrillness caught Max's attention. She was used to judging emotions through the voice. She glanced back. The younger boy was pointing the rifle loosely in their direction. She didn't feel entirely sure he wouldn't use it. She called to Dubois and they waited for the soldiers to catch up. When the boys walked by, their heads were higher. They cradled their rifles in front of them. The power shifted to those who held the guns.

It was almost six-thirty before they reached the research station.

Hiding in the bushes, Dubois and Max looked out across the clearing. All appeared quiet.

"The dark does not matter. We get Pip and Yoko and climb down now," said Dubois. "*Allez on y va.*"

Max nodded in agreement and they sprinted across the clearing, scanning the jungle around them. When they burst into the cabin, Yoko and Pip—soup bowls in front of them—stared at them and then at the two boys with the rifles arriving behind them. Max told them quickly the Kutu were possibly climbing over the mountains at this moment, these were Rwandan soldiers to protect them, and they had to leave the station *now*. Gesturing toward the door to emphasize the urgency, her hand got a little carried away with the gesture and flapped up and down a few times, a childhood habit. She let it. This was not the time to get fussy about details. The two researchers hurried into their boots and jackets, while Dubois grabbed the few handfuls of papers she considered crucial. It was only when they turned to leave that the younger boy stepped deliberately into their way.

During the climb to the station, neither woman had truly considered the boys as individuals, as decision-makers who could impact their future. They had assumed the boys were soldiers under orders, predictable, here to protect them.

Flash-glancing at this scrawny adolescent with his jittery bloodshot eyes, Max realized they'd made a bad mistake.

Standing between them and the door, he shook his head.

"What's his problem?" asked Pip.

Dubois addressed the boy in French and gestured toward the door. The boy looked out the window at the growing dark and shook his head again. "*Animaux dehors*," he said.

"*Mais les Kutus*," responded Dubois and the boys' reactions were strong. It was as though they'd somehow forgotten about the possible appearance of thousands of Kutu soldiers. They swiveled toward the door, holding their rifles at the ready. One moved the wad in his mouth from one side to the other. Unfortunately neither of them seemed any more motivated to venture outside.

"Dubois," said Yoko quietly. "They're chewing qat."

Dubois looked at the boys afresh. "*Non*," she said. "That is qat?"

"I don't know where you rustled up these soldiers, but they're fucking high." Yoko kept her voice calm and smooth, could have been describing what she had for breakfast. "And carrying Kalashnikovs. Let's not scare them anymore than they already are, OK?"

Just as some people had an aptitude for instinctively grasping algebra or how to handle animals, others had an aptitude for dangerous situations. Yoko had comprehended in a minute what Max and Dubois had missed all afternoon.

Whatever happens, Max thought, I'm sticking with Yoko.

"What is it I should do?" asked Dubois.

"Don't make sudden movements or startle them," said Yoko. "Don't talk loud or use an angry voice. Try to persuade them calmly that walking down to town right now would be safe and easy."

"Don't mention the forest buffs," said Pip.

The older boy flinched and Max wondered how close the word, "buff," was to the French and if they'd just scuttled their chance of walking down tonight.

For ten solid minutes, Dubois talked in French, her voice patient and low, her sentences simple and repeated. The other women sat down in the chairs, hands folded in front of them, trying not to move at all. Meanwhile the boys bolted the front door, helped themselves to large bowls of soup and ate hungrily. Finally, tiring of Dubois' voice, the younger boy lazily rested the barrel of his rifle along her sternum. The rifle lay there like a metal finger, pointing upward toward the soft underside of her chin.

In mid-syllable, she stopped talking.

He took his rifle back and returned to his meal, muttering something in French under his breath.

Shakily Dubois lowered herself into the seat next to Yoko. She whispered, "He says we climb down at first light. Their officer tells them if they return without us, they get a beating. The boy says do not worry; they make sure we are OK."

Probably thirteen years old, Max thought. He should be in middle school, playing with video-game guns, not real ones.

"Stay here all night?" said Pip. "No way." And she took two steps toward the door.

The boy machine-gunned the door just in front of her. No one knew if he wanted to scare her by getting that close or if he'd missed by mistake. Either way she stopped, staring at the bullet holes through the wood in front of her belly. In the small cabin, the sound of the gunfire echoed in their ears long after it had stopped.

In this moment, Max understood the Kutu so much better, their preference for children. Until now she'd always assumed a large man holding a gun was one of the scariest things a person could face. Now she realized that a child with his finger on the trigger was much much scarier.

Pip lowered herself into a seat, placed her hands on the table. Her breathing was fast and audible.

Within half an hour, the researchers had settled down for the night, lying on the bed or the floor, wearing all their clothes, ready to leave the moment they were given permission. The two soldiers took shifts during the night, sitting in a chair by the door with a rifle—whether to keep the women in or the Kutu out, Max didn't know.

Max woke, her heart pounding. It was dark enough that the only way she realized it was predawn was by the birds calling. At first she wasn't sure what had woken her. Then she heard it again. From this distance, it sounded like one rock ricocheting against another, a slight echo following.

A gunshot. At least two miles down the mountains. She could hear the change now in the other women's breathing. It had woken them, but they were too scared of the boys to move. Cautiously they peered through the dark to the chair by the door. It took them a moment to be sure neither of the soldiers was in the cabin.

"*Bonjour?*" whispered Dubois. "*Il y a quelqu'un?*"

"They've deserted us," said Pip. "Thank God."

"Must have realized their chances were better without us," said Yoko. "Didn't care as much this morning about their sergeant whipping them."

Now the *pada-pah pada-pah* of assault rifles drifted up the mountain, many firing at the same time. The women crept to the window, peeking over the sill, but could see nothing moving in the swirling mist of the clearing. Yoko eased the door open half an inch. The distant boom and crunch of larger guns reverberated, coming from somewhere down near town.

"Jesus," said Yoko.

"*Les Kutus,*" said Dubois. "We must run."

Max found she was breathing quickly through her mouth, half crouched over as though in some cheap cop movie. This felt unreal. Why exactly was she here in this cabin? A few weeks ago, she'd never even heard of these mountains. Consciously, she made herself step back from the door, lean against a wall and breath deeply. Into her mind floated the smell of her mother's winter coat, the feel of its corduroy trim. Pressed against the wall, she found she was still hyper-aware of the room around her, the sound of artillery. In case of gunfire, she repeated to herself, fall to the ground. Fall to the ground. She wanted to hold her mom's coat in her arms for a few minutes, bury her face in it. Then she'd be able to deal with this so much better.

"The question is where do we run to?" asked Yoko. "It's suicide now to try for town."

Dubois talked fast, her accent worse in the rush. "We make a circle around the guns. Go through the jungle to the road to Karago. We pay money to someone there to drive us to safety."

"You're crazy," said Yoko. Her voice, while still whispering, was harsh. "You've no idea how wide the Kutu are spread out down there or where you might bump into them. Twenty-thousand killers can take up a whole fuckload of space. Even if we got to the road safely, we'd be blinking neon signs saying, 'Foreigners, Eat Me.' Most of the Rwandans around here speak just Kinyarwanda. We wouldn't be able to find out where the danger is or how to stay safe. We'd be helpless."

"What else can we do?"

Yoko stayed still, facing the window. From the length of the pause, it was clear she had no idea.

Dubois continued. "We can't stay here. Everyone knows the station exists and that it has whites in it. They will come."

Max spoke. "The gorillas."

"What?" said Dubois. "No, we must save ourselves before we can help them."

"No, the gorillas can help *us*. We can hide with them."

There was a pause while they absorbed her idea, then Yoko grabbed her by the ears and planted a kiss hard on top of her head. "Fucking brilliant." She remembered whom she was dealing with and let go. "Sorry about that, Tombay."

"Brilliant?" asked Dubois.

Yoko was swiveling already, grabbing a knapsack and stuffing the radio in it. "Look, we carry as much food as possible, enough to last a few weeks, until things quiet down or the UN arrives." She yanked the blankets off Pip's bed and began ramming them into the bag. "With all that firepower, the Kutu aren't hiking over the top of these mountains. They're driving around, along the roads. Sure, a few might climb up to the station to search for us, but there's a hundred and fifty square miles of jungle around. They're not going to check every square foot of it. With the gorillas, we'll be safe from predators. We bring the radio so we'll know when it's OK to climb down." She stepped fast over to the food cupboard.

"Perhaps it is months," said Dubois. "Perhaps years."

Yoko spun, her arms full of sweet potatoes. "Better than strolling down through a jungle full of underfed cannibals." She began funneling the potatoes into her bag.

Dubois said, "Before you say you do not think they eat people."

"I was lying," said Yoko. "Made us all feel better."

The distant pops and explosions drifting up from town were coming faster now, the battle truly engaged. Max stood against the wall. She was rocking back and forth. At the moment, she needed to rock—that was OK—but she worked not to forget herself in the motion, not to lose focus on what was happening.

From Pip's direction came a small but continuous clicking—like a tiny, very fast typewriter—and she turned toward it. Pip's arms were wrapped tight around her ribs. Glancing upward, she saw Pip's teeth chattering, her eyes staring out the window, searching the jungle.

Dubois was only a little better off. She was moving from window to window, watching for soldiers, but not preparing to flee.

Yoko, on the other hand, was filling a canteen and clipping it to her knapsack. She grabbed another blanket off a shelf and threw it to Max. "Tombay, snap out of it," she said. "We don't have time for any aspie shit. Pack fast."

Max continued rocking, but at the same time awkwardly shoved the blanket into her knapsack with her one working arm. The knapsack still contained all the canned food she'd bought yesterday in town. "Can you take these too?" she asked and gestured to the bags of mangoes. Yoko tied them onto the straps of her backpack. "Don't forget raincoats. We'll need them."

Dubois rubbed her temples with her fingertips, pain in her voice. Probably getting another migraine. "I do not know what to do. I must get help for the gorillas. They are my responsibility. *Je ne sais pas.*" Scientists weren't trained for this sort of situation. "I think I must go down the mountains. Try to get to Karago. Remind people of the gorillas. I walk quiet through the trees. I listen. It will be OK."

She continued, "I do not have authority to tell you what to do. I cannot tell you to follow me. Each of you must choose your direction."

Max grabbed some socks and a fleece sweater from Pip's bureau and packed them, scanning the room for anything else that might be of use as she stepped over beside Yoko. Yoko buckled her knapsack closed, threw a pair of binoculars over her neck.

Pip stood there. Her head swiveled back and forth between Yoko and Dubois. She muttered, "If I disappear for weeks, my kid'll think I'm dead."

"You come with me or them?" asked Dubois.

Pip coughed out a small laugh—not filled with humor, more surprise—and stepped over to Dubois.

"You should take some food," said Yoko.

"You keep the food. You will need it." Dubois said, "By dinner time, we will either be in Karago. Or not."

Yoko stood there for a moment, her hands slack by her sides. Then she nodded and turned away.

With a magic marker, she scrawled on the wall in Japanese—a language it seemed unlikely the Kutu would know—that two researchers had gone up to hide with the gorillas and two other researchers were walking down to Karago. She dated and signed it.

With a final look around, the four of them crept out of the cabin. Dubois grabbed Max fast into a hug. "*Bonne chance.*"

Pressed against her, Max found Dubois came only to the level of her nose and smelled of espresso and some type of strawberry shampoo. Max was still rocking, if anything harder, so Dubois swayed with her once—back and forth—then let go and stepped away.

The others hugged. Pip stood to the side, her breathing fast. Her hands clenched. Max didn't look, didn't step toward her. Rocked harder.

Then before any of them could really absorb what they were doing, they split into two groups and stepped away from each other. Yoko and Max strode across the clearing toward the path that headed up the mountains.

After a hundred feet, they looked back. All they could see through the morning mist was the gleam of Pip's blue jacket and the silhouette of Dubois' head moving down the path in the direction of the gunfire. Dubois' stride seemed unnaturally smooth; perhaps she was trying not to jar her migraine.

The jacket and Dubois faded away into the mist.

"Good luck," Max whispered.

Climbing the mountain, she and Yoko moved through the undergrowth. Every few minutes they stopped to check if the guns sounded any closer. The two of them felt like such a small group, no Mutara, no Dubois, not even Pip. Just two women walking on alone. Probably it would be this way for many days. At this hour, the mist was thick. It completely erased them from the waist down and little vortexes of it curled and twisted in their trail, especially where Max's right hand flapped through it like she was paddling. Her other hand flapped in its sling, patting her chest as though to comfort her. In the jungle, in this situation, there was no reason to pretend she was other than she was. She'd forgotten how calming this habit was, how much it could help.

Into her mind came images of her aunt in a tattered wedding dress trailing them up the path.

The two of them began to push their way through a thicket of bamboo, the shafts bony, the whole of the leafy sky wobbling on its stalks with a rustling clatter.

Yoko jerked to a halt, her head cocked to listen. Max stopped behind her, unsure of what had alarmed her. They grabbed as many of the bamboo stalks as they could, hugging them to silence their clatter. The stalks quieted enough for them to hear the cheery ruckus of a jungle at dawn. Still they waited. Max concentrated on standing still, not making any motion that could attract attention, not rocking or flapping. She mouthed swears instead. Yoko's head was to one side, her eyes closed in concentration, listening.

This was a new situation for Max, to feel terror like this. Certainly she'd at times experienced adrenalin—what felt to her like short moments of extreme physical alertness—but extended terror like this, true terror, deep in her gut, was different. She observed her reaction with interest. Her joints felt airy and her limbs were trembling. Her heart had been pumping audibly in her ears for an hour. This situation might last for weeks.

It was, she decided, distinctly unpleasant. The pressure inside of her was building. The silent swearing was not enough. She clenched her left hand to keep it from flapping, stuffed her right hand in her pocket. Her fingers bumped into the *féticheuse's* pouch. On their own, they grabbed it. It fit snugly into her palm, its fur silky as a cat's. Her thumb rubbed over the pouch fast and repetitively. She hooted silently.

Yoko still made no motion forward, intent and waiting. No sound of humans except for the distant *kuhkuh kuh* of guns.

Inside the pouch, seeds shifted, stems rolled, leaves crinkled. The feel of plants between Max's fingers. She rubbed harder, trying to concentrate on plants, how accomplished they were at survival.

Yoko took a step forward to peer out from behind the bamboo. She scanned all around, then waved Max on, and they began to climb again, moving now into a clearing of ferns. The fronds, as high as their waists, rustled and cracked around them.

Max continued to rub the pouch, like she was a child and this was her favorite stuffed animal. Stroking the pouch, she could feel a few roots in there too, ropy and fibrous. There was something that might be a cushion of moss. Moss had a true talent for survival. When samples of it—dried out for a hundred years—were misted with water, they started to grow again.

Rubbing the pouch, she glanced behind them.

The broken ferns. Their path as clear as the trail of a gorilla. A child could track them.

"Problem," she said.

"What?" Yoko said, turning. Stood there staring, motionless, looking for a moment as helpless as Pip.

This path must lead all the way back to the station. As soon as the Kutu got there, they would see the path and know some of the scientists had fled upwards into the mountains. They would trail them. Find them.

Max closed her eyes. Plants, she thought, our position is being betrayed by plants. She concentrated on the rhythm of her thumb over the seeds inside the pouch, hard and round as beads. Before today, she'd always considered prayer a classic byproduct of the neurotypical tendency toward wishfulness, clinging to the belief that the geometric causality of the universe could be shifted by sheer hope.

In this moment though, standing here in this jungle, her eyes shut for fear of what she might see, she found herself strangely willing to put faith in this pouch. For the first time she understood old women stroking their rosaries and mumbling.

She could fix this, she told herself. She knew enough about this habitat. She could think her way out.

She rocked back and forth, like a davening Rabbi. Prayer came in all forms.

She rubbed the pouch, thinking. Then opened her eyes.

"A stream. We need a stream," she said.

"Why?"

"Walk up the center of it for a while. Hide our trail."

"OK, Tombay. Alright," Yoko inhaled. "I like it." She looked at the mountain peaks above them to get her bearings. "Follow me. There's one this way."

They located the stream within a quarter of a mile and tied their boots together to sling them over their necks. The water was icy cold, fed from the snow melting above. They picked their way up the river, looking back many times to make sure they were leaving no clues of their passage. The clouds of underwater gunk swirling with the movement of their feet were quickly washed away, as well as any indents in the mud.

Occasionally their toes slipped on unseen rocks and they twisted around, struggling for balance. After maybe half a mile, Max spotted a large mat of scrubby vegetation on the river-bank. The grey-green foliage was four inches high and as thick as though it had been poured over the ground.

She stopped and pointed. "We can climb out here. That's *Thymus serpyllum*. It stands back up even when crushed. It'll hide our prints."

They stepped out on the spongy mat, avoiding any spots of bare mud that might leave an imprint. The thyme ran out after twenty feet, but by then they were up and over the side of the riverbank, so their tracks would be out of sight of anyone who might follow them up the river. Sitting on a log, she started to pull on one of her boots.

"Bad idea," said Yoko.

"Why?"

"Your prints, think about your prints. Barefoot, they can pass as a juvenile gorilla's. The moment you put on your boots, even a partial print will betray us. Anyone who spots an inch of tread knows exactly what he's trailing."

Max weighed her boots in her hand. "You know spending the next few weeks on these mountains in bare feet is going to suck."

"Got a better idea?"

She slung her boots back around her neck.

Climbing, they occasionally swore and hopped about, having stubbed a toe or stepped on something sharp. They began to move slower, eyeing the ground, giving a wide berth to thorny plants or thick shrubs, their path becoming more roundabout, like the gorillas'.

Midmorning something crashed through the bushes hundred yards below, parallel to their path. Both of them froze in mid-step, awkward statues, staring downward. To stop herself from rocking, Max rubbed the pouch. Whatever was below them, it plowed along with enormous power, breaking branches. She saw a flash of movement through the trees. If she let go of the pouch, she would start screaming.

An explosion, faded with distance, echoed its way up the mountains. On this vast continent, she was thousands of miles from everything she'd ever known, in a situation she'd never imagined.

Her lips moved silently, mouthing the words, "Please God please God please.'

She marveled once again at how chameleon was the human mind—capable of shucking off a lifetime of values fast as a dirty shirt—able to angle the facts toward whatever it found convenient. She was quite surprised to find this capability inside her own mind.

Below, the crashing arced away and they heard the lowing of a forest buff. Yoko exhaled in relief and they began to climb again, searching for the gorillas.

I t was close to the hottest part of the day. The cicadas whined, doves called. Watching the men work, Jeremy felt almost hypnotized by the noise of his own breathing. *Otombe*, some small part of himself constantly whispered in his head, *Otombe*. He kept replaying this morning's scene with Otombe stretching after the long night in the tree, but no matter how he imagined the scene, each time it ended in the same way, with him turning away from Otombe. The loss beat in his throat.

This morning, in the mirror, his skin had appeared a trifle yellow, the whites of his eyes a little lemony. It might be lack of sleep, he thought, or his imagination, or his eyes permanently seared by this fevered yellow sun.

It did not necessarily have anything to do with the malaria.

In front of him the men were supposed to be rolling boulders into the river, building up a dam across the old riverbed to force all the water to flow into the new canal. As soon as the old riverbed was emptied of water, they could start building the feet of the railroad bridge.

Mostly, however, the assembled boulders were not moving. The men grunted mightily, leaning into their work, but the rocks seemed stubborn, almost glued to the earth. He watched two of the men heaving at a medium-sized boulder. It did not appear more than a hundred weight, still their strain was obvious, their necks corded with effort, their bodies pressing into the work. Only after a moment did he notice that their legs were not angled back for traction, but stood straight up, relaxed, not bothered in the least by the theater in the rest of their stance.

"Work, you men. Work!" he yelled, getting to his feet. His anger, his frustration, all of his emotion from the last few days coming out.

The men turned to him. Their faces, this time, were not as startled at this tone of voice from him.

Stung by shame, his voice got louder. "Stop this damnable playacting. Why are you determined to cheat the railroad? You want to get away from the lions, do you not? Then work hard and fast. Block this river, build the bridge, and move the railroad away from this cursed place."

This time Singh translated his words, calling them out over the rushing waters of the river. Before this week, Jeremy had never yelled at others in this way, the way in which he had yelled at Alan and these men. He had always sought to speak with the kind of respect and enthusiasm he found most effective in motivating himself to work. As he bellowed, he weaved on his feet with the rhythm of his voice, as though a trifle drunk. If he wanted to, he was not sure he could stop this sway. In his mind's eye, he saw again Otombe at the base of the tree, stretching after the long night, while the vein in his neck beat on, untouched.

"You are shirking the work you signed up to do. Not earning your pay. You are imperiling yourself and others. You will do it no longer. I'll not stand for it."

The sea of dark faces was turned to him, their expressions closed and watching. It was the same way in which they had looked at him weeks ago, when during his opening speech a fight broke out among them so he had shot his rifle into the air.

They looked at him as though they had always suspected he would act this way.

From the malaria, twenty-seven men had died thus far. On average, three a day since they had arrived at this river. Lions, yellow fever, and complications from jungle ulcers had taken the total of another twelve. Thirty-nine deaths he was responsible for, thirty-nine. He imagined, back in some dusty hamlet far outside Jaipur or Delhi, the mother of one of the dead men grinding out the spices for the evening meal, going about her life as normal while the telegram was carried by foot the ten or fifteen miles from the nearest telegraph office, passed from traveler to traveler, getting crumpled and dust-stained, closer and closer, ready to inform her the structure of her life had been destroyed.

He remembered the warmth of Otombe's hand cradling his ankle as he prepared to cut the worm eggs out of his foot.

His head throbbed. He raised a hand to his forehead. "I want to save your miserable brown hides," he screamed, "so you can be shipped back to India to starve. You get those boulders in the river this morning or there will be no lunch this afternoon for the lot of you."

Something in the personality of the group changed, as the coolies pressed their weight against the boulders, beginning to roll them with an effort close to real energy. As the first rocks splashed into the water below, no one cheered or even smiled.

He was tired, deeply bone tired. His greatest fear was that he would fall asleep during a night's hunt, so deeply asleep he would not hear the lions when they charged, not wake when Otombe shook him, leaving the N'derobbo to face the animals alone.

Sheer will and tea was all that kept him awake now, ten to fifteen strong cups a day. The little time he had to sleep, between dawn and when work started, he mostly lay on his cot, pulse jittery, temples ringing from exhaustion, staring up at the tent's canvas roof.

Now, leaning back in his chair, he asked for a pot of tea from Singh. His lips felt thick.

Singh looked at him, his eyebrows raised, unsure what he had just said.

It was almost sunset. Already the night monkeys were calling and some jackals yelping. The insects throbbed at the same pace as Jeremy's headache. He stared at the riverbank's thick jungle, hypnotized by the great green heat all around.

Next to him, Otombe got undressed for their pre-hunt bath, dropping his cloak to the ground, neatly placing his spear and knife on top. Jeremy began to fumble with the buttons of his shirt. From two steps away he could smell the other man, his scent of sweat, wood smoke, and red dust, of grass and the fur of his cloak. He inhaled, savoring the smell, trying to memorize it and store it away for the long years ahead. He had retained the scrap of Otombe's robe that the hunter had placed between his chattering teeth two nights ago. He kept it tucked in his cheek, sucking on it secretly. He watched the man's naked body against the shimmer of the sun on the water.

In the river, he copied the extra care Otombe showed, running the soap and then the herbs twice over his body, rinsing three times, working to get off all smells, even the slight scent of the soap's fat and lye. The lions knew they were being hunted now, knew the smell of Jeremy and of Otombe's trick of hunting from in a tree.

Jeremy heard his own voice announce, "Tonight will be the most dangerous hunt of all."

Otombe glanced at him, surprised by the calm prescience in his voice. "Yes, tonight, we will hunt in a new way." The man turned and headed toward the shore. "I thought of it this morning."

Jeremy would always remember this moment, replaying it again and again in his mind. He walked after Otombe, the warm silt of the river squishing beneath his toes. On shore, the askaris—seeing him leaving the river—had already turned and were hurrying away down the path, scared to be out of the bomas this close to sunset.

A leopard coughed raspily somewhere past camp, a fox

barked downriver, a passing strand of lakeweed caressed Jeremy's calf. He worked to memorize each detail of this, his Africa. Ahead of him, Otombe was striding out of the river, his body in a watery striptease, gleaming black. His straight back. His buttocks. His thighs. For the first time Jeremy noticed he had long raked scars along the small of his back. He focused on them, wondering if these were tribal scarification marks or clawing wounds from an animal.

He did not notice the slight movement in the bush on the far side of the clearing, the sense of a presence, the dappling of light on haunches tensing into readiness.

And so they stepped onto the riverbank, walking toward their clothes, naked, moving easily, delightfully cool. Jeremy stared at those pale scars on the dark skin, their slight sway, the raised marks reminiscent of the tracks the railroad left upon this land.

The creature bolted forward.

A cannonball of motion, of weight and size, a fanged beast, low and mean and limber, the lack of mane revealing so clearly its driving purpose.

"Rifle," screamed Jeremy, rolling his legs forward through the slowness of time, running toward the firearm where it lay on his towel and moving thus toward the animal. Those heavy paws swinging up into another stride. Those yellow eyes flicked to him, locking on like the scope of a gun.

"Tree," yelled Otombe, sprinting away.

The motion caught the lion's eye. There was a pause, a small bubble in the fabric of time. Then, in midair, the animal's muscles rippled, his weight shifted in his shoulders as, like any cat, he chased what ran away. He galloped by so close that Jeremy heard the raspy *huff* of his exhale, noted the scars that years of nyika thorns had gouged into his skinny flanks. The animal pared down to muscle and bone and desperate hunger. Not a ghost at all, but terribly physically real.

Jeremy reached his rifle in two slow-motion strides. He turned holding it—already loaded with the round he had chambered out of sheer habit early this evening—thumbing the safety back, rolling the barrel up. The scope floated over to reveal the lion knocking Otombe over, his arms flailing for balance as his whole body fell, disappearing behind the lion, the animal's head rolling down, his haunches bunching as his claws began to cut in.

Jeremy had no other option, no other target available. He shot the creature's haunches.

Bowled forward into a somersault by the impact, the lion screamed. Not roared, not whined. He screamed thin and high as a person. Jeremy's shaking fingers were levering the next bullet in even as the creature spun toward him. He pumped the cartridge into place as the lion galloped at him, his speed great even with one of his hind legs flapping loosely, broken at the hip by the shot, those thick front arms clawing him forward.

He shot the animal in the head. Such a modern power, the gun.

The lion was slapped flat onto the ground. Then surged right back up onto his elbows, the corner of his skull clipped off, his ear dangling by a thread to one side. The blood so red. His front legs spasmed, struggling to pull him up. In this quiet moment, they both listened to the rasp of his claws in the dirt and to the snick and clink of Jeremy chambering that final round.

Turning his broken head to face the gun, the animal snarled defiant.

Jeremy took one step closer. He aimed and shot out a gleaming yellow eye.

The lion's head flopped loosely onto the red earth.

He heard someone shrieking loudly in what sounded like his own voice, "I've done it. I've done it." The voice kept yelling, but it seemed as though there were no need, so quickly did the whole camp stampede up the path, galloping forward at the rifle fire and the animal's scream, all the coolies so triumphant at the death of one lion that they momentarily lost their fear of the other. Many hands scooped Jeremy up into the air to dance around victorious; other men swarmed forward to kick the bloodied carcass. He shouted for Alan, twisting in the determined grasp of the mob, trying to reach Otombe, trying to get him medical help.

When the crowd lifted Otombe, raising him high in the air, Jeremy noted his head was up and his arms flailed strongly. Jeremy fought and called upon the coolies to fetch the physician, but his cheering throng danced about as it wished, separate from Otombe's mob, never close enough for his arms to reach in spite of how he leaned and stretched. Later, when he thought of himself and the hunter, the image that always came to mind was of these separate screaming crowds propelling them in different directions.

By the time the mob finally put Jeremy down, Otombe had been carried away to the physician. As Jeremy's feet first touched the ground, he nearly collapsed, hard rivers of shivering running down his legs from the malaria or the excitement or some mixture of the two. Head down like this, concentrating on remaining upright, he glimpsed his own nudity and began to cast about for his clothing. However men's feet crowded the ground everywhere and, after a bit of searching he could locate only his trampled shirt. He knotted it as a semi skirt around his loins.

At least partially clothed now, he straightened up and caught sight of the dead body of the lion through the crowd surrounding it.

It was huge, somehow looking even larger sprawled there, so unmoving. Curious, he took one step closer, then another. Even in death, power shimmered off the corpse, muscled and tawny. He found he could not force his feet any closer than three yards. At that distance, his lungs constricted and his vision began to narrow. It lay on its side, face turned away.

And for a single moment, glimpsed this way in flashes between the shoulders of the jostling crowd, it seemed almost human, only built on a bigger scale: bent knees and arching ribs, bony hips and arms akimbo.

In the darkness, the fur was smoothed into amber skin.

Emaciated and prone, it looked like a slender woman.

Horrified, Jeremy held up his hand, to make what gesture, he knew not. Perhaps to wave away the crowd or signal for help or magically tug out the bullets he had shot. The other men did not seem to perceive any such resemblance. The crowd stepped forward to stomp on the head, kick at the ribs, yank on the ears and tail. Against the size of the lion's limbs, they looked like a mob of maddened children. Their ferocity surprised him. A man bent over the face with a spoon, struggling to pop out the remaining eye. Another punched a knife repeatedly into the belly, the hilt thumping against the flesh.

Then Jeremy blinked, and saw again it was just a lion's body.

Still, he continued to stare at this unfettered violence he had never suspected the coolies contained within them. And the crowd was not made of only Indians. He spotted a WaKikuyu man trying to saw off the lion's testicles with a spear. Looking now through the crowd, he found a few other Africans, men and women, even children. Had they heard the lion's scream from some nearby village and dared to run through the nyika in what was now complete night? Or were these the Africans who lived as companions of the Indians in camp?

Sarah was here also. Her head thrown back, she laughed with joy at the sky, smeared with blood, a chunk of flesh on her cheek, while he, light-headed, backed up to lean against a tree.

Alan appeared beside him. He was dressed immaculately in freshly ironed linen. It seemed strange, as a physician, he never had the slightest stain of blood or pus on him. Did he change each time he left the hospital or was he careful to keep a distance between himself and his patients?

"Congratulations," Alan said. "Brave shooting. Proud of you. You must tell me the blow-by-blow at teatime tomorrow."

With Alan, Jeremy no longer felt any shame. This time it was the physician who turned away, facing the crowd rather than Jeremy's naked chest and improvised loincloth. Alan was careful not to ask what activity Jeremy had been in the midst of when the lion attacked.

"And," the physician added as an afterthought, "I just examined your hunting chappie. Some nasty cuts along his belly, but nothing pierced the abdominal wall. It appears he will be fine."

Hearing this, even leaning against the tree, Jeremy had to clamp one hand onto a branch to stop himself from sliding slack-kneed to the ground. "Thank God," he whispered.

He was still holding the piece of Otombe's cloak inside his mouth. With it tucked in the pocket of his cheek, the fluidity of his face was somewhat restricted. He did not believe this would be a problem, for his mother had always complained that his face had a tendency toward a greater expressiveness than was proper. He was worried however that the piece of leather might create a bit of an impairment to his pronunciation, so he took care to hit each consonant sharply. Working to keep this secret in his mouth, it was possible his face and voice appeared a bit more restrained and forceful than before, perhaps a trifle more like his Grandpapi.

Alan, continuing to direct his gaze away, nodded in agreement. Now that the lion was dead, the power had shifted. Jeremy would be a hero with the railroad authorities and the Africans. For the coolies, faith in him would be restored, the problems he had encountered with indolence would diminish. The railroad tracks would push quickly onward, leaving this area far behind.

He should feel elated.

Over the tangled thicket of the nyika trees, a call quavered through the air. Different from a roar, it took him a moment to recognize. The other lion was calling for his companion, a sad moan rising into the growing night of a day already past.

The animal was not roaring, but crying. His power gone. His companion dead. Soon Jeremy, or someone else with a gun, would shoot him too.

Jeremy stood there another moment, simply breathing, leaning against the tree, watching the scene he had set in motion. A man swung the lion's cutoff tail through the air like a whip, two others played catch with a bloody paw. Their yells sounded shrill with the last few weeks of pent-up terror. This was the first time he had witnessed any of them act so savagely. He wanted to stop them but could not seem to muster the energy. He told himself it did no real harm. This violence must have always been inside of them. His mother had repeatedly foretold this scene: wild dark-skinned people, bloodthirsty savages.

He had killed the lion on the first day of this new century, this century that stretched ahead of them, empty and waiting.

About midmorning, they found the trail of Titus's group and began to follow it. For once, the family's prints didn't wander roundabout through the jungle from edible bush to edible tree. Instead the trail climbed straight up the mountainside, the gorillas moving single-file and without stopping to eat.

"The gunfire," Yoko said. "They heard it and they're scared. They're heading up, away from town."

After an hour of hard climbing, following the trail, the women still hadn't spotted the gorillas. This was much further than the group normally wandered in a day. Max had at least two cuts on the bottom of her feet now and a puncture in her left ankle that felt deep. Yoko was limping, seemed unwilling to put any weight on her right heel.

At this altitude, the foliage had begun to change. Fewer *Vernonia* and *Hagenia* trees and for the first time Max saw giant heather, a scrubby tree rising thirty feet into the air, the twisted branches shaggy with lichen. The higher they climbed, the shorter the trees grew, the jungle beginning to transition to alpine grasslands.

Around two pm, they caught their first glimpse of the family through the heather from about two hundred feet. The gorillas had stopped fleeing, were clustered in a patch of wild celery and eating hungrily. Max came to a halt, drinking in the sight of their dark muscular weight. Everything, she thought, everything will work out fine.

Yoko pulled her behind a giant heather tree. She whispered, "We shouldn't get any closer today. They're scared and we don't want to spook them. We'll approach them gradually tomorrow."

The emotions of the morning as well as the long climb had exhausted both women. They took turns lying splayed in the sun and snoring, while the other stood guard. At this altitude sometimes a wind from the west momentarily erased the sounds from town.

While Yoko took her turn sleeping, Max watched the gorillas with the binoculars. She felt calmer when she looked at them than when she searched the slope below for any signs of Kutu. She tried to pretend this was just a normal afternoon with them. She took comfort in how they knuckled from spot to spot just like they always did, chomping through the celery, their roving messy tea party.

Turning back to the trees below, she caught the flash of something red, but training the binoculars on it, saw it was just a bird flying by.

Her heart was beating fast and her head hurt. How did neorotypicals deal with fear like this?

She looked back to the gorillas. Working on breathing normally, she tried to think only about these apes, to observe them. This was when she noticed how closely they were clustered, all within thirty feet. Generally they left a much greater space between each other. A few of them sat just inches apart. Although most were eating, they didn't seem as concentrated on the food as they normally were. Twice she saw a gorilla let a few stalks of celery fall to the ground and not bother to pick the food up even though there wasn't that much to eat at this altitude.

Several times, Titus snorted and stared down the mountain. At first she was worried he was catching their smell, but the wind was moving the wrong way for that, and he wasn't looking toward them, but further down the mountain.

At one point he stood up to his full height, drummed his chest and pig-grunted. Uncle, the second silverback, roared fiercely from a spot safely behind Titus. The others stared toward town, sniffing the air, the gunfire and explosions reverberating distantly.

From behind her, Yoko whispered, "The last war in this area was just a few years ago. All the gorillas, except the babies, remember what gunfire means."

Searching, Max found Rafiki after a moment, slightly uphill of the group, holding Asante in her arms. Normally they didn't touch like this. Rafiki's chin was cupped over her child's head, rocking their bodies gently back and forth, both of their eyes closed tight. Rocking and rocking.

For dinner, Yoko and Max ate two mangoes each as an appetizer. Having hiked through a lot of the day, their hunger was immense. Max managed to down the orange-colored flesh by closing her eyes and thinking about cream of wheat. From being banged around in a bag all day, the mango flesh was nearly liquefied. They would have to eat the mangoes in the next few days before they went bad.

Once they'd finished sucking the mango skins clean, Yoko pulled out two sweet potatoes and then froze. "Shit."

Max threw herself to the ground, hands on top of her skull, hoping to protect it against any bullets that might fly by.

She stared downhill, from bush to tree to bush, searching for any movement, but could spot nothing. She flash-glanced to Yoko.

Yoko was sitting upright, staring at the potatoes, not the bushes. "We can't cook these. We don't have matches, and even if we could get a fire going, the smoke would betray our position."

Max rolled over onto her back, holding a hand against her chest. "Fuck, don't scare me like that."

"Nice duck-and-cover you did, Tombay."

"Fuck."

Yoko handed a potato to Max. "Are these going to poison us if we eat them raw?"

Max considered hers. "No, it'll be better for us. More vitamin A and C." She looked at it with regret, then closing her eyes and thinking hard of a peeled Idaho potato, pure and white, took her first bite.

They crunched through the food with determination. They hadn't spoken a lot today, too stunned by all that had happened, too scared of whom else might be in the woods listening. They communicated as much as they could with gestures. At any unusual noise, they froze, heads cocked and waiting, before resuming chewing. When they were finished, they licked their fingers clean.

Yoko whispered, "I think we got maybe thirty potatoes in my bag, as well as the bag of mashed mangoes."

Max added, "I've got twenty cans of what I hope is soup in my knapsack."

Yoko leaned forward, excited. "And a can opener?"

Max froze, self-disgust on her face.

A distant explosion boomed like thunder.

"Alright. That's OK. We can manage," Yoko said. "We can smash them open with rocks or something. We'll lose some food to the smashing, but we'll still be able to eat most of it."

"This food won't last us long."

"Nope. We're going to have to forage as much as possible."

"Well," said Max, "we can eat anything the gorillas eat. However we can't break down cellulose like they can, so a lot of what gives them calories won't do us any good. The best things are probably the berries. I'll think about it and see if I can come up with a tuber or two." She held her canteen above her mouth for a moment to drain the last of its water. "We're going to get skinny."

Yoko said, "What I worry about is water."

"Why? There are streams everywhere."

"You haven't spent the last few months combing through the poop around here, counting parasites. From the streams, we can get guinea worm, amebiasis, and giardia. We can't boil the water clean because we can't build a fire. Spending a few months up here won't be a lot of fun if worms start popping out our—"

"No," Max said, shoving her thumbs into her ears. Her dislocated arm could just make this motion when she angled her head that way. "Can't hear that."

Yoko started to say something more, her voice amused.

Her eyes shut tight, Max spoke over her. "No, I'm serious. That info I can't have. It won't leave my mind." The image of something inside her, eating her.

Yoko heard her tone of voice and stopped.

Max cautiously pulled her thumbs out. "What you're saying is we need a source of clean water?"

"Would be nice, Tombay. You think we can dig a well?"

Max started scanning the plants around them. "No." She stood up and walked in a slow circle, discarding options almost as fast as she thought of them. "Better than that. Give me a minute." This way, thinking hard, she felt more in control and less scared. Finally she spotted a small pygeum and walked over to it. "Can you break this branch off, close to the trunk? I can't do it with my arm in a sling."

Yoko ripped the branch off with a grunt and Max held her empty canteen under the gash in the tree. After waiting a moment, a small ker-plink echoed from inside the canteen. Then another.

"Tie the canteen in this position. You can use the strap and run it over the branch above," Max pointed. "The canteen'll be full by morning. The sap is pure enough for our purposes and we'll get a few calories from drinking it.

There are other trees we can do this with. I'll find them."
She was glad they weren't down in Karago, wandering through town pleading for help in a language no one could understand. Up here among the plants, they had at least a fighting chance.

"Stick with me, kid," said Yoko. "We make a good pair."

Above them, the gorillas started to build their nests for the night. While Max set up the other canteen so it would also get filled while they slept, Yoko began to construct a nest, mounding the branches and leaves high enough to keep the blankets off the damp ground, as well as to create a bit of a cushion to lay on. Then she took all their blankets and spread them on the pile to make a single bed.

"What do you think you're doing?" Max asked.

"At this altitude, it's going to get close to freezing at night. We only have three blankets. No tent. We're going to have to bunk together."

Max stared at the blankets. The sun was on the far side of the mountains. She was already shivering, even in all her clothing. She tried to imagine sleeping next to a shuffling kicking human. A long moment passed. "You lie down facing away from me. You can't move during the night."

"Jeez, you're like my ex-husband."

"I mean it. I can't take it. Not in the middle of all this." She closed her eyes, figuring out how to say it. "My nerves, right now, they're tight. Humming. They can't take much."

"Alright, alright."

They lay under the blankets, facing away. Yoko was stiff and still, trying to help out. So uncalm.

After a long moment, Yoko said, "It's time for the BBC broadcast. Permission to move so I can wind the radio up?"

"No, you stay still. I'll do it."

At the first buzz of static, even two hundred feet away, they heard Titus's snort of fear. Max fumbled the radio off fast.

Then she plugged in the ear set before turning it cautiously back on, her and Yoko each getting one earbud.

Experimentally, Max tried scanning the airwaves, but aside from the BBC, she found no other broadcasts they could understand. On most of the stations, she wasn't even sure of what the language was. So, she returned to the BBC, hoping for an update on the Kutu.

Unfortunately that day the President had visited London, and reports on the protests and speeches took up most of the broadcast. No mention at all was made of any country in Africa.

At the end of the broadcast, Max snapped the radio off.

Yoko asked permission to readjust the blankets for the night. Max agreed; the only part of her that was warm was where their backs pressed together. Yoko sat up and tucked in the blankets as tightly as a sleeping bag around them, then lay back down. The sky darkened and the jungle around them quieted, the calls of nightjars, hyrax and a few monkeys. In comparison, the distant sounds of battle seemed to get louder, reverberating, tidy as fireworks. Max was glad she could hear no human sounds behind the noise.

"Yoko, stay still."

"I am."

"Are not."

"Am too."

Max was quiet for a moment. "This is hard for me."

"I know, Tombay. I'm sorry." Yoko said, "I *am* trying."

She rubbed the *féticheuse's* pouch between her fingers in order to ignore Yoko's small shifts and her shivering, in order to calm herself.

From the angle of Yoko's back, Max thought her head was probably turned so she could look down the slope, keeping an eye out for danger even in the darkness. They were silent for a while, waiting for sleep. It wasn't even eight o'clock.

Yoko said, "My boyfriend right now, Patrick, have I talked about him? Since my ex, he's the first guy I really . . . " She paused. "I've been gone for months. I email and phone when I can, and it sounds like he hasn't changed, you know, or met someone else, but it's been a long time." Her voice vibrating through her back irritated Max, but at least while talking, Yoko wasn't as rigid with constricted energy. Max tried to concentrate on the words.

"I've dreamed," Yoko said, "about the moment when I get off the plane at home. Not daydreamed, but dream-dreamed, at night. I see Patrick in the distance, just the back of his head and shoulders. He's standing there in a crowd of all these strangers. I walk closer and he starts to turn around. I know in a moment I'll be able to see his face, tell from his expression just how he feels."

She added, "Then I wake up. Several times I've had that dream."

The two of them fell quiet. Yoko seemed calmer now and that made Max calmer. Neither of them spoke again that night, just tried to sleep as much as they could. The air got colder quickly. The two of them pressed so tightly together, it was difficult to tell which one of them was shivering.

At one point, wafting up the mountain came the smell of what might have been burning hair. Then the wind changed and it was gone.

The later the night got—as her mind drifted in a state of half sleep—the more difficult it became not to imagine what might be happening down in town. At the slightest sound below her, she visualized what might be climbing toward them through the darkness. Occasionally she pictured tomorrow's dawn, the sun rising to reveal her head, lying by itself on the jungle floor, all the flesh knifed off of it. She imagined herself part of a Kutu's jittery system, never at rest.

Her fingers rubbed the pouch mechanically without stopping.

Above her, the gorillas seemed to be even more restless. She heard them rustling or whining uneasily. Occasionally there was the *pok-pok* of Titus slapping his chest, displaying his power to the dark night.

The flexibility of the neurotypical mind had always amazed her, its lack of loyalty to any inconvenient fact, its willingness to convince itself of any blatant untruth simply because the untruth would make life easier.

Her lips were silently mouthing again, "Please God please God please." Perhaps her work at becoming normal had been a trifle too successful.

That night, she heard Uncle the most often, pig-grunting roughly at the dark, determined to scare everything nearby away.

Late in the night she finally drifted to sleep by imagining it was Titus's back she rested against. His vast muscular body breathing, lying there calm, ready at a moment's notice to leap up at any threat.

Even asleep, Max held the pouch tight in her hand.

When she woke, the sky was just lightening. In the grey light, she could make out the dark form of Uncle on the slope, pacing back and forth. Titus was on his hind legs, motionless and majestic, staring at the surrounding jungle, smelling the air. Over the next twenty minutes as she watched, Uncle never stopped pacing. He jerked around to stare at each noise. He'd always been a bit jumpy, even before the gunfire started. Maybe he'd been pacing all night. Overnight he'd developed the nervous habit of tugging on the short beard under his chin, then wiping away the hair he'd jerked out on nearby leaves. When the wind moved in the right direction, she could hear the rasp of his breath. Sometimes he tapped his knuckles against his left breast, as though from indigestion. He was older than Titus. He might have lived through several wars. She didn't think either silverback had gotten much sleep.

As the sun came up, Uncle roughly roused the family by

coughing and grunting. He led the way down toward the jungle, stopping to look back and make sure they were following. From behind, Titus herded the others along. They didn't loiter to feed, but walked along quickly single file.

The women packed up and followed the group from a distance, out of sight. The gorillas' trail proceeded for a mile, angled slightly south and down the mountain, straight as an arrow. Everything about their actions seemed unusual and Max wondered about their destination.

After an hour, the women caught up with them. The family was spread out and feeding hungrily, near a small waterfall. Max and Yoko hid behind a *Hagenia* about a hundred feet up the mountain, peeking out from behind it to watch the group. Although the rest of them fed hungrily on their normal foliage—*Vernonia, Galium,* and nettles—Uncle stood right by the water's edge, tugging leaves off a ground vine and folding them into his mouth. At this distance, Max couldn't identify the plant, but could see his concentration. After rolling the leaves around in his mouth for a moment, he leaned forward to spit the leftovers into the water, then plucked some more leaves and started again.

Max remembered the vine she searched for was supposed to be spat out, not swallowed.

"Can I borrow the binoculars?" she whispered.

When Yoko didn't respond, she flash-glanced at her.

Yoko's chin was thrust forward and her eyes averted. She made no move to hand over the binoculars.

Max sucked air in. Looking back at Uncle holding the vine, she said, "This is it, isn't it?"

Yoko said, "If you bring back that plant, people'll swarm over these mountains, harvesting all of this plant the gorillas need. Searching for other plants. They'll scare the gorillas up higher and up there they'll starve."

Max's face felt hot. Although she still whispered, her voice was louder. "What are we, like an hour and a half from the station?"

"Hey Tombay," Yoko said, low and harsh. "Hey, we didn't keep you from the search; we just didn't help you. You never expected us to."

"Oh, *come on.*" She spoke loudly enough the gorillas heard. There was a single startled cough from them and they bolted into the bushes while Titus charged toward the women, roaring. About forty feet away, he recognized them and angled off, his sheer momentum taking yards to dissipate. His gut made *galumph-galumph* noises like a horse when it cantered. Once he'd come to a stop, he rested his face against a tree and breathed heavily. It was his responsibility to protect his family, to charge toward possible death. After several moments, he pulled himself up and knucklewalked slowly back toward the waterfall. Several of the others peeked out of the bushes on the far side of the clearing. He grunted and they gradually drifted back into view, peering up at the women.

Feeling guilty, Max shuffled out on her knees from behind the tree so they could see her and she pretend-foraged, trying to look unthreatening, until all the gorillas were eating again.

Only then did she whisper, much more quietly, "Do you understand what this drug could mean? Hand over those binoculars." Her face was still hot with anger.

Yoko made no response, her stubbornness apparent in the silence between them.

Max drew in a breath. "My dad died of a stroke when I was a kid. In front of me. I was the only one in the house. That vine might have saved him."

When Yoko spoke, her voice had lost all its fierceness. "Oh Tombay. I'm sorry."

Her tone released some tightness in Max's gut. The heat in her face moved to her eyes. She stared at the jungle for a moment to gain control. "Thank you. Now hand over those binoculars."

"I can't." Yoko said. "I'm sorry about your dad—really sorry—but neither of us can help him now."

"This plant could save thousands, if not tens of thousands, of lives every year."

Yoko scrubbed her hand through her hair. At her movement, Max caught the smell of her sweat, sour from a day of fear.

"This is the way I think about it," Yoko said. "As a species, we have it all. We have cars, central heating, and cruises to the Caribbean. We have a million pharmaceuticals. We can be a bit generous here. We can do without one thing. Let this family have a few square miles, some trees, a few more years."

Titus sat down next to Uncle and began to pick leaves off the vine. He was still breathing heavily.

Involuntarily, Max remembered that moment in the tree, swinging from his grasp, how he waited until she'd gotten her balance before he let go.

When she spoke, the depth of her rage surprised even herself. "Forget your binoculars. OK? I don't need them."

She knucklewalked/ toward the vine, her arm in its sling pressed against her belly. At her direct path, the gorillas flash-glanced over. When they saw who it was, they watched her, but nothing more. She saw their trust in her. She forced herself to make her path more circuitous, but was still powered along faster than she should, especially since she wasn't stopping to forage. As she got closer to Titus and Uncle, they sniffed the breeze and looked past her for what might be making her move like this. They assumed she wouldn't do this without good reason.

Ashamed, she made herself stop. She foraged for a minute before proceeding, moving slowly enough that at least she wouldn't cause them alarm.

Once she'd gotten within five feet of them, she got a glimpse of the plant in their hands. A compound pinnate, the leaves cordate and lobed, the vine had a strong rhizoid spreading pattern and a tiny white flower.

Searching the ground near her, she found a sample of the plant, crushed a leaf in her hand and waved it under her nose. Astringent.

Touching the leaf to her tongue, bitterness flooded her mouth. Alkaloids. The first heart medicine ever discovered, digitalis, came from a plant high in alkaloids. She spat the taste out, felt a momentary numbness in her mouth—probably it affected the central nervous system too.

She looked down at the leaf in her hand. This vine was what brought her to this jungle, these gorillas, this danger. She turned to the gorillas, their lumbering backs. Asante was munching through a large clump of ferns, feeding hungrily.

I won't tell Stevens where it came from, she thought. I'll pretend I got it down in town, that someone gave it to me.

She watched her hand collect ten feet of the vine and loop it into a small bundle.

Better yet, she thought to herself, she'd keep it secret. She'd quit Panoply and figure out how to synthesize the compound on her own.

It would take a lot longer to get to market because the clinical trials wouldn't be run concurrently using extracts from the wild-harvested plant. But in a way that would help. By the time the drug was ready to announce, no one would ever associate it with her trip to this country.

She held out the vine, examining not so much the plant as her hand continuing to hold it. This is my hand, she thought.

She watched it stuff the vine into her pocket and zip it shut.

Afterward she knuckle-walked slowly back to Yoko. "Let me guess. They only use the plant after a lot of stress, right? Not all the time."

Yoko nodded. She didn't mention what Max had done. Her voice was tight. "A silverback will come to this waterfall three or four times a year, after a fight with a rival or a close brush with hunters. They only touch the plant in the very early morning, before seven. Dubois has a theory the leaves are less toxic then."

Max said, "The chemical's probably manufactured in the roots and lifted into the leaves in the morning once transpiration's started."

Yoko scrubbed her face. Her voice was tired. "Look, I want to be clear. I don't blame you. This is your job. It's my fault. I worked hard to bring you here, to convince Dubois. It was a calculated risk."

She decided to ignore Yoko's statement. "So I could have spent my life hiking up every morning to observe what they eat, and I'd never have found the plant."

Yoko nodded. "Normally we never get to the gorillas before eight. It's what we were counting on. The only way you could see them use the plant was to sleep up here with them. Be with them at first light."

"Dubois slept with them?"

"She'd camp nearby. With her workload, it was the only time she had with them. She'd hike up just before sunset, then come down in the morning. That's how she found it."

They both sat there, staring down at the gorillas.

"Jesus," Max said. Looking down at the gorillas, she pictured Dubois and Pip in a beat-up Toyota driving over the border into neighboring Burundi, yodeling out the windows with relief.

Then, unwillingly she pictured them instead in town just a few miles from here, face down in a huge pile, everyone's limbs tangled together in stiffened intimacy.

"Jesus," she repeated.

The morning mist had dissipated. The early morning birds and monkeys still called. The gorillas seemed perhaps a bit less jumpy today. There didn't seem to be as much gunfire. The apes foraged, hungry after their long walk. They made little noise, the occasional crack of a branch or a social grunt. Once in a while they glanced over at the humans, their expressions unreadable.

Her stomach grumbled. "OK, let's get breakfast."

Wordlessly, she and Yoko moved into a nearby thicket to pick blackberries. They ate with a fast intensity.

After they'd finished off all the blackberries, she showed Yoko two or three other plants she could eat and then she moved off to forage. She gradually knuckled in among the family. Sitting among them, she chewed methodically through leaves and stems just like they did. She tried not to think about the vine in her pocket.

The gorillas accepted her without comment, their ranks closing around her.

Around noon, she was sitting on a log with Rafiki, pulling off clumps of *Usnea lichens* and chomping through it. *Usnea* looked like Spanish moss and tasted a bit like watercress. Eating food this low in calories was real work. Her jaws got tired from the sheer chewing and she still felt a little light-headed from hunger. However she applied herself to the task. She knew, over the next few weeks, she would need every calorie she could get. In a way she was well prepared for this, for she'd never considered eating a pleasure, more a task that needed to be powered through and, since she normally ate a very narrow set of possible foods, she had no problem with a monotonous diet.

She and Rafiki sat with their backs to one another, one leg on either side of the log, heads down and concentrating on the *Usnea*. Back to back was how the gorillas tended to sit if they were within a few feet of each other because it decreased the chance they might glance into each other's eyes by mistake.

Rafiki shifted backward a few inches, closer to Max, in order to pull some piece of moss out from under her leg. This close, Max sat inside her shadow, her smell all around: a dense combination of sweaty horse, chewed greenery, and pungent adolescent.

She touched her pocket with the vine. Perhaps, once she had synthesized the compound successfully, she could persuade some researchers to pretend they'd invented it from scratch. That she had nothing to do with it. Then no one would ever connect the resulting medicine with the gorillas or these mountains.

Still chewing the last bit of moss, Rafiki leaned back, settled her weight against Max. A solid deep pressure, none of the uneasy fritter of humans. The quiet contact Max had always wanted. She leaned back into it. Rafiki inhaled—the long draw of breath filling her ribcage—and then sighed out.

They relaxed there against each other, the only motion their breathing. Staring out at the dense jungle.

In the background was the gunfire.

They were eating berries aroud midday when they heard the first voice. Both the women and the gorillas stopped in mid-chew. There was the cracking of underbrush under many feet, male voices, perhaps two hundred feet away.

At these noises, Titus made no attempt at defense, but whirled and galloped up the mountain, leading his family away. The gorillas bolted after him. The velocity with which they moved was shocking. The researchers stared, then belatedly sprinted after them. The approaching soldiers might not be Kutu, but the women weren't going to wait around to find out.

The men called and crunched forward through the underbrush. Perhaps, considering all the noise they made, they might not hear the gorilla's rushing retreat.

Barreling up the muddy slope, over rocks and logs, yanking her way through the foliage, Max was deeply conscious of the clear target her knapsack made swaying through the bushes. She scrambled fast, kicking the insteps of her feet into the mountain for traction and grabbing at tree branches to pull herself along faster, but her dislocated arm didn't have the strength to help much. She was slower than the others. Her breath rasped, her heart thudded. The apes galloped over the ridge. Even Rafiki lumbered out of sight. Over all of her own noise, Max couldn't tell if the soldiers were still marching or had stopped and were raising their rifles. Thirty feet from the ridge. Her legs felt strangely light, flying effortlessly through the undergrowth. A high-pitched vibration rose in her ears. Time ballooning out. Ten feet to the ridge.

She dove over the edge, threw herself down beside Yoko. Pressing her cheek against the rough hip of a tree, she gasped for air. Below, the soldiers talked and called and marched forward through the bushes. They didn't pause, didn't shoot.

One minute passed, then two. The sounds of the men gradually faded away round the mountain. In the slow silence that followed, she noticed her pants were stained wet and dark down to her knees. For a moment, she stared mystified.

"The gorillas crap when they flee too," Yoko murmured, so quietly Max could barely hear her. "It must lend some evolutionary benefit."

For breakfast, she'd eaten handfuls of blackberries, followed by the roughage of all that *Usena*, and then two mangos at lunch to stop her belly from aching. They hadn't packed any toilet paper and, even as she'd eaten the mangos, she'd known she'd pay for this later.

Adrenalin is an effective diarrheic. She lay where she was, flat against the mountain.

"My guess is shit works as a deterrent," whispered Yoko. "Yuck, says the predator, I don't want to eat *that* one."

Max stared up at the jungle canopy far above, at the distant leaves twinkling in the wind. Embarrassment seemed an emotion well beyond her at the moment. Her nerves realigned. Her hearing rich with her continuing breath. The air tasted green, moist, and deeply alive. Her pulse beat with a tight *bam-bam* in the tips of her fingers. Her body hummed on, functioning and whole.

She felt lighter. Not only in the obvious physical way, but as though she'd also dropped something less tangible behind. Strangely enough, she felt cleaner. More herself.

After a few minutes they found a stream to wash her pants in. She took them off and scrubbed at the stain with a rock.

Afterward, she sat down in the brook and watched the water pouring over her legs. The river rippled and shifted. She touched the surface with one fingertip, just enough that a shallow dimple was formed in the water, the cohesive bonds ribboning underneath. The water so transparent, it glistened like solid air. It smelled metallic and cold. All her senses heightened.

She wasn't proud of herself, not of how she'd acted in several ways over the last few days.

She took the *féticheuse's* pouch out of her pocket and left it by the side of the brook, soaked and abandoned. She didn't need it anymore. She would manage on her own.

Then she got up, wrapping a sweater around her waist as a sort of skirt. She wrung her wet pants out and tied to the outside of her pack to dry. Without soap, they weren't bacteriologically clean and wouldn't they smell very nice. Still, there was nothing she could do about it. Pausing frequently to listen for patrols, she and Yoko found the trail of the family again and followed it up the mountainside. The gorillas' trail shot straight up, higher and higher, not bothering to forage or stop for a nap.

Climbing, Max's bare legs moved freely, more easily than she could remember. Sounds struck her as sharply as light, the rocks glimmered in the sun.

Glancing up, she spotted the apes, still climbing at what must be twelve thousand feet. The slope around them was only sparsely vegetated. They seemed to be moving slowly, perhaps from the altitude or maybe from hunger. Normally they ate constantly. The last few days they'd hardly had time to forage. Climbing the rocky slope, the researchers moved even slower, their feet bleeding, their walk awkward and limping.

She watched her right hand grab hold of a clump of grass to pull her up. She realized she'd never really looked at her hand before, not hard enough: the blunt nails, the amber skin, a mild keloid scar left from a fall in fifth grade. This so-familiar pocket of muscles, tendons, and bone.

Her lungs moved, her legs climbed. She blinked around at the world. She felt a part of the gorillas and Yoko, this red soil and equatorial sun.

Uncle was leading the family. The researchers followed. The brush at this altitude was sparse enough they could keep the family in sight even from several hundred feet. Occasionally, the gorillas glanced back at the humans, at first startled, then resigned. They climbed on. The air got colder. At this altitude, Max began to find it difficult to breathe, sucking air in through her teeth. The gorillas had their heads tucked down into their effort. She concentrated on each step. That twig, this step, that hand. This moment here.

There was less and less mountain for them to climb up. No trees lived this high up except for occasional samples of heather and even these were stunted. They now clambered up among *Lobelia*, flowered spiny stalks rising six feet high, oversized so they wouldn't freeze solid at night. A few cabbage-like ground-sels in a barren world of lichen and moss. Bare scree clattered away under their feet. Nowhere was there any foliage big enough to hide behind. Just boulders, patches of snow, and these Martian-looking flowering stalks.

Some type of scarlet bird alighted on a *Lobelia* and pecked at its seeds, glancing nervously around. The gorillas seemed just as jumpy, ripping stalks down with watery cracking sounds, eating only half of each and then moving on. Titus and Uncle wouldn't let anyone stop for long. Uncle was still tugging on his chin, then wiping his hair away on the ground. The two silverbacks kept glancing back down the mountain, searching for soldiers, then they'd turn back and grunt ferociously at dawdlers.

Baring their teeth and thumping the ground, they herded the others up and up until there was nowhere left to climb.

The family stood on the peak, milling around and confused. The point farthest on all sides from civilization.

The air was cold up here, a brisk wind whining in from the south, the snow carved by the wind. Yoko and Max stayed a hundred feet down from the peak, kept their movements quiet, heads lowered. The animals didn't look at the women much, seemed dazed with exhaustion.

As the sun sank behind the mountain, the family settled down to sleep on the bare ground. There were no branches to make nests from. Shivering, Max pulled on her pants and bundled up in the blankets with Yoko. She didn't know how Asante and Rafiki would survive the night on the windswept peak without anything to keep them off the frozen rocks and snow.

Below her, stretched the vast landscape of jungle and, beyond that she could see a patchwork of many farms, diminutive and neat. From this altitude, the distance didn't seem all that great, almost as though, if she took a giant running jump off this mountain, she could reach the nearest homes, perhaps find safety.

The sunset cycled the sky through every possible hue and shade as the shadow of the mountains stretched out further and further over the land below. Max stared at it, unblinking.

Then the sun disappeared, darkening the world. On the peak, one of the gorillas groaned. A sad elongated note of cold and worry. Max looked up at them. Unable to discern individuals, she could see just the lumpy silhouette of the family huddled together for warmth.

A different gorilla answered, a lower mewl extended for a long moment in the growing dark.

A smaller voice—probably Asante—hummed back, and then another called, and another.

Together, they sang, their voices rising, long moans, eerie

whines, rumbling calls, discordant and low, chaotic and communal, crying out into the night.

Max watched the silhouette, transfixed by this alien chorus.

Long after the night had descended, long after the gorillas had fallen silent, perhaps sleeping, perhaps not, she stared around at this world, the stars brilliant and twinkling in the thin air, the moon rising bright as a bone, lighting this landscape so it gleamed.

T en days after the first lion's death, Sarah had stepped into Jeremy's tent after the camp had retired for the night. He had been sweating and tossing with the malaria that came and went no matter what medicine Alan gave him. For days at a time he would be fine and then, as the sun set, shivers would begin to roil up from deep in his gut and he would shut himself in his tent so the workers would not see him weakened and trembling.

That night, the slither of the goatskin off her body had reached him through his delirium, making him open his eyes and sit up in bed. In the darkness in front of him, stood the silhouette of a naked African body.

The day before he had bid goodbye to Otombe. Beside them the train had idled, waiting for Jeremy, ready to cross the newly built bridge to the far side of the river. Since the night of the first lion's death, the second lion had not been spotted, had not killed again. In the windows of the train were the faces of several hundred workers. He had not meant for his good-bye to be this public, had been searching for Otombe all day, but only now, as the train was about to leave had the hunter appeared, stepping out of the nyika. Jeremy watched him stride closer. Feeling his own face tighten with emotion, he directed his eyes at Otombe's feet as the man stopped three feet away. By staring only at those dark toes spread wide in the red dust, he was able to contain his own expression, but he had no idea what Otombe's face showed.

Speaking, the man's voice sounded relatively normal, neither rushed nor choked up. "I thank you for helping me rid the area of the lions. You have saved many of my people." His words were measured and clear, as befitted an important occasion, the kind of words Jeremy so wished he could issue from his own throat right now. Instead there was only this heat tightening in his neck, his ribs working to pull air in. He remembered Patsy's open mouth struggling to breathe.

Out of the corner of his eye, Jeremy glimpsed Alan stepping into the doorway of the train, lighting his pipe, and watching this scene with straightforward curiosity.

"I thank you also for saving my life and treating me fairly," said Otombe. Beneath these words, there was more feeling. Perhaps he was warming up to something, something demonstrative. Jeremy had seen African men holding hands in public without embarrassment, as well as standing with their arms draped over another's shoulders. In a moment Otombe might step close, pull him into a tight hug or—like the French—a kiss on each cheek.

And then he would step back. Let go. Jeremy's chest or cheek beginning to cool where the warmth of Otombe had been pressed just a moment before.

The rest of Jeremy's life stretching out in front of him.

So Jeremy jerked back harshly, from this moment, from whatever other words Otombe might say, from whatever gesture he might make, from all these men staring. He chopped one hand up in farewell and stalked away, shoving past Alan onto the train and locking himself into his own compartment.

He had no idea how Otombe reacted; with what expression he watched Jeremy's stiff-backed retreat.

In the day since, Jeremy's furious loneliness and self-reproach were close to a physical assault. All he had left were his memories and the scrap of Otombe's robe, the lump of it becoming so much a part of his mouth that he knew not how to live without it, the way it filled his cheek with its load of wet sorrow. However, he knew already its taste had faded and changed, begun to be sucked away and infiltrated by the flavor of his own flesh. He had to work increasingly hard to remember how it had been, reconstructing its tang of sweat and dust. He knew his memories would fade in the same way, becoming bland and overexposed. With every hour that passed, the paucity of his life stretched out in front of him.

And now standing in the darkness of his tent was this naked African body.

Blinking, he decided it must be Otombe who, confused by their farewell, had paced across the bridge to visit him in the railroad's new campsite on the far side of the river. The bravery of Otombe had always been greater.

Awkwardly pushing himself to his feet, his head pulsing with fever, Jeremy felt desperate with the need to take back his graceless good-bye, to make his feelings clear. The criminal bravery of the condemned. Here in his tent there could be no further reason to prevaricate. No one was watching. Otombe must already understand him for what he was and, obviously, this was Jeremy's last chance with him. If, God forbid, any complaint surfaced about what might happen here, few would take the tribesman's word over his own. Stepping forward, he laid one hand on the person's shoulder. The African made no movement away. Lowering his nose to the neck, Jeremy inhaled sweat, wood smoke, and red dust, closed his eyes to savor it. Since the malaria had started, his sense of smell worked so well, better than his vision, which sometimes fuzzed and flickered. Even from this small motion of his head, his skull felt as though the river were sloshing around inside, making every thought bob about, confused. Scared he would faint before he could demonstrate his intentions, uncertain of how to do this, he ran his hand hurriedly down the ribs to the hip.

Still the person did not move away, but only swiveled to offer the rump.

Jeremy gave up trying to dissuade himself. He grabbed her and pulled her to him. In the drunken moments that followed, in the midst of his unpracticed rubbing and grinding, he found her quite sufficient. The dark flanks, the narrow hips and spine.

By the time in his delirium he began to comprehend his mistake, he was far beyond the point of stopping.

Afterward, his reaction was gratitude.

So intense.

He pressed upon her all the money he had in the tent. Her eyes opened wide at the bills he shoved into her hands. Quickly she tucked the money into her robe and swung out the tent flaps, disappearing without a word.

An unspoken understanding was reached. Sarah visited his tent every few nights. After a little experimentation and a few humiliating failures, he found the best formula. It was easier when the malaria was upon him. Then, by simply closing his eyes he could find himself back in the river, everything so clear. It was more vivid than the rest of his life: cool water to his waist, Otombe staring at him, those dark eyes. He sucked on the piece of leather in his mouth. He breathed in her smell.

But whether the malaria was present or not, in the darkness he always approached her from the back, touched only that side of her body, far from the breasts, pretending. She inserted his manhood with as little fanfare as one might slide an envelope into a mailbox. He used her shoulders to guide her motion, while he buried his face in the tuft of wooly hair at the back of her skull. He never had to learn what expression her face wore, whether desire or disgust or simple endurance.

When she visited, before he touched her, he always tied the tent flaps open with trembling hands, so only the mosquito netting and several miles of recently laid railroad tracks remained between him and the distant water. Since the malaria, his powers of imagination had increased, could recreate whole scenes. Every day the coolies laid more of the tracks, moving the camp further on, yet he found in the tent at night he could still smell the river's water, hear its low gurgle. He could watch Otombe wading toward him, the waves rippling round his hips, the askaris mysteriously gone, the lions not around. Otombe placed his hand softly on Jeremy's chest, leaning closer. All his life, Jeremy had trained himself to be satisfied with so much less than this.

The joy each time took his breath away.

But then afterward, afterward . . .

He would open his eyes to see this stranger panting on her knees in front of him, head down, waiting for him to pull out so she could collect her money.

In this intimate moment, he felt more alone than ever.

Unable to speak for the tightness of his throat, he would remove himself quickly. She would get to her feet, pick up the purse he left for her on the desk, and leave. At no point during this interaction did either of them say a word. There was no point. They did not share the same language.

He would wash off, sometimes two or three times, swearing to himself never to do this again.

He would have assumed that this regular physical relieving of the tension within him would make him more relaxed and easygoing, but instead, especially the day after a visit from her, he found a restless irritability near the surface, this emotion that could erupt with no notice into rage. One afternoon when his men were working with a sluggishness that seemed egregious, the feeling bubbled up inside of him and he lost control, screaming at them that they were embarrassments to humanity, abominations, that their families would feel disgust at how they shirked their work. His face got hot, his lips wet, his voice shrieking.

Of course afterward he deeply regretted this scene, his statements. He stayed up late drafting a short speech of apology, but the next morning at the worksite, while he unfolded his speech, preparing to deliver it, Ungan Singh pointed out how quickly the coolies were laboring. In his voice was approval. In a single day they had laid three-quarters of a mile of track, nearly double their normal achievement.

Surprised by this, Jeremy looked back over the distance they had traveled since yesterday. He knew that this much farther from the river, there would be fewer mosquitoes.

The next day, in the daily post that arrived with their supplies, came a note of congratulations from the head engineer in Mombasa, Preston. Since the lion had been shot, Preston had been writing him upon occasion, consulting on details, asking his opinion.

And so he forced himself to remonstrate the coolies at times, especially on the days after Sarah visited. He was motivating them to labor away from the malarial river, working to safeguard their lives. Each time he doubted his actions, he considered that brutal scene of the coolies stabbing the lion's body. They had different mores than he did. Who could tell if his yelling bothered them? The critical point was this was the best way to save their lives.

And bellowing at them had the additional benefit of releasing the emotion knotted inside of him so he could sleep at night.

With each day, lashing out at the men became a little less forced. Wishing not to yell at them any longer than necessary, he learned which threats were most effective at motivating them. No lunch being served until enough work was completed certainly got the men moving (especially once there were a few days where no lunch was served at all), and soon they seemed almost to expect him to castigate them while they began laying railroad tracks in record time. At that point, trading in on the new esteem Preston held for him, he had a second doctor brought in to help care for the infirm. This decreased the mortality rate somewhat. With the coolies' new speed, he was also able to arrange to have them paid more. He was figuring out how to subsist in this land, working out an effective if unpleasant mode of behavior, trying his best to be responsible.

At the worksite, the sense of isolation was not that much worse than before. It was something he knew how to endure.

Tonight, he remembered seeing Otombe walking out of the river, his skin gleaming. Pumping quickly now, Jeremy ran his hand along the spine of the person bowed in front of him, feeling the bones and sinewy muscles. He could do this because the malaria sometimes still returned, the evenings flickering and fevered. He could do this because he did not feel he had a choice; there was his physical need and this interaction was the closest he could get to Otombe now. He could not give it up.

During the daylight hours, it was hard to believe in these surreal visits, that he had performed such an act with a woman, that he had paid for her services. So many of his life's wishes and desires had resided solely in his head that this dreamlike quality felt right to him.

Thus, perhaps it was not surprising, that a number of visits had occurred before he first considered the possibility her womb might quicken.

In the beginning the idea had a certain ludicrous quality to it, but as the weeks passed and her visits continued he was forced to consider the possibility more seriously. Never before had this potential existed for him, and he found his mind dwelling upon it until it felt almost predestined. He realized that if Sarah were to conceive, he would unfortunately have few lines of action to choose from, none of them appealing.

As her body swelled and ripened, Alan would comprehend her situation. He would argue—never implicating Jeremy directly—that the increasingly obvious example of her past behavior would be damaging to the moral development of the coolies in camp. Alan would advise she be let go as the cook and sent back to her people. Implicit in his advice would be his conviction that no man who had lain with her could have any certainty her condition was the result of his seed.

Of course Alan's solution would be the one most men chose, the reaction expected. However Jeremy would find it extremely difficult and distasteful.

An alternative would be to have her remain in camp, but that choice would be frowned upon. Sarah's offspring would be relatively pale and, in terms of potentially responsible parties, there were only two white men residing within twenty miles.

Perhaps Jeremy could stomach returning her to her village if he sent along a regular stipend. On this continent, a few coins could change a life.

However, even then, the child, possibly of his issue, would have to survive in a mud hut, in a land where famines happened, where malaria and lions killed, where no one wore trousers or attended school. Other men might not be as bothered by the idea of this kind of upbringing, but, then, they knew they were likely to sire other children who could be raised in a more conventional manner.

If Sarah did have a child, once it had passed the age where it critically needed the mother (British boarding schools he believed waited until the age of six or seven), maybe he could transport it to the relative safety of New England and arrange for the gift of civilization and an education (probably in Boston, where the more cosmopolitan schools had experience with students of many backgrounds). After the child had reached his or her majority, Jeremy was not sure what the future could hold. The important point was the education, the offering of the wonders of the modern age.

However, with this solution there were still the dangers of infancy in Africa, the distress of separating the child from the mother.

One night, after Sarah left his tent, he was unable to sleep.

He lay perspiring on his cot, wondering what kind of man he had become, a high whine in his ears, a metallic taste in the back of his throat. At last, somewhere near dawn, he fell asleep and to his mind came a fevered dream in three short scenes. Although usually his dreams appeared in grainy black and white similar to a cartoon in a newspaper, this vision swirled through his head, as vivid and full of saturated color as a tropical garden. At times even smells wafted delicately through the scenes.

He stood in the customs building in Boston harbor, at a wood counter, his pen hovering over a form. He had just finished writing "Sarah" and was pausing to consider the empty field of the surname. He could feel the woman herself, pressing in tightly against his back, her hard huffs of fear. With one hand, he tried to ease her back to a proper remove, but in the vast marble rotunda a crowd bustled by, all sculpted clothing and clacking shoes, attended by porters and wheeled conveyances; her throat let out an almost tea-kettle whine as she wrapped herself around him. Turning to pry her off, he noted that at least she was not wearing her goatskin toga, but a blue dress with a small bustle. Still, there was her shaved scalp as well as her bare feet and calves visible beneath the dress's hem as she worked to scale him like a tree.

In the next scene he was in Africa, weeks earlier. He was trying to convey the concept of Maine as best he could. It was impossible to know what she made of his repeated words and explanatory props. The only point at which he was sure they were communicating was when her eyes lit up as he held up the cash. After this, while he continued talking, she stared at the sketch he had drawn of his family's house in Maine, running her fingers over it. His map of the continents—the ocean intervening—she barely glanced at. The calendar which he flipped through, muttering "years and years," she was not distracted by.

In the dream's last scene, she did not appear. He was walking down Hammond Street, the day's purchases in his arms. He could hear the creak of the wood sidewalk under his heel, feel the gentle Maine sun upon his face, smell the manure of a bustling metropolis.

He became aware that across the street two people were staring at him. As he started to swivel toward the pair—Mrs. Greeley and Nathan Bartleby—he could see the way they leaned in toward each other, exchanging some confidence. He felt the familiar horror rising in his throat; they must be sharing the old gossip of his unnatural shame.

But regarding them directly now, he saw their expressions held not the disbelieving disgust he so vividly remembered. Instead the eyes of these two were wide and their mouths slack. Their expressions that of children during a ghost story, caught somewhere between horror and delight.

Even in his dream, he felt certain he would never, even in passing, have mentioned the African woman, nor her light-skinned newborn to anyone in town or in his family; he surely would not reside in the same neighborhood or district, nor have any contact with them, aside from the regular money his solicitor's agent delivered and his own occasional visits on the darkest of nights. In spite of all these precautions, there was Mrs. Greeley leaning in to whisper into Nathan's ear.

Of course the tale of the lion hunt would have changed as it moved through town; this Jeremy expected. Otombe nowhere in it, aside from perhaps as a sort of dusky shadow, the spotlight on Jeremy and his gun, his bravery unquestioned. The white hunter's character in this narrative becoming the type of person Jeremy tended to feel cowed by, steely and brave, his expression through it all stalwart and closed, similar to that of his Grandpapi.

Staring at Mrs. Greeley, he understood the story of his interaction with Sarah had also been transformed.

As Nathan leaned toward Mrs. Greeley, caught in the midst

of being scandalized, Jeremy found—at least in the dream—
an unusual reaction inside himself. Instead of the humiliation
and self-loathing he was familiar with, he felt a trembling commencing in his gut, a vibration that grew stronger as it rose
inside his torso, forcibly taking his whole body over, shaking
his shoulders, rolling his head back, opening his mouth. The
laughter bursting from somewhere deep and dark inside.

At the idea that—considering all that was actually true about
him—the rumor of fathering any child could embarrass him.

Laughing so hard he woke himself up, the African sun high
in the sky, the sound still vibrating in his throat.

For days, the dream remained with him, while he watched
the coolies work, while he ate, while he lay in his bed at night.

Even now, in the tent, sucking on the piece of leather from
Otombe's clothing, pumping above the body crouched before
him, the dream was so powerful, not just the laugh at the end,
but that first scene. The customs form in front of him. His pen
hovered over the paper, the puzzle of that empty white space.
That image haunted him. In some way, the surname had become
magical, the key for him. If he could only figure out an appropriate name, he believed that if the pregnancy ever did occur,
he could find his way through all the difficulties that would follow, be able to make choices that were not entirely distasteful.

Distracted, his actions began to lose some of their urgency.
He pounded harder, with a slight sideways twist, trying to con-
jure up the river and Otombe wading toward him.

In a way the lion had given him so much—not what he truly
wanted, but at least more than he had thought he could ever
have. Its death had allowed everything to happen: being separated from Otombe had created his reaction to Sarah's visits,
which led to the possibility of his someday fathering a child.
Each of these results following the previous one like the cars of
a train followed the engine's lead. If Sarah's womb did quicken,
then years from now, when Jeremy looked back at his own life,

it would appear from the point the bridge had been completed, with every additional railroad tie that was pressed into the ground, more distance had been established between him and the way in which he was different.

Perhaps he slammed into her a little hard. On her knees in front of him, she grunted a noise somewhat similar to *Oh*.

Following that first syllable, the rest of Otombe's name automatically tumbled into his mind. Of course. Without him, the child could never happen. Sarah's surname had to be some variation of that name, slightly Americanized. Tombet, Tomber.

Tombay.

The name rang out in his head, eclipsing all other sounds in the tent. Tombay.

With this name on his tongue, he felt a surge of confidence and the pleasure of his release started to shiver up his spine. He knew no matter what happened he would find an answer; the repercussions could not be as difficult as the last few years. Nothing in comparison to that, not since he had the memory of a few weeks of happiness, this scrap of leather, the returning fever.

And in this moment, his lips parting in an animal groan, he opened his eyes to see through the tent flaps the embankment of his railroad, the tracks gleaming in the moonlight, the force of the future riveted with steel and wood into this red earth, his bridge and railway which would funnel in trains and machines, colonists and attitudes, carrying in all the freight of this next century.

T he sky was just starting to lighten. She sat on the slope by herself, at a distance from both Yoko and the gorillas, watching the sky through the morning mist. She'd been unable to sleep, needed to be alone. She sat on the cold gravel mountainside, holding the vine in her hand and thinking.

Then below her, a stone fell, clattering down the slope. The noise loud in the silence.

Staring in that direction, she saw something glitter in the fog, perhaps gold lamé. Then it was gone in the mist.

Run, she thought, run. In this fog, in her grey clothes, she might get away. Run. But rising to her feet, she glanced up at the gorillas on the peak. They were visible—so visible—large and dark against the mist.

Bushmeat.

More scree clattered down, kicked by a boot.

She found her hands rising, then waving around, her arms signaling frantically back and forth—even the dislocated one as much as it could in its sling—trying silently to warn the family of danger. The vine flapping in her hand like a flag, forgotten.

Titus jumped up at the falling stones. All the other gorillas followed, rising like a single body, looking downward. She could feel their fear inside herself, their hearts pounding inside her chest.

From the corner of her eye she could see the Kutu now, heads down, emerging from the mist. Guns and dresses, skinny limbs. They seemed to move so slowly, time ballooning outward.

She yelled up with all her strength, "Get out of here."

The gorillas swiveled as one and began to run down the far side of the mountain. Utterly silent. Even Titus not roaring.

She was turning now, the boys standing there below her in the mist, staring at her. Above her, she heard a single rock tumble, kicked by a fleeing gorilla and she yelled again. Yelled the first thing she could think of, to cover up the noise.

"I'm American," she screamed. "From Bangor, Maine."

Probably the only word they understood was "American," but they got the concept. Young boys in tattered finery.

There was a rising shrill in her ears. She could barely feel her body. Like in the moment after jumping off a too-tall diving board, she was surprised at the ease of this. She only hoped it would be fast.

The fear utterly gone. The clarity of mind returned. The freedom intense.

It was possible Yoko was using this moment too, sprinting away, low and serious. She might make it. Max couldn't spare the moment to check. For time was moving on.

The Kutu were pulling up their rifles now, yanking back on the safeties. So busy with their yelling and their jittery anger, she didn't think they'd notice what she did in this moment and so she glanced a final time after the family. Rafiki the last one, her shambling two-legged run. Asante just in front.

They disappeared. She was left alone.

Waving her hands now harder and wider, feeling the release of this movement, truly herself, flapping her arms through the air, her voice somehow rough with joy, she screamed into the morning light, "Fuckity fucking fuck."

The majority of the facts in this book are as accurate as I could make them. Much of the world's coltan for cell phones does come from the Democratic Republic of Congo. Gorillas do sing.

Although the Kutu are a group I made up, the details of child soldiers, wedding dresses, drugs, and cannibalism, are based on several tribes existing in Africa today, such as the Lendu in the Democratic Republic of Congo and the Lord's Resistance Army in Uganda.

Finally, the United Nations Environment Programme predicts that by 2030, 90% of the remaining habitat of the gorillas, chimps, bonobo, and orangutans will be destroyed, and these species unlikely to survive in the wild.

For some of the botanical information and images in this book, I'd like to acknowledge Colonel Patterson's *Man-eaters of Tsavo*, as well as Francis Hallé's book, *In Praise of Plants*.

Aside from having been to Africa, I read over seventy books to write this novel. Some of my favorites are as follows:

The Railroad across British East Africa:
The Lunatic Express, Charles Miller
Man-eaters of Tsavo, Lt. Col. J. H. Patterson

Democratic Republic of Congo:
In the Footsteps of Mr. Kurtz, Michela Wrong
Africa in My Blood, Jane Goodall
The River Congo, Peter Forbath
King Leopold's Ghost, Adam Hochschild

Rwanda:
The Key to My Neighbor's House, Elizabeth Neuffer
We Wish to Inform You That Tomorrow We Will Be Killed With Our Families, Phillip Gourevitch
Shake Hands with the Devil, Lt. Gen. Romeo Dallaire

Lions:
Ghosts of Tsavo, Philip Caputo
The Serengeti Lion, George Schaller

Gorillas:
Gorillas Among Us, Dawn Prince-Hughes
Gorillas in the Mist, Dian Fossey
Woman in the Mists, Farley Mowat
In the Kingdom of Gorillas, Bill Weber and Amy Vedder
Year of the Gorilla, George Schaller
The Dark Romance of Diane Fossey, Harold Hayes
Gorilla, George Schaller

Botany:
In Praise of Plants, Francis Hallé
Life at the Limits, David A. Wharton
Botany of Desire, Michael Pollan
Medicinal Plants and Traditional Medicine in Africa, Abayomi Sofowora

Africa:
No Mercy, Redmond O'Hanlon
The African Slave Trade, Basil Davidson
Travels in West Africa, Mary Kingsley

The Zanzibar Chest, Aidan Hartley
Famine Crimes, Alex de Waal
Across African Sand, Phil Deutschle
Wild Africa, John Murray
Guns, Germs, and Steel, Jared Diamond

ABOUT THE AUTHOR

Audrey Schulman is the author of three previous novels: *Swimming With Jonah*, *The Cage,* and *A House Named Brazil.* Her work has been translated into eleven languages. Born in Montreal, Schulman now lives in Massachusetts.

www.europaeditions.com

EUROPA EDITIONS BACKLIST
(alphabetical by author)

Fiction

Carmine Abate
Between Two Seas • 978-1-933372-40-2 • Territories: World
The Homecoming Party • 978-1-933372-83-9 • Territories: World

Simonetta Agnello Hornby
The Nun • 978-1-60945-062-5 • Territories: World

Milena Agus
From the Land of the Moon • 978-1-60945-001-4 • Ebook •
Territories: World (excl. ANZ)

Salwa Al Neimi
The Proof of the Honey • 978-1-933372-68-6 • Ebook • Territories:
World (excl. UK)

Jenn Ashworth
A Kind of Intimacy • 978-1-933372-86-0 • Territories: US & Can

Beryl Bainbridge
The Girl in the Polka Dot Dress • 978-1-60945-056-4 • Ebook •
Territories: US

Muriel Barbery
The Elegance of the Hedgehog • 978-1-933372-60-0 • Ebook •
Territories: World (excl. UK & EU)
Gourmet Rhapsody • 978-1-933372-95-2 • Ebook • Territories:
World (excl. UK & EU)

www.europaeditions.com

Stefano Benni
Margherita Dolce Vita • 978-1-933372-20-4 • Territories: World
Timeskipper • 978-1-933372-44-0 • Territories: World

Romano Bilenchi
The Chill • 978-1-933372-90-7 • Territories: World

Kazimierz Brandys
Rondo • 978-1-60945-004-5 • Territories: World

Alina Bronsky
Broken Glass Park • 978-1-933372-96-9 • Ebook • Territories: World
The Hottest Dishes of the Tartar Cuisine • 978-1-60945-006-9 • Ebook • Territories: World

Jesse Browner
Everything Happens Today • 978-1-60945-051-9 • Ebook • Territories: World (excl. UK & EU)

Francisco Coloane
Tierra del Fuego • 978-1-933372-63-1 • Ebook • Territories: World

Rebecca Connell
The Art of Losing • 978-1-933372-78-5 • Territories: US

Laurence Cossé
A Novel Bookstore • 978-1-933372-82-2 • Ebook • Territories: World
An Accident in August • 978-1-60945-049-6 • Territories: World (excl. UK)

www.europaeditions.com

Diego De Silva
I Hadn't Understood • 978-1-60945-065-6 • Territories: World

Shashi Deshpande
The Dark Holds No Terrors • 978-1-933372-67-9 •
Territories: US

Steve Erickson
Zeroville • 978-1-933372-39-6 • Territories: US & Can
These Dreams of You • 978-1-60945-063-2 • Territories:
US & Can

Elena Ferrante
The Days of Abandonment • 978-1-933372-00-6 • Ebook •
Territories: World
Troubling Love • 978-1-933372-16-7 • Territories: World
The Lost Daughter • 978-1-933372-42-6 • Territories: World

Linda Ferri
Cecilia • 978-1-933372-87-7 • Territories: World

Damon Galgut
In a Strange Room • 978-1-60945-011-3 • Ebook • Territories: USA

Jane Gardam
Old Filth • 978-1-933372-13-6 • Ebook • Territories: US & Italy
The Queen of the Tambourine • 978-1-933372-36-5 • Ebook •
Territories: US
The People on Privilege Hill • 978-1-933372-56-3 • Ebook •
Territories: US

www.europaeditions.com

The Man in the Wooden Hat • 978-1-933372-89-1 • Ebook •
Territories: US
God on the Rocks • 978-1-933372-76-1 • Ebook • Territories: US &
Can

Anna Gavalda
French Leave • 978-1-60945-005-2 • Ebook • Territories:
US & Can

Katharina Hacker
The Have-Nots • 978-1-933372-41-9 • Territories: World (excl.
India)

Patrick Hamilton
Hangover Square • 978-1-933372-06-8 • Territories: US & Can

James Hamilton-Paterson
Cooking with Fernet Branca • 978-1-933372-01-3 • Territories: US
Amazing Disgrace • 978-1-933372-19-8 • Territories: US
Rancid Pansies • 978-1-933372-62-4 • Territories: USA

Alfred Hayes
The Girl on the Via Flaminia • 978-1-933372-24-2 • Ebook •
Territories: World

Jean-Claude Izzo
The Lost Sailors • 978-1-933372-35-8 • Territories: World
A Sun for the Dying • 978-1-933372-59-4 • Territories: World

www.europaeditions.com

Gail Jones
Sorry • 978-1-933372-55-6 • Territories: US & Can

Ioanna Karystiani
The Jasmine Isle • 978-1-933372-10-5 • Territories: World
Swell • 978-1-933372-98-3 • Territories: World

Peter Kocan
Fresh Fields • 978-1-933372-29-7 • Territories: US, EU & Can
The Treatment and the Cure • 978-1-933372-45-7 • Territories: US, EU & Can

Helmut Krausser
Eros • 978-1-933372-58-7 • Territories: World

Amara Lakhous
Clash of Civilizations Over an Elevator in Piazza Vittorio • 978-1-933372-61-7 • Ebook
Divorce Islamic Style • 978-1-60945-066-3 • Ebook • Territories: World

Lia Levi
The Jewish Husband • 978-1-933372-93-8 • Territories: World

Valerio Massimo Manfredi
The Ides of March • 978-1-933372-99-0 • Territories: US

Leïla Marouane
The Sexual Life of an Islamist in Paris • 978-1-933372-85-3 • Territories: World

www.europaeditions.com

Sélim Nassib
I Loved You for Your Voice • 978-1-933372-07-5 • Territories: World
The Palestinian Lover • 978-1-933372-23-5 • Territories: World

Amélie Nothomb
Tokyo Fiancée • 978-1-933372-64-8 • Territories: US & Can
Hygiene and the Assassin • 978-1-933372-77-8 • Ebook • Territories: US & Can

Valeria Parrella
For Grace Received • 978-1-933372-94-5 • Territories: World

Alessandro Piperno
The Worst Intentions • 978-1-933372-33-4 • Territories: World

Lorcan Roche
The Companion • 978-1-933372-84-6 • Territories: World

Boualem Sansal
The German Mujahid • 978-1-933372-92-1 • Ebook • Territories: US & Can

Eric-Emmanuel Schmitt
The Most Beautiful Book in the World • 978-1-933372-74-7 • Ebook • Territories: World
The Woman with the Bouquet • 978-1-933372-81-5 • Ebook • Territories: US & Can
Concerto to the Memory of an Angel • 978-1-60945-009-0 • Ebook • Territories: US & Can

www.europaeditions.com

Audrey Schulman
Three Weeks in December • 978-1-60945-064-9 • Ebook •
Territories: US & Can

James Scudamore
Heliopolis • 978-1-933372-73-0 • Ebook • Territories: US

Luis Sepúlveda
The Shadow of What We Were • 978-1-60945-002-1 • Ebook •
Territories: World

Paolo Sorrentino
Everybody's Right • 978-1-60945-052-6 • Ebook • Territories: US &
Can

Domenico Starnone
First Execution • 978-1-933372-66-2 • Territories: World

Henry Sutton
Get Me out of Here • 978-1-60945-007-6 • Ebook • Territories: US
& Can

Chad Taylor
Departure Lounge • 978-1-933372-09-9 • Territories: US,
EU & Can

Roma Tearne
Mosquito • 978-1-933372-57-0 • Territories: US & Can
Bone China • 978-1-933372-75-4 • Territories: US

www.europaeditions.com

André Carl van der Merwe
Moffie • 978-1-60945-050-2 • Ebook • Territories: World (excl. S. Africa)

Fay Weldon
Chalcot Crescent • 978-1-933372-79-2 • Territories: US

Anne Wiazemsky
My Berlin Child • 978-1-60945-003-8 • Territories: US & Can

Jonathan Yardley
Second Reading • 978-1-60945-008-3 • Ebook • Territories: US & Can

Edwin M. Yoder Jr.
Lions at Lamb House • 978-1-933372-34-1 • Territories: World

Michele Zackheim
Broken Colors • 978-1-933372-37-2 • Territories: World

Alice Zeniter
Take This Man • 978-1-60945-053-3 • Territories: World

Children's Illustrated Fiction

Altan
Here Comes Timpa • 978-1-933372-28-0 • Territories: World (excl. Italy)
Timpa Goes to the Sea • 978-1-933372-32-7 • Territories: World (excl. Italy)

www.europaeditions.com

Fairy Tale Timpa • 978-1-933372-38-9 • Territories: World (excl. Italy)

Wolf Erlbruch
The Big Question • 978-1-933372-03-7 • Territories: US & Can
The Miracle of the Bears • 978-1-933372-21-1 • Territories: US & Can
(with **Gioconda Belli**) *The Butterfly Workshop* • 978-1-933372-12-9 • Territories: US & Can

Non-fiction

Alberto Angela
A Day in the Life of Ancient Rome • 978-1-933372-71-6 • Territories: World • History

Helmut Dubiel
Deep In the Brain: Living with Parkinson's Disease • 978-1-933372-70-9 • Ebook • Medicine/Memoir

James Hamilton-Paterson
Seven-Tenths: The Sea and Its Thresholds • 978-1-933372-69-3 • Territories: USA • Nature/Essays

Daniele Mastrogiacomo
Days of Fear • 978-1-933372-97-6 • Ebook • Territories: World • Current affairs/Memoir/Afghanistan/Journalism

www.europaeditions.com

Valery Panyushkin
Twelve Who Don't Agree • 978-1-60945-010-6 • Ebook • Territories:
World • Current affairs/Memoir/Russia/Journalism

Christa Wolf
One Day a Year: 1960-2000 • 978-1-933372-22-8 • Territories:
World • Memoir/History/20th Century

Tonga Books

Ian Holding
Of Beasts and Beings • 978-1-60945-054-0 • Ebook • Territories:
US & Can

Sara Levine
Treasure Island!!! • 978-0-14043-768-3 • Ebook • Territories:
World

Alexander Maksik
You Deserve Nothing • 978-1-60945-048-9 • Ebook • Territories:
US, Can & EU (excl. UK)

Crime/Noir

Massimo Carlotto
The Goodbye Kiss • 978-1-933372-05-1 • Ebook • Territories:
World
Death's Dark Abyss • 978-1-933372-18-1 • Ebook • Territories: World

www.europaeditions.com

The Fugitive • 978-1-933372-25-9 • Ebook • Territories: World
Poisonville • 978-1-933372-91-4 • Ebook • Territories: World
Bandit Love • 978-1-933372-80-8 • Ebook • Territories: World

Giancarlo De Cataldo
The Father and the Foreigner • 978-1-933372-72-3 • Territories:
World

Caryl Férey
Zulu • 978-1-933372-88-4 • Ebook • Territories: World (excl. UK
& EU)
Utu • 978-1-60945-055-7 • Ebook • Territories: World (excl. UK &
EU)

Alicia Giménez-Bartlett
Dog Day • 978-1-933372-14-3 • Territories: US & Can
Prime Time Suspect • 978-1-933372-31-0 • Territories: US & Can
Death Rites • 978-1-933372-54-9 • Territories: US & Can

Jean-Claude Izzo
Total Chaos • 978-1-933372-04-4 • Territories: US & Can
Chourmo • 978-1-933372-17-4 • Territories: US & Can
Solea • 978-1-933372-30-3 • Territories: US & Can

Matthew F. Jones
Boot Tracks • 978-1-933372-11-2 • Territories: US & Can

Gene Kerrigan
The Midnight Choir • 978-1-933372-26-6 • Territories: US & Can
Little Criminals • 978-1-933372-43-3 • Territories: US & Can

www.europaeditions.com

Carlo Lucarelli
Carte Blanche • 978-1-933372-15-0 • Territories: World
The Damned Season • 978-1-933372-27-3 • Territories: World
Via delle Oche • 978-1-933372-53-2 • Territories: World
Edna Mazya
Love Burns • 978-1-933372-08-2 • Territories: World (excl. ANZ)

Yishai Sarid
Limassol • 978-1-60945-000-7 • Ebook • Territories: World (excl. UK, AUS & India)

Joel Stone
The Jerusalem File • 978-1-933372-65-5 • Ebook • Territories: World

Benjamin Tammuz
Minotaur • 978-1-933372-02-0 • Ebook • Territories: World